MAID FOR MAJESTY

BLACK SWAN

AJ PHOENIX

MAID FOR MAJESTY

BLACK SWAN

Book Three of the Maid for Majesty Series

When cunning servant Madeline Black stole the heart of King Alexander, little did she know that she had set into motion a love affair that would change the future of the British monarchy, as well as endanger all the subjects of England...

Alex is now in crisis. Not only must he protect the woman he loves; but he must also save his countrymen and his best friend Greg Umbridge, who is in the throes of his own forbidden love affair.

All the while, Madeline is hellbent to avenge the murder of her late mother, Elizabeth Swan. However, the truth-which Alex has secretly found out- hurts Madeline more than anyone else....

FREEBIE FOR READERS

https://www.maidformajesty.com/free-novella

INTRODUCTION

Apologies to my North American friends, if you're still here despite the UK English, thank you! Yes, I'm Canadian for anyone wondering.

To every phoenix

STOLEN SHIP

*S*usanna Bathory rolled her eyes at the man lying next to her. He wasn't what she had hoped for. He was disappointing on many levels. She slinked off her bed and walked over to the large porthole window and watched the English Channel waves pass by. She hated her room. Prince Carlos was territorial and had taken over the Captain's lodgings. *He isn't a gentleman. By the end of this short voyage, I'll have to kick him out of there.*

She imagined by now, Alex had found out that she had escaped with Carlos and the Duke of Axford's ship. Not that it mattered. With the head start she and the crew had there was no way Alex could get a message or ships out in time to catch them before they reached Santander. Especially since she and a few of her father's supporters destroyed some of the semaphore towers from London to Portsmouth.

She looked over at the man laying on her bed. "You can go now," she said abruptly.

"But-" he stopped confused. She had invited him there. He'd spent the last hour giving into every one of her requests.

She gave him a look of disgust that made him feel foolish.

"Out," she said in a flat tone.

"I thought we were going to-" he paused. He was sure this would eventually lead to his pleasure as well.

She laughed derisively, "We? Who said this is a 'we' situation. It's a 'me' situation. You're here to please me. I'm done with you now. Off you go," she said shooing him with her hand.

Shocked, he said nothing. He stood up and discreetly put his clothes back on. She watched him as he did. He felt hot as her eyes burned onto his skin. When he finished, he rushed out.

"Such a shame when they look so heavenly but don't work divinely," she whispered to herself.

She fixed herself up and headed out of her room, but the waves tossed the ship. She grasped the doorframe, stabling herself to her feet.

Prince Carlos was waiting in the hall leaning against a steel column.

"Another one? Or did this last one not meet your standards?" He crossed his arms over his chest, "I thought you were a Princess. Oh wait, technically you aren't, are you? You never were. My father told me King Charles stripped your family of those titles."

A sarcastic smile spread across her face, "I understand. It must be difficult to be on a ship with a bunch of men, and the only enjoyment you can get is standing next to my door...listening."

He turned away. When he had first met Susanna, she was covered in dirty and her hair was a knotted mess. But before they got onto the ship, he discovered she cleaned up beautifully. He had regretted his earlier treatment of her, and it pained him, but she was the most striking woman he'd ever laid eyes on. He sighed. "Once we get to Madrid, I'll have the company of women of class."

She snorted, "I guess that means I will also have the company of high-class men. Can't wait. I'd like to know what Spain has to offer a blonde girl. Is it a rather large court? Will it take time to find my favourites?"

His jaw dropped, he had heard English women were proper. He never met a woman so crass. "If we are to rule England together, you won't make me a fool, Susanna. Stop this, or I'll-"

Unexpectedly, she pressed her lips against his. He responded, grasping her blonde curls in his hand, cupping her head. She pushed him back. "Or you'll what?" she laughed. She tried to walk past him, but he raised his arm across the corridor, blocking her path.

"I want an obedient wife. You need to be shown what it means to belong to a man." He moved forward and kissed her again, "I find it impossible to concentrate on attacking England if I'm to be made a cuckold."

"You make an excellent point, your Highness," she said realizing an opportunity to get the upper hand. "Are you suggesting we start getting familiar with one another?"

He nodded and casually walked into her room. She followed behind him. "I don't like England much," he said as she shut the door.

"You'll like me," she said with a closed lip smile.

"Will I? What will I like most about you?" he asked as he headed toward her bed.

"I always get what I want."

"Am I what you want?"

He wasn't. Though Carlos was an attractive man, she couldn't help to think he was a demanding bastard. After helping him escape the dungeon, he had the audacity to take the best room on the ship. Now, it seemed as though he thought she should be excited that he was interested in her.

"All I care about is how comfortable I am," she said.

"How comfortable you are?" he repeated.

"Yes. You see, I'd be comfortable with having England, Spain, and royal heirs. In time, I'm sure I'll get them. But I won't get them if I don't have a man that respects my wishes."

"And what are your wishes?" he asked suggestively.

"Well, the last man that was here, hardly respected my wishes. If he did, I would have invited him to stay longer."

"Don't worry. I'm capable."

She watched him for a moment sizing him up. What mattered was how a man handled a woman. Horsemen were usually perfect in this regard. Most of them were built like steel from training their horses.

They knew when to gently stroke and when to pull the reins. Susanna had never been with a prince. His power alone was an aphrodisiac, but the idea that he wanted to lay with her in such drab surroundings was detestable. "I hardly think that this room is an appropriate place. You and I are future royalty. We should be in the nicest room on this ship."

"You're a true Princess," he smiled.

"I'm glad you agree."

"Let's go."

Once they reached the Captain's room, Carlos took out his key, put it into the lock and pushed open the door and extended his arm, forgetting to take the key from the lock. "Here we are, my lady," he said invitingly.

Susanna saw her chance, deftly slipped the key from the lock, and discreetly put it into her pocket. "In," she ordered, shutting the door behind them.

He got onto the bed and lay on his back, his hands behind his head, his legs spread. "Come here," he said, as he began to fumble with the buttons of his trousers. "I'm going to settle your urges."

"Not like that you aren't. Do you really expect me to just crawl on top of you, peel off my clothes after the disgusting room I was just in? That's not pleasing to me."

His jaw dropped, "Susanna-"

"You think you'd be trying to get me comfortable with my new surroundings," she argued.

"Fine," he huffed. "I'll help you with your dress." He got up scowling.

"It'd be good to have a drink," she said stiffly.

He glanced about the room, "There are none in here."

"Of course, there aren't. The Duke of Axford never drinks and this is his ship."

"Is that what you need before our little romp?" he teased.

"At least you're quick with the hints."

4

"I'll be back," he said exasperated.

He walked out the room planning to ask the crewmen if any of them had brought any alcohol for the journey. But moments after he was beyond the threshold, he heard the door shut behind him.

CLICK

Carlos whirled about, his expression turning to dread. She had locked him out! Several crewmen nearby chuckled beneath their breath.

"Get the hell out of here, you peasants," Carlos snarled. "One more breath out of any of you English filth and I will throw you off this ship myself."

The men quickly left, knowing it wasn't an empty threat. Susanna had her ear pressed to the door and overheard his words.

"They may be filthy peasants, but you're hardly better," she called. "You came down to my room and expected me to sleep with you after you listened to me be with another man. That's vile!"

"I'm vile?" he bellowed. "We've been gone a couple of days and you've already acquainted yourself with a few men on this ship!"

"I may be promiscuous but I'm not your whore," she said stern. "Get the drinks and then come back in here and conduct yourself like a gentleman. You're royalty. Act like it."

He stood there with his mouth hanging. Her telling him to act like royalty when she couldn't do the same was hypocritical. But there was no point in complaining; he could see the ruse. He had known when they had left England, Susanna was not happy that he had taken the Captain's lodgings, and now she had hoodwinked him and taken the best room on the ship.

HOLYROOD HOUSE

"Sofia!" Greg grunted beneath his breath.

She had been doing it for days now. Even though she did every morning, it still caught Greg by surprise. He grunted again, "Princess ... if McFadden comes in – " he abruptly exhaled. "He doesn't ... always knock."

Greg let out a sharp gasp as she explored him under the bedsheets. She liked hearing his reaction. Every caress always elicited a sigh or yelp. It was funny to listen to him object. She knew Greg wanted her to continue, but he didn't want McFadden barging in and ruining it.

He clasped his fingers around her soft brown curls. "Come to me, Princess." She rose from the sheets and gave him a soft kiss on the mouth.

McFadden stormed in. "Got a letter from tha King."

"McFadden, you shouldn't come in here without making your presence known," Greg said in embarrassment. "Sofia or I could be getting dressed."

"Ya said tha' yesterday."

"Give me the letter. But ya know I was 'ere before ya."

McFadden grinned and set it down on the nightstand and stepped back.

"Are you going to stand around here all day?" Greg said cross. "We'd like to get dressed and we don't want you watching us as we do."

McFadden was immovable.

"Leave McFadden," Greg demanded.

"Ah right, ah right, I was just anticipatin' what the King might say," McFadden said waving his arm before he headed out the door, shutting it behind him.

"Curious of what his Majesty has got to tell us?" he asked as he tried to reach the letter.

"Not really," she said kissing his neck.

He turned, gently cupped her face and looked into her eyes, "It may have something to do with your family, you never know."

"That's what I'm afraid of," she murmured. "I don't want to be forced to leave."

"I wouldn't worry," he said, caressing her face. "You're the Princess of my world now. I don't care what any king says. Your place is with me."

She smiled, reached out for the letter and handed it to him. He tore it open, "Hm, it's long," he said annoyed. "Great."

He read it aloud to her:

GREG,

I hope this letter finds you well. I would have written you earlier, but it's been a busy time.

The wedding was beautiful. Madeline was breathtaking. Everything was perfect. But maybe I just felt that way because I knew I was marrying the right person for me. I always thought I would marry as a duty to my country. I'm glad I didn't. I feel complete now. I know I'd be lost and unhappy for the rest of my life if I didn't marry Madeline.

At our wedding, she was graciously accepted by the nobles. They had no issues that we had invited common folk, either.

There is nothing but praise for Madeline in The Society Pages. These past few weeks Mr. Ackers and other writers continue to compliment what she wears. They sometimes compare her to her mother, I don't care for it, but I suppose this means she's become a fashion plate.

Since most of the English subjects like her, I feel confident that our baby will be welcomed by the nobles. We haven't made our exciting news public yet. Though I'm sure the servants know, she's been sick from time to time.

I must confess that though the pregnancy has been going well, I worry about her. Lately, she's been reading through her mother's diaries quite often. I know she wants me to imprison the Duke of Axford and put him on trial. She hasn't demanded it yet, but she's convinced the Duke of Axford killed her mother and mentions it from time to time.

However, the real reason I'm writing you is to warn you. Unfortunately, Prince Carlos escaped with Susanna Bathory. They are heading back for Spain as I write this. By the time you receive this, they will be making their way across the Spanish countryside to Madrid.

As you know, the Royal Navy is spread across several parts of the world. I have sent messengers with instructions to prepare a naval blockade down the English Channel, but it will take weeks if not months, to get my ships organized; there isn't enough time. If I could hold the Spaniards off from attacking Windsor and London for several more weeks, I could arrange a blockade and counter-attack. There are men in northern France, I've sent for them to return, but there won't be enough men to secure both London and Windsor.

It may be time to consider Sofia's safety as well as your own. I doubt King Fernando would attack Edinburgh, but I'm sure he intends to collect Princess Sofia in time.

Alex

SOFIA LOOKED UP AT GREG, "I'm not going back to Spain," she said simply. "My father doesn't care what happens to me. And I doubt he and Carlos would come here."

Greg squeezed her, his eyes falling on her sympathetically. His family would give anything to have him back home in Aylesbury Vale. She sounded certain that she had been forgotten.

"Over the past several months, I have only received one letter from my father," she said. "But it wasn't a letter, it was just orders to marry Alex. I'm happy here with you, Greg."

"Then we'll stay here."

"What about Alex? He thinks we're in danger."

"Maybe we are. From the sounds of things, he needs to buy himself some more time, but there's nothing we can do about that."

She looked at him astounded by his attitude.

"He'll be fine," Greg reassured her. "He always is. I'm sure he'll find a way to get more time. It's not for us to worry about."

"But–"

"For now, we can have all the fun we want. No one here can stop us," he said suggestively.

She giggled. He lowered his head, looking down at her dark peaks protruding out the thin cotton layer of her chemise. He cupped her breast with one hand and teased the tip between his fingers. She murmured, looking down at his hands and the near see-through material. She could sense the tingling heat between her legs, her hunger growing. She absentmindedly spread her legs, inviting him to take advantage.

Greg looked down, noting her legs parting, and let out an involuntary groan. These days even the suggestion of intimacy had her fired up in anticipation; she wriggled her hips. Though he wanted to please her and give in to his Princess' demands, she would be much more euphoric if he insisted on grooming her body for what would come in due time.

He loosened the laces of her chemise and pulled it down, exposing her hard peaks beckoning to be pleasured. He drew soft circles with his tongue, capturing each nubbin playfully. As he tasted her between his lips, she purred appreciatively, clawing into the bedsheets like a kitten. She felt a heat surge between her thighs in her eagerness to have him.

His fingers swept down her belly, and he leaned back onto his side and slid the chemise down her legs and off her feet. She watched his hand slowly slid up her legs and settled into the furrow of damp curls. He coaxed the sensitive flesh, massaging gently. She perched onto her elbows and captured his lips with hers, and smoothed her hand across his length, enticing him further. Her scarlet gaze met his, and he yielded to her appetite. He slipped one finger inside the hot crease, then another.

BANG!

A clatter came from the window, and her brow lifted, "What was that?"

"Nothing," he assured her. "Groundskeepers starting the day."

A scurry of footsteps could be heard in the distance.

"Looks like Holyrood House is getting ready for the day," he continued, his large orbs staring into hers. She knew his urges were to be reckoned with at the moment. But the pair stared at one another for a long moment. Sensing her objections, he slowly pulled his hand.

She grasped his wrist, "Please," she whispered breathlessly. She couldn't deny that her appetite was as ravenous as his. He heeded and delved into the deep wet folds. She delighted in his affections while biting her lower lip. She hadn't a clue what she would do if someone walked in, nor did she care. She needed to relieve the coiling desire within her and didn't care about the social repercussions. She panted, her body growing hot, and he knew she was seconds away, his hand working at a feverish pace, the tender wetness contracting around his fingers.

"Stop," she muttered.

"Only a moment longer."

She grasped his length again and stared at him wantonly. He said nothing but stared at her scarlet expression and released his hand from her intimated grip. She spread wider, and he complied, leaning over her. Her eyelashes fluttered up into his, they stared at one another, the tension filling their nerves as they could hear another flurry of footsteps again.

He gently pressed into her, and in a string of passionate and possessive kisses, he claimed her. She clung to him aching to be fulfilled; her murmurs were soft as she resisted the urge to cry out.

He muffled her sound with his mouth, relishing in the taste of pleasure from her lips. His blood was inflamed, and he felt the heat of her increasing, her breath becoming haggard. The intensity of it over-flowed, and she yelped as her eyes welled up. He gazed down at her skin, now a fleshy red. A whirlwind overtook him as he tried to hold off, but a sweet sound rang out from her, one of pure ecstasy, which broke him. His foot spasmed as he relinquished himself in her.

They lay for several minutes, him inside her, watching one another. There was nothing in the world beyond them. No kingdom to save. No king to fear. No servant near their door.

PRINCELY BEHAVIOUR

$\mathcal{I}$t was evening in Santander. On the outskirts of the city, Susanna sat next to a fire, surrounded by the crew. She warmed her hands, as some of the men cooked whatever small game they could find. Several tents had been set up, Carlos and Susanna's being the biggest, held some of the Duke Axford's personal possessions. There weren't enough tents for everyone, so half the men had to sleep outside in the grass under the trees.

One of the men, whose name Susanna had forgotten, was cooking a small squirrel. Chills ran up her spine; the thought of eating a small rodent was horrid. "Make another fire and cook that little beast somewhere else," she ordered.

Carlos walked over in time to witness the scene. "Susanna, in Spain squirrel is a delicacy," he said haughtily.

"Well, in civilized England it isn't. I hope you don't plan to put that on the menu once we take over, Carlos. I refuse to eat an animal that looks like a rat."

He sat next to her. "Strange. You won't eat a rat, but you'll sleep with one," he said, gesturing to the men around them.

"Every man is a rat," said Susanna stiffly.

"Really?"

"Yes."

"What makes one rat better than the next?" he asked curiously.

"I think that question has an obvious answer. Status, power, and money."

"You're a shrew."

She laughed, "Have you come to tame me?"

A part of him wanted to say 'yes'. He loved a challenge. But there was nothing innately good about her. She was striking and intriguing but she was made of stone. It was as if she felt no deep emotion toward anything or anyone.

"I don't want an unmanageable wife," his eyes gleaming as he looked into the fire. "If we are to rule two countries together, you need to learn your place …"

He continued to lecture her, but Susanna rolled her eyes and stomped off to the tent. He ran after her. Once he reached the tent, he grabbed her arm and whirled her around, then grasped both her shoulders shaking her.

"Ow. That hurts," she said her voice cross.

"Don't walk away from me while I speak to you," he growled. "I'm the Prince of Spain, you hellcat!"

She swiftly kneed him in the groin. He keeled over onto the ground. "ARGH!" he groaned before he cursed in Spanish beneath his breath.

"No one treats me that way," she said putting her hands on her hips. "If you expect me to be your wife, to attack my own country, provide you an heir and another country to rule, you'd better respect me, Carlos." She stormed past a bathtub and large makeshift bed to a dresser with an oval mirror. Though they weren't staying long, Carlos had insisted on purchasing some furniture so they could be comfortable during their stay. But now she regretted that they were sharing a tent. She grabbed a wineglass and a bottle from the dresser, and poured herself a drink. She plopped down on a nearby chair as Carlos continued writhe in pain on the ground. "Pathetic that you think you need to discipline me as if I were a petulant child," she grumbled before taking a sip of wine.

As Carlos looked up at her, he realized that there would be only one way to get through to this woman; he'd have to please her for now. When they got to Madrid, he could discipline her behaviour and teach her what it meant to be an obedient wife. "Susanna," he said weakly, "I'm sorry."

Her expression softened and she turned to him. "Don't take what I'm saying personal, Carlos. But I just want to make it clear. I saw your mother at court. She's quiet, mousy, and always at your father's side. She barely says a word. I'm not going to be anything like her."

He steadied himself onto his feet. He walked toward her and put his hands on her shoulders. He bent down, lifted her blonde hair to his nose and smelled it setting it back down, "If we are to spend a life together, we should try to find things we like about one another. I have to admit, despite the condition I first saw you in when you helped me escape from the tower, I *did* find you attractive."

A smile crept over her face. "I suppose you're right," she admitted. "But it's going to take me some time to think of something I like about you."

He took her hand and placed it on his crotch, guiding it up and down. He came to life in her hand. "I think there is something you like about me. Or at least, I'll make an effort to make sure you do."

"I don't really like to exhaust myself giving you attention that you don't deserve," she said pulling away her hand.

"That's fine. I'll tire myself to give you the attention you want. Because I know that's what you want. You like it when it's about you."

Finally, he understood. Susanna hated when a man expected her to pleasure them. In her opinion, any man that laid with her should be thankful for the privilege. She refused to have sex with a man who couldn't please her first.

"Just how do you plan to make it about me?" she asked.

"Tell me what you want," he whispered into her ear and kissed her neck.

She thought about it, tapping her finger to her cheek. She hadn't liked how disrespectful he had been to her during their voyage. A little humiliation was in order.

"Are you sure you're going to be enough?" she asked setting down her glass of wine on the vanity table next to her. "I mean, I've been with a prince before," she lied. "And to be honest, I found him to be terrible. It was as though he expected me to wait upon his every need. I don't want you to make me feel like I'm a servant fulfilling your needs. Get on your knees."

There was nothing Carlos despised more than being told what to do. He felt cornered. He needed to marry Susanna to capture the British crown. He sank to his knees, "What can I do for you?" he asked feigning interest.

"You can start by kissing my feet."

"Kissing your feet?" he said aghast.

"Yes," she smiled. "If you're really going to make me your Queen, show your loyalty and treat me like one."

Carlos wanted to smack her. No woman should have the audacity to speak to a man that way, especially a prince. Begrudgingly, he lifted one of her feet off the floor and began to unlace her boot. He pulled it off. "Truthfully, your feet smell awful," he said.

She sighed, unimpressed, "That's the kind of comment a silly boy makes. Do they really smell awful? Is that a surprise? We've been on a ship for days, I haven't the chance to clean myself up. I am guessing your feet smell like a peasant man's arse."

He'd never been so insulted. He opened his mouth to speak but then thought better of the words that came to mind. "I'll get something to soak your feet in," he said curtly.

"Well, if you're going to go through that trouble, you should just get me a tub full of water and bathe me."

He grinned, though it was servants' work, having her naked in a tub was much more enticing, he stuck his head outside the tent and called to one of the crewmen.

"Hey you," he said to the man eating the squirrel. "Drop that rodent and bring in a tub full of warm water."

The man did as he was told and an hour and a half later, a deep tub was sitting in Susanna's tent, full of hot water. Carlos sat on a chair, "Is that better?" he asked.

"You're improving," she said wryly, "but don't get haughty about it."

She stood up and began to peel off her clothing. He gaped, aroused by her confidence. She looked like an alabaster sculpture. Her skin was flawless. Every detail down to her nipple was a poet's ideal. Then again, she was related to the house of Warwick. The English royal family had a reputation for being striking. Carlos's looks had often been compared to Alex in his youth, which he hated. He grinned triumphantly, it was going to be fun claiming Alex's cousin.

She tested the water waving her hand through it. "It's a little too hot. Another pail of cool water should do it."

"Why don't you get in and wait for it to cool?"

"Hot water dries out the skin. Speaking of which, find me some oils."

It was a shame that such beauty was so demanding. More than anything, Carlos wanted to put her in her place. The way she spoke to him without reference to his title, as if he was her own personal servant, was abhorrent. He peeked his head out of the tent and ordered what she needed. He turned toward her.

"Lord knows how long that bucket will be," she said, shaking her head. "I might as well get on with it. She picked up a loofah that had been floating on the surface of the water in the tub. "Wash me," she commanded.

He scowled.

"Or you could just get one of the crewmen to do it," she said. "I mean, really Carlos, that's all you've been doing, ordering other men around. I doubt I would have this tub of water if it had not been for the crewmen on the ship."

He took the loofah from her hand, "I suppose this is the only duty you've given me that's worth doing," he said suggestively.

She smiled as he offered his hand to help her into the tub. He pulled up a stool next to the tub and dipped the sponge into the water. He swept her blonde hair behind her shoulders and squeezed the loofah. It poured water down her back, and she sighed, her muscles relaxing.

Though there was no soap, he scrubbed her back.

"Why don't you drop some oils into the bath?" she asked sharply.

His temper was about to blow, but he knew if he could hold back a little longer, he might finally get the upper hand. He dropped the loofah back in the water and begrudgingly walked over and grabbed some vials of essential oils off the vanity table. "There are a few different kinds here, lavender, jasmi-"

"Oh, for heaven's sake, just grab one," she said impatiently.

He picked up the jasmine and poured some into the water. He then sat back on the stool, fished the loofah out, and began to clean her while she sat in the tub. Unexpectedly she stood up.

"Make sure you get every part," she said simply.

He looked at her bottom at his eye level and smirked. "I'll make sure that I wash you properly." He slid the loofah back up her leg, drenching her leg as he squeezed it. He moved it up to her bottom and began rubbing circles; he could feel himself stiffen. He was tempted to drop the sponge and grab her and ravish her, but he had to show some restraint. He breathed heavily. Moving the sponge up her back, he stood up and looked into her eyes.

Her eyes were intense. He'd never seen crystal blues like them before, and she was staring straight at him as if she could see through him. He moved the loofah between her chest. She stood patiently, the animalistic expression on his face striking no intimidation in her. She knew what was to come. He wanted it more than she did; she was certain of it.

The loofah dropped, slipping down between their bodies and back into the water. He stood back and began tearing off his blouse. He pulled off his boots, then his trousers, his gaze not leaving her naked body.

He quickly embraced her, crushing his lips to hers. They pawed one another frantically, their mouths moving about one another's faces.

"I want you," he grunted.

She pulled away from him and stepped out of the tub. She lay down on some blankets on the makeshift bed. He followed her to the bed, grinning. There was no confidence in his stride. To Susanna, he seemed to be like an over-excited puppy with a new bone, and she didn't find it charming.

He lay next to her in the bed and gazed at her, and for a minute. It was awkward, and she wondered if he knew what he was doing. Then it hit her. Carlos was used to having women pleasure him. She rolled her eyes; she could only imagine the women he had already been with putting forth their best efforts and enthusiasm. Title of Queen, wealth, and privilege beyond measure would motivate most noblewomen.

"Ladies first," she said, hoping he'd comply. It'd be a horrible marriage if he couldn't.

There was a slight look of surprise, but then he put forth his effort. Sort of. She stared above her, trying to contain her frustration. His touch was blundering as if he were touching a woman for the first time. She was tempted to ask if this had been the first time he had been with a woman but given previous conversations, she doubted that. His movement was more than just clumsy; at some points, he was pinching and kneading his fingers and hands in a way that hurt. She hadn't made a single gasp of pleasure. She needed to do something to remedy the problem.

She pushed his hand away from her, "Carlos, intimacy with me is like dancing. If there isn't a sound, you haven't got a rhythm to move to."

"Huh?" he said, cocking his eyebrow.

"If I'm not making a sound, whatever you're doing isn't working. Listen."

"I was listening," he whined.

"Listen to my breathing and my body. If you can't make my heart pump faster at any point, chances are you're not succeeding."

A dead stare came across his face. *Is this woman serious? There are women in every court across Europe who would be thanking God for the attentions I am giving her.*

"Let's try something different now, shall we?" she said as she pushed his head toward her body.

There was a part of him that wanted to storm out of there. But he couldn't; if they could overthrow England, she held the keys to the Kingdom. He continued with his usual performance. It had worked on other women, and he was certain that her body would yield as well in time.

She sighed and looked up at the ceiling of the tent, thinking of Cedric. He was a boy that had worked in the Royal Mews that she'd always been fond of. She closed her eyes. It was hard to believe that she was fantasizing about some common boy while she was with a prince! She had always imagined that being with royalty would be heaven. Every noble girl that had been with Alex seemed to rave about his expertise to no end. Even Miss Hampton, despite their differences, would admit to it.

She rolled her head on the pillows in disbelief. Was Carlos so terrible that her thoughts would wander to her cousin? She glanced down, watching his stiff movements and then to the tent ceiling again.

Other gentry. She needed to think of other wealthy, handsome men of status. With the thought of Alex, Greg Umbridge came to mind. He wasn't wealthy, but he did have status as the King's most trusted advisor, and he was handsome. If the rumours were true about Princess Sofia being abducted by the rebel, she had no sympathy. She could only imagine how exciting running off with Greg Umbridge would be. A sultry smile cornered her lips at the thought. There was another deliciously tempting thing about Greg; if she ever spent a night with him, it would anger Alex. There was a time she had tried it. Though Greg was drunk, he managed to remain noble and witty at the same time.

"BUT WHY WOULD a lady of your noble birth want to be with a scoundrel like me?" Greg said. "Wouldn't your father disapprove?"

She chuckled to herself.

"YOU LIKE THAT?" said Carlos encouraged. She looked down at him. She had completely forgotten he was there.

19

"Mm, yes," she lied, wanting to get lost in her thoughts again. With a hopeful expression, he began nibbling like a rat. She shivered. She didn't want to spend much more time with Carlos. Since he wasn't accomplishing anything, she'd have to take over. "How about we have some more fun," she said, pushing his chest with her hand; he fell back onto the blankets.

With a steely look in his eyes, she climbed on top of him. He wasn't keen on her perched above him. He hated aggressive women, and Susanna was outspoken. He was about to object but didn't. If he said anything, she'd find a way to humiliate him, and that might cut the night short.

She was still unaroused. She pressed him to her entrance then impaled herself upon him. It pinched, and she let out a slight cry. She grasped his shoulders and squeezed her eyes shut. She knew she would have to imagine someone else to get through this. Drowning out everything around her, she directed him to hit her most intimate places. Since she was familiar with her body, she knew it wouldn't take long.

He could barely take her intensity; she was moving so quickly, the tightness clenching down on him. He had never been with a woman as beautiful as Susanna Bathory. Her golden hair swaying across her exquisite breasts as she bounced up and down him was a heavenly sight. He could barely stand it.

"Mmm," she murmured, her excitement finally growing.

"Haahh," he said, finishing.

Her eyes popped open. *Is this over? It hadn't lasted a minute!* She glared down at his satisfied face.

"That was amazing," he said earnestly. "I don't think I've ever gone so fast."

How nice, she thought with a sarcastic expression on her face as she got off him. Not only did she not enjoy herself, but even when she attempted to take over to please them both, he cheated her out of it.

"Unimaginable," she whispered to herself, crawling off the bed.

"What?"

"Nothing," Susanna said dismissively. " Go to sleep, Carlos."

Feeling dirtier than she had before she had taken a bath, she stepped back into the tub and grimaced in his direction. He was already sleeping.

She lowered herself into the water, her eyes narrowing at him, "The absolute worst I've ever experienced," she said, drenching the loofah in the water. "I shall look forward to every other man I'm with for the rest of my life. No man could possibly do worse than that sorry act."

OTHER ROYAL DUTIES

Alex's eyes soaked in the beautiful sight before him. There was part of him that wanted to wake Madeline, but he couldn't for appreciating the moment; his beautiful wife, lying asleep on the bed, a little bump protruding from her abdomen. The natural light from the large windows flooded the room, making her skin glow.

He had royal duties that he attended to earlier in the morning and had thought she would be awake by now. But she wasn't; she was still sleeping peacefully in her four-poster bed.

He stripped off his clothes and gently dropped them to the floor, and crawled into the bed next to her, trying to be careful not to wake her.

"Alex?" she whispered.

"Yes dolcezza, it's me. Just go back to sleep if you want," he said huskily.

He curled up next to her, but it was too late; she was wide awake. She glided, her hand up to his chest, feeling his rippling muscles and smooth bare skin. "Alex, are you not wearing any chemise?"

"Does that surprise you? I rarely do."

It didn't surprise her. Since they'd gotten married, he never wore anything to bed. He didn't pressure her to be intimate, but it was clear the offer was on the table … every night. Often she took it. Now it seemed he was extending that offer into the daytime. Usually, she would fulfil her needs. But now, she felt timid. In the natural light, every scar on her back and curve of her body would be seen. She trembled, intimidated by the thought of seeing Alex's marble-like perfection against her changing body and scars.

He rose above her, leaning on his elbow; he combed through her tresses with his fingers. "Are you tired?"

"No," she said, yawning. She lightly skimmed his muscles with her fingertips.

He chuckled, "No? Can I talk to the baby then?"

She smiled, "That's sweet, but I don't think the baby will understand."

"I'll just kiss baby then."

He threw back the covers, but she pulled them back up, covering herself again. She looked away, blushing.

"Madeline, what's wrong?"

"I'm getting bigger," she said, not making eye contact.

He slowly pulled back the covers again and looked down at her middle, "You're going to get a lot bigger than that I hope. You're having a baby," he said cupping her face.

"Soon I won't look the same. There will be more marks."

"Dolcezza, you are the most stunning woman I've ever laid eyes on, but that's not the reason I married you."

Since the wedding, he had noticed she had gotten more emotional about everything. Now that her body was preparing to go through serious changes, she was becoming self-conscious. He watched her, but the awkward silence made her more emotional as her eyes welled with tears.

He lowered his face next to her tummy, "There are many things about a pregnant woman's body that I know I'm going to appreciate," he said between soft pecks on her bump.

"Really?" she said cocking her brow, "such as?"

"I've noticed your breasts are beginning to swell."

"What?"

"Madeline, you allow me the pleasure of satisfying you most nights. I know every inch of your body, and I know when things are changing."

He went back to pressing more kisses to her belly.

"If we do this, I want you to shut the drapes of the bed," she said.

He didn't know what to say. He could tell her that he didn't prefer the drapes shut and wanted to indulge himself in her beauty. However, even if she did believe him, she might still feel too embarrassed to expose herself in the light. He sighed, there was only one way out of this no-win situation, and that was to tell her it was a no-win situation for him.

"Madeline, I'm going to be really honest," he paused. "I want to make love to you with the drapes open. Since our wedding night, I haven't gotten a good look at you, and I'm eager to see you naked. Your hair is silky, your skin is glowing, and I think you are more desirable now than you ever have been."

Her mouth hung open, she was about to object, but he continued.

"I also understand that maybe you don't feel comfortable revealing yourself to me." He sighed, "If you don't want to, you don't have to, but if we shut the drapes, I don't want you to think that it was my idea. This morning I sat in my meeting, and all I did was fantasize about my pretty pregnant wife that I-" he stopped, not wanting to humiliate her with the thoughts he had been having.

Her eyes searched his, and she knew he was being honest. Seeing her pregnant made him frisky.

"How about you stay naked, and I'll leave my chemise on?" she compromised.

His shoulders fell. Damn. But it was better than closing the bed with the drapes.

"All right. Whatever makes you comfortable." He pulled back the covers and sheets to the edge of the bed.

"Why are you pulling the sheet back so far, Alex?"

"You want to see me naked."

"Right," she murmured.

She looked up as the sun lit up his skin. If he thought showing his flaws would make her feel comfortable to take off her chemise, it wasn't working. He had no flaws. But seeing him was rousing her. As she took in his solid muscles, tan skin, and lower, there was a stirring in her centre.

She rose from the bed and reached out to touch him, but he guided her back down to the mattress. "I suppose you need a little more attention, now that you are pregnant," he said. "I shouldn't just expect that you are ready for me."

Not that he ever did. A generous lover, he usually looked after her before himself. His hand carefully slid up the chemise, and his knuckles grazed across the dampened curls. He pressed the nubs of his knuckles lightly, and her knees grew weak. He softly kneaded them into her, emitting tiny hums from her throat. He gently pulled back the chemise as if he were unwrapping a fragile gift and rested the material above her abdomen.

She hadn't noticed. Not when his tender lips wandered up her thigh. Not when his tongue exquisitely pleasured her. She was spellbound by his touch and hadn't noticed that her skin, her most intimate areas had become exposed. Her nerves delighted in his every move as he conducted waves of pleasure building and releasing. Her skin quivered as the light beyond the window cast over her beautiful and vulnerable frame. The one thing she did notice was his touch had become more delicate and precise.

He rose above her and gazed at the delicious sight before him. A light lined the curves of her body. His arousal heightened, his urge for her growing. Her swollen breast peeking out from the front of her chemise, the drawstring loosened. He leaned over her. Through hooded eyes, her emerald pools gazed up at him, eager for what was to come. She extended her arm to him, and he closed his eyes as she threaded her fingers into his black hair.

"By God, Madeline, you're are so stunning," he said breathlessly.

She exhaled, her breath shuddering as she did the last shocks of his attentions finally ebbing. His large handheld her jaw, and he brushed the pad of his thumb across her deep red lips. He lowered himself into her, their mouths dancing as he delved deeply. He took his time, devouring her lips, her cheek, and her jawline. He found her earlobe and softly tugged and nibbled, sending tingles through her body, settling in her core, where he slowly stroked deeper. She let out a helpless moan as his lips explored her neck, nibbling at the hollow of it. Then lower.

He cupped her breast. She hadn't realized her chemise had become so loose. Both pert, dark harden tips were in the sunlight. He had removed the drawstring that held the v-shaped opening together. Being so enraptured, she lost track of the moment she became exposed, her chemise now only covering the skin between her chest and belly.

He tantalized each with his tongue as her hands clasped his temples, encouraging his touch. She whimpered at the strokes of his tongue as he cradled her body in his affections, his lips sealing to the most sensitive parts of her flesh, his thrusts pulsating against the apex of her thighs. His sole purpose was to please her, galvanizing every part of himself to her needs, being attentive to each moan and quiver.

His breath became rapid along with his movement as her inviting flesh clenched around him. His throat became dry like a desert, but her indulgence would be his oasis. She gasped and panted; the heat of it became unbearable, engulfing her. She held herself tightly to him as she lost all control, her swirling urgency throwing her into oblivion.

He wriggled his torso deeper, and another whirlwind ripped through her. Eager to please, he had almost had no energy left for himself, but his body was already breaking from the taut heat within her. He lurched forward and came to completion, his warm breath caressing her neck as he did.

He eased himself away from her grasp and spooned next to her as she lay on her side. He nuzzled close to her neck and kissed her, "Are you all right?" he asked, his voice ragged.

"Yes," she said breathily.

He grabbed the blankets at the foot of the bed and covered them both with them. His hand wandered to her belly, tracing his fingers across it.

She felt tired and warm and quickly fell asleep as he rubbed her tummy.

AFTER A SHORT NAP, Madeline awoke to find Alex combing through her hair.

"Alex," she muttered.

"Hm?"

"I've been thinking. Remember you said you'd take me to Swan Manor?"

"I did," he muttered.

She gave him a look.

"Dolcezza, in your delicate condition you shouldn't be going to Swan Manor," he said as he placed his hand on her stomach.

"My delicate condition?' she scoffed. "How can you say that after what you just did?"

"I was gentle. Besides, it's not just that, Madeline. It may be very emotional to see. I don't think that would be good for you or the baby."

He rose from the sheets, thinking his comment had settled the discussion. She sat up, throwing her fists into the pillows around her. "Alex! Don't dismiss me."

"Madeline, I need to get dressed. I do have another meeting to attend. Frogmore to Windsor is -"

"I don't care. If you don't take me, I'll go myself," she said glaring at him.

He stopped buttoning his trousers, approached her and embraced her tenderly. She felt his hard chest as her head naturally fell to his pecs.

He pulled back. "I care about you," he said looking deeply into her eyes. "I understand why you feel the need to go. I just don't think this is the time."

"I don't think there will ever be a good time," she reasoned. "It's driving me crazy. I don't care if I get lost a thousand times before I get there, I'm going."

He bit his lip. He always knew he'd have to take her there, but he dreaded going. "Fine. I'll take you after you give birth. But we are not touring the whole manor. It's dangerous. Upstairs is off limits."

She nodded.

"I really don't wish to go," he went on. "I think it will be something you'll regret later."

"It's my choice. They were my family. If I wish to go, I -"

"I know," he said pushing his finger against her mouth. "Just promise me you won't be angry with me if you see something that's disturbing."

"I promise," she nodded.

He moved away from her and dressed in silence.

She felt horrible for giving him an ultimatum, but it really wasn't one. It was reality. She couldn't go on in her life without seeing the place, so she had to be honest. If he wasn't going to take her, her curiosity would bring her there.

He kissed her on the cheek before leaving, "I'll see you. Don't think about it too much, dolcezza."

"I love you," she said softly.

He rubbed her belly, "You too." He gave her one last peck on the forehead then headed out the door.

AFTER ALEX HAD LEFT, Madeline got out of the bed and went to her closet. There were still plenty of dresses she hadn't worn yet. Because she was beginning to show, she was sticking to the empire waist style dresses. Wearing anything with a corset felt restricting. She saw a light green chiffon dress and pulled it out. "Your Majesty?" She heard a voice call behind her. She hated being called that, especially by her friends.

"Come in, Martha," Madeline mumbled.

Martha walked through the bedchamber and into the closet and did a curtsy.

"I really wish you wouldn't call me that," Madeline said as she entered. "Or curtsy."

"It's proper etiquette."

"It feels weird," Madeline said looking down to the floor awkwardly.

"I'd say," said Martha slightly annoyed. "You're supposed to call for me to help you get dressed. It seems I have to guess when you feel like getting dressed."

"I'm sorry Martha, but it's ridiculous. Most my life I've waited on other people. Now I have someone that I've become friends with call me a proper title. Being called 'Lady' was strange. Now ..." she trailed off her eyes cast downward.

"I understand. But you don't want people to start talking about how you don't follow-"

"I know. I just, when it's just you, me, Marie or Sissy, I'd like things to stay as they were. Casual. Greg Umbridge calls Alex by his first name."

"Greg Umbridge has a reputation for being rude," Martha said pointedly.

"Please call me Madeline."

"All right, but I can't do it publicly. I hope you understand."

Madeline nodded. At least, she was getting somewhere with Martha; Marie and Sissy had been quite stubborn on the subject since she had married Alex.

"I'm going to go with this dress," Madeline said pressing the green chiffon against her body.

"Lovely. Oh, did you want this handkerchief as well?" Martha asked as she bent down and picked up a blue silk handkerchief off the floor. It had some dark green leaves embroidered into it. It didn't match the dress.

"This isn't mine," she said taking it from Martha's hand.

"Maybe it belongs to another dress in here?"

"I don't think so. I don't have any dresses with this colour or pattern. It looks like it might belong to a man."

"Probably his Majesty's then," Martha said as she folded it and put it in one of Alex's drawers.

"Mm," Madeline muttered doubtfully. It looked quite feminine and didn't match any of his ensembles.

"Let's get ready, shall we?" Martha said brightly.

"Yes."

TRUTH OF A DARE

*I*t was a typical dinner at Holyrood House. McFadden, Sam, and Belle sat with Greg and Sofia in the Royal Dining Room. When they had first arrived Sofia and Greg had dinner alone, but he soon grew tired of it. It was too quiet. He loved Sofia's company, but when there were only three servants in Holyrood House, it felt strange. They socialized with them the rest of the day; it made sense to eat together.

Since arriving, neither McFadden, Belle nor Sam seemed to catch on to the fact that Sofia was the Princess of Spain. Though Greg called her 'Princess' from time to time, they continued to believe it was only a pet name, and she was a Lady.

Though Belle couldn't communicate well, listening to the conversation was helpful and Sofia would often translate so Belle would understand. Nonetheless, English continued to be difficult for Belle. Interestingly, Sam had picked up some French phrases and from time to time when she asked for something in French, he'd immediately get it and hand it to her. Her pale cheeks always went red when he did this. Sometimes, she'd ask for several things. It was obvious she liked his attention.

"Passez les pommes de terre s'il vous plait," Belle said in her sweetest tone.

Sam stood up, reached far across the table and handed her the bowl of potatoes. Greg and McFadden glanced at one another knowingly.

"Eh boy," McFadden said, as he chewed on a piece of pheasant. "Why don' ya be a man? Give 'er what you really want her to have."

Greg burst out in laughter, which quickly turned into a howl as Sofia kicked him beneath the table.

"Com' on lass, Sam can take a joke," McFadden said.

"Go ahead make your jokes," Sofia said, "but at the end of the day, Sam's more likely to get a woman than you."

"Oh. She got you there McFadden," Greg said laughing again.

"Ya laugh at any joke yer lass makes. Yer a smart arse. Yer charming. That is why the King likes ya."

"Mr. McFadden, how did you become in charge of Holyrood House?" Sofia asked.

"Tha' King don' know me, if that's what ya asking, lass."

"Right. We guessed that," said Greg taking a sip of wine. Sofia smirked in his direction.

"Years ago, when they posted for tha job. There were jus' a couple things ya needed. Firs' ya had to know all the families of Edinburgh, as well as the town itself. Next, ya had to be able to drink tha competition under the table."

Sofia's jaw dropped, Greg and Sam smiled.

"He's just kidding Sofia," said Greg.

"Actually, he's not," Sam said. "That's really how he got this post."

"What?" Greg said. "Does that mean if I can drink you under the table, I can have your job, McFadden?"

"I'm not takin' tha' challenge. I wouldn't be surprised if ya beat me. Yer crazy enough. Runnin' about here in nothin' but a kilt."

"Running around in nothing but a kilt?" Sofia said, her eyebrows rose at Greg.

Greg sat speechless, glaring at McFadden.

"All righ' that be 'nough fer me then," said McFadden. He quickly grabbed some more pheasant, a few asparagus, and left the room. Sam quickly grasped Belle's hand and they made a quick exit.

"Heh," Greg said sheepishly. "For a big man, he sure can move fast."

"What was he talking about?" Sofia asked turning to him.

He closed his eyes, "We made a bet. I lost. I had to run around Holyrood House in a kilt."

"When was this?" she stammered, "Did Belle see?"

"Uh, well now I don't think so," he said his eyes moving about the room.

"When? Who saw?"

"The night of Alex and Madeline's wedding."

"ALL OF EDINBURGH SAW YOU?"

"Just anyone that was still there the wee hours of the morning."

"This is humiliating," she cried. "Just because we're in another place, where we don't know anyone doesn't mean you get to make an arse of yourself!"

A thousand witty comments were floating about Greg's head, but he knew he was better off keeping his mouth shut.

"It was just a bet," he murmured.

"Oh, that's all well and good," she said, "but if we are going to be together, remember what you did makes me look foolish."

"How?"

She paused, "Should I run around Holyrood House in nothing but a kilt to prove a point? I'm sure I could get an audience."

"Point made," he said waving his hand. "But there's no need for that."

"Are you going to act like an oaf because we're here? Please don't tell me you're going to start acting like McFadden," she said shaking her head.

"I'm sorry, Sofia."

She paused, deep in thought. Feeling a little guilty, she shrugged, "Maybe it's because I had a privileged upbringing."

"So did I," he grinned.

"I'm guessing everybody found it hilarious," Sofia said. "Maybe, I'm just being a prude."

"No, Sofia. You're not. You're right. I mean, everybody did find it quite funny, but I shouldn't have done it. If you and I are going to be together, I need to consider your feelings too. Will you allow me to make it up to you?"

She raised her eyebrow, and scoffed, "Just how do you plan to do that?"

"Well, now Princess, I do know how to impress."

"Ha! You think you know how to impress me?"

"I know I can," he said, confident. "Alex took you to all sorts of different places and he bored you to tears."

She tittered, "All he talked about was history and all things uninteresting. But there were things we did that were entertaining. Alex can play an instrument."

"True. But he plays the most droll classical pieces. I think you liked my Scottish jig more. You enjoyed going to the theatre too, which was also my suggestion."

"Everyone loves the theatre," she said.

"Yes, but you also let me help you get over your fear of birds. Admit it, you've always enjoyed my company."

She thought about it. It was the reason Alex picked Greg for a friend; he could make anything interesting. "So how are you going to entertain me Sir Gregory?"

"I got a few ideas, Princess," he winked. "But for now, I promise I will no longer act so foolish."

SNEAKY GUEST

❦

*M*adeline sat at a writing desk in the library at Windsor, reading her mother's journals. She had been spending a lot of time reading and rereading passages, thinking that maybe she could find a clue to what happened to her mother. The last words of her final entry; *When I'm dead, I won't be alone, but I'll be free.*

Clearly, Elizabeth knew someone was going to kill her soon. She wrote about death as though she knew it was coming. The words made Madeline cringe. Elizabeth knew she wouldn't die alone; she expected other people to be with her. But how could death make her free? Free from a marriage arrangement with the Duke?

Elizabeth wrote about him from time to time, but there wasn't much said. In the beginning, it seemed that she was fond of him, but as time went on, she wrote of him less and less. Suddenly, Madeline noticed her father mentioned. But strangely, not much was written about him either.

She wrote a lot about other people at court and conversations she had with them. It was interesting to see her thoughts on them. She seemed to think that English people were far too concerned with gossip; there was always plenty of it to fill the pages. Madeline didn't want to say anything to Alex, but it seemed that his father had often cheated on his mother with other ladies at court. But Madeline doubted that would surprise Alex; he most likely knew, just didn't want to speak of it.

"I thought we agreed you wouldn't bring those here today," Alex said to her, looking over her shoulder. "We came here to get books on pregnancy."

That was the plan, Alex had invited Marie to come along. She, Mr. Tinney, and Sir Ashton were there, looking about the library, too. But Madeline could see the confused look on Marie's face as she looked at the books on the shelves, unable to read their titles. Madeline felt ashamed, but the journals were beckoning her to read them, or at least, she felt they were.

"Doctor Sheffield has been good about seeing me," Madeline said simply. "He seems to think everything is okay with the baby."

"You've got a little life growing inside you. Aren't you curious at all?" Alex asked.

"I am," she said sheepishly. She looked back down at her mother's handwriting, "It's just-"

He shut the journal she was reading and set the stack of journals aside.

"Alex," she said in a harsh voice.

Just then Marie sauntered over. She curtsied, "Excuse me, your Majesties, uh, what kind of information about pregnancy are we looking for?"

"That's a good question," said Alex, folding his arms, glaring at Madeline.

Marie eyed the journals, "Why did you bring those?"

Alex said nothing, Madeline shifted uncomfortably in her chair.

"Oh, did your mother write anything about her pregnancy with you?" Marie gushed, as she grabbed the journals.

"No," Madeline said realizing for the first time that her mother never made a single mention of Madeline or being pregnant in the diaries. Madeline's heart sank.

"Everyone, I'd like a word alone with my wife," Alex announced reading Madeline's face.

Sir Ashton and Mr. Tinney stopped searching through one of the shelves nearby and quickly left the room. Marie followed them out, shutting the double doors behind her.

"Dolcezza, this is madness," Alex said softly.

Madeline began to cry. He got to his knees and she cried as she rested her head on his shoulder.

"You understand that whatever she wrote is only a small fraction of her life," Alex said consolingly. "Has it ever occurred to you that maybe the most precious things in her life were things she wanted to keep protected? Writing secrets about things you care about is dangerous you know."

She sniffed and whimpered, "But there's absolutely no mention of me. None at all. You would think she'd say she just found out she was pregnant."

"If you were an unmarried woman, would you write that in a journal? Did you tell the girls before we wed that you were pregnant?"

"No," she said. "Sissy calls it our 'honeymoon baby,'" she laughed.

He smiled. "When the baby comes, I'm sure she'll stop saying that. Do you think Marie or Martha knew we were pregnant before the wedding?"

"I'm sure they knew we were pregnant before the wedding. But they wouldn't dare ask me about it. I didn't tell them until a few weeks after the wedding. Telling them right after the wedding would have seemed …" she trailed off, tapping her finger to her mouth.

"Exactly. Usually, people don't speak about such things. I'm sure that there was a lot of things happening in your mother's life that she left out of her entries."

"Then why write?" asked Madeline perplexed.

He rubbed circles into her back, "Never mind that, Madeline. There may never be any clear answers to what happened to your mother and your grandparents. But you're going to be a mother in six months. What do you know about being a mother to a small infant?"

She felt ashamed. He was right; she would never know what happened. If the culprit was still out there, they had twenty years to cover their tracks. Her emerald eyes reflected a dark sorrow that he couldn't bear.

"We'll go to Swan Manor on Friday," he said without thinking.

"Really?" she asked hopeful.

"Yes. It may give you some closure. But you must promise me that after that, you will try to let go. You need to move on from this," he said patting the stack of journals.

She nodded knowing he was right. He helped her to her feet. "You know, there are other ways of getting some closure, too," he went on. "You should try taking an interest in some of the things your mother used to do. You told me she used to play the harp. Maybe you should head to the Music Room more often."

"That might help," she agreed.

"But for now, let's find some books," he said giving her a hug.

She wiped away her tears and followed him over to the shelves.

Several hours later, Marie and Madeline returned to Frogmore by coach. Though she had taken some books about pregnancy with her, she gave them to Marie as she continued reading through her mother's journals.

When they arrived at Frogmore, Madeline noticed something strange. Tracks of mud were on the floor, and carpet in the entrance.

"What on earth?"

"Whoever it was, had big feet," Marie said.

Madeline said nothing but followed the wet, muddy tracks. They led up the stairs through her drawing room and into her room. The room had been destroyed. The curtains to her canopy bed were slashed, and pulled from their rings, the mattress flopped over the side. All her vanity drawers had been pulled out and her makeup thrown about the floor. She saw her and Alex's clothes strewn about the floor by the closet door. Next to the fireplace, all the cushions from the couches were tossed about. Her armoire had been broken into, each box within it, opened. The only thing left untouched was her dressing screen.

Marie sighed, "Did they take anything?"

"It doesn't look like it."

"Maybe they were looking for something?"

"Maybe these," Madeline said, gesturing to the journals in her hands.

"Maybe," Marie said reluctantly. Marie hated to admit it, but since nothing was taken, what else could the trespasser want?

They left the room and found Mr. Barry. Immediately, he had all the servants in Frogmore report to the kitchen, but they were quickly dismissed. Unfortunately, no one had witnessed anyone come in.

MR. SHEFFIELD

*I*t wasn't easy, but Madeline followed Alex's advice and tried to experiment with some of the interests her mother had. Alex had some footmen bring some instruments over to Frogmore, and he tried to teach her to play the harp. But since Alex was so busy, it was hard to find time for lessons. So, Madeline decided to give a few of Elizabeth's other hobbies a try. Of course, there were things she knew she couldn't do, like attend parties. Given that the country was under threat, it would be dangerous for her to go gallivanting at parties. It would also look bad on the crown's reputation. She wanted to try gambling, but that too was done at social events.

But her mother was a very social person. Everything she did involved seeing or being around people. Madeline had always wanted to be that type of person, the one everyone was dying to meet and talk to. In that sense, she and her mother were nothing alike. Madeline loved being with people, but she also needed time away from them. Through her journal, Elizabeth was always describing conversations she had over tea with friends, watching horseback racing, and going to see a show of Punch and Judy. Madeline could hardly imagine herself doing those types of things. Though she did have afternoon tea with friends, Elizabeth consistently invited people she didn't know around for tea because she simply wanted to get to know them.

Though there were plenty of people at court Madeline knew she should start getting familiar with, the idea of inviting a stranger over was daunting. In some cases, awkward. She had been a servant most her life, what kind of conversation would she and a noble have? She had never entertained strangers on her own either. She'd much prefer someone she was familiar with. Then it hit her. She hadn't seen him in ages and he was someone that her mother may have had over for tea, Mr. Sheffield.

It took several days to make the arrangements, but eventually one of the royal carriages made its way to London and brought Mr. Sheffield to Frogmore. He arrived early afternoon and though Madeline wasn't supposed to see her guests in, she sat in the entrance, anxiously awaiting his arrival. It had been so long since they had a real conversation. The last time she had seen him was briefly at her wedding and she felt ashamed that she hadn't thought of inviting him then.

The footmen by the door stood staring at her. She knew they had probably found it strange that she was there, but she didn't care. She wondered if it would be inappropriate to have a conversation with them. They had been at Frogmore since she had started living there, but Lord Walsh had made it plain that speaking to servants was rude. He had told her that servants didn't want to have conversations with their masters; trying to socialize as though servants were equals made servants disrespect their masters. He also said it made servants feel awkward because they are not comfortable speaking to someone much more educated than themselves. Of course, when he said this, Madeline reminded him that she was a servant once, to which he retorted, "Did you ever start a conversation with Lady Watson?"

She didn't answer him. Her reason for never speaking to Lady Watson in a casual manner was because she didn't like her. As she sat there staring at the men, she pondered if they felt the same way about her as she did about Lady Watson. *Why am I questioning this? I used to be a servant, I don't see myself above them.* Alex himself knew the names of most of the servants and addressed them by name before commanding them. What harm could there be in having a pleasant conversation? "It seems odd; you both serving me, and me not knowing your names," she began. "What would you prefer to be called?"

Both men looked at one another, shocked. It took a moment but the gangly one with red hair spoke, "I'm Henri Carver."

"Where are you from Mr. Carver?"

"Plymouth."

"Oh," she said. She had no idea where that was.

He immediately recognized her confusion, "It's quite far from here, across the country, by the sea. It's a port town."

"Really? I'm sure you had the opportunity to go sailing abroad then?"

"Yes, I did. But I get seasick quite easily. I'm a land lover."

She chuckled. "And you," she said directing herself to the other footman. "What's your name? Where are you from?"

His eyes widened. It seemed as though he was startled at her lack of manners. "Caldwell," he said shortly, his eyes glued to the wall in front of him. "I'm from Liverpool."

She carried on the conversation with Mr. Carver, and they talked for a while about Plympton and his family. But she noticed that Mr. Caldwell kept to himself, an expression of disdain on his face as he stared ahead of him. She tried to ignore it, but she knew that there was some truth to what Lord Walsh had said. But she wasn't sure whose lack of manners Mr. Caldwell was more repulsed by, hers or Mr. Carver's.

After several minutes, the carriage approached Frogmore, "I suppose I should get back to work," Mr. Carver beamed.

"That's right Mr. Carver," Madeline joked. "Working at Frogmore should not be all fun and games."

He nodded. She knew she had crossed some boundaries. More than Alex would have. But going from the life of a servant to a queen wasn't easy.

Mr. Carver left to retrieve Mr. Barry. There was a silence between the two as they waited. Mr. Barry arrived, "Gentlemen, the doors."

Both Mr. Carver and Mr. Caldwell opened the double doors as Mr. Barry went outside to invite Mr. Sheffield in. She watched from the threshold excitedly as Mr. Sheffield stepped out of the carriage and pressed his glasses higher up the bridge of his nose.

As she stood waiting, she was itching to run out and greet him. But to do so would look poorly on her. She waited.

"Your Majesty," Mr. Sheffield said, as he entered and bowed. She felt a twinge of sadness, usually when she came into his shop, he would say, 'Madeline, my dear,' brightly, then comment on how she was looking more and more like her mother.

"Hello, Mr. Sheffield. I'm so glad you could make it." The words and her manner felt so unnatural, she couldn't help herself, "But I think I'll always be Madeline to you."

"Would you prefer that?" he asked.

"I may have become Queen, but I prefer to keep my dearest friends casual."

"Of course, you do my dear," he said winking.

"Come this way," she said taking his hand. "They'll be serving us tea in the Green Pavilion."

He followed her down the Colonnade and he immediately noticed the beautiful life-sized vases and stone planters. There were lavish red and gold drapes hung about a row of windows. As he walked past he looked outside and got a view of a gorgeous blue pond surrounded by lush greenery. When they reached the Green Pavilion, he noticed a circular table in the centre of the room. The walls were filled with large paintings with thick gold ornate frames. Of course, the walls were green, but the chairs and curtains were a beautiful red fabric with a gold leaf weaved pattern. The room also had some beautiful ornate mahogany dressers and he couldn't help but ponder how much they would sell for.

"So it seems the last thing you stole was worth it," he said taking a seat.

She looked around the room curiously, "Oh, the vase?"

"No. The King's heart."

She blushed.

"I have to be honest Madeline, I've often wondered how it all unfolded."

He was one of the few people that had asked her how she and Alex came to be, and she knew why. Such personal questions would never be asked to a royal, but she knew there was nothing she couldn't tell him. In the darkest times of her life, he was always there. She felt a pang of guilt. *Why did I take so long to invite him over?* "I'm sorry I didn't talk to you at the wedding," she said.

"That's fine, Madeline," he said earnestly. "You were the bride of the King of England. I doubt you had much time for anyone that evening."

It was true, the schedule of the day left little time for socializing. The time she did have, she had spent alone with Alex, and she wouldn't change that. "Thanks for being so understanding. How have you been?"

"I'm very well. But you seem to keep changing the subject. How did you and the King come to be?"

"Oh, I'm sorry," she said half-laughing. "I suppose it looks as though I'm trying to avoid that. We met at Lady Watson's anniversary party, do you remember the day I came into your shop and Miss Susanna was there?"

"How could I forget? The look on her face when you didn't address her as a Lady was priceless. I think of it from time to time whenever I'm down."

She chuckled, "That's an excellent idea."

Two servants entered and served them their afternoon tea trays. Mr. Sheffield looked down in amazement. The way the sandwiches, scones, and desserts were presented on their trays made them look like pieces of art.

"So you met King Alexander at Lady Watson's anniversary party?" he said picking up a cucumber sandwich. "Did he immediately ask you to work for him?"

"No. I displeased Lady Watson that night. She had Will sell me at auction the next day."

He looked at her sympathetically, "I'm sorry I couldn't find someone better to take you in Madeline. I would have done so myself if I could have afforded to."

"I know that," she said.

"Do you know why I couldn't?"

She nodded. Though he never told her, she knew that his wife was not well and needed around the clock care.

"Is that-" she felt embarrassed for asking, so she stopped.

"Go on Madeline, ask."

"I read in my mother's journals that her mother wasn't quite well either. Do they suffer from the same thing? My mother did not -"

"Yes. They have the same problem it seems."

"Does Margaret communicate well?"

"Margaret communicates better than your grandmother did. When I met Elizabeth, she told me that the poor woman could only say one or two words at a time. The words she did say were quite disturbing."

"Oh. Do you know how my grandmother came to suffering from it?"

"Your grandfather had said she had fallen out of the carriage while they were riding, hit her head on a rock."

"That's horrible."

Madeline didn't need to ask about Margaret. She knew she suffered many fits a day and was slowly deteriorating.

"There's something else we've never really talked about," Madeline began, "because I've always ignored the subject."

"What would you like to talk about your Majesty?" he asked with a smirk on his face.

"My mother."

"I was beginning to think you wouldn't ever ask," he said, choked up.

"Who was she?"

"Your mother was the most compassionate, kind hearted person I ever met."

"How did you become such good friends?" Madeline asked, setting her teacup on her saucer.

"I was just starting my business. My father thought I was crazy. I suppose I should probably explain my background a bit. I didn't grow up in London, I grew up on a farm in Aylesbury Vale. You probably have no idea where that is."

She chuckled, "Actually I do. Sir Gregory's family lives there."

"Yes, my family know the Umbridges quite well. Our families had always helped one another through bad seasons."

"Small world," Madeline said in amazement.

"Indeed, it is."

"It seems you know so many people I know."

"Sorry to correct you your Majesty, but I think you know everyone I know."

"You're right. I suppose you knew the Umbridges and my mother before I did.So you were starting your business?" Madeline said returning to the subject.

"Yes. Margaret had just suffered her accident on the farm. She could no longer help."

Madeline nodded in understanding. Though he never talked in detail about what had happened to Margaret, she had once met her and understood Margaret may have suffered a brain injury. Her speech was slurred and sometimes she had difficulty completing sentences.

"There wasn't enough money in farming to have someone look after her, so I moved us to London. I thought if I could start a successful business, I could pay for someone to take care of her and set some money aside for retirement. I sold off all the land my father bestowed me. It was enough to get us settled in London."

"Did Margaret have a hard time adjusting?" Madeline asked.

"At first, she did. It was a trial finding a caretaker that was patient and understanding. Some of them treated her like a child. The ones that did, I couldn't stand. I knew the accident had addled her mind, but she still had her dignity. She was still my Margaret."

"You're a very good man," said Madeline as she put down her tea.

"Your mother was a very good woman. That's how I met her. You see when Elizabeth first returned to England, she was getting accustomed to her mother again. The accident happened when she was so young she couldn't remember your grandmother. Unfortunately, your grandmother couldn't remember her either. She had completely forgotten who Elizabeth was."

Madeline felt a deep sadness, "That must have been so hard. Did she have much to say about it?"

"Elizabeth didn't prefer to talk about depressing things. But the first time she came into my shop, she opened up to me, once I told her about Margaret, of course."

"Really? What did she say?"

"Elizabeth had come in to get a gift for her mother. She hadn't the money to spend to go to one of the ritziest shops, so she gave my shop a try. She shared with me that she had recently come from France and was trying to communicate with her mother. Lady Swan would scream when Elizabeth entered the room. She thought buying a gift might help Lady Swan understand that she had no intentions to hurt her."

Madeline's eyes widened, "Lady Swan thought her daughter would hurt her?"

He sighed, "I think Lady Swan was just fearful of unfamiliar faces."

Madeline nodded, "I suppose that makes sense."

"After that visit, your mother brought in all her friends from the court. Soon I had regular visitors from many of the upper nobility. Because of Elizabeth, Margaret and I were able to establish ourselves here in London."

"I suppose it was fate that you met then," said Madeline as she realized that had her mother not forged a relationship with Mr. Sheffield, there was no telling where she would have ended up. Most likely at Madam Ravine's brothel. She took another sip of her tea.

Mr. Sheffield watched her, "All the years I've known you Madeline, you've never been curious about your mother. I've always noticed that whenever I brought her up, you'd either change the subject or pretend you hadn't heard what I said. I always thought her death had bothered you, and you just didn't prefer to talk about her. What has changed?"

She bit her lip, "The truth is Mr. Sheffield, I never knew about my mother's death. My father never told me."

He gaped unblinking, his face turning a dark red shade, he tried his best to calm himself, but he spoke his intonation harsh, "Isaac never told you?"

"No, he didn't," she said embarrassed though she knew it wasn't her fault. "He told me my mother was dead, but he never explained what happened. I always assumed she had gotten sick after my birth."

He put down his tea, "Please, forgive me. I should have told you more about her, even if you weren't willing to listen."

"Don't be hard on yourself. Perhaps it was better that I grew up not knowing, I think it would have made me a bitter person," she said. "When I first learned about it, I was shocked and then in time I became angry because my mother wasn't the foolish girl that I thought she was. Now, I want to know the truth of what happened that night. I want to know who thought she didn't deserve her life and I didn't deserve a mother or grandparents. It bothers me that the killer has gotten away with it." She started to cry, "She and my grandparents still haven't had a proper burial." Madeline dropped her hands to her lap and tears began streaming down her face.

Mr. Sheffield stared in astonishment. He had always known her to be such a brave, strong girl. Not even when Madeline had been sold into slavery by her father did she shed a tear. Nor did she feel sorry for herself for the abuse Lady and Lord Watson had put her through. Elizabeth's tragic and mysterious death had rocked Madeline to her core. But he understood why; she was a bright girl and knew not to allow horrible people like the Watsons or her father affect her. Elizabeth's death was different. Whoever had done it robbed her of a better life and to some extent her identity. He took a handkerchief from his coat pocket and handed it to her.

She wiped her eyes with it, "Thank you," she said meekly, "I'm sorry I'm so emotional."

"Don't feel sorry, Madeline. If it's any consolation, I think your mother would be very proud of you."

She raised her head from her hands, "Why?"

"You've overcome so much to get to where you are."

"What do you mean?" she asked, "Frogmore?"

He laughed, "No, no. You're happy. You're not living your life in fear. Just before she met Isaac, your mother started to act strangely. Very scared. Very paranoid."

Madeline could imagine why. If Elizabeth was living in fear, it was likely because her relationship with the Duke wasn't going well. Perhaps he had a dark secret. Maybe he preferred the company of men and Elizabeth had found out; it was common knowledge that the Duke hadn't courted any other woman before or since Elizabeth's death. "What are your thoughts on the Duke of Axford?" Madeline asked.

"I knew him well. But after he and your mother stopped courting, we had a bit of a falling out."

"Why?"

"He was asking questions. He wanted to know where your mother and father were residing."

"You didn't tell him?" Madeline assumed.

"Heavens no. I was your mother's friend. I wouldn't betray her trust like that."

"Do you think the Duke really loved my mother or do you think it was all an act?"

"The Duke has always been a mysterious sort of man. Weeks after the deaths, so many strange rumours floated around about him."

"Like what?" she asked intrigued.

"Any bizarre theory you could imagine," he admitted. "There used to be a farmer that lived not far from Swan Manor, the man claimed to have seen the Duke that night running through a field down to a small pond, covered in blood. There was also a rumour that for weeks after, while the investigation was commencing, the Duke spent his time hiding in the forest around Swan Manor."

"Hiding out in the forest?" she asked in disbelief. "Why on earth would he do that?"

"I doubt either rumour to be true," Mr. Sheffield said shaking his head. "What person would incriminate themselves by spending time nearby the crime scene?"

"Right."

"Of course, there were other rumours that he was seeing other women just after the deaths, spending time at some of the brothels. Apparently, he behaved rather oddly."

"How so?"

Mr. Sheffield cringed, then hesitantly began to speak, "Well, I'm not certain about this, you understand how sometimes rumours can be exaggerated. It was rumoured that he once went into the brothel, and requested to see all the ladies with black hair and green eyes. Naturally, black hair and green eyes are an unusual combination. There was only one lady there with black hair, but she had blue eyes."

Madeline could feel herself growing sick. She wished she hadn't asked. He noted the expression on her face.

"Oh no. It wasn't quite like that. He didn't want to sleep with the girl," Mr. Sheffield said quickly. "He had requested that she put on a dress. I imagine it must have belonged to your mother. Then he asked to sit down and talk with her."

"Do you know what the conversation was about? What he asked?" she asked swallowing hard, worried of what the answer might be.

"No one quite knows. But the conversation left the lady in such a state that immediately afterward she began to dye her hair blonde. She was anxious that he might come back to have another conversation or possibly want something more from her."

"Do you know who the name of the woman, Mr. Sheffield?"

"Sorry Madeline, I don't know. It was twenty years ago. I'm sure whoever she was, she isn't working the brothels now."

"True," she said. She looked away into the gardens outside the window. Madeline would give anything to know whom she was. Whatever the Duke said, it must have been disturbing. Possibly a confession. She continued to pry further into what Mr. Sheffield knew, "What's the oddest rumour you ever heard?" she asked curiously.

"There was a rumour that the Duke had hired all the servants that had worked at Swan Manor immediately after the murders." Madeline's jaw dropped, but he shook his head. "I doubt it's true, though. There was such a dark cloud following that man during that time, I don't think any servant that served the Swans would be able to work under his roof."

Madeline nodded in understanding. She knew that the Swans were known for treating their servants well. They servants wouldn't feel comfortable working for someone thought to be their killer. She took a deep breath, nervous about her next question, "Do you think the Duke of Axford is the killer?"

He hesitated, "I know many think that he was the killer. For the most part, the theories make sense. No one has ever found the bodies, and the man owns so many residences, he could have hidden them in a number of places. But-"

"But what?"

"While that is a very logical explanation, there is one thing that doesn't make sense."

"What might that be?"

"His servants."

She dropped her scone on her plate, dumbfounded, "His servants?"

"Yes. I mean, it would be quite scandalous, a murderous Duke. With all the servants he has, you'd think one of them would know something. It has been over twenty years and you never hear any gossip or word on the subject from any of them. No confessions, nothing."

She understood what he was hinting at. If the Duke had killed the Swans, the servants that waited upon him at the time would have known something: what time he came home that night, if he had a murder weapon, or any odd behaviour. "Do you think he paid them not to speak about it," she asked.

"I suppose that's possible. But you'd think one of them would have let something slip to a newspaper or The Society Pages by now. Many of the servants that had worked for him at the time of the Swans deaths would have gone into retirement by now. If they knew something they'd have something to gain, why haven't they talked?"

"I suppose he paid them a lot," she said shortly.

"Possibly. Or maybe they did have a good master and he politely asked them never to speak of the matter. If he did do it, and one of them shared the information, he would never be able to catch up with them to punish them. There's a good chance, he'd be sitting in jail awaiting torture and hanging for killing the Queen's mother."

Madeline was speechless. She had never thought of it that way, she had forgotten the power she now wielded. If someone had information on her family's deaths, they would be generously rewarded, but no one had come forward. She tapped her finger to her chin, contemplating if she should advertise a reward for information that would lead to the killer's capture. But that would likely lead to all sorts of folks coming forward spinning any lie for the chance that it might lead to the Duke's capture. When the baby was born and the war was over, she would have Alex organize a search for the woman that the Duke had seen in the brothels. Though she desperately wanted answers now, she knew Alex had far enough stress already.

"What's going on in that head of yours, Madeline?"

She blinked, "Oh well, I just thought you made an excellent point. If the servants knew anything, they would have come forward by now."

He looked at her sceptically, "You know if you really think it was the Duke, why don't you just ask him? The man is like the walking dead. Almost soulless. He might be carrying around so much grief now, confessing might relieve him of that burden."

She hardly knew what to say, the thought had crossed her mind, "I can't deny that I have thought of confronting him, but I can't."

"Why?"

"I'm afraid of what he might tell me."

"I can understand that," he said grimly.

They continued to eat and talk and Madeline asked him more about Margaret, "So how is Margaret these days?"

He gave a well-practiced smile, looking into Madeline's eyes,

"She's doing well. She's taken to taking walks with Harriet."

"That's good to hear, so Harriet is still her nurse?"

He nodded, trying to hold back his emotion. Madeline looked so much like her mother and had it been Elizabeth, he would have told her the truth. Margaret wasn't doing that well. With each passing day, she was finding it more challenging to communicate and was forgetting words. That was the reason they wanted to take her out for more walks, to remind Margaret of what things were, to watch people move and describe to Harriet what they were doing, hoping some of what was discussed would stick. There was a time he only needed to read to Margaret to help her remember words. But now she needed visuals, it was tiring for her to try to imagine stories in books. Everyday Harriet would take her out for a walk in the morning, and when he arrived home in the late afternoon he'd take her for another.

It was also getting harder to get her the care she needed. At home nurses were becoming more expensive now that Napoleon's war was over and they were in high demand. Harriet had already been offered more money to go elsewhere. Mr. Sheffield wasn't sure what her price would be, but he knew that if offered enough, there was a good chance Harriet would leave them.

But he couldn't bring himself to tell Madeline that. People that lived in his kind of situation were not allowed to be honest. The truth depressed people and made for awkward conversations.

"So how is it being a queen?" he asked, pouring himself and Madeline more tea. "Do you feel the pressure? I've read The Society Pages; they seem to be quite interested in to know if you're pregnant yet."

"Are they?" she asked intrigued.

"Yes, having you seen all the articles written about you lately?"

"Actually no," she said, shaking her head. "Alex doesn't like to have The Society Pages in the royal residences. He only reads articles if one of the Lords or advisors think that something needs to be brought to his attention."

"And this doesn't need his attention?"

"Why? Is it something terrible? What's being written?"

"Nothing terrible has been written. They have interviewed plenty of people at court and some Lords and Ladies have been discussing their thoughts of whether you're pregnant or not and what sex the baby might be."

Her mouth hung open, "Oh, my. I suppose this is part of being royalty though. So, anything interesting?"

"Naturally because you used to work for the Watsons, they were interviewed."

Madeline rolled her eyes, "Blast, I can't imagine what they might say."

"You know Lady Watson always has to make things about herself," he said in distain.

"Oh yes. Let me guess. She thinks I am pregnant and I'm going to have a girl and name it after her."

He howled, "That's a good guess, but not quite. She claims to have seen you here at Frogmore and that you have confided to her that you are pregnant."

"Ha!"

"She also claims that she introduced you to the King."

"She really is something, isn't she?" she grimaced.

"Yes, I suppose that's why the King hasn't been informed."

"No. I'm sure someone would tell him of those remarks," said Madeline placing her cup in her saucer. "He just doesn't want to worry me with that rubbish."

"Does it bother you?"

"Absolutely not," Madeline giggled. "She's not well liked at court. Chances are no one will buy her nonsense."

But then Madeline realized that Lady Watson's claims weren't nonsense; she was pregnant and though the court didn't know, in time they would. Madeline didn't want Mr. Sheffield to find out through The Society Pages or a noble that she was expecting. She would have to tell him now. "I should be honest with you though," she paused trying to hold back a grin, "Alex and I are expecting."

His lips curved, "Congratulations, Madeline," he said quietly. "I'm happy for you. I'm sure if your mother were here she'd be over the moon."

"But very few know," said Madeline cautiously.

"I understand," he said knowingly. "I won't tell anyone."

They talked for a few hours and soon the sunlight began to fade.

"Would you like to stay for dinner?" Madeline asked. "I can give you accommodations for the night."

"I would Madeline, but as you know, it's a long trip back to London and I have to see that Margaret is taken care of."

"Right," she said feeling ashamed of herself. He had spent the morning and part of the afternoon there, taking his time with Margaret away, hardly thinking of how his visit may disrupt his schedule.

Then it dawned on her; if he left now, he wouldn't arrive back in London until dark. Harriet was working a late night. What had that cost him? Having his store closed for a day to see her, what had that cost him?

Her heart sank, but at the same time she was grateful he came. He was her oldest friend and was always there for her despite how burdensome it was for him to do so.

"You should get going then," she said. "It will be hard for Margaret, you not coming home at your usual time."

He nodded, thankful that she understood.

"Wait here a moment," she said, "I'll ask someone to get your carriage prepared for you."

He gave her a confused look as she quickly got up and scooted out of the room. She walked down the Colonnade, her eyes searching about. There had to be something worth more than its weight in gold, something for a retirement. She looked at the vases between each of the windows but had no idea of their worth. She considered giving him the Ming Dynasty vase she had stolen, but decided against it. She knew Alex had a bit of an attachment to the vase now. Though Frogmore was one of the more modest royal residences, there had to be something of substantial value.

She spotted an exquisite clock sitting on a pedestal. She had noticed it many times before. It was one of a kind, made of mahogany, ebony, silver and gold, she knew that it chimed beautifully and from time to time when walking down the hall she would hear it. She'd miss the sounds, but their absence would remind her that her friend Mr. Sheffield no longer had to worry about the future. She went to the front hall, both Mr. Carver and Mr. Caldwell bowed.

"Your Majesty," they said in unison.

"Mr. Carver, could you and Mr. Barry take the clock in the Colonnade to Mr. Sheffield's carriage. I'm giving it to him as a gift."

"Yes, your Majesty," he said bowing.

She went back to the Green Pavilion, but said nothing about the gift. She knew that if she handed it to Mr. Sheffield during the visit, he wouldn't accept it. Putting it in the carriage and then telling him before leaving that she had gotten him a gift would be easier. "I'm so glad you came," she began. "It was good to see you."

"Thank you, Madeline, it was wonderful being here. It's such a relief to me," he said, almost on the verge of tears. This took her by surprise. "There were many nights I worried for you."

Her lips trembled, feeling a lump in her throat, "I wouldn't be here if you didn't do everything you did. You gave me food when my father didn't come home from the pubs. You saved me from a life in a brothel. You told Alex that I was the child of Elizabeth Swan. If you didn't do those things, I don't think I would be here." Her eyes filled, a teardrop escaped down her cheek.

"You were always a good girl," he said softly. "You didn't deserve the situation you were born into. I had to help."

"I didn't deserve the circumstances I was born into," she admitted. "But you didn't have to help me, you chose to."

They hugged, squeezing each other tightly. It was miraculous. Despite all the obstacles they had both had, somehow their lives had turned out better than they could have planned. It was at that moment Madeline knew that it was divine intervention that they had been a part of each other's lives. Neither of them could have imagined when she was still a child that they would save each other from poverty.

Madeline escorted him back through the Colonnade. He didn't notice the clock missing and they continued through the foyer. Mr. Carver and Mr. Caldwell opened the double doors, bowing. The carriage was prepared, ready with a driver and Madeline escorted Mr. Sheffield to the carriage.

Mr. Caldwell followed them and opened the door to the carriage. Mr. Sheffield saw the clock sitting on one of the bench seats. "What is that?" he said in amazement.

"That is a gift from me to you," she said casually.

"Madeline, no. Do you have any idea of how much that clock would be worth?"

"I do," she said, "but I want you to sell it. I want it to be the last thing that your shop ever sells. It bothers me that you spend your nights worrying about your circumstances. It is time you live life with your wife, not stuck in a shop hoping you can provide her one."

"It's such a beautiful piece I'm not sure that I should accept it. Surely you don't want to part with it?"

"I won't miss it. But its absence will give me comfort. Every time I don't see it there or don't hear it chime, I know that you will be home with Margaret, having a life with her. Not stuck in a shop trying to afford her care. You deserve this. If you ever need more, or it's not enough, don't hesitate to come back."

He gaped at it knowing it was more than enough. He could sell his business and live quite comfortably with Margaret for years. "Madeline, I- I-" he stumbled, his eyes filled to the brim.

"Don't say anything. You've done enough."

He nodded, "Thank you."

She hugged him, "You have a nice evening with Mrs. Sheffield."

"I'm certain we will."

He climbed into the carriage, "When you and his Majesty decide to visit London again, let me know."

"I will," she smiled, "we'll keep in touch."

She stepped away from the carriage and Mr. Caldwell shut the door. The driver snapped the reigns into the air and the horse took off at a trot. As she watched, she felt a swelling in her heart. Though she knew she couldn't fix all of the Sheffield's problems, she did make things much easier for them.

PRIVATE MEETING

⚜

*S*ir Ashton was briefing everyone on the rumours of Susanna and Carlos in the House of Lords meeting, "It seems that the Prince of Spain and Susanna Bathory arrived in Santander and are now heading back to Madrid. We've had a few of our ships return from the Mediterranean, and many of them reported spotting the Duke of Axford's ship on the coast. It will be a matter of a couple of weeks before they meet with King Fernando if they haven't already. It doesn't give us much time, but I imagine King Fernando will be able to organize his army and fleets and attack Windsor, within a few weeks of their arrival."

Alex wasn't paying much attention. He was busy staring down at the Duke of Axford from his pulpit. The Duke of Axford had returned in the sneakiest of ways. It started several days earlier when Lord Winthrop claimed to have 'witnessed' one of Bathory's men follow Madeline into the secret passageways the night of her debutante ball. A full, signed confession came from one of the imprisoned men in London Tower quickly thereafter. A Spanish man by the name of Emilio Abaroa claimed to have threatened Madeline in the secret passageways with a knife.

Soon afterwards, the Duke started going to public events claiming that he had been staying at his residence in Edinburgh for some time and that he had never disappeared. He managed to create several alibis for Madeline's debutante ball as well. Some of the Lords backed up his story and one of his head butlers claimed that only he of his servants knew of his vacation to Edinburgh, and was unaware that Alex's men were searching for him.

It incensed Alex that the Duke had so much control over his own court that even Alex himself could not question him. Lord Winthrop, Alex's personal lawyer was one of the Duke's witnesses! It was a testament to how much power the Duke had, even though he spent much of his time in isolation.

Alex hadn't the courage to tell Madeline. He knew that even if he did put the Duke on trial, Madeline would lose. It would be her word against the Duke and everyone willing to lie for a bribe. What price he paid them, Alex had no idea. How he got a signed confession from one of the Spanish prisoners was beyond him as well. Alex couldn't imagine how angry the situation would make her. The break-in at Frogmore had her only speaking of one thing;

"HE OBVIOUSLY WOULD KNOW how to get in here Alex," Madeline said yesterday over dinner. "He was a close friend and cousin of your father's, wasn't he?"

"There weren't many guards around Frogmore," he tried to reason, "it wouldn't be hard for someone to sneak in."

"Oh, please," she said, slapping her fork down. "The person who came into Frogmore knows the grounds inside and out. The Duke does, I'm sure. He came straight to my room. His tracks led directly there! I want you to find him and imprison him."

ALEX SIGHED to himself as Sir Ashton continued with the meeting. Ashton began discussing rumours of Napoleon. Some of the Lords began to speak, describing things they had heard about Napoleon in their social circles and how he had planned to return. Alex was annoyed by this.

"Stop, Lord Pye," Alex interrupted. "Does anyone have any information about Napoleon that can be backed up with facts? There will always be whispers of him returning, but unless there is evidence to back up these claims, this talk is a waste of our time. Many of these rumours contradict one another. The sightings are beyond ridiculous, as we have men reporting to us from Elba."

"But your Majesty," Lord Pye began, "you don't want your subjects to think that you aren't taking any kind of action."

"I assure you that many qualified men are at Elba with Napoleon," said Alex abruptly. "His activities are being watched closely. I have been receiving reports daily. Is anyone here willing to offer who their sources are, and why we should trust these sources over mine?"

No one answered.

"Let's move on," Alex continued. "There are several Lords here that I would like to meet with concerning the battle plan for the Spaniards when they come. I'm certain they will. Sir Ashton will contact you to let you know when our first meeting will be scheduled. It will be within the next couple of days."

"I will do so immediately after this meeting, your Majesty," said Sir Ashton.

The meeting went on for another hour, then the Lords were dismissed. Afterwards, Alex went directly to Sir Ashton, "Tell the Duke of Axford I'd like to speak with him immediately," Alex whispered to Ashton.

"Where shall I take him, your Majesty?"

"The Green Drawing Room."

As Alex waited for the Duke to join him, he questioned how he should bring up the subject of the Duke's disappearance. He sat on one of the green silk couches by the fireplace watching the candles in the chandelier above him burn. It wasn't going to be an easy conversation; he was certain the Duke would lie and remind him of how much control he had over the court. The Duke entered, and Alex's eyes dropped from the chandelier.

"Your Majesty," he bowed, "you wished to speak to me?"

"Yes Walt," said Alex clearing his throat, "have a seat."

The Duke sat across from him on a green silk upholstered chair, nervously tapping its gold gilt arms. He looked over at the doll's house.

"Still have the doll's house, hm?" the Duke said uncomfortably.

"Yes."

"Keeping it for future little ones?" he asked.

It was now Alex who felt uncomfortable. He and Madeline decided not to tell the court that she was pregnant just yet. *If the Duke knows, how did he find out?*

"Yes, someday I suppose," Alex said casually.

"Your mother was certain you'd be a girl, Alex," the Duke said smiling.

"Yes. I know."

"She was an odd woman -"

"You're not here to discuss what my mother was like with me," Alex said curtly.

"You didn't know her well," the Duke said, "I thought I would-"

"She didn't seem to care to know me," Alex interrupted brusquely. "I asked you here to discuss my Queen among other things."

The Duke moved about in his chair and scratched his nose, "Go on, your Majesty."

"Why did you attack Madeline at her debutante ball? You deliberately risked being seen going into the secret passageways and held a knife to her throat."

"You believe rumours and idle gossip, your Majesty?" he asked staring into Alex's eyes.

Alex raised his brow, "I believe my wife, your Grace."

"You do know there is not a trace of evidence that ties me to Swan Manor the night of the murders?" the Duke said his eyes intense. "I'm sure Madeline would imagine that it was me in the passageways. Many are convinced that I murdered the Swans. I'm sure she is no different."

Alex continued, "Stop lying or trying to change the subject, Walt. You disappeared after threatening her. Why?"

He rolled his eyes, "Let's say hypothetically speaking, I did enter the passageways and threatened her. Well then, why didn't I kill her? It would have been easy, if I did have a knife to her throat." He frowned. "It should be obvious that whoever threatened the Queen, may have been trying to take her to a safer place. But it backfired because she managed to get away."

"It doesn't look good Walter," Alex said understanding the Duke's true intent, "you must admit."

"I know. That's why I decided to lie low for a while. I had hoped that as time passed, she would realize that I'm not a threat to her. Or perhaps I would find an opportunity to prove that I do not intend to harm her."

Alex shook his head, "You should have come to me then," he steepled his fingertips, "Walter, you're an odd man. I never know where your loyalties lie."

"My loyalties lie with one person and one person alone," he said calmly. The words sent a shiver up Alex's spine.

"Not me?" said Alex knowingly.

"No."

"Not Lord Bathory?"

"No," the Duke said simply, half-laughing. "I know you have reasons to believe that I might support his ideologies, but for the record, I've always thought the man was a fool. Why would I have ever considered Elizabeth Swan, the daughter of a lowly Baron, if I believed in his rubbish?"

"When Lord Bathory escaped Curfew Tower, did you know it was through the tunnel that leads to one of your residences in Windsor?"

"That's impossible!" Walt exclaimed. "I have the only key that would open that tunnel."

"Have you seen that key recently?" Alex asked.

The Duke paused and closed his eyes, "No. No, I haven't. It has been some time," he admitted in embarrassment.

"Why did you come back now?" Alex continued. "Susanna and

Carlos stole your ship. Now, more than ever, you look guilty of treason. Not to mention that Frogmore has been broken into twice since your disappearance."

The Duke furrowed his brow, "Do you know who the culprit is?"

"No clues, just a shredded wedding dress, muddy rugs, and a bedroom overturned. What were you looking for?"

"Don't be ridiculous Alex," he said waving his hand dismissively. "I have no reason to intrude on the Queen. Why would I destroy her wedding dress? Am I insanely jealous with love for you, your Majesty?" he chuckled.

Alex hesitated, coming to a revelation, "You gave Madeline Elizabeth's wedding dress, didn't you? Who else would have had her wedding dress all these years? Elizabeth had no family to leave it to."

The Duke said nothing but shifted uncomfortably in his chair, he looked over at a decanter on one of the tables, wishing he could pour himself a drink.

"Madeline's convinced that you were the person who tore her wedding dress to pieces, you know. She also believes you tore apart her room searching for something. Were you looking for Elizabeth's diaries, Walt?"

Again the Duke said nothing. Alex was growing frustrated. He couldn't understand what the Duke's motives were. He decided to change tack.

"You knew Elizabeth quite well. Madeline's quite curious of knowing more about her mother, but the diaries are confusing to read. Perhaps you could sit with her and answer any questions she may have."

"I'm not discussing Elizabeth with you or her," the Duke said firmly.

"Don't forget your place."

"Nor should you forget yours. Elizabeth Swan is not your business."

"No. Elizabeth Swan is not my business, but she is the Queen's," Alex said his voice rising. "Elizabeth was her mother. Don't act as though you are the only person mourning Elizabeth's death."

"Madeline never knew her," the Duke spat.

"Could you imagine what it would be like never to know your mother, to just know that she was brutally murdered, her body never found, nor her killer?"

The Duke sat with a hardened expression on his face.

"I have no proof to throw you in a cell, Walter. But with all the interesting evidence floating about, and a very anguished wife, I'm sure I could invent some," Alex threatened.

"If you were to do that, it would anger many of the Lords and Ladies of England. When you did a couple of months ago, even then you would only allow it a few weeks, Alex. There is no solid evidence. If you were to create some, the nobles would no longer respect you. Don't forget, I've also helped many of these families financially during trying times. I've helped many Lords politically. Many that hold office are there because I backed their campaigns and sometimes even mentored their careers. Who will they go to now? Not the King. Nobody would have the audacity to ask a King for money or a favour. I've given so many favours, I'm owed many. You may hold the crown, but I hold the purse strings of this court. It's been twenty years since Elizabeth's death. Nothing can be proven now. And my ship being stolen and that tunnel being used isn't evidence that I committed treason. Many Lords have used my residences as a place to stay while attending to political matters. My ships and carriages have been stolen before."

Alex clenched his teeth; it was seldom Alex wasn't in control. All his life the Duke of Axford made Alex question his power over the nobles. He remained calm, "Perhaps I should have someone investigate Swan Manor. Tear the place apart."

The blood drained from the Duke's face. But he quickly recollected himself, "That's already happened. They found nothing but that ghastly parlour."

"No one has dismantled the manor," Alex went on, staring hard at the Duke.

"What's the point?" the Duke asked his face turning green, his hands began to shake.

Alex glared at him, "I think it would be wise that you leave England for a while."

"Leave?" he repeated, curiously. He thought Alex might throw him into Curfew Tower again.

"Yes. I'm giving you an opportunity to go. That is what this meeting is actually about. My wife is very distraught by your presence, so I want you to leave England. Don't come back."

The Duke stood up shakily, his eyes not moving off Alex. He said nothing, and exited the room.

MEANWHILE, Madeline, Marie, and Martha sat in Madeline's drawing room at Frogmore. Madeline lay across a chaise longue, leaning on its back, her feet outstretched. Marie sat on its end, with pregnancy books surrounding her, pretending to decipher the words but just looked at the pictures. Martha sat across from them.

Madeline had a pregnancy book in her hands, but wasn't reading it. Between the pages, she had slipped in one of her mother's diaries.

"These books are nasty!" Martha said. "The lady that wrote this one said she had seven children. Who is crazy enough to have seven children? The only thing she has written about is how to lose pregnancy weight. She said the best way is to wear a corset during your pregnancy."

"Well, she's coming from lots of experience," Marie said. "Wearing a corset makes sense."

Madeline raised her eyebrow and looked up from her mother's writing, "Actually, Doctor Sheffield told me that I shouldn't wear any kind of stays or corsets as I get bigger."

"I've worked for a few ladies that did," Martha said. "I think it's true, but after seven kids I doubt using a corset would still work."

"Alex and I feel we should do what's best for the baby," Madeline said. "I was thinking of wearing my stays, but as soon as Doctor Sheffield mentioned that it was too restrictive for a growing body, Alex has been against it."

"Humph! He's just trying to make things easier for himself. I'm sure removing a stay isn't much fun for a man," Martha said. Marie blushed and giggled.

"Martha!" gasped Madeline in embarrassment.

"What? I'm sure his Majesty thinks that sex is still okay."

"We are not discussing this," Madeline said and went back to her mother's diary.

They were all silent for a few moments. But then Marie piped up, "What are the signs of pregnancy? I've been looking about this book and there isn't much. What did you feel?"

"Nothing at first, but then I threw up a few times. I was nauseous for a couple of weeks. I thought I was coming down with a bug."

"What would you have done if you got pregnant before? You know, when you first got to know him." Marie stopped, knowing she asked something far too personal.

Martha looked up in surprise.

"I don't know," admitted Madeline. "But I don't think Alex is the type of man to abandon a woman in that situation."

"Yes, they all seem that way," Martha said sarcastically.

"Do you think Harold would abandon me if I were?" asked Marie.

The two stared at her.

"Are you?" asked Martha.

"No," Marie said, "but lately we've been talking and Harold really wants-" she softly sucked her bottom lip.

Martha howled, "Harold's trying to lay with you? You mean you haven't yet?!"

Marie's humiliated expression said it all.

"You don't have to do anything you don't feel ready for," Madeline said. "If you want to do the honest, proper thing, I'm sure he'd wait. He's smitten."

"I know he'd wait," Marie agreed. "It's just I'm afraid of getting pregnant. I mean, what would I do?"

"I know lots of girls, some from France, even some in this court that have gotten abortions," Martha said in a hushed tone.

Marie looked aghast, "That's not something I could do."

Madeline looked out the window, lost in a daze. She was lucky

that Alex was a stand up man. She never felt he would force that decision on her. Guilt came over her. Everyone was making a fuss over
her being pregnant. Alex mostly. He was always concerned with how
much rest she was getting, what she was eating, and waited on her
when he was in her presence, forgetting that he had servants to call
upon. She exhaled ashamed of her behaviour. She needed to be more
involved. She closed her mother's diary and discreetly tucked it
between her leg and the longue chaise cushion.

Just then, a thought sparked in her mind. Elizabeth never wrote
about Madeline in her journals; but Elizabeth didn't abort Madeline.
Someone must have suggested it at some point during Elizabeth's
pregnancy. Her grandparents? Elizabeth's friends? Madeline doubted
her own father wanted to have her. But Elizabeth had decided to keep
Madeline, though it would ruin her reputation at court. Reading
about pregnancy for the rest of the afternoon was difficult.

It wasn't until Alex came back later in the evening did Madeline
feel comfortable to say something. The thought of her mother
deciding to not abort her was all Madeline could think of. As Alex
tucked her into bed, he kissed her softly on the lips. "Do you need
anything before going to sleep?" he asked.

"No."

He turned to blow out the gas lamp on her nightstand.

"Alex."

He stopped, "Yes?"

"Do you think my mother ever considered having an abortion?"
she said her voice cracking, her lips trembling.

"I don't know," he said running his fingers through her hair.

"Do you think she was pressured by anyone? I mean I could
imagine my father-"

"Dolcezza, I don't know if she considered it. She was probably
pressured to at some point. But I thank God that she decided not to.
She loved you before she knew you." He rubbed her arms and crawled
into the bed next to her. He wrapped his arms around her. "You have
to stop worrying about things you'll never have an answer to," he said
his lips brushing against her ear.

"I know. But how do you stop thinking about something like that? I mean, how do you stop thinking about what happened to you when you were in Ireland, Alex?"

"It took time, but I don't have the dreams anymore."

"How did you get them to stop?" she asked.

"I dream of you now."

"Oh."

"It used to be whenever I was alone with my thoughts; I thought of my country, the stresses of my day, Bathory, and what had happened in Ireland. But when I met you I realized I would much rather think about the things that I love. You make me happy. I'd rather think about you and my future with you, than waste my life worrying about things I can't control."

"I love you, Alex."

"I love you too, dolcezza," he said rubbing her belly, "I love you both."

She turned to him and massaged her lips with his. They kissed one another for a while until they drifted off asleep in each other's arms.

INVITATION

※

Sissy hadn't seen much of Madeline in the past few weeks. Madeline had become quite busy with planning a wedding, becoming Queen, and being a pregnant newlywed. It was difficult for Sissy to know what to do with her time. She was one of Madeline's unofficial ladies in waiting. But she didn't know proper manners or the duties of a lady in waiting. When Sissy wasn't around Madeline, she wasn't sure what to do with herself. At first, she followed Marie about. Marie visited Buckingham Palace and Windsor and often spent time with old friends. Sissy felt comfortable being with Marie, but if Marie had plans with Harold, Sissy had to find something else to do.

She had tried to spend time with Martha, but Martha had her own established routines and tight-knit friends and Sissy quickly sensed that Martha didn't enjoy being shadowed by someone much younger. The longer Sissy spent at Frogmore, the more out of place she felt. Sissy often found herself wandering the royal residences unsure of what she should do with herself. When she watched the maids cleaning, she was often tempted to join them. Even if it were for the sake of making friends, but she didn't want to embarrass Madeline.

In time, Sissy realized that she needed to establish her own circle of friends outside the residences that she could visit on her own time.

She decided to go into London and Windsor and looked for opportunities to make friends. But it was near impossible; most of the ladies travelled with other women. Sissy often got strange looks from people when she walked down the streets of London and Windsor by herself.

One afternoon while walking down the Strand, she had seen a group of ladies having afternoon tea inside the Twinning's tea house. Sissy sat in the establishment hoping for an opportunity to speak to some of them, when a striking girl with blonde hair walked in and sat next to her. It was the first time in months Sissy hadn't had to approach someone else and make friendly. Her name was Delilah, and she too had been looking to meet new people.

The two quickly became friends and began to meet one another in Windsor and London. Sissy had never met anyone quite like Delilah; she knew just about everyone in London. She was even familiar with some of the Lords that frequented court. They'd often spend their time talking about them and Sissy's castle life, of which Delilah was very interested.

Sissy entered the Twinnings tea house on the Strand and she looked around, hoping she'd spot Delilah. Unfortunately, she hadn't arrived yet. There were several small alcoves in the walls with tables and chairs where guests could sit and talk. But Sissy had decided not to sit in one of them. Upper-class society came here often, and she knew that many of the nobles favoured those seats. Sissy sat at a small table, not far from the counter, looking about at the pretty noble women drinking their tea with perfect manners and decorum. Sissy's life had changed so much; before moving to Frogmore, she would have never have thought of entering Twinnings. But dressed in her new clothes, she didn't feel out of place. Despite leaving everything she knew and having to adjust to a new social life, there had been many benefits.

"Hello!" said Delilah, her voice booming as she entered the tearoom. She crossed over to Sissy. "I hope you haven't been waiting too long. On the way here I ran into Lord Chatswick, do you know him?"

Sissy lifted her brow, "I think I've seen him," she lied.

"I'm quite sure he went to the King and Queen's wedding."

Delilah sat down in the booth with her, "You haven't ordered anything yet? There's no need to wait for me. Sissy, you should have got yourself something."

"It's all right, Delilah. Besides, I know how busy your schedule is. Who did you entertain this morning?"

"Oh, I saw Lord Pye this morning. We had brunch and he took me out to see an afternoon show at Drury Lane."

"Really? I've never been I've heard it's lovely."

"Oh, you should go. Life can become boring if you haven't any entertainment. You would think the Queen would fancy seeing a show. She's never taken you, Sissy?"

"No, but she did attend once with the King."

"Does the King like the theatre?" she asked, her eyes wide.

"I've heard he prefers opera. But her Majesty is, well, I suppose she's more of a homebody."

"How awful for the King!" Delilah exclaimed, flipping her hair.

Sissy laughed, "Why is that so awful?"

"Just think of it, Sissy. This man can offer her the world, but she'd prefer sitting around reading journals all day. That is what she is doing, isn't it?"

"Well, yes," Sissy hesitated, "but wouldn't you be curious? What happened to her family was tragic."

"No reason to live life wallowing in self-pity," said Delilah aghast. "Really, she's in the company of a man women dream to be with."

"True," said Sissy nodding as she looked down at the menu, "but the King is a very busy man."

"Does he make time for her?" she asked interested.

A server came to their table. "What would you like today, ladies?" she asked as she curtsied.

"Oh, um I'll have the Earl Grey tea," Sissy said weakly.

Delilah paused before ordering, "Is that all Sissy? Just tea? Earl Grey tea? I'll take something a little more exotic myself. I'll have the chai tea with the afternoon tea special. Oh, and serve it with honey, please."

"What about you miss?" the server asked looking at Sissy. "Anything else?"

"I'll just take my tea with a little milk, thank you."

The server's eyes shifted from side to side as she curtsied again and left.

"So you were saying," Delilah asked.

"I'm sorry, what?" Sissy said confused.

"I asked you if the King makes time for the Queen," she pressed.

"Yes. He's always been a gentleman."

"Do you know what the diaries say?" Delilah questioned. "I mean, to spend all that time reading them."

Sissy looked about nervously, sometimes Delilah asked very personal questions about Alex and Madeline.

"I don't know," she finally answered.

"What do you mean you don't know?" Delilah said, her voice filled with attitude.

"Well, I just don't think it's safe to talk about these things in such a public place. There are so many people here, look around."

Delilah looked around at all the faces. Everyone there was someone of means; tea at Twinnings wasn't cheap.

"Yes, there are people here. But I doubt they care much what we girls talk about," Delilah giggled.

"But they are all aristocrat types. If anyone hears what we are talking about-"

"You're afraid to get the Queen in trouble?" Delilah said tapping her fingers to the table.

"Yes."

"Sissy," she laughed. "Don't be so silly. There are far more scandalous things going around than what King Alexander and Queen Madeline do with their time. I entertain many of the Lords myself. The gossip in court is far more intriguing."

Sissy sat thinking for a moment. "Why do those men always wish to be with you? I mean they take you about, show you London and expect nothing in return?"

Delilah raised her brow. "Now Sissy, I told you. The men I entertain are true gentleman, they expect nothing but my company. Many of them have older wives that are homebodies like your Queen. They want someone that is lively. You know, just fun company. They pay to be seen with a young, pretty woman. Only that."

Sissy looked Delilah up and down. She was pretty with her blonde hair and petite frame. She could imagine that the men that saw her enjoyed her energetic personality. The server came back and set down their tea trays in front of each of them, then set a three-tiered plate full of petite fours, scones, and desserts next to Delilah.

"Go on have some," Delilah said to Sissy. She grabbed one of the sandwiches and set it down on a small empty plate while the server prepared their teas. Once the server left, Delilah continued to press Sissy, "Okay no one is within earshot. Now tell me what about the King and Queen. How are they really? I mean is the King bothered by the diaries? Do you know what they say?"

"I can't say, Delilah," Sissy said shrugging and took a small sip of tea.

"Oh well, in that case, I guess I can't tell you my little secret. It's a big one too." Delilah said with a wicked smile.

"Who is it about?" Sissy asked putting her teacup down in her saucer.

"Well, I've taken on a new client. I would love to tell you who. But if you can't trust me with a secret …" She took a sip of her tea.

"Well, there isn't much to really say," Sissy offered. "I know it bothers the King. Madeline is quite obsessed with what happened to her family. I think she wants to know who did it."

"I can understand that. Does she suspect anyone?"

"She's certain that the Duke did it. I think the King wishes she wouldn't care so much."

"What about you, what do you think of it all?" Delilah asked leaning toward Sissy.

"I think the Duke did it. I mean everyone says so. They've been saying it for years. Madeline just wants to prove it."

"Did her mother write something that makes her think so?" she whispered.

"I don't know. But she seems very determined to find out what happened. His Majesty doesn't want her to get too emotionally wrapped up in it."

"How could she not be emotional?" Delilah said sympathetically. "That is her family that died."

"Well, don't tell anyone, but the Queen is pregnant. The King doesn't want her so upset in her delicate condition. They don't want word to reach Spain, either."

Delilah paused, deep in thought, "I suppose I should tell you my secret. I'm going to be entertaining the Duke of Axford."

"What? Oh, promise me you won't tell him anything I told you. The Queen fears him! She thinks he's after her."

Delilah shook her head, grinning. "Don't be silly, Sissy. I wouldn't dream of it. I wouldn't want to endanger the Queen, or ruin our friendship."

Sissy was relieved.

"But it does make me wonder,"Delilah went on. "How far along is the Queen?"

"It was a honeymoon baby," Sissy said brightly.

"Well, that's lovely," Delilah said straining a smile. "Will they have a party to announce it you think?"

"I'm sure they will in time."

"You think you could get me an invite?"

A VISIT TO SWAN MANOR

*lex had decided to make his and Madeline's excursion to Swan Manor private. They took a carriage. He drove it while Madeline stretched out across the seat in the back. She knew he was trying to avoid any holes in the dirt road by slowly going over them. They were a couple of miles outside of Windsor when she saw that they were in a field. The grass had grown so long she could see the tips of it through the coach window.

They would be there soon. She'd finally see where her mother had spent the final year of her life. There was a part of her that felt she would get an answer in the manor. It was odd, but she felt as though her mother wanted her to come. Her spirit had been waiting all these years for Madeline to reveal what had happened the night she died.

The carriage made a slow, steady stop. Madeline looked out the window and saw a small house. She raised her brow.

Alex opened the door and held out his hand. She took it, "Where are we?" she asked.

"At Swan Manor," he said, "I decided to not take the door to the front. I thought it would be better to enter from the back."

"Oh. Then what's that small house over there?"

"I suppose it was a place for the servants to stay while they were here," said Alex simply.

"Really?"

"Yes, some of the older manors had separate servants' quarters."

Madeline looked about and saw the Swan Manor house further off in the distance.

"The servants' quarters might be kind of interesting to see," she said pushing through the grass.

"I don't know how safe that is, Madeline," he warned. "I doubt the servants' quarters are much sturdier than the manor, and it's not doing so well."

"But the quarters are made of stone. I would think it'd be okay."

"All right. Let me check it first."

Alex pushed down the grass with his feet moving toward the house. It was fairly small, and could only house several workers. It had a small wooden porch and a short stone chimney that was missing some stones at the top. Madeline watched as he went inside. Several minutes later, he came out and walked toward her. "It looks a bit safer than the manor. Do you want me to carry you?"

She laughed. "It's okay, Alex."

"Well, maybe you should take off your boots?"

"Good point."

He got down on his knees and removed her boots.

"Your feet will get dirty," he said, gesturing her to get on his back.

She took the hint that he didn't want her walking through the rough field and grass. She wrapped her arms and legs around him and he took her boots. Once they got there, she sat on the derelict wood porch and put her boots back on. The porch was weather-worn and weeds were growing through the spaces between the wood planks. Some planks were split in two.

"All right, I think I'm ready," Madeline said and took his hand, he wrapped one arm around her and escorted her inside. It smelt awful. "Why does it smell so bad?" she asked.

"I think some animals have made this their home," he said looking about. "Watch where you step."

He was right, there were lots of birds' nests along with feces. It was repellent. The room she was in was bare. Vandals and thieves had come in; the furniture was gone, all the windows had been smashed. She knew that the room she was looking in must have been the kitchen. The fireplace mantel along with its stones had been torn out. All the cupboards had been ripped from the walls, except one. The wood door to the cupboard had a large split in it, and the finish was bubbled and the wood warped. She could see an outline on the wall and the floor of where the rest of the cupboards had been. She could imagine what it used to look like. It was nicer than the Watsons' servants' quarters. She moved carefully over the debris on the floor.

Alex followed, "What are you doing?" he asked.

"I want to see if anything is in that cupboard."

He moved in front of her and opened it. It, like the rest of the room, was dusty, dirty and bare. "Nothing. I looked in the two bedrooms, there was nothing in them either," he said matter-of-factly.

"I'd still like to see them."

"I know," he said quickly and scooped her up in his arms.

"Ohh! Alex!"

"You shouldn't be walking through all this rubbish."

He took her into the other two rooms. But they were the same. Bare. Each had one window broken.

"Is there anything you want to take a closer look at?" he asked.

"No," she said disappointed.

He quietly carried her back outside, she could hear the creaks of the wood floor beneath his feet as they went. He set her down on the porch and helped her down to the grass. Staring at the ground, she looked solemn.

"What's the matter?" he asked concerned.

She pursed her lips.

"Nothing," she lied. Something about the old abandoned house gave her the creeps. They seemed to be nice quarters for servants. The house was sizeable, had a decent kitchen and a fireplace. Obviously, her family saw servants as people. But the shabby place looked so dismal. It was hard to believe that any life or happy times had ever been had in it.

"Are you sure you're ready to go in the manor?" he asked. "If you change your mind at any point, you can say so. I'll take you home."

"No Alex. It will nag at me until I do."

He sighed. He picked her up and plodded through the grass, bending the blades down. It was a long walk from the house to the manor, but as they came closer, she could see the veranda at the back. It was run down to, most of the white paint on the wood had chipped off. He set her down to her feet and climbed onto the veranda.

"I'm going to go in first, see what rooms are still safe to enter. I don't think we'll go upstairs. If you fall through the ceiling like Greg did, I'll never forgive myself."

"But Alex-"

"No, Madeline. You promised me. You aren't going upstairs and I don't want you to see the parlour either."

"I'm not a child," she protested.

"I know."

"I'll agree that we won't go upstairs today," she compromised. "But after I have this child, I'd like to go. I will see the parlour today," she said placing her hands on her hips.

"If you see the parlour ... Madeline, please don't. For me?"

"Don't try that with me, I won't be manipulated," she said, her voice cracking.

He didn't know what to say. His eyes full of emotion, he held out his hand, "We'll go in together. But if it's too much, please tell me."

She took his hand and hoisted herself up on the veranda with him. The large double doors to the inside were stripped off their hinges, taken by looters. She looked at the threshold miserably. "How is it that everything was taken, but you managed to find those diaries and that tiara in her hope chest?"

"People did loot her hope chest. I think that they considered the chest itself bad luck considering what happened to her. I mean, she was supposed to marry the Duke before she ran off with Isaac. But I found the diaries in a secret compartment in the chest. I'm sure if someone had found them before I did, they would have taken them."

There was a small part of her that was jealous. It was evident that many people had visited, but he had found Elizabeth's most personal thoughts written on paper. A small part of her felt she needed to find something. She was going to. Why else would she be so drawn to seeing the place? Maybe she was meant to find the Swans' remains.

They went through the entry way. Inside was a large dining room, that could entertain around twenty guests. The wallpaper was peeling off the walls. The mantle to the fireplace had been removed and there was a large hole in the wall. Hanging above it was a large broken glass case, the shards of glass beneath it on the floor. In the case was a moth-eaten, weathered coat of arms. The patch of the harp had been slashed, and the white swan had holes punctured all over its body.

"Why would someone tear up the coat of arms?" she asked softly.

Alex said nothing. She moved across the room into the kitchen. Alex followed her in. It was half the size of the dining room. But, like the servants' house, all the cupboards and flooring had been torn out. There was nothing in the room but a small pile of cobblestones on the floor.

"Are people dumping things here?" she asked looking at the pile.

"No," Alex said, eyes fixed on the pile. "No, I think that may have been used for an oven or fireplace."

She nodded.

The place felt violated. Many people had walked through the manor since her family had lived there. She felt angry. It felt as though everyone had visited to take a piece of the Swans. They had even tried to remove the wood floor, "Why do you think people didn't remove the wood floor?" she asked looking down.

"Too difficult to remove without damaging it," he said, pointing to one of the removed planks. It was split.

They walked down a corridor that led into the foyer and she could see the stairs next to her. He was right, they were rickety and unsafe. She continued toward the foyer but he stopped her, "Wait," he said.

He grabbed her arm and she turned, "What is it?"

He pointed to the boarded-up room several feet from them. She couldn't see inside, but she could see a large hole in the boards.

"I need you to reconsider this," he said nervously. "That room. It's dreadful."

"I know," she said softly.

"Knowing and seeing are two different things."

She stepped forward, but he rushed in front of her.

"Don't please."

"I'm sorry Alex, but I have to." She pulled away from him and moved toward the hole. She stopped by the shards of wood and peeked inside. She gasped, and stumbled back. Twenty years had passed, but the blood remained dark red and black, set into the damask wallpaper. The Persian rug on the floor had several large black stains on it, and it looked as though some bloodied bodies had been dragged across it. There was a large gothic style cabinet on the opposite side of the room, with gargoyles carved into its wood. Some of the detailing had been chipped off, making some of the gargoyles noseless and mouthless. Next to the cabinet was a grandfather clock, its dead hands pointing to ten. Some old mouldy chairs and couches had been tossed about the room, their upholstery ripped and stained, and a coffee table with broken legs, lying flat on the floor in the centre of the room. She smelled death and rot in the air. She felt sick.

"Don't look," he whispered as he pushed her head to his chest.

But the image was seared into her mind.

She broke into a fit, shaking and crying loudly.

He closed his eyes, feeling her warm tears through his shirt. "I'm sorry," he repeatedly said, as he rocked her, trying to soothe her. In the corner of his eye, he could see the room. He felt an uneasy feeling. It looked as though something or someone had chipped away at the wall and the cabinetry in the room. It made him sick. No other room had parts of the wall removed. It was obvious that people had come in and taken pieces of the room as souvenirs. He heard gruesome stories of people stealing parts of gravestones of famous people. He turned his head away, disgusted. He heard her as she began to gag.

She ran through the front door and he went after her. She held one of the porch pillars and vomited over the side. When she finished, she lowered herself onto to the porch, leaned against the pillar, and began to cry. He sat down next to her and rubbed her back.

"Why?" she began gasping between words. "Why was it left like that?"

"My father had ordered it to be boarded up. Several Lords moved to have it dismantled in the House of Lords."

"Why wasn't it? Why didn't your father-" she stopped sniffling, trying to catch her breath.

"Some people felt that it would be disrespectful to the Swans to tear the place down. Many people felt that if their remains were lying somewhere in the house, they didn't want to disturb them."

"That's a pathetic excuse. If they were found, we could have finally named the murderer. It was the Duke of Axford's opinion that it shouldn't be taken down, wasn't it?"

He looked away, "I'm guessing so."

"I want this place taken down, Alex!"

"Madeline," he tried to reason, "I don't think the evidence is there anymore."

She clenched her teeth and glared at him, losing herself, "YOU GET HIM! I DON'T CARE WHAT IT TAKES! THIS BUILDING IS STILL HERE! IT'S A MONUMENT TO WHAT HE DID!" she cried beating her fists into his chest.

He clutched her wrists stopping her, and she fell into his arms wailing, "Shh," he whispered softly, cradling her. It pained him to see her like this, "I'll take care of it," he said calmly.

"What will you do?"

He took a deep breath, "I'll have the Duke thrown in prison. I'll invent a reason."

"Why don't you use the manor? The evidence is right here, I'm sure!"

"Because, the case has already been tried. He wasn't convicted. I can't unless there is evidence that proves that he did it. Everyone has searched this manor. No one found evidence. I don't think the remains are here. If they were, I'm sure he's moved them by now. He's had years to do whatever he needed to do to detach himself from this."

"But everyone knows-"

He held her chin, "I know everyone knows. But no one proved anything. There's a reason for that. He managed to stay a few steps ahead. We'll throw him behind bars, force a confession, where upon he'll tell us the exact location of the remains. Then we'll respectfully take down the manor."

She paused. *Why hasn't Alex tried to do that before?* "Why are you trying to do this now?" she questioned.

"When I was here before, it wasn't a personal matter to me. But I can't bear to see you like this. If putting him in prison and proving your case will give you some peace, then I will do it. I don't want to spend the rest of our lives together, you moping about reading those diaries, looking for answers."

She nodded in agreement.

"Madeline?"

"Yes?"

He sat silent in thought before he finally spoke. "Never mind. We should head back. This has been a long day for you."

"Alex, I do want something from here."

"What is it?"

"I know everyone thinks it's cursed, but I would like to have my mother's hope chest."

Alex remembered it being rundown and rugged, but it was the only thing of her mother's that she could take that hadn't been taken by someone else.

"Of course," he said. "I'll have some men come down and retrieve it."

The ride home was a long one. Alex stopped from time to time to check in on Madeline. He could hear her cry as he drove and felt terrible. Of course, the first time he had stopped and gone into the coach, she had pretended she was fine. Holding back her tears, she tried to smile and had insisted that he continue driving. But seeing her eyes welled up in pain, he sat next to her and told her it was normal that she cry, "It's better to let it out, I think. It's not good holding these things in. Trust me, I know."

She thought of him as a young boy inside the Irish stronghold. By himself, surrounded by death. She broke down, crying hysterically falling forward.

He caught her and held her. Each time he could hear her sob as he drove, he would stop the coach and see her again.

She couldn't say much, and she usually would cry to the point of exhaustion. Her chest and body ached. On one occasion, she had fallen asleep from exhaustion.

He left her there to rest and went back to driving the coach. An hour later, she woke up and he could hear her again. He stopped again, regretting that they had gone, "Madeline, I'm sorry. I shouldn't have taken you," he apologized.

She shook her head. "I wouldn't have listened, Alex. I'm glad you came. If I went on my own ... I couldn't handle that on my own."

LES LIAISONS DANGEREUSES

It was around midnight. The Duke of Axford was sitting casually next to his fire, reading a copy of Les Liaisons Dangereuses. He had never understood the book much. He hated having to read the original French version; it forced him to brush up on the language. As a boy, he had always found languages difficult to learn. But, he always thought French sounded beautiful.

He had an English translation, but he knew stories in their original language were always the best version. Besides, he loved recalling the time he first got the book.

It was years ago. His cousin, King Charles, seemed determined to get him a wife before he fled back to Tahiti. Of course, Charlie tried to disguise it as a dinner party to celebrate Valentine's Day. But since it wasn't something the King or anyone celebrated, it was obvious that the King wanted to introduce him to every woman at court.

It was annoying at first. Charlie took him from group to group around Buckingham Palace's Ballroom trying to get him to chat to all the young debutantes. Walt eventually stopped him.

"Charlie, Charlie," Walter said as the King tried to drag him across the room. "I'm not a fool, I know what you are trying to do. But there isn't a woman in this room I'd ever be interested in."

"But you've got to see Baron Swan's daughter. She's gorgeous. You won't regret looking at her."

"Charlie, I don't care how beautiful she is. It doesn't matter. English ladies aren't my type."

"She's not exactly English, Walt. She's lived most her life in France," Charlie said as he tried to pull him along.

But Walt planted himself to the floor. "Stop Charlie. I'm not going to meet some girl that just wants to make a good match with a wealthy Duke. Honestly, Lord Swan is only ten years older than myself. I can't imagine how young his daughter is."

"She's twenty or so. Ripe. Besides, she's heard all about you. She's told me she has something she wants to give you, Walt."

They darted through the crowd. Walt spotted Bathory, drinking and conversing with several other Lords. "Hey, it's your nephew, perhaps we should say 'hello'."

"Not a good idea," said Charlie. "He's angry with me."

"Why? Is he ignoring you?"

"There have been some embarrassing situations. He has been bitter since Alex was born."

"Well, he grew up thinking he'd be a king," Walt reasoned. "All that's come to an end. I can't say I blame him."

"Never mind him," Charlie said. The King spotted Lord Swan and the two went toward him. "Lord Swan!"

"Your Majesty!' the Baron said, bowing. "You look well. Elizabeth has been wondering why you haven't said hello to her yet."

"Oh she thinks she's the belle of the ball," Walt whispered hoarsely to the King.

"She just went to get us some punch," Lord Swan continued.

"Your Majesty!' said a bright voice with a French accent. Elizabeth Swan, came through the crowd with two glasses in her hands, and dramatically bowed to King Charles.

"Half the night has gone by. You haven't said a word to me," she said pretending to pout.

The King blushed and Walt looked to the floor. She was striking, with glowing skin and long, thick black locks. Her deep red lips and pearly white teeth lit up her face. Walter hoped he wasn't blushing too.

"So this is the Duke?" she said passing a glass of punch to Lord Swan. "How have you been finding England since you've been back, your Grace?"

"Well. And you? Obviously, you haven't been back long," Walt said noting her accent.

"He can recognize a French accent," Elizabeth joked.

Charlie laughed, "Give him the gift, Miss Swan. I think he'd like it."

She pulled out a book from the pocket of her large ballroom dress. "Here you are, your Grace."

It was a well-read book. But as he went through the title he realized he wouldn't be able to read it. He shook his head, "I suppose you think I'd be impressed by this, Miss Swan? A French book?"

"Hardly," she tittered. "That's the joke. I thought since you're one of the few English men living in Tahiti that doesn't know French, you can, at least, make a good impression for the rest of England, and make it look like you're trying."

Charlie and Lord Swan laughed.

"I won't read it," Walt said seriously, trying to give it back to her.

She giggled, "I know that, your Grace. But like I said, to make the rest of your countrymen look good, I want you to carry this about with you when you go back to Tahiti."

Other guests around them overheard the conversation and began to chuckle.

"I'm sorry, Miss Swan. The French people and French culture have always disgusted me. A bunch of heathens," he smiled.

"Walt, it's just a joke," Charlie said.

But Elizabeth laughed. "You don't like French people or French culture, yet you live in French Polynesia, surrounded by a bunch of French settlers?"

"I spent most my time with the tribal people," Walt said curtly.

"Oh yes, they are sophisticated. Not savages like the French?" Elizabeth said sarcastically.

"The tribal people of Tahiti never stormed onto someone's land and claimed it as their own. Not like the French," Walt said inflamed.

"Are you trying to entice me in a conversation about politics, your Grace?"

"Not at all. I know a well-bred woman knows her place. Politics isn't something you'd speak of," he challenged.

She smiled, "Well-bred woman? I was brought up by the French, so if you are correct about the French, I must be a heathen. If I'm a heathen, then I will give my view on your silly politics."

"The French's brutal takeover of the Tahitian way of life isn't 'silly politics'," he said severely.

"Tell that to all English colonies whose cultures have been dominated by the English," she retorted.

There was a silence as he gawked at her, speechless. He couldn't believe her audacity to say those words in front of the King. "Very nice that you got me a gift Miss Swan," he said uncomfortably. "But there is no need for it." He held the book out to her to take again.

"Oh no your Grace, though you won't read it or carry it with you, I still think you will find it of some use."

"Really?" he said, annoyance uttered in his tone.

"Yes. I imagine that there are lots of flies and insects in Tahiti. You can use the book to swat them when you visit the tribal villages."

"Brilliant," Charlie said pretending to laugh. "Walt, I don't know how you can accept this gift from Miss Swan and not invite her to dance with you."

"Miss Swan is busy having her punch, your Majesty," Walt said between gritted teeth.

"That has never stopped you before," Charlie said his eyes narrowing.

"I'll take your drink dear," said Lord Swan reaching out taking her drink from her hand. The bright smile on her face turned to a frown. She didn't like the idea of dancing with the Duke either.

"It seems the King thinks we should dance Miss Swan," said Walt angrily. He swiftly grabbed her hand and pulled her to the dance floor.

"You certainly have a tight grip," she said.

"Let's just get this over with," he said taking his position.

"If it makes you feel better, I have no interest in you either," she spat back with a scowl.

He said nothing and they began dancing the allemande. But he was curious, "No interest in being with a wealthy Duke?"

She answered seriously, "No."

"Then why the gift, Miss Swan?"

"Well, if I got you something, it would look like I'm trying. I hope you do go back to Tahiti."

He still doubted that she didn't want him. She was only bitter. "It would greatly please your father if you found a man of means, wouldn't it?" he asked.

"Might make him happy. But I don't want to marry you."

"Why's that? Is there a younger gentleman?" he chided.

"No."

"Then what is the problem, Miss Swan?"

"You're English. I actually do prefer the company of the French."

"You are actually English Miss Swan," he reminded her.

"I wasn't raised English," she said, her accent becoming harsh.

He twirled her about. "The French are a bunch of crazy revolutionaries and libertines," he said as if he was stating a fact.

She didn't answer. Not that she needed to, the look in her eyes said that she still preferred the French.

Those eyes. They were the last thing Walt had imagined before Sir Ashton Giles barged in with a group of Alex's men, taking him out of his reverie. He dropped his book to the floor, eyes widened in amazement.

"What is the meaning of all this?" Walt bellowed rising from his chair.

"Your Grace," said Sir Ashton, holding out a document, "by his Majesty the King, you are hereby placed under arrest for treason."

"What? What have I done?"

"For aiding Miss Susanna Bathory and Prince Carlos of Spain by means of a ship."

"My ship was stolen!" he bellowed.

"His Majesty has reason to believe otherwise." Sir Ashton gave a quick nod and several men surrounded the Duke, grasping his arms.

"This is ridiculous and you know it, Ashton," Walt argued.

"I have a duty to my King," Sir Ashton said. "Gentleman, take this man to London Tower. Make sure he is chained in his cell."

The Duke laughed, "London Tower? Seems there's a bit of a security problem there. Miss Bathory escaped not too long ago."

"True. His Majesty will be sealing the tunnels at Curfew Tower, so your stay in London Tower will only be temporary. In the meantime, his Majesty will have your home and the rest of your estates searched."

The men dragged the Duke out of his estate, but he didn't bother to fight back. In a state of shock, he stared into the darkness as they shackled him inside a carriage.

* * *

It was the early hours of the morning. Alex watched Madeline sleep, her soft skin glowing in the pale moonlight. They were at Windsor Castle in his private apartments. After taking her to Swan Manor, he felt that she should spend the next few days there. At Windsor, he could attend to his duties and if she needed him, he could be there in a moment. At Frogmore, her mother's diaries were sitting in her room.

Alex yawned. He was tired, but he didn't plan on sleeping that night. He didn't want Madeline to start having nightmares like he had. He decided if she started to moan or move about, he'd wake her. If she started the habit he once had, he wasn't sure what he'd do. Waking her before they started seem to be a logical solution.

To his surprise, she slept peacefully. Perhaps it was because she was pregnant and needed rest. But, he doubted that. Madeline was strong. She had been through a lot before he had met her. Her treatment by her father and the Watsons was traumatizing. But it never broke her.

The grandfather clock in his room struck four. He heard some shuffling about happening in his drawing room. He quickly slipped out of the bed, then he heard a familiar voice, "YOUR MAJESTY!"

It was Sir Ashton Giles. He began knocking on the door.

Madeline awoke with a jolt.

"Don't worry, it's Sir Ashton," Alex said reassuring her. "Enter," he called toward the door.

Sir Ashton Giles opened the door and bowed, "Sorry to disturb you so late, your Majesties."

"It's fine," Alex said.

"We found the Duke of Axford at his estate outside of Windsor. We will be searching all of his estates."

"Excellent, thank you, Sir Ashton," Madeline said, her expression filled with relief A perplexed expression came across Alex's face. He had ordered the Duke to leave England, he wasn't expecting him to still be at one of his estates.

Sir Ashton Giles raised his brow, "I'm sorry, did you think the Duke wouldn't be there, your Majesty?"

Alex looked down at Madeline his eyes bulging.

"What is it, Alex?" she asked confused.

"I just thought he might be in London," he said, making a quick recovery. He curled back under the sheets.

"You've taken him to London Tower then?" asked Madeline.

"Yes," Sir Ashton confirmed.

"Once Curfew is suitable, transfer him," Alex ordered.

"Of course, your Majesty," Ashton said then bowed and left closing the doors behind him.

Alex's gaze was fixed on Madeline.

"I can always count on you," she said smiling as she nuzzled into his chest.

He laid back onto the pillows and sighed. After several minutes, she drifted off, but he lay awake, worried. He was counting on the Duke being gone. He had no intentions of beheading him or even putting him on trial. Killing him would anger many of his noble subjects, but that's not what was bothering him. Alex was fairly certain that the Duke didn't kill Elizabeth Swan.

He patted her back as she murmured. A blubbering mess, her hair was a fright, strands of it stuck to her face from her tears.

He pulled them back, "I think you need your rest. It was a bad idea to go to Swan Manor at this time. I don't know what I was thinking," he said, glancing at her belly.

"No, I had it in my mind that I was going," she said recognizing how stubborn she had been. "I wouldn't have waited so many months."

"I'm not going to attend the House of Lords for the next few days," he said. "I'm going to stay with you."

"But what about the Duke of Axford? If you intend to throw him in prison, isn't this something you'll have to discuss with the other Lords?"

"I don't intend to. I'll just allow the Lords to assume he's missing."

SPANISH COUNTRYSIDE

*S*usanna poked her head outside her carriage window, admiring the scenery. They had been traveling for weeks across the countryside. Though they went through many hills and valleys, making the trip a long one, she didn't mind. She was traveling in style.

In Santander, Susanna and Carlos had bought several horses, a carriage, food delicacies, weapons and a new wardrobe for each of them. They had bought so much they had to buy another wagon to pull what their carriage could not take. At first, this angered Susanna; she had felt that some of the men could have carried the boxes of clothes and food. After tying some of the cargo to the horses, there was still a pile of boxes. She suggested tying the rest of the boxes to the men as they had with the horses, but Carlos thought this was a bad idea, "Do you honestly think they won't steal things from us?" he asked shaking his head.

"Your father would have them shot if they did," said Susanna.

"Maybe so, but waiting for these men to carry the luggage on their backs will lengthen our journey to Madrid. I'd like to get there before Christmas."

So they bought a wagon to match their carriage. Both were made of cherry wood and had a lacquer finish. The wagon was larger with a wooden roof that held a canopy with drapes hanging over its sides. Of course, some of their items poked through the drapes, and because it was such a heavy load, they had to get four horses pull it. The carriage had the same drapes as the wagon, but the entire structure was made of cherry wood with large gilt wheels. It too had four horses pulling it.

Though they were comfortable, the men in their company weren't. While the two napped in the carriage, ate well, and dressed in fine clothes, the men were provided with bread for their troubles. They stopped at small rivers from time to time to get a drink, but they were never allowed to rest for long. Both drivers feared every pot hole they saw in the dirt road. They couldn't imagine what kind of punishment they would receive if a wheel broke. None of the men were given a weapon. Not trusting the common English peasant, Carlos kept several rifles inside the carriage with him and Susanna.

Though Susanna didn't appreciate much about Spanish culture, she found the countryside breath-taking.

Carlos sat across from her, staring at her as she took in the scenic view of the green hills around them. The sun shone on the hills' rocky tops and the fresh smell of the air was enticing. He moved from his bench and sat next to her.

"What are you thinking?" he asked.

"How all of this will be mine too," she smiled.

He laughed. "We'll take England together, but we can't just take Spain, my father is still King."

She pulled back from the window and looked him straight in the eye. The carriage went over a bump, but she had somehow managed to keep staring at him. "I think if we take England, it would be a wise idea for your father to step down, don't you?" she asked, her eyes searing into his.

"Why?"

"Face it Carlos, if you don't take the Spanish crown, your father will try to run England, too. You'll have to wait years until he dies to have any power."

Carlos knew she was right. If he could take England by killing Alex and marrying the person next in line to England's throne, Spain should be his too. He nodded in thought.

"You agree then?" she asked.

"Yes. But I don't want to usurp my father. I'm not killing him if that's what you have in mind."

"I don't think we need to do that. When we get back, you need to take control. When it's decided how we will invade England make sure that the plan set in place is set by you. If the nobles of your court see strong leadership skills in you, you'll be more respected than your father."

"I don't know," he said hesitantly. "I think even if I were to lead Spain in battle, my father would still-"

She grabbed the collar of his cravat and tugged, bringing his face close to hers, "Carlos, England is an empire; it has many colonies. Spain is losing its empire. Have you noticed that recently many of Spain's colonies are gaining independence? It's obvious that your father doesn't know how to rule. Leave it in his hands and we'll lose everything." She released him.

"Didn't England lose America?" he challenged.

"That was almost forty years ago. Besides, I'm simply pointing out that your father has proven he can't keep control of his colonies. I imagine his nobles must be frustrated-"

"All right. But how can I show my father's advisors that I'm the stronger leader?"

"I know England," she said with a haughty expression. "I know its people, and I know how to defeat Alex. When we get back, I want you to see to it that I am part of planning the attack."

He howled, "That's no place for a woman to-" He stopped mid-sentence as he watched her eyes darken. He held his breath.

"Why should I marry a man that thinks my opinion doesn't matter?" she said appalled. "Tell me, when we take England, will I have any say in my kingdom's matters, Carlos?"

You won't, he thought. But he didn't want her to figure that out just yet. "Sorry," he relented, knowing he was going to have to keep her believing they were a good match. "You're right. You do know England and its King."

"I'm glad you see reason."

He rubbed her thigh with his hand. She looked down at his hand on her dress and turned up her nose. "What do you think you're doing?" she asked.

He removed his hand, "I know it doesn't always seem so, but I do want to be a good husband to you."

She rolled her eyes. "Carlos, I'm no fool. This marriage is more of a business contract."

"I'd like it to be real," he said in his sincerest tone. "I mean if we are to be married, maybe we should give it an opportunity. It would be good if we could grow to care for one another. Do you think you could care for me?" He slowly placed his hand on hers, his dark eyes looking up innocently at her.

"Trust is earned," she said unsure of his true intentions.

"I thought I already earned your trust."

"Why?" she began, her voice indignant. "You think because we've had sex that means I trust you?"

"Most women don't have sex with men they don't trust."

"I'm not most women. Just because I was with you, doesn't mean I care for you."

He felt so awkward. He never met a woman so unemotional.

"Carlos, do us a favour. When we arrive in Madrid, we should be greeted with a beautiful homecoming. If we are going to be loved by the people, we have to make a grand entrance."

He nodded in agreement.

"We'll pen a letter to your father," she continued. "Make several demands of what kind of welcome you should get. Mention that you and I plan to wed."

"Did you buy a quill and some ink in Santander?"

"Yes, but I believe it's in one of the boxes in the wagon."

"Good. We'll stop, let the men take a short break, and they can look for it."

It took a few hours, but the men found the supplies in one of the boxes on top of their carriage. Of course, they tore through every-thing in the wagon first while Carlos looked over their shoulders. It was dusk by the time they found it.

Carlos and Susanna went back inside the carriage to write the letter.

"Once we're finished, send one of the men to go ahead of us and take it to Madrid," Susanna said. "He'll have to ride day and night to give your father a fair warning, but it will be worth making an impression on the people."

Carlos nodded and began the letter, writing in Spanish.

"What are you doing? Why are you writing it in Spanish?" Susanna said, irritated.

"This is Spain," he said shaking his head.

"But how will I know what you write?"

"Didn't you learn Spanish? I learned English, even your King knows-"

"I don't care what Alex knows," Susanna barked. "I'd like to know what you're writing. My father didn't think I'd have any use for Span-ish. I focused on Italian and French. If you must, write in English first, then translate it to Spanish." It was a lie. Susanna did know Spanish, but she didn't want Carlos knowing that. Earlier, she had decided she wasn't going to speak Spanish. Not when she could express herself better with English. A lifetime of speaking and learning the nuances of another language would be limiting to her. If she and Carlos always spoke in Spanish, she was certain he would win every argument.

It was irksome, but he did as he was told.

FATHER,

With the help of Miss Bathory, I have managed to escape England and I am making my way to Madrid. Of course, I take along with me, Miss Bathory and she and I have gotten along quite well. We'd like to marry, and once we do, she and I both think we should continue with the plan to usurp King Alexander.

When we reach Madrid, we are hoping that the subjects of Spain feel as excited about our future as we do. A warm welcome would be greatly appreciated.

"There," he said and handed it to her.

She read it quickly, but an annoyed expression came over her, "Demand exactly what we expect. I want to be sure that your father does this right. It's important. Also, I'm 'Lady' Bathory, not 'Miss' Bathory."

He sighed as he took the letter from her. "What else would you like me to write?" he asked yawning.

"Let's see," she said tapping her lip. "Ah, when we arrive, we will need a kind of parade. If someone could meet us outside the town walls with some appropriate transportation. I mean – this carriage is all right, but I'm sure your father has something more fitting."

"What else?"

"We should be welcomed in by the subjects. Maybe holding some festivities or a feast. If it's a day of celebration, our subjects will warm up to us."

He had to admit there was a method to her madness; if he wanted his people to favour him and Susanna's union, this was a good start.

"There should also be a ball, and towards the end of the night, it can be announced that you and I plan to wed and unite both countries under one realm."

"Anything else?"

"There has to be some sign that both of your parents approve of this."

"You want a gift from them?" he asked surprised by her demand.

"It makes sense, Carlos," she said exasperated.

"What did you have in mind?"

"A title."

"Susanna, I don't think it's possible to hand you a title."

"I've rescued his heir, the future King of Spain. There must be some title or honour for my deed."

He nodded in thought, "There is an honour for services to Spain. I suppose my father can present you with that."

"He should want to," she said firmly.

He stopped and looked down at his words, thinking of his father. "I don't know, Susanna. Women are never presented with such honours."

"Do you think I really care about an honour from Spain?" she asked in disdain. "It's the respect of your subjects I want. Your father rewarding me with something will give me that. Besides, I rescued you and brought you home. I deserve it."

Carlos knew she was right; if a man had done this, there would be a ceremony and a presentation of the award. But, his father was traditional; giving a woman that kind of honour would be absurd in Fernando's eyes. He could picture his father thinking that such honours would be useless to a woman. Carlos needed it to sound like rewarding Susanna would benefit his father too. He wrote:

I feel it would be wise to give Susanna an award for rescuing me and taking me back to Madrid. If we do so, many subjects will warmly accept her before she and I wed. It is important to me that she be liked, father. If she isn't, any children that she bear, may not be favoured.

Once the letter was finished, Susanna read it over. It wasn't how she would have liked it written, but she knew he was trying to persuade his father. Susanna gave it to one of the crewmen, Eliot.

"No sleep, until you hand this to King Fernando, Eliot," Susanna ordered. "If what is demanded in here does not happen, it will be your head."

Carlos watched in disapproval, "We should stab him in the leg," he whispered. "Madrid is the closest city to find the help of a doctor, and that will make him ride as quick as he can."

"What if he succumbs to the injury during the journey?" Susanna mumbled beneath her breath. "Then the letter will never reach Madrid before we do."

"We will send another man with him," Carlos said. Raising his voice, he turned to Eliot. "Have you made a friend among these men?"

Eliot nodded and pointed to one of the peasants loading the cargo back onto the wagon, "That man over there, his name is Dean."

"You there!" Carlos called, "get a horse and go with this man."

Dean mounted himself onto another horse and galloped up to Eliot.

Carlos withdrew his dagger from his coat and stabbed Eliot.

"AHH!"

"I hope you trust this man," Carlos said casually to Eliot. As Eliot continued to yelp in pain, Carlos looked at his friend. "If he dies, leave him on the side of the road and continue to Madrid. Of course, if my father never receives this, there will be consequences."

Dean nodded shakily and the two left as the sun set in front of them.

THE QUEEN'S BEDCHAMBER

*G*reg and Sofia were taking an evening walk through the Great Gallery looking at the paintings; some had been ruined by the parties they had been having. Sofia glanced at a canvas that had been sliced with a sword by McFadden.

"What will you tell Alex?" she asked biting her lip.

Greg observed the room, "Well not all the works are ruined. Just a couple. I suppose I could find someone in town to fix them up."

Sofia gave him a look.

He smiled, "Don't worry Sofia, I used to wreak havoc in the Billiards Room at Buckingham Palace all the time."

"This isn't just one room," she scoffed. "It's all of Holyrood House!"

"Well, I'm sure I can come up with something," he said pausing in thought. "I know! I'll say I found the place like this. He has never been here before."

She grinned shaking her head, "What are you going to tell him? All of Edinburgh partied here before you came along?"

He considered it a moment, "Not a bad lie, love." He took her hand and began leading her through the hall.

"Seriously Greg, what are you going to tell him?" Sofia pressed.

"Like I said, I'll tell him I found it like this."

"Oh? But that still doesn't answer the question of how Holyrood House got like this."

"Oh yes Princess," Greg began jokingly imitating Alex's refined accent, "Let me tell you the history of Edinburgh and Holyrood House. It started several centuries ago when the selkies found Edinburgh."

She howled, "The selkies? You mean the humans that can change into seals?"

"Yes," he said matter-of-factly, "they had been on a long voyage at sea, and Nessie was threatening them. They landed on the shores here and sought refuge." He didn't smile, waiting for a reaction from her.

She didn't give him one. She wanted to see what other ridiculous ideas he'd come up with. "Go on, tell me more," she said.

"They built Edinburgh of course!"

"Oh."

"They stayed human for so long, that some of them forgot how to change back to seals."

"I suppose some of them are still living here?" she asked raising her brow.

"Not exactly. The selkies of that time have died off, but their ancestors live among us. You see, it was forgotten for years that selkies could turn to seals. The only way they could was if they had a good time."

"So you're saying the people of Edinburgh, have never had a good time and have never turned into seals since founding Edinburgh?"

"Not until recently. You see, the selkies lived as humans for a long time, until a cute Spanish Princess came along with a heroic, dashing English man."

She pressed her lips with her finger, trying not to laugh, "I suppose the Princess taught the people to have a good time?"

"Not really," he chuckled. "You see the Princess was cursed. She didn't know how to have a good time either."

She gave him a light shove, "So it was the heroic English man?"

"No, no. It was the magic of Edinburgh. You see, part of the problem was that she was a princess, and was told to act a certain way.

It was boring to her. But when she and the English man came, they decided not to tell anyone she was a princess so she could have a wonderful time, and she did."

"So then what happened? All the selkies turned to seals?"

"That's exactly what happened!" he said throwing his hands up in the air. "They did it in Holyrood House! When they turned to seals, they were so confused that they tore the place apart."

"What happened to the Princess?" she asked softly as they entered the Queen's Lobby.

"She was just fine. It was a little scary seeing humans turn into seals, but she didn't mind the people being selkies."

"What about the English man?" she asked as she casually glimpsed at the silver dishes and weaponry in the floor-to-ceiling glass cases.

"The English man had to tolerate all of it because he didn't want to leave the Princess."

"So did they stay there, in Edinburgh?"

He kissed her softly, "They're still there now." He gently pushed her back into one of the glass cases and lifted her hands above her head, firmly restraining her wrists. He melded his lips fervently to hers. She responded murmuring, roughly kissing him back.

He slowly pulled away, his eyes smouldering. Then he grinned and glanced at the staircase leading to the Queen of Scots Chambers.

"Don't even think about it, Greg," she warned.

"What? I think it's the only room in the house we haven't, uh, thoroughly enjoyed yet."

"I told you we need to stop doing this," she said, cracking a smile. "This isn't some kind of mission. I mean, we don't have to be intimate in every room in the house. That's all we've been doing since we got here."

"I know, but none of it was planned," he said, trying to reason with her. "It just happened. Besides, Mary's bedroom is safer. When we were in the Great Gallery, Belle nearly walked in on us."

Sofia gave him a worried look, "I don't know, I just-"

He grabbed her arm and bolted up the winding, narrow staircase with her.

"Greg! Don't you think it's a bit disrespectful? I mean, that room used to be-"

"I don't think the Queen cares," said Greg quickly. They reached the bedroom, and he released her, shutting the door behind him. He turned, his eyes turning dark with desire.

"Tell me Sir Gregory, what do you consider disrespectful? I think since meeting you, you've broken every rule of etiquette I know, and always go against anyone with status or authority."

"I always give *you* what *you* want," he said pointedly.

"Ha! Hardly," she said, realizing his words were true.

He always tried to make her happy. He walked toward her, his soft eyes capturing hers. She took several steps back.

"Admit it Princess, I know what you want, and I always surrender to your needs," he said seductively. As he continued to approach her, she continued to step back, bumping into a window behind her. "Even now. You say you don't want this, but I know that look in your eye."

He stopped inches in front of her and leaned his arm against the glass pane. She felt his hot breath against her skin, and blood rushed to the apex of her core.

Slowly, he undid the buttons to her dress and began tugged her dress down. It dropped to her hips, then to the ground. As she glimpsed out the window, her hairs stood on end; she wore nothing but open crotch pantalettes and a corset.

She felt his hand slip between her thighs; then, his fingers sank into her. Her breath hitched as he circled inside of her, stirring a range of emotions from lust to fear. The vulnerability of their situation worried her but also heightened her excitement. His insatiable desire for her drove her arousal. There had always been this tug-of-war between them, but what was becoming clearer with time was that she was letting him win. She rather enjoyed it when he did.

She felt his fingers briefly brush against her bud, and she murmured. She placed her palms up on the window, feeling the coolness of the glass, her eyes closed as soft sounds emanated from her. If anyone were to pass by and happen to look up at the window, the vision they'd have of her would make only too obvious what was happening. But the thought hadn't crossed her mind. Her focus was brought to every caress on her thigh, the graze of his thumb to her pearl, and the depths of his fingers. She eagerly wanted to release, not just for herself, but also for him. He loved her satisfaction as much as she did.

Inflamed to see her body twisting and crumbling, he dropped his hands from her and grasped her hips, roughly twisting her around. Gasping, she gripped the stoned walls at either edge of the window, stabling herself. He loosened the drawstring to her pantalettes, and they dropped to her ankles, revealing her womanhood to the damp castle air. She let out a shuddered sigh instinctively, drawing her legs together. He peeled them back gently, nuzzling his head next to her peachy flesh.

He enveloped his mouth to her, tasting her, and she almost lost balance from the sheer intensity of it. She moaned as his kisses consumed her, the warmth within her spreading to each limb. Growing dizzy with his motions, holding her weight was becoming laborious. Her legs trembled uncontrollably. She knew she was seconds away from coming apart. She clasped the stoned walls crying out. He continued the fiery caresses of his tongue, her sweet noise music to his ears. His efforts were rewarded when she crooned again, her small figure just barely holding to the wall.

He rose from the floor and watched as her body slumped down the hard stone wall. Before her bottom hit the floor, he scooped her up in his arms.

"Easy there, Princess," he whispered. "Perhaps it's time for bed."

He pulled back the sheets to her bed and set her down. The satin sheets were frozen against her skin, and she shivered as she watched him wander to the wardrobe.

He pulled out a chemise and set it down on the bed. She watched him as he slowly unlaced her stay, then lifted the chemise above her head. She rose her arms into the garments, and he pulled it down over her. She watched him in a sort of awe. There had been plenty of servants in her life that had looked after her, but never had she thought much of them dressing her. They did it because they had to.

He did it because he loved her. He crawled into the bed next to her, his warm mass a furnace compared to the sheets. She curled up to him, intertwining her legs with his.

He pressed a kiss to her forehead, closing his eyes, "Good night, Princess."

"Good night," she whispered back.

SEÑOR ASTUCIA

When Carlos and Susanna reached Madrid, King Fernando was prepared for them. Outside the city, they met with some servants and guards that gave them what Susanna had demanded; the extravagant carriage painted in gold reminded her of the one that was commissioned for Alex when he had been crowned King of England. It wasn't as large or detailed as the Gold State Coach, but she wasn't being crowned. Yet it would do for her grand entrance into Madrid and make a good impression on the people of Spain.

It was pulled by eight magnificent horses, all in their own uniforms. Each horse was ridden by a horseman and the coach had a driver, with two footmen standing on two small platforms on each side.

Along with their carriage, there were other carriages and wagons similar to the ones that they had arrived in. Susanna wondered who they were for. She pulled Carlos aside, "All the rest of these coaches and wagons? What do we need them for?"

"The coaches will be holding the things we bought in Santander," he said watching the guards as they began to load the carriages.

"And the wagons?" she asked.

106

He sighed. "I was talking to one of the guards. Father seems to think it would be a good idea to take the rest of these men and hold them prisoner. We will shackle the men to the wagons and carriages." His eyes quickly dropped and he stared at his feet.

She pursed her lips, her eyes narrowing. She understood what King Fernando was trying to do, "Your father wants to make you look like you conquered the English?" she asked appalled. "Fact is, I rescued you."

"That's not what Madrid wants to hear," he said indifferently. "If we want the support of the people, we have to make it look as though England is weak."

She tapped her chin in thought, "I think it's cowardly that your father won't admit that I rescued you. On the other hand, I see how this can work in our favour; I doubt Spaniards want a prat that was saved by an English woman, do they?"

"Obviously not," he said in a harsh tone.

"I'll get into the carriage then."

"Father thinks it'd be best if I ride alone in the gold coach," he said.

"That's all right," she said making her way toward the coach. "When we get there, you can simply explain there was some sort of miscommunication." She stood next to the gold carriage door and snapped her fingers at the footman next to it. "Open it, you dolt." The footman obeyed and she stepped inside.

"Wait. You want me to lie to my father?" he called chasing after her.

"One good lie deserves another," she said sitting on the coach bench. "King Fernando has lied to Spain to make his son look good. You're going to lie to make me look good."

"And if I decide not to?" he asked.

"If you don't lie, I'll speak the truth." She arranged her skirts and patted the velvet next to her. "Come, Carlos."

He sat down. Outside they could hear the yelps and gasps of the sailors they had travelled with from England, as the Spanish guards took them and shackled them to the wagons. Susanna briefly thought of the messengers they had sent a couple days earlier and guessed that they were already in cells. After the Spanish guards had finished shackling the men and packing the other coaches, they began their tour into the city.

As they pulled into the streets, Susanna peeped her head out. It was a beautiful city. People lined the streets and threw flowers at the carriage as it passed. The sun shone on the buildings, many looked new. Some of them had a more humble exterior, with simple brick, not decorated with all kinds of statues and columns like much of London. But as they went deeper into the city she saw more elaborate structures with balconies and decorative windows. They entered the town square and the street was crowded with people, shouting and celebrating. Susanna couldn't help but smile and wave at the subjects.

"What are you doing?" Carlos asked appalled at her behaviour.

"Making friends with my future subjects," she said smiling.

"Part of being royal is acknowledging the fact that you're better than your subjects. Not many royals wave you know."

"Maybe you don't wave in Spain," Sofia said, "or maybe you're just a prat. In England, we wave. It's a good idea to be a favourite amongst your people."

He rolled his head against the red fabric. "If you rule well, you'll always be remembered."

She said nothing but continued to wave. Finally, they came to the palace. The gates opened and the entourage entered. There were statues that lined the drive as they made their way to the entrance. Sofia looked at them in awe, noticing that some wore crowns. "Are all these statues past royals?" she asked hoping she might be among them someday.

"They're Gothic kings. No recent monarchs are among these statues."

They reached the entrance and entered the courtyard.

"Father expects us to go to the Throne Room immediately," Carlos said. "The court will be there, waiting for our arrival."

"Good. You can introduce me as your fiancée to the nobles then."

"Sorry Susanna. My father would be the one to make that kind of announcement."

She sat silently questioning if King Fernando would only announce the engagement if he approved of it. A cool sensation came over her body, and she could feel a shiver crawl up her spine.

They entered the palace and walked up a large entrance staircase. At the top, she could see three large arches. In the middle arch was a statue of King Fernando behind a gold balustrade. A large tapestry with the royal coat of arms hung from the gold rail. On either side of Susanna, she noticed several gold branches coming out of the walls, each holding three candles. As the footmen led her and Carlos, she squinted at Carlos's arm clutching hers, "Are you always going to hold my arm like that?" she whispered. "A little tight."

"I didn't think so," he said shaking his head. It didn't take much for her to get annoyed, but that didn't matter. He knew her stubborn, opinionated ways were soon to be put to rest.

"Is the Throne Room through one of those two arches?" she asked.

"No," he said as they reached the top of the stair. He turned her around and there were two more large staircases on either side of them. "Up these stairs."

She looked about. She hated to admit it, but the Grand Staircase in Madrid Palace was the most impressive she had ever seen. She looked up at the ceiling which was full of paintings that reminded her of the Sistine Chapel. Large circular windows at the top lit up the room.

Carlos led her up the next flight of stairs and to the Throne Room. All around the room, the court waited to greet them. Their presence was announced to the court in Spanish and the two entered the room. Carlos led Susanna down the red carpet aisle to the thrones where King Fernando and Queen Isabelle sat.

Susanna curtsied, "Sus Majestades reales," she said in perfect Spanish.

Carlos gave her a strange look, before bowing to his parents. After he had bowed, King Fernando stood up and hugged Carlos hard. He whispered something in his ear in Spanish as the Queen looked on.

Then Fernando turned to Susanna, "My son has told me he plans to marry you still?" he whispered.

"Yes, I-"

"It is time to get to know you then," he said sternly.

It was then she knew that she wasn't going to be given any honours. She was being put under a microscope instead and would have to be cautious of everything she said and did.

"Let us have dinner then," King Fernando said.

Carlos took Susanna's arm again, "Sorry that you didn't get any honours," he said half smiling as they exited the Throne Room. "But like I said, my father doesn't think a woman would have any use for honours."

Susanna held his arm tighter, pulling him closer to her, "How does he expect me to win favour then?"

"Watch my mother, you'll figure it out."

They walked through several rooms. But Carlos held her back as the rest of the court entered the Royal Dining Room.

"The court will seat themselves before we enter," he said roughly pulling her back. "Of course, we will be announced."

As the two waited, King Fernando came up to them, "Let Susanna take her seat with the rest of the court, Carlos," said King Fernando as he looked sideways at Susanna.

Susanna wanted to punch King Fernando. She knew that he had spoken his words in English so that she would understand. She was getting the feeling that King Fernando didn't like her.

"Where should I sit your Majesty?" she asked sweetly in English. If she were to be treated like this, there was no way in hell she'd lower herself to speak Spanish again. She peeked her head into the room, looking for the most handsome noble to flirt with. Carlos immediately took notice, "I think she should sit next to me, father," Carlos said quickly. "Señor Astucia can escort her inside."

"Who is Señor Astucia?" Susanna asked.

"One of my advisors and my closest friend," Carlos said.

She nodded. It was better that than the humiliation of entering alone and having no idea where to sit. Carlos ordered a nearby footman to get Señor Astucia. A few minutes later a very tall, dark handsome man entered from the Royal Dining Room with the footman at his side.

"Susanna, this is Arsenio. You can call him Señor Astucia," Carlos said, "he'll take you to the seat next to mine."

She smiled at him. Arsenio was gorgeous. He had wavy black hair, tan skin, and big dark brown eyes. "Good to meet you, Señor Astucia," she said.

He kissed her hand, "My pleasure," he said in his Spanish accent.

Her toes curled as he spoke. He took her arm and led her into the room. It was nothing like the dining rooms at Windsor or Buckingham Palace. Though it was smaller, the lengthy room had walls that were green with gold trim and sculptures embedded into the walls and ceilings. The drapery around the windows and doors were red and gold. There were eight giant chandeliers, each holding more than a hundred candles, and there was a large arch in the middle of the room, supported by several marble pillars. Beneath the arch, a life-sized table ran down the centre of the room.

Enthralled with the artistry, she hardly noticed Señor Astucia gazing at her, "I've never been to England," he began, "are most women pretty and blonde?"

She giggled and patted his arm, "Señor Astucia, I think the question that should be asked is why haven't you been to England?"

"Have not been invited, Miss. Are you inviting me?"

She didn't respond. If she could have her way, she'd invite him to her bed now. He pulled out her seat, "Miss Bathory," he said.

"It's Lady Bathory," she said correcting him.

"Sorry, my Lady. You look too young to be a Lady."

"You do know how to flatter, don't you Señor Astucia?" she tittered.

"Flatter?" he repeated, unsure of what the word meant. "This is your seat," he said putting his hand on its back. She stood next to it, her eyes following him as he went around the table to his seat, which was across from hers. Carlos walked in the room once his name was announced. He stood next to Susanna and she looked away from him to Señor Astucia's penetrating gaze.

King Fernando and Queen Isabelle entered after Carlos. When they sat, everyone followed suit.

Servants and footmen entered with different platters of food. There was stuffed chicken along with some side dishes. Susanna looked on in disgust.

"Carlos, don't Spanish people enjoy appetizers?" she whispered in disappointment.

"I'm not sure why there are no appetizers," he said. "But that is not a reason to be rude."

"I wasn't rude," she said between grit teeth.

"Susanna, what news of England? Before you left?" King Fernando asked interrupting them.

"Well, I'm sure you've heard the King recently wed."

"Yes," he said slowly, cutting his meat. "We've heard some odd things here. It seems no one really knows much about the woman he married."

"Hardly anything," Susanna said. "But she-"

"What of Princess Sofia?" Fernando interrupted asked cutting her off as he chewed on his food, "Do you know anything about her whereabouts?"

"I heard that the Princess was taken away to Edinburgh by-"

"Edinburgh? Scotland?" the King said in astonishment, "that's not possible."

"Yes, King Alexander has a residence there," Susanna said nodding.

"It's true," Carlos confirmed. "Before kidnapping Sofia, Greg Umbridge told the servants at Frogmore that he was going to Edinburgh."

Queen Isabelle, murmured as she brought out her handkerchief and quickly wiped away a tear from her round cheek.

"I'll give that boy a warning," said Fernando stuffing a hunk of chicken into his mouth. "If Sofia isn't returned safely to us, he'll be sorry. Along with all of Edinburgh."

King Fernando continued talking in Spanish, disregarding his conversation with Susanna. She looked down the table at Queen Isabelle. The Queen still looked quite emotional; it was obvious that Sofia's kidnapping was bothering her. The round woman stared down into her lap, her mouth trembling slightly. She slowly reached over for her glass of wine and took a small sip.

"How do you like Spain?" Señor Astucia asked, capturing Susanna's attention.

"You have beautiful countryside here," she answered.

"I have heard England is quite beautiful. Do you like Spain or England more?"

"That's difficult to say," she said putting down her fork. "Spain is quite stunning. The people are very welcoming. But I do miss the courts at Windsor and Buckingham Palace."

"I'm sure you'll make friends at the court in Madrid. You can consider me a friend. I've known Prince Carlos a long time."

"Oh, I suppose you might have a few interesting stories then. Anything I should know about the Prince?" she laughed.

"His Highness can be rather, what's the word …" he trailed off, in thought. Then he grinned, 'It seems my English isn't so good."

"Arsenio," Carlos began, "have you missed me at all? As I sit here, you've paid more attention to my future wife. You haven't asked me how England was."

"By the looks of it, I think you enjoyed England," Señor Astucia said, his eyes grazing over Susanna as he took a sip of wine.

Carlos continued talking to Señor Astucia in Spanish. Susanna quietly ate as she looked down at her plate, listening to their conversation.

"How has court been?" Carlos asked, emphasizing the word 'court'.

"Court? Are you asking about court or–"

"I think she may understand Spanish," Carlos abruptly said, slightly nodding his head towards Susanna.

"Really?" Señor Astucia continued in Spanish, "Why doesn't she speak it?"

"Don't ask," Carlos said. "So, how is court?"

Señor Astucia breathed heavily through his nose, "Well, if you've noticed, the entire court isn't here."

"I noticed," he said. "I was hoping you might have a message for me regarding that," he said testily.

Keeping her face down Susanna discreetly watched Señor Astucia, trying to understand who or what the conversation was really about. Señor Astucia had an uncomfortable expression as he tried to find the right words,

"I don't think the court is very happy with the, uh, development that has recently taken place. Court has never liked the idea of-" He paused gazing at Sofia. "Uh, tea. You know that."

"I haven't been that fond of tea, either," Carlos said glaring sideways at Susanna.

"Really?" Señor Astucia said in surprise raising his brows.

"But we must make tea a part of society here in Spain if we are to progress as a country," Carlos continued. "There's good money in tea. Most countries in the world do well when they decide to do business with tea."

Susanna clenched her napkin in her hand. She knew their marriage would be loveless, a contract they would both benefit from, but she couldn't help her curiosity. Obviously 'court' was a love of Carlos's. But how much he loved 'court' and how beautiful she was mattered to Susanna.

Susanna pushed her potatoes about with her fork. She never thought she would be true to the man she would marry anyway. She had never had an exclusive relationship with anyone, though she had fooled some men into thinking that she was true to them.

Susanna had always found it impossible to focus on one man when there were so many. She had always figured that when she married it would be a business arrangement. But as she listened to Carlos speak of 'court,' she felt mortified. Not that she had plans of being faithful to Carlos, but she was going to be discreet about her infidelities. She had hoped he would try to have their courtship appear authentic before they married. Instead, he was talking about his soon-to-be mistress casually at the dinner table.

Of course, Susanna could confront Carlos later. But that would mean admitting knowing Spanish fluently and that would lead to having to speak it.

"Ugh," she muttered under her breath.

Carlos glanced at her.

"Um ... the potatoes are cold," she said quickly.

"You should have eaten them faster."

She grabbed her wine glass and took a sip. She couldn't confront him now. If she caught Carlos with 'court', she might say something to humiliate him. But for now, ignoring the issue would give her freedom to be with whoever she pleased.

She smiled and lifted her glass towards Señor Astucia and winked at him before taking another sip.

MANY GIFTS

$\mathcal{M}$adeline had never seen a room full of so many gifts. Usually, the Garter Throne Room at Windsor was spacious. It was a room for presentation. Other than its caved ceiling with moulded designs and chandelier; along with its wood panelled walls decorated huge paintings of previous monarchs it didn't hold much furniture. The dozen blue upholstered chairs with their detailed wood arms and legs were gone. The carpet was now covered. There now only a narrow blue strip of carpeting leading to their thrones. It was hard to believe that this was once the spacious Throne Room that had welcomed Sofia to Windsor … and where she and Alex had consummated their marriage.

"What is all this?" Madeline asked turning to Alex, who was standing next to her.

"These are wedding gifts from the different colonies of Britain."

"Did they all come at once?" she asked, looking around her feet.

He laughed, "No, they've been arriving here the past few weeks," he said uncomfortably. "They were probably sent when they found out that we were going to get married."

"But it has only been a few weeks. Some of these must have come by ship."

"Yes. I think a few more will be coming."

She stood perplexed.

"You're wondering how they arrived so quickly, your Majesty?" Ben said to Madeline as he walked into the Throne Room. He bowed to both of them. Richard and Jack followed him in and each bowed in turn.

"You're here to help with the gifts, gentlemen?" Alex said quickly, "Thank you."

Madeline looked at the room full of gifts, some of them looked quite exotic.

"Wouldn't it take months for some of these items to get here, Alex?" Madeline said and she immediately noticed the valets snickering.

Alex closed his eyes, "Madeline, please don't be offended."

"This is going to be good," Jack nudged his brother, Ben in his ribs.

"There are many colonies, you know, some of the empire is all the way across the world," Alex said uneasy.

She put her hand on her hips, "So?"

"Well, there are always miscommunications, you know, much has happened in these past six weeks. Not everyone knows or can keep up with what happens here in Windsor and London. Some of these gifts may have been sent even before we wed."

"Why would anyone do that?" she asked furrowing her brow.

"To impress I'd imagine," Alex said shrugging.

The valets laughed at once.

She noticed a large, red, crystal-like orb, sitting on a gold gilt stand.

"Red. Sofia's favourite colour," she said slowly. "People in other colonies think you married Princess Sofia?"

"Either that or they expected it. I'm sorry Madeline," Alex said sympathetically. "But I don't think every gift was confused. Sir Ashton has been sending back anything that may have been specifically for Sofia."

She knew she should be grateful for the gifts, but it was beyond humiliating. "So," she sighed, "I suppose it would be rude not to accept them?"

"Well, not everything was personalized. I don't think every colony was misinformed," he said trying to comfort her.

She somehow doubted that.

"If you don't want to accept them I understand," he said. "But-"

"It would make a bad impression if we didn't accept them," Madeline concluded. It was true. If the first impression that the colonies had of her were that she was picky, the monarchy would lose some respect.

"It was an honest mistake, Madeline," Alex said consolingly.

She stood silent.

"You know your Majesty, you should have gone with the 'red represents love and royalty' approach Sir Ashton suggested," Richard whispered to him.

Alex put his hand to his forehead and shook his head in embarrassment.

Madeline tried to suppress her hurt feelings. Not one to feel so emotional over material things, she felt ashamed. She was offended by the gifts meant for Sofia. Mortified, she hoped she wasn't turning into Lady Watson and the other prissy women at court. But something else was worrying her; she had never been forced to think of her reputation before. It was a double-edged sword; if she accepted the gifts, she would be seen as foolish. On the other hand, if she returned them expecting the colonies to give something else, she would be seen as demanding. The pressure was awful.

"We can send them back, Madeline," Alex said evenly.

"That's not a good idea and you know it," she said glancing up at him. It was then she saw him with new eyes. She always felt sympathy for the tough decisions he had to make, but now she had an idea of how it felt. He lived his entire life, everything he had done, analysed and judged. This was what royalty was really about. "This is what we will do," she began, "we'll accept them and send thank you cards explaining that we understand the confusion, but are very pleased with the gift. That way, we seem gracious."

"Thank you," he said in relief and kissed her on the cheek.

She smirked. It was the least she could do. Alex had sacrificed and risked so much to make her his wife. He would have done the same for her.

"All right gentlemen," said Alex brightly, "we'll sit on the thrones. Please present the Queen and I with the gifts."

"Isn't there a representative from each country that is supposed to present these?" Ben whispered to Jack and Richard.

"Yes. But Lord Walsh and Mr. Tinney didn't believe the Queen would accept the gifts," Richard said in a hushed tone.

"She does have humble beginnings, she didn't grow up a princess or Lady-to-be," Jack pointed out under his breath. He grabbed one of the gifts, then turned to Madeline and Alex, "This your Majesties is from the island colony, New Zealand."

Jack pulled off a red silk cloth with gold tassels at the corners. Beneath the silk was a plant Madeline had never seen before.

"A silver fern," Alex said recognizing it, "I don't believe we have one at Frogmore, we can have it planted there."

Jack looked at it amazed, "Wow, does it really grow all white and silvery like that?" He reached out to touch it.

"Don't touch it, Jack. I imagine it wasn't easy to care for on its journey here," Alex warned. "Yes, it really does grow like that."

"Neat," Madeline commented.

"This is from Malta," said Ben before opening a large detailed carved chest, inside were linens.

"Oh," said Madeline picking out a small square linen. "I think it's lace."

"It must be handmade lace," said Alex. "Malta is known for that."

"It's a table setting," she said as she dug deeper into the chest, "How many do you think are here?"

Ben scoffed, "Enough for a large party."

Richard came up with the next gift, and though they weren't originally intended for Madeline, she began to grow excited.

"This is from the New South Wales," Richard said, and opened a chest. Inside were two white, glossy pieces of rock that looked like icicles.

"What is it?" Madeline asked, picking one up.

Alex took it into his hands, "Looks to be some kind of rock."

"It has a note," Richard said and he began to read it aloud:

Presenting their Majesties of England with pieces from the mystical caves in New South Wales. The natives of the country believe the caves to have mystical healing powers. A wish to their Majesties that they are always in good health.

"Thoughtful," Alex smiled and set it back in the box.

The gifts went on and on, all of them were interesting and in some way represented the places from which they came. India sent some fine silk and cotton fabrics. Ceylon had sent tea leaves. Many allied countries sent gifts as well; blue Delft vases were sent from the Netherlands; Russia had sent several large wax medallions by the artist Fyodor Tolstoy. They looked like Wedgwood pieces and the details were stunning.

It took most of the day, but they finally reached the last gift, "This one comes from The Canadas," said Ben.

He opened the box and Madeline gasped. She had never seen anything like them.

"What on earth are these?" said Ben almost laughing.

There were four. Alex pulled one out of the box, inspecting it. It was made of leather and fur and had intricate beading. "I think they are boots," said Alex.

Ben pulled out a card, "Says that they are 'muk-luks'?" he raised his brow.

Madeline couldn't help but to laugh, "Well, I suppose it can get quite cold in the Canadas. But I don't think we'll ever have any use for them here. It doesn't get so cold here to need boots with fur."

"Could be good for hunting," Alex offered.

"Well, that's it then," said Madeline happily, looking about at the room full of gifts with a satisfied expression. She would never have dreamed being given so many gifts.

"Not quite, I got you a little something," Alex said grinning.

"After all that?"

"It's something I've wanted to give you for a while. Jack, can you go get them?"

Jack nodded.

Madeline leaned toward Alex, "You spoil me," she said softly.

"You never act spoiled, that's why you get spoiled," he winked.

Jack opened the doors leading to the courtyard and left momentarily.

"There not exactly rare," Alex said, "but I think you'll enjoy them at Frogmore."

Jack escorted two footmen into the Garter Throne Room. Both men were carrying a black swan. They set the pair down and they began waddling about. Madeline giggled, "That's cute. I'm guessing one's a male and the other's a female?"

"Yes," Alex said, then he whispered beneath his breath. "The female's pregnant."

"Aww," she gushed.

"It's an odd time of year for her to be pregnant," he said, "but I suppose not everyone does things according to custom."

She laughed.

"Black swans mate for life too," he said, squeezing her hand in his.

She melted. It was so sweet and thoughtful she hardly knew what to say. Both swans cuddled next to one another on the carpet.

Richard tried to pet one.

"I don't think you want to be doing that mate," Jack said pulling him back. "If they aren't familiar with you, they might start nipping at you."

"Have them taken down to Frogmore garden," Alex said. The footmen took them back out.

"That was so cute," Madeline grinned.

"I'm glad you like them. But, I was also thinking we should get away for a couple of days," Alex went on. "I think it'd be good for us."

"What about Spain? Are they not planning an attack?" she asked looking at him, surprised that he would suggest leaving.

"Yes. But," he sighed, shifting in his chair, "in the private meetings about the Spanish, the Lords, Colonels, and myself agree that you and I should discreetly leave for a week or so. You know, in case the Spanish do attack, Windsor and London aren't well secured just yet."

She pursed her lips and crossed her arms, irritated. "Isn't that risky to leave and go to another place that has no protection at all?" she asked.

"We'll only be gone a week or so," he said reassuringly. "We won't be too far."

"Where were you thinking of?"

"They haven't told me, yet. Sir Ashton is going to let me know when it's decided."

"What about the Duke of Axford?" she asked cross. "When are we going to take care of matters involving him? Or is he just going to sit in London Tower? When will justice finally be served for what he has done?"

Alex bit his lip, "Actually the Duke has been moved to Curfew Tower recently. But Madeline you must admit, with the war that is about to happen, there is no time to punish the Duke. We will deal with him after."

She sighed knowing he was right; for their safety, they'd have to leave and put the Duke on trial later.

LION'S DEN

King Fernando rounded about the table in his Royal Armoury. He looked down at the map of England and the small model ships and an evil grin emerged.

"My son couldn't have come home at a better time," he said in Spanish as he patted Carlos on the back. "Now, we can go over these plans together and perfect our strategy."

Susanna sat quietly on a chair off to the side, listening intently. Though she knew the entire conversation would be in Spanish and she could ask Carlos what the battle plans were later, she wanted to hear all the suggestions. She doubted that King Fernando noticed her there. If he had, she was sure he would have kicked her out by now.

"Your Royal Highness," began one of the Coronels, "we had a solid plan to free you from the English."

Carlos raised his brow, "How come that never happened?"

"Well," King Fernando said sheepishly, "we needed to be certain that we could get into the castle. "

"Yes," the Coronel continued, "we had just received some intelligence from several men we had sent. We had just learned from some sources that you were in Curfew Tower and were planning a way to break you free."

Susanna rolled her eyes. These men weren't efficient. All the commoners of England knew where Prince Carlos was.

"Yes, we had talked to several friends of Lord Bathory. They had told us there was a secret tunnel. We were trying to locate it," King Fernando said as he brushed the miniature ships and men from the map. "But that is no longer needed."

"No, it's not. You see your Highness," began Señor Astucia, directing himself to Carlos, "we were going to take a large fleet of ships, land in Brighton like we did when we attacked with Lord Bathory; trek the countryside and attack Windsor. It seems that the English don't know how we entered England before. There isn't any English military stationed in Brighton or the countryside we went across. This may be because after Napoleon was defeated, the English Royal Navy that was occupying the English Channel sailed to other parts of the English empire. Our Coronels feel that it would be best to attack England now before King Alexander can reorganize his men to come back to England."

"But, now that you're here Carlos, we can use you to lead some of the men and devise a new plan. Your upcoming marriage to the heir Miss Susanna will ensure domination of England when we take Windsor."

All the men nodded in agreement.

"We can attack next week," said one of the Coronels, "several fleets of ships around Brighton."

"Next week?" King Fernando shook his head, "No. We shouldn't be too hasty. Remember when we went in with Lord Bathory; I insisted on getting more men. Bathory believed that we would conquer Windsor with a surprise attack and look where that got him. It appears that Windsor can take a small battalion of men."

"Your Majesty, I think it would be wise to take advantage of our situation. We know that King Alexander has sent a message to his men in Europe to return. I mean, I'm sure he's expecting an attack," Señor Astucia said.

Susanna nodded in agreement. Giving Alex too much time wasn't wise. It would take Alex several weeks or a little over a month, but if the men in Windsor and London could hold the Spanish off long enough, Alex's reinforcements would arrive.

"Señor Astucia, you're not a military man," King Fernando countered. "With Carlos here, we don't have to worry so much about Carlos's life being threatened. We can properly prepare ourselves, storm into Windsor, kill King Alexander, his new Queen, and take over. Carlos's return gives us the upper-hand. We can wait a couple more weeks, build a stronger plan, army and fleet. If we wait for extra men, the English will have no prayer in defeating us. England's men are scattered. It will take King Alexander much longer to get his navy and organize a counter-attack or defence against our armies. We should continue to work on a plan and improve it before taking fewer men and hoping for a victory. There is no room for error. We need a guaranteed victory."

Anger built in Susanna. She remembered her father once telling her he felt King Fernando was a procrastinator. No wonder King Fernando was losing many of his colonies. She wanted to say something, but she waited for one of the Coronels to speak up. Unfortunately, they didn't.

"We'll take a large fleet of ships. Every ship we can find on the coasts of Spain, and its colonies" the King continued. "We'll depart in a month for Windsor and London."

"London, your Majesty?" a Coronel asked in surprise.

"Yes, London," King Fernando confirmed. "If we are going to take over this country, we should take hold of its capital. To demonstrate to the rest of Europe a clear victory."

"Your Majesty, are we certain of King Alexander's whereabouts?" one of the Lords piped up curiously.

"Good question, Señor Menendo. By the time we leave, he might be at Buckingham Palace, not Windsor. Another reason to invade both places at once. I'll lead the invasion on London, Carlos will lead the invasion on Windsor."

Susanna clenched her fists. What King Fernando was requesting made no sense. He wanted to wait longer to take a bigger fleet? Killing Alex was a certain victory now and they didn't need a big fleet to do it, only a crafty plan. She looked around at the expressions of the other men in the room. She noticed the Coronel that had just spoken was pursing his lips looking down as the King split the fleet of ships and men on the map, placing half of them in London and the other half in Windsor. She wasn't given an education in military tactics, but even she knew this move was counterproductive.

Señor Menendo spoke up, "You know your Majesty, if we decide to split the fleet, perhaps we should have more ships head to London. Windsor is a small town and-"

"Ah, you forget Señor Menendo, the King will most likely keep most his guards near where he is staying."

"But the civilians-"

"Civilians will flee," King Fernando said dismissively.

Susanna shook her head, she doubted every man in London would flee. Some might. But it would be seen as unchivalrous to do so, and no true English gentleman would do that. She looked at the men, curious if any one of them would speak up. But she knew they were 'yes' men. She had to say something.

"Your Majesty?" she said getting up. King Fernando turned, hearing her foreign voice ringing out in English. Until then, he hadn't noticed her.

"What is the plan once you reach Windsor, your Majesty?"

King Fernando looked at Carlos and in his native tongue said, "What is her concern here?"

But Susanna ignored it and continued, "I know Windsor Castle very well-"

"You think I don't?" King Fernando asked heatedly.

"I know you've visited," Susanna said timid. "But your Majesty, I do believe that the reason why the battle was lost at the castle was because the underground tunnels were not invaded first. If you-"

"How did a woman get in here?" King Fernando boomed. He stood next to Carlos and said something beneath his breath.

"Someone please take Miss Bathory out," Carlos ordered in Spanish, "this is no place for a woman."

Two footmen stood on either side of her, "Carlos," she said irritated.

"Your Highness, the proper way to address Carlos is 'your Highness'," King Fernando said correcting her with his heavy accent, his eyes blazing.

The footmen grabbed her arms and escorted her out. She was about to yell out, but she knew there was no point.

She sat outside the Royal Armoury on a bench waiting for the meeting to finish. As soon as Carlos came out, she would give him a piece of her mind. But as she heard the Spanish voices in the next room, she realized something; it wasn't that she was English that King Fernando was rude to her. It was clear that King Fernando had no respect for women. She had no power here. In fact, she wouldn't have any influence until she and Carlos married and took over England. It was frustrating, but she needed to tolerate how she was being treated for the time being. She needed to find something else to do instead of dwelling on how she was being ignored. For a moment, she questioned if she should find Queen Isabelle and do some needlepoint with her. She chuckled at the thought.

Instead, she decided to go to Carlos's drawing room in his private apartments. She couldn't wait outside the Royal Armoury, ready to pounce on him. Nagging Carlos in front of King Fernando wouldn't be smart.

* * *

A COUPLE HOURS LATER, Carlos entered his drawing room and spotted Susanna, sitting on one of his green silk couches next to the fireplace. He sighed, "You've been waiting for me?" he said awkwardly, trying not to make eye contact.

"I can't stand Sofia's apartments," Susanna said, "so many small rooms. Most of them red."

"What's wrong with red? Red is royalty," Carlos said smiling, "and passion." He stroked her cheek, hoping this would help her forget what had happened earlier.

She grabbed his wrist and tossed his hand away from her. "Carlos, how could you let your father speak to me like that? If I'm to be your wife-"

"He is the King of Spain. No one talks to royalty like that," he said clenching his fists at his side.

"But-"

"You want my father to like you?" he said, raising his voice. "You have to understand something. He's a traditional man and doesn't like opinionated women. Actually, most men don't." He took off his navy blue waistcoat and threw it onto the couch next to her.

"Why? Because more often than not, we have something intelligent to say?" she barked back. "I suppose it must be insulting to a man when a woman has better ideas about war. I think if we were to find out more about Alex's new Queen, Madeline Black, we might be able to use her. Possibly hold her for a ransom of the empire."

"Please," Carlos said massaging his temples. "A king is not going to give up ruling his empire for the head of his wife. If that scheme could work, that's how all the wars in history would have been fought. If we were to capture the Queen, King Alexander would wage war on Spanish grounds and we don't want that. You clearly have no experience in battle. All the men in that room, myself included have a background in the military and experience on the battlefield. What do you have that they don't?"

"A brain."

He looked at her in disgust, "A woman's brain is not as large as a man's."

"Maybe. But a woman doesn't have two heads to think with, so she never gets confused."

He stared in shock, "That's a vulgar thing to say."

"It's the truth," she said crossing her legs and turning away from him, gazing at the fire. "Anyway, I know the enemy much better than anyone in that room. Isn't knowing the enemy a good tactic?"

He said nothing.

"Admit it, Carlos," she said trying to persuade him, "even you find the plan ridiculous. Waiting to do a double-attack and then not using the tunnels to our advantage makes no sense."

He was silent as he walked toward the fireplace and watched the flames. So far the plan wasn't great. She had made some valid points in the Royal Armoury.

"My father is a stubborn man, but honestly, this war will be impossible to lose whether we leave now or in a few weeks. King Alexander has fewer men." He sat down on a couch across from her, "Why do you care so much? Leave it to us."

"I care because you don't know King Alexander. He always has a trick up his sleeve. Always wriggles himself out of tough spots. I think my father's biggest problem was that he underestimated Alex again and again."

"Did you ever tell your father what you thought of how he handled King Alexander?" Carlos asked.

She held her breath. She never had.

Carlos shook his head, 'It's not easy to tell a headstrong man what to do," Carlos continued, "I met your father. That man was near impossible to work with. I'm surprised that he and my father managed to storm Windsor together."

"Carlos, I want to know the details of everything that is being said in your meetings,' she said sternly. "Is your father deciding every course of action? There are other men in there that have experience and could give good advice. Is there any man your father listens to?" she asked, a keen expression on her face.

He gave her a nasty look, "Planning to seduce someone, Susanna?"

"It's difficult to be with a Spaniard," she dismissed.

"Doesn't matter. I can't really say that there is anyone," he lied. "Anyway, my father believes that all royalty is chosen by God. He believes that any man that is a king is a god amongst men."

"So there is no one he will listen to then?" she said discouraged.

"Like I said, you have to be destined."

"Doesn't he see you as destined?" she asked. "I mean, you will eventually rule."

"He will listen, but only take the advice if he likes it."

She sat in thought. She knew Carlos wasn't going to take her advice and start trying to persuade Fernando to do what she wanted.

"Well, what do you think should be done?" she asked, hoping to get an idea of what the final battle plan might be.

He considered her for a moment. Her eyes were so eager and full of longing; too ambitious for her own good. It was easy to take advantage of a woman when she wore that desperate a face, it was familiar to him. Like many of the ladies he knew at court, she had a weak side. He had finally reached it.

"I agree that we should invade the tunnels," he lied, "barricading the men inside the castle and defeat them. It makes sense. It pains me to admit it, but taking Windsor first would be easier than a double-attack. Going earlier, I don't think makes much of a difference. But as the English say, the sooner, the better."

She clasped her hands together, beaming. "Good, you agree."

He nodded.

She walked over to him, she began running her fingers through his thick black waves. "You and I are alike you know," she kissed him, "we think alike."

He tucked some of her loose blonde tendrils behind her ear as she looked deeply into his eyes. *Fool*, she thought. There was one man she could sleep with to get what she wanted; he was it.

She caressed his cheek, "So what else did you men talk about after I left?"

"My father just decided how many men should go and when we would depart," he said casually.

"When does he plan to do so?" she asked her eyes widening.

"Well, now that he knows where Sofia is, he plans to write Sir Gregory."

"Why?" she asked curiously.

"My father wants to make it clear to Sir Gregory that Sofia does not belong to him and if he doesn't release her, my father will kill him after we take London and Windsor. But ..." Carlos trailed off.

"But what?

"My father plans to torture and kill Sir Gregory even if Sofia returns home safely."

"Why would he bother to write if he plans to kill him anyway?" she asked confused.

"He wants that fool to shake in his boots. He also thinks it sends a strong message to the commoners not to mess with Spanish rule."

She cuddled to his chest, "Doesn't he worry that Sir Gregory might kill her?"

"Losing Sofia wouldn't affect our take over," Carlos said casually.

She was disgusted. Lord Bathory was stubborn, but her father did respect her and wouldn't leave her life to chance. On the other hand, Sofia wasn't Susanna's problem. Susanna had to convince Carlos that leaving earlier was a good idea. She needed him to persuade King Fernando.

"Enough talk of politics. You know Carlos, I've been doing some thinking and we haven't had much of a chance to be together," she said glancing at him suggestively.

"I've been thinking the same. I enjoyed our time together in the tent," he said smiling.

"So did I," she lied, her eyes piercing his.

"I thought so."

"I never got the chance to show you how grateful I am."

"I thought you weren't interested in pleasing me," he teased.

"I am very interested in pleasing you. You have no idea."

"Excellent," he said unbuttoning his trousers, glancing up at her expectantly. "On your knees."

She refused, "I'm a Lady, Carlos, and that's something I don't just do for anyone."

"I'm the Prince of Spain!"

"There are other ways I can please you," she offered.

She straddled herself on top of him and fumbled with the front button of his trousers. He reached out for the decanter on the table next to him and poured himself a glass of brandy. She felt humiliated as he took a sip from his glass, watching her.

He began to stiffen. He put his brandy back down and ran his fingers through her hair. She could feel pressure at the nape of her neck, his hand pushing her down, her face lowering. She grabbed his hand, "Stop. You a hardly a gentleman, much less a prince."

He glared at her, "You seem to forget where you are and the situation you're in. I don't care if you want to or not. I'll order you to do it by royal command."

She sprung to her feet, "Think again Carlos, you can't force me to do anything without making yourself look like a laughingstock. What are you going to do? Call your guards in here to force me?"

"You're right. I don't have to command you," he said staring blankly at her. He rose to his feet. Sensing he was about to lunge at her, she quickly grabbed his glass of brandy thew it in his face and kneed him in the groin.

"ARGH!" he cried out lurching in pain.

She walked out of the door, huffing as she did. When she reached outside, she turned to one of the guards, "Gentlemen, his Highness is not feeling well. Could you please escort him to his bedchamber?"

FESTIVE TIMES

It was a fall day when McFadden skipped through Holyrood House happily. It was comical to watch; it was only two in the afternoon and he was already drunk, bumping into everything within a five foot radius of him. As he danced and frolicked about, Sofia sat in the Morning Drawing Room, trying not to laugh aloud as she read Scottish myths on a settee. The settee was covered in silk and had wool embroidered images. Like the tapestries around the room, it told a story in three separate panels. Sofia had no idea what story was being told, but there were several nobles and knights. She had found the book of myths in the Queen's Ante Chamber. She had read a few stories and was certain she had seen some art pieces around Holyrood House depicting the Scottish myths she was reading. She was searching the book for the myth that related to the settee.

McFadden bumped into the settee and Sofia dropped her book. "Mr. McFadden! What are you doing?" she said shocked.

Sam rushed in. "I'm sorry Miss Sofia," Sam began, "I've been trying to get him to-."

Sam tried to hold McFadden up, but McFadden pushed him away.

"Sir, you can't be like this," Sam began cautiously, "we have duties to do."

"When have I ev'r worked lad?"

Sofia giggled. She often wondered what McFadden's job was.

McFadden grimaced.

She stopped, bringing her hand to her mouth.

"What you tee heeing aboot?" McFadden asked stabling himself.

"What are your duties McFadden?" she asked sincerely, trying not to offend him. But he didn't seem to hear her. He was staring off, his eyes centred on something outside. She followed his gaze, but there was nothing. Turning back, she saw him teetering on his feet again. Sam pushed on his shoulders, trying to hold him up.

"Aye, neva really look at the description, but I think I do well," McFadden said, planting his feet firmly on the ground. "No one complainin'."

"But you must report to someone. Who is your superior?" she asked.

"I am," Greg said entering the room.

"Na ya not. Ya the King's arse."

"True," Greg acknowledged, "but you forgot that the day I came here, I came here with an order from the King. You are to follow all my orders." He noted McFadden's drunken state, as McFadden continued to struggle to keep his balance. "It's not even dinner yet, mate," Greg said aghast. "When did you start drinking?"

"I dunno. But I kno' I'm not the only one."

"No one but you is drunk, Mr. McFadden," Sofia said.

"That's not true Miss," Sam said. "McFadden's been on the Royal Mile all morning."

"What's on the Royal Mile? Where is that?"

McFadden slapped his thighs laughing, nearly falling over. "It be tha street outside of this house lass! But I suppose you and tha' arse haven't been out yet."

"There's a festival going on," Sam explained. "Lots of drinking and dancing. Edinburgh has it every year 'round this time. Last one before the cold weather comes."

"There's a festival today and you didn't tell us, McFadden?" Greg asked somewhat insulted.

"Ya arse, I'm not tha only bloke here! Ya got Sam and tha daft girl, Belle."

Sofia was growing more irritated by McFadden's ignorance toward Belle. She wasn't stupid. She was from a culture he didn't know, and a language he didn't speak.

Sam frowned.

"Ooohhh, I think I offended tha lover boy."

"You offend me too, McFadden," said Sofia. "Belle isn't daft. Why would she know that Edinburgh has a festival today? She struggles to communicate with everyone here, including you. I have no idea why she bothers with you. If I were her, I wouldn't give you the time of day."

"No, the girl jus' can't do her job," McFadden said.

"If you don't know what your own duties are, how do you know Belle's?" Sofia said laughing.

"She makes a good point," Greg said. "But you don't care what Belle does, McFadden. You just like to give her and Sam a hard time because they've got a soft spot for each other."

Sam stared at his feet blushing, trying to think of an excuse to leave the room.

"Soft spot? That's puttin' it mild. They've been battin' eyes at each other fer months!" McFadden exclaimed. "She's tha one with the courage. This boy's too shy ta do a damn thing."

Sofia cocked an eyebrow, "So because she's got the courage, she has to ask him? Isn't it a gentleman's job to ask the fair maiden?"

"No lass, not in this case."

"Why not?" Sofia asked flabbergasted.

"She still be wantin' him. He's a scared lil' arse. If she'd be stoopin' low enough to wan' that arse, she should be doin' something."

Embarrassed, Sam looked away but said nothing.

Greg laughed, "That's a fair point, McFadden."

"I don't understand that," Sofia said folding her arms. "It's not funny, Greg. Sam's just a little shy."

"That's what McFadden's trying to say," Greg reasoned. "Belle knows Sam isn't man enough, in that case, she should put us all out of this misery. Sorry, Sam but watching you two bat your eyes at one another is getting old."

"It's a little hard to communicate," Sofia said defending them both. "She hardly knows English. He barely knows French."

"Lass, there be a language they both know," McFadden said nodding his head, a smirk on his face.

Sofia put on an air of disgust.

Greg's mouth curved as he observed Sofia, and her upper lip cracked slightly. "So, McFadden, when is this festival?" Greg asked changing the subject. "What is Edinburgh celebrating?"

"Ta hell if I know," McFadden said.

Sam shook his head, "It's not really celebrating anything. The first time I went was when I first came here four years ago. There will be storytelling, games, highland dancing competitions, and theatre."

"Don't forget the drinkin' lad."

"Yes, there's drinking," said Sam. "Everyone goes. There's some music too. They've had some operas some years."

McFadden blew a raspberry, "Nobody cares 'bout opera!"

"It sounds interesting," Sofia said excitedly, "Has Belle ever been to it, Sam?"

He shrugged, "No."

"I know a lady that might like to go," Greg began, "Sofia will you accompany me to the festival?"

"Of course, Sir Gregory," she said. "What time did you want to go?"

"What time does this all start, McFadden?" Greg asked turning to him.

"It's happenin' now," McFadden replied. "It'll be nothin' but a good time for the next week. Or when all we decide to go home."

"Want to go now, Princess?" Greg asked shifting his brow up and down at Sofia. Sofia smiled knowingly.

McFadden rolled his eyes, "Hear tha' Sam? It's not that hard to ask a lass. Just call 'em 'princess.'"

Sofia tried not to laugh, "I'll get dressed now."

"Don't be getting all gussied up lass, no one really cares," McFadden said as she turned to leave.

"Wear whatever you'd like," Greg said, ignoring McFadden's comment.

"See, again Sam. Let 'em think they are the boss," McFadden advised, pulling out a flask from his belt, he took a swig.

"Think? I am the boss," Sofia said with a coy expression before walking out of the Morning Drawing Room heading back to the Queen's Chambers.

Sam glanced at Greg and McFadden, waiting for them to make fun of him. But they said nothing. When he realized they weren't going to tease him, he spoke, "McFadden, if you know so much about women, why don't you have a woman?"

"That'd be a lotta work lad. Makin' a lass think she's boss," McFadden said as he patted Sam's back. Taking another gulp from his flask, he left the room heading back to the festival.

Sam stood awkwardly looking at Greg. Sam had been wondering something since he had met Greg Umbridge, *how did Greg get Sofia, being in the shadow of King Alexander?*

But Greg answered his question before Sam could ask. "Either she likes you or she doesn't. If you feel something, do something. Ignore it long enough and some other bloke will muster the courage you don't have."

"Didn't Sofia fancy the King at all?" Sam asked incredulously.

"Sure. All girls fancy a man that has power, wealth, and good looks. But there was no chemistry. I waited around until she finally realized that. Lucky you, Belle wants you. The best part is, you could say anything you wanted to her, and not make a fool of yourself."

"You think I should invite her to come with me to the festival?" Sam said wide eyed.

"You're hopeless, mate," Greg sighed.

* * *

A COUPLE HOURS LATER, Sofia was almost ready for the festival. It had been weeks since she had enjoyed any culture. Though the parties they were having were fun, and she had learned a little about Scottish

137

culture, the festival sounded as though there would be all sorts of things to appreciate. She had decided to go against McFadden's advice and don one of Madeline's beautiful green velvet dresses. She loved to wear red, but she wanted to surprise Greg. She still had the string of pearls that she had been wearing when they had left Windsor. She hadn't worn them since arriving and decided that this would be the perfect time. After she had applied her reddest lipstick, she went to find him. Since she had spent much of the afternoon getting ready, she figured he had gotten some fresh clothes, and was likely in one of the drawing rooms waiting for her. Sofia found Greg in the Evening Drawing Room.

But he hadn't freshened up. He was playing cards with Sam. A stack of money was next to him and just a few shillings next to Sam. Sam was pale as he looked down at his cards.

She should have been furious that she had spent all that time trying to look nice for him. But she knew it was useless and she didn't want to pick a fight before going out.

"Give up? Put your cards down," Greg ordered looking intently across the table at Sam.

"That's it, no gambling. Greg, give Sam his money back," Sofia insisted. "Why don't you get dressed before we go out?"

Greg lifted his brow, staring hard at Sam, "You're more concerned about what I'm wearing?" he asked. "I'm sure this festival will cost us something. Why do you think I'm playing with Sam? I want to be sure that my Princess has fun." Finally, Greg looked up, noticing her for the first time. She was breathtaking. He murmured softly, his eyes ogling her. He seemed lost.

"You're going to pay for our fun by taking Sam's money?" Sofia asked astounded.

Still gawking at her, Greg didn't answer.

"I don't agree with that," she said. "What if he wants to treat Belle?"

"Hm?" Greg said in a daze. "You look beautiful in green."

Sofia blushed, "Greg, maybe Sam wants to treat Belle. You should give him his money back."

Greg laughed, "Sofia you're so cute." He lowered his voice to a whisper, pulling her close to him, "He won't invite Belle out, Princess."

She glanced over at Sam as he was about to lay down his hand. She grasped Sam's wrist before he could put his cards on the table.

"How about this," Sofia began, "I'll take Sam's place. If I win, he has to ask Belle to the festival."

"What if I win?" Greg asked.

"Well, then I suppose you'll have more money."

"Ladies don't bet," Greg said simply. "Besides, what do you have?"

She took off her string of pearls, "Can you match this Sir Gregory?"

"I don't think you should play," Greg said unsure. "If I win, I know you'll be expecting those back. I'm not sure I can match it anyway."

"How about you deal the cards again. Even though you can't match what I put down, we'll call it even," Sofia said. "I promise if you win, I will never ask you for them. You can sell them or do whatever you like with them."

He sat in thought, then shook his head, "No Sofia, you're betting one of the last pieces of jewellery you have on one hand."

"Move over Sam," Sofia said confidently.

Sam moved over to an empty seat at the table. Greg folded his cards and put them on the table.

"I don't want to do this. You'll be angry when I win."

"That's *if* you win," she giggled.

He shook his head smiling. "Princess, you've never played cards before."

"I've watched you play."

"Yes. Have you noticed more often than not, I win?"

"Enough excuses, Umbridge. Shuffle the cards and deal them."

Reluctantly, he gathered the cards and began shuffling. "Ladies choice, what game would you like to play?"

She grinned. He could be an English gentleman. She knew he'd let her choose the game, "Euchre."

"That's not a gambling game, Princess."

"Why can't it be?" she asked. "Besides, you said it was my choice. What's wrong? Not comfortable with Euchre, Sir Gregory?"

He pressed his lips together, "It's not my usual game."

"Good. It happens to be mine."

He dealt the deck, "If at any point, you wish to stop -"

"I'm not going to change my mind," she said. "I can beat you. Sam keep track of the points. Whoever reaches ten first wins."

Greg took the fives out of the deck and handed them to Sam. He shuffled the cards some more before he placed a card on top of the kitty. It was an ace of diamonds.

"Pass? Or would you like diamonds to be trump?" Greg asked.

She looked down at her hand and at the cards in front of them. She had the left bower and a few lower diamonds.

"Pick it up," she said.

"Fine. I suppose I'll get to go first."

Greg laid down the king of spades. He won a couple tricks, but she took the round. Greg had the nine of diamonds and the ace but didn't have any other trump cards. She had most of them.

They played another round. A queen of spades was on the kitty. She picked it up and won again.

"No points yet, Greg?" she asked playfully. "In a few more hands, I'm sure I'll win the game."

Sam smiled wide, looking hopeful. Several minutes ago, he wasn't sure how he would make it to his next pay day.

Greg drew the ace of spades on the kitty. He didn't have many spades and by the looks of things, neither did Sofia. He passed on the opportunity and turned the card over.

"I'll make it hearts," Sofia said.

"Are you sure?" Greg asked. "I mean, you should have at least two trumps to call it."

"I'll be fine. By the looks of things, you don't have a heart."

"Oh Princess, I've got a heart," he winked.

"Really?" she teased, "I hope it doesn't break when I win."

All the cards she held in her hand were hearts, and she took it again.

"I'm winning," she said haughtily afterward. "You haven't a single point yet, Sir Gregory."

"You may have won a few battles. But you won't win the war," he chuckled.

But after a couple more rounds, she did win.

Greg buried his face in his hands. "How?" he asked. "I didn't get a single hand!"

"I warned you, Euchre is my game," she said grinning from ear to ear.

Sam put his hands around the winnings and gathered it to his chest.

"Sam, what do you think you're doing?" Sofia asked.

"Um, we won Miss," he said sheepishly.

"No, Sam. I won. The deal was if I did, you'd ask Belle to the festival."

Greg began to laugh. Sofia picked her necklace out of the pile and put it back around her neck.

"I'm not giving you all the money either, Sam," Sofia said. "You can have half your share now. If I see you with Belle, I'll give you the other half." She divided the winnings, putting the other half of the money in her dress pocket.

Greg took the money he didn't lose off the table.

"Don't be so greedy next time, Greg," Sofia said. "If you are going to rob someone of their money, it should be McFadden."

They both rose from the table. Greg extended his arm, "Shall we, Princess?"

The two left the Evening Drawing Room and headed for the festival.

Sam sat alone and dropped his head to the table. He didn't have to invite Belle out; losing half his pay for the week didn't seem so bad. On the other hand, Sofia might demand the money she just gave him back if he didn't.

FUTURE PLANS

*W*hile festivities were had in Edinburgh, Susanna looked around the dinner table at the nobility as King Fernando addressed them in Spanish.

"Before Carlos escaped from Windsor, he came upon the King's secret tunnels," he bragged as he cut into his steak. "Carlos made some notes about them. We will take advantage of this. The first men to make it to Windsor will immediately invade the tunnels. That's how the English counter-attack you know, they have their men go into the tunnels and attack their enemies from behind. That's why they won last time."

Susanna looked down into her lap, her lips curling. It had taken weeks, but once Susanna had drawn some maps of the underground tunnels, Carlos had finally convinced his father that using the tunnels to their advantage would be necessary. Of course, Carlos was taking credit for her brilliance, but she would have to allow for that if they were going to defeat England.

It still irked her that King Fernando was procrastinating the attack, but luckily, it didn't sound as though Alex had done anything to prepare for Spain's coming. There was word that some of his men were mobilizing across Europe, but his armies in Europe wouldn't be able to defend against the large fleet of ships King Fernando was planning on.

"Carlos also feels we should go sooner rather than later," Fernando continued. "Eager, of course, to take out the English. But we can't be too hasty. I think if we leave it a couple more weeks, we'll have more men and cover more territory."

Carlos chuckled, "My father would like to advance on Edinburgh as well. Teach that scoundrel Greg Umbridge a lesson, and of course rescue Sofia."

Susanna glanced at Queen Isabelle. There was no kind of emotional reaction at the mention of her daughter this time. The Queen continued to eat her meal, as though nothing was said.

Carlos addressed Susanna in English, "Miss Susanna, how do the English nobles feel about Greg Umbridge?"

She sat in thought and set down her wine glass. "Your Highness, there is no easy answer to that question."

Everyone chuckled.

Susanna saw Señor Astucia's eyes tasting her body again. He had done so repeatedly at every meal for weeks. She had grown used to his stares and didn't mind. She still had not figured out who 'court' was, yet. But, she was certain Carlos had already met with her. Several days ago while searching about for Carlos, Susanna eventually found him in the garden. He was by himself a table full of food in front of him, along with two empty plates. Whoever the woman was, she had taken off before Susanna had found him. When she asked Carlos what company he was keeping, he told her that it was Señor Astucia. A lie. Before she had left the castle to search the garden, Señor Astucia had come to her looking for Carlos, too. In time, Susanna was sure she could get Señor Astucia to reveal the identity of 'court'. Susanna continued, "I'll try my best to answer your question about Greg Umbridge. There were many nobles that did not like his lack of etiquette. Many don't like his close relationship with the King. When he was a teenager, many people called him the 'King's clown.'"

Laughter rang out in the room.

"I suppose he still is?" Fernando said.

"I hate to admit it your Majesty, but as time went on, he gained some respect from the nobles," Susanna explained.

Fernando looked perturbed by this, "How could that be?"

"Trust me. I was never one of them," she said waving her hand. "But then some of the men learned that the best way to have your opinion heard by King Alexander was to be friendly with Greg Umbridge. Yes, he made a few friends. A lot of the younger Lords like him. He's a good card player and drinking mate."

"The man's a fool," Fernando said, his tone argumentative.

"Couldn't agree more, your Majesty," Susanna grinned.

"What do you mean Miss Susanna?" King Fernando barked. "You just said that he's a good card player and drinking friend? I can see you think he's good company."

"What?" she said in surprise. "I don't think-"

"Miss Susanna, I'm not deaf," King Fernando interrupted. "I heard what you just said." She opened her mouth to explain that she didn't care for Greg Umbridge, but King Fernando went on, his face beet red, "It's not a good idea to feel that way about King Alexander's best friend. It makes me feel uncomfortable. Are you really willing to storm England? Or should I be questioning your motives, Miss Susanna?"

She couldn't believe what she was hearing. She looked over at Carlos. She knew there was no point in trying to reason with King Fernando. Only Carlos could clear up this misunderstanding. But as she gazed at him waiting, he sheepishly rubbed his neck and ignored her plea.

Thankfully, Señor Astucia came to her rescue, "Your Majesty, I doubt Miss Susanna has come to Spain to insult you and your court by favouring Greg Umbridge. I think she was just letting you know how the younger noble gentleman in the English court feel about him. Is that the way of it, Miss Susanna?"

"Yes," she said, all eyes on her. "No proper woman would think Greg Umbridge was 'good' company."

"That's a relief," Fernando said. "I was almost certain you liked him, Susanna. Do you think any of the men with influence would come to his aid if he were attacked in Edinburgh?"

She was about to answer 'yes'. Lord Davis made a point to play cards with Greg at every court event. The Duke of Axford was known to have a soft spot for him too. If Sir Ashton Giles survived the attack on Windsor, he would send whatever men available to Edinburgh. But as she observed the stern look on Fernando's face, she knew she shouldn't tell him that. She could only tell him what he wanted to hear. Otherwise, he might have another tantrum. "I doubt anyone would come to help him," Susanna lied. "Besides, the few men that he is friendly with have not much power. Most of them are barons."

Fernando nodded, "I imagine those barons are only friends with him in hopes to become viscounts or earls? I sent Sir Gregory a letter you know. A few weeks ago."

"Do you think he has received it yet?" Carlos asked in Spanish, and the conversation continued in their native tongue.

"If he hasn't yet, he will in a few days," Fernando said chuckling. "I'm sure the moment he reads it, he won't get a good night's sleep." He turned to everyone around the table and shouted in Spanish, "You see, I told Greg Umbridge that if he sent Sofia back, I might not tear him to pieces! But what kind of example would I be setting if I didn't?"

All the men laughed.

"You think he'd be a gentleman and allow Sofia to write to her family," Carlos said.

"I don't think he knows he should allow her to," Señor Menendo commented, wiping his mouth with his napkin. "Poor Sofia is probably going crazy. She is a delicate thing."

Fernando nodded. "I should have followed your advice in keeping her with me, Menendo. I regret trying to secure a union between her and King Alexander. We've all heard what an odd fellow he is."

"The rumour is true then?" asked Señor Menendo.

"Yes. Carlos confirmed it with me. He did marry a common girl. Worse of all, she used to be his servant."

Many heads around the table shook in disapproval. King Fernando looked up at Susanna and addressed her in English, "Do you know anything about this servant girl the King has married?"

"Dreadful woman. I used to see her in the marketplace from time to time," said Susanna as she put down her fork. "English subjects have such respect for my family; they don't refer to me as 'Miss' over there. I'm known as 'Lady Bathory'. Once she saw me and ignored the pleasantry. She didn't curtsy to me. The woman never knew her proper place."

"When we take England, you won't have to worry about anyone not giving you the proper pleasantries," said Carlos smiling. "We will remind King Alexander's new wife how she should properly address her superiors."

Susanna nodded and took a small sip of wine. Normally she would raise her glass and make a toast at this point of a discussion, but she knew King Fernando wouldn't see it fitting for a woman to do that.

Fernando raised his glass and made a toast in Spanish, "To teaching England a new level of sophistication," he shouted.

Susanna barely managed to smile as she lifted her glass. Carlos considered her and began to question how much Spanish she knew. He gathered that she must know a little; when she addressed his parents in Spanish the first night and the next day when they were going over the battle plans. He was almost certain she could carry a conversation.

After dessert, Susanna retired to Sofia's drawing room. Earlier in the day, she had taken a map of England as well as some miniature ships and men out of the Royal Armoury. She sat at a writing desk, placing each miniature piece in a plan that she thought would work; taking the entire fleet to Brighton, securing Windsor and usurping Alex was the most tactical, logical course of action. Why Fernando wanted to split the fleet made no sense.

Alex seemed to prefer Windsor to Buckingham Palace these days and he wasn't one to retreat from a fight. If they stormed Windsor, he would stay until his men secured the castle. On the other hand, his new Queen might sway how he would normally deal with things. She tapped her chin. Though Alex didn't have any men stationed near

Brighton, it was possible he already had some men on the coast of England, keeping a lookout for them. It only took several men to light a pyre to warn Windsor. They'd spot the ships hours before Spain attacked. Knowing Alex, he had probably sent for all his men across Europe to come back. But there wasn't enough time for him to set up a strong front, it was doubtful Alex could get them all back in time. However, Alex could organize a small fleet back to Windsor if King Fernando didn't act now.

She glowered at the map and ships. It was wiser to invade sooner. *Why can't King Fernando understand the benefit of going now? Why does he feel he needs most of his men to take on England?* She was certain Alex didn't have enough men to take on what King Fernando had already prepared.

King Fernando wasn't going to change his plans either. In the past several meetings, Prince Carlos and all the Coronels had already suggested they go earlier and he had refused. They also suggested not splitting the fleet. But, he was a stubborn man, the type that insisted things be done his way.

There is only one way of defeating Alex. Someone has to make King Fernando think the ideas are his. She sighed. *But how?* He didn't want to talk to any woman concerning war or politics. Nor could she work her charms on him. The situation was impossible. Carlos didn't seem to have the power of persuasion, either. He had tried to convince King Fernando of the wisdom of attacking sooner; both he and Señor Astucia were quietly talking about it over dinner that evening. But it seemed the two were just as frustrated over the King's decision to leave later as she was.

Carlos entered and she turned in her chair with a toothy grin. "Hello, Carlos."

"Susanna," he said curtly as he walked toward her. He peeked over her shoulder and saw the map of England with the miniatures scattered about. "What are you doing?"

She glanced over at her plans.

"You know how my father feels about you getting involved in these things," he said stiffly.

"Yes. I know. He doesn't like to hear what a woman has to say."

"Well. It's not really a woman's place. Besides, you're English. How does he know you won't betray him?"

She blew a raspberry, "Really? Are you joking? What was the point of freeing you and bringing you back here then? Or does your father really believe you escaped Curfew Tower on your own?"

He ignored the comment, "So what are you thinking?"

"Your father is a fool if he is going to wait. It makes no sense."

"I'll admit, he does prefer to be well prepared. But there is not much difference between now and two or three weeks from now. King Alexander can't set up a solid battle plan either way."

"It's still risky. This is the most opportune time," she said pounding her fist on the writing desk. "Worse of all, he wants to go to Windsor and London at once."

"What's wrong with that?" asked Carlos somewhat bemused by her intensity.

"I'm next in line to the throne. It's simple. Kill Alex. Take the throne. What does London matter?" she said.

"My father wants to secure the strongholds."

She shook her head.

"Susanna, what do you know of war?" Carlos laughed. "Did your father educate you in combat and tactics?"

"What do you know of your enemy?" she challenged. "If you knew Alex well enough, you'd know waiting isn't an option. That's what the problem was last time." She stood up from her chair. "Actually for years, my father kept waiting for the right opportunity. He should have just done it!" She wailed clenching her hands into fists.

"You make it sound easy," he said, rubbing her shoulders. "If it were that easy, we'd do it as you say. But there's politics, too. The rest of Europe and England's allies to think about."

"The rest of Europe is too weak dealing with the aftermath of Napoleon," she countered. "There isn't politics. I'm the next in line to the throne anyway."

"True. But you have no way of knowing where King Alexander

will be. If we can control the largest city, and take over Buckingham Palace and Windsor, it's a secure win."

"I know where he will be. The King will hide his new Queen," she said. "Wherever she is, I'm sure he'll be close by."

He laughed, "Even if that were true, you have no idea where he would hide her."

She tapped her chin and paced back and forth in front of him. "I doubt he'd take her far from Windsor."

"Frogmore?" he asked.

"Ha! No," she said. "He'd use the tunnels to take her to a safe place within the town. Which is why the tunnels need to be invaded."

"My father has agreed to that. The original plan was to just block them, but in our meeting today, he agreed they need to be invaded."

"Why? Because you suggested it?" she said in contempt.

"Don't get angry," he said, standing in front of her stopping her pacing. "You take this all too personally. But he listens to no one."

She paused and looked at him. There was something unusual about his manner. He was being kind. He hardly ever was. The few times he was, she could tell he didn't want to be. In the past few weeks, he had rarely come to visit her.

"Why are you here, Carlos?" she asked.

"I've been thinking," he put his arms around her waist. "We talked about getting married, but we never talked about when."

She was silent for a moment, "When were you thinking?"

"Before we depart for England."

Obviously, King Fernando had put him up to this. She knew he wasn't over 'court'. She had overheard him the other day on the Grand Staircase talking to Señor Astucia about trying to have another secret meeting with 'court'. But she still wasn't going to confront him; if she wanted England, she'd have to ignore the 'court' situation for a while longer.

"I suppose it makes sense," she said trying to sound agreeable. "If you invade England as my husband, it will be unquestionable that we have taken power."

"Since it is quite last minute, there won't be much pageantry with our wedding," Carlos quickly added.

"Ha!" she said smiling, "I wouldn't want to have my wedding party here. I'd rather have a large party in England."

"You want a second wedding?" he asked shocked.

"Wouldn't you? Our subjects will love us for it. Everyone likes a good party."

He nodded, "I'll go tell my father. How does next week Friday sound?"

"Fine. But I want to wear something fashionable. I don't want to walk down the aisle in something a noble could wear. Not when I'm to become royalty."

"We'll have a few designers come in from the city. I'll go tell my parents now." He turned to leave the room.

"Tsk. Not going to give your future wife a kiss before parting?" she asked giving him a look.

"Of course," he said. He turned and pecked her on the cheek, then left her alone in the room with her thoughts.

She turned her attention back to the map of England and the miniature ships and men. His proposal wasn't romantic. It was laughable. But then again, he was in love with another woman, their marriage would only be a business transaction. The conditions of her marriage did bother her. She had a solution to it. She figured that once they had taken over England, she would see less and less of him. She'd try to stay at Buckingham Palace in London. In time, she'd somehow spoil his reputation with London's court. Then, he might be inclined to stay in Windsor. She doubted he would go back to Spain. King Fernando wouldn't allow it.

Her eyes grew narrow with her thoughts. She hated thinking about King Fernando being a part of her future. She remembered how her mother had always complained about her in-laws while they were alive. Lady Bathory would brood for days before they arrived at their home. When they had passed away, Susanna remembered her mother telling her that if she happened to marry with intolerable in-laws to put as much space and distance between them as possible.

King Fernando was pretentious, stubborn, and not very intelligent. Queen Isabelle was weak; she had barely uttered a word since Susanna and Carlos arrived. The Queen was like a quiet, tired, old mouse scurrying about the castle, trying to remain invisible to everyone around her. It was nauseating to watch. Most people would have sympathy for a woman like that. But Susanna didn't; in her mind, those that surrendered themselves in such a repugnant manner asked for the abuse they got.

Though Susanna found the Queen's mousy ways pathetic, she had to admit, she would rather be rid of the King than the Queen. Then Susanna remembered something and a new plan began to form in her mind; killing royalty like her father had done. She could get rid of King Fernando, and it wouldn't be that hard. Once she and Carlos ruled England, she could invite them over, and poison him with belladonna. Belladonna had proven helpful to her family before. "Perfect," she said softly, "Carlos would have to go back and rule Spain."

LETTERS AND THREATS

"This is quite possibly the best festival I've ever been to," Greg said arm in arm with Sofia as they walked down the Royal Mile, McFadden following in their wake.

"Tis a grand day!" McFadden cheered. "One of the best of the year if yer a Scotsman."

"I just can't believe all the different kinds of entertainments and games there are," said Sofia as her eyes searched the street.

"Most tha drinks ya can get fer free too," said McFadden emphatically as he took another swig from a mug of beer.

"Free?" Greg repeated in disbelief.

"Well, depends on who ya know. I know 'em all. I'll get 'cha a couple glasses. I'll be back!"

McFadden sped ahead of them tripping on his own feet, but still managing to keep from falling. He walked up to one of the vendors.

Sofia looked at Greg with a warning expression on her face.

"What? I've only gotten really drunk once since we got here. The King's wedding night. You did, too."

"And what happened later that night?" she scolded, tapping her foot. "After our last party, you promised me you would only drink if we were drinking together."

"What? You're not going to have a drink? This is a celebration, Sofia. It's our first Scottish festival."

"Well, I hadn't planned on drinking," admitted Sofia.

"We won't get drunk. Just one drink for the each of us. Hm?" he asked.

"One," she said holding up her finger with a stern expression. "That's it."

"Great. Besides, when you go to a party, you should let loose a little. You know none of these people will be working tomorrow," he laughed. "By the looks of things they may be in recovery for a few days."

"I don't care how drunk everyone else is," she said slightly miffed. "You know I don't like it when you're drunk. Do you know why that is?"

"Well, guessing from what Alex used to say ... it's embarrassing for you?"

"Exactly. Alex used to say that?" she asked surprised.

He laughed, "When we were younger, Alex didn't mind so much. But then there were nights he'd have to ask someone to get me off the floor."

She looked at him aghast.

"Believe it or not, I'm not as bad as I used to be," said Greg in his defence. "But to be honest, I'd hate to do that to you. I don't want you picking me up off the floor, or ordering someone else to."

"I'll tell you right now Greg Umbridge, you ever do that to me and I'll take advantage of your drunken state."

"Oooh, you'd do that?" he asked raising his brows.

She laughed, "Not in the way you're hoping."

McFadden ran back up to them passing each of them two beers.

"Just one this evening McFadden," said Greg. "I'm in the company of my Princess."

"Aww," Sofia gushed as Greg gave his extra drink back.

"What abou' ya Sofia, you gonna be handin' back that second drink?" McFadden asked.

She passed it back to McFadden.

"More fer me," he bellowed, drinking from each glass he held in his hand. He stumbled off and the pair continued walking down the street.

"So how is this the best festival you've ever been to?" Sofia asked Greg. "I mean London is so fashionable and exciting, how could this be more than what London has to offer?"

"Are you serious?" he asked, his jaw dropping. "We're you not amazed by those men tossing those cabers?"

"Oh, you mean those burly fellows running around throwing tree trunks? What were they trying to accomplish?" she asked, trying to irritate him.

"What? It wasn't just running around with a tree trunk! The man had to make it flip in the air and land on its end. That's not impressive to you?"

"I couldn't stop thinking about something Belle told me earlier," Sofia said.

"What did she say?"

"Well," Sofia began, her eyes falling onto the cobblestone street beneath her, "she told me that the men wear nothing under those kilts."

"Why should they?" chuckled Greg.

"It's called modesty."

"Don't be surprised if later in the night, the men get so drunk they start lifting them."

Sofia bit her lip, she had a feeling Greg was right.

"Are you really telling me that this hasn't been the most enjoyable festival you've ever been to?" Greg asked. "You have to admit, the bagpipes were spectacular."

"Yes," she nodded, "the Gaelic music was great and all the contests of brute strength were … amusing."

"Yes," he said emphatically, "where else would you find people throwing hammers, weights, and tree trunks?"

She tittered; it was funny when he put it that way.

"Not in London," Greg continued. "Look at those men over there, playing the fiddle. They're doing a jig, having a laugh, and stomping all about that stage. Now if we were in London, would it be like that?"

"No," she said.

"What kind of music would they be playing in London?" he asked knowing the answer.

"I'm guessing classical. Probably several string instruments."

"Yes, there'd be a cello, a piano, and any other instruments that scream sophistication. But look at the crowd surrounding the stage of fiddlers, it's more fun. If it were London or even Windsor, people wouldn't surround the stage. The men would be expected to ask some noble girl to dance some boring traditional dance."

"So you didn't like dancing with the noble girls?" she laughed. "Do all men hate dancing?"

"Oh. It's not so bad. There's only one man I know that hates it more than anything."

"Who?" she asked taking a sip of her beer.

"Alex."

She stopped mid-stride, spilling some of her drink on her dress. Greg stopped and pulled his handkerchief out of his pocket, wiping the spill.

She quickly swallowed her beer. "Thank you," she said softly. "Alex hates dancing? He's so good at it though."

"I don't think he hates the dancing. He just hates that it never stops for him; he goes to a party and every girl is waiting for the opportunity. When he tries to take a break, the girls pout."

"That happened to Carlos, too. He loved the attention, though."

"He never grew tired of that?" asked Greg. "If it were me, I know I'd find it annoying."

"Carlos? Not exactly. He always liked the girl that would go to desperate lengths." Sofia said. "The more obsessive and jealous they were, the more he seemed to like them."

"Are you serious? I don't think I've ever met a fellow like that. The desperate type are kind of scary," he sniggered. "Some noble women and girls used to pay off a guard to sneak about Buckingham Palace and Windsor. They wanted to try to find Alex to get some alone time.

Of course, footmen or someone else working in the castle would find them before they could find Alex and ask them what they were doing."

She giggled, "What did they do? Run off?"

"Sometimes. Usually, they lied. They would say that Alex was expecting them."

"Did they get away with that?" she asked incredulously.

"Oh no. Most times the girls were taken to Sir Ashton, who escorted them out."

"So did any reach Alex before that happened?"

"Very few. Alex would typically tell them he was busy. They'd whine. He hated that. Eventually, the guards that were taking the bribes were fired."

"Funny," Sofia said amused at the differences between Carlos and Alex. "Carlos had girls come to the castle to see him, too. Any noble girl was to be brought directly to him. If he thought they were pretty, he would allow them to stay."

"Your brother is an odd bloke. Most men I know don't fancy women that are so needy."

"I think Carlos is like that because of my father," she admitted. "He always told Carlos that the happiest relationships were the ones that the man was in control."

"Well, someone desperate enough to make themselves look foolish is easy to control. But what did father expect of you then?" he asked crinkling his brow. "How did he want you to behave with men?"

"My father was particular about the men I could see. I couldn't talk to anyone he didn't approve of."

"What kind of men did he approve of?" Greg asked knowing he wasn't one of them.

"Mostly his own friends. They were all older than me. My father only considered a younger man if he-" she stopped, clasping her fingers to her lips. Her eyes welled up and a few tears streamed down her cheeks. But she didn't cry. She was silent.

Greg wrapped his arm around her waist. Holding her close to him, he rubbed her back. It was clear that King Fernando used her to gain power or other favours he wanted. He saw her as property.

She let him hold her for some time. She inhaled him, a sense of safety and happiness coming over her. Just being held by him was a sort of therapy. Finally, she pulled away and continued walking.

"What about your mother," Greg said changing the subject. "I didn't really get to know her when she came."

"She doesn't say much in public," she said her voice cracking. "I hated being alone with her.'

"Why?"

"She would talk to me about all her problems. Complain about court life."

"Did she complain about your father?"

"I don't-" she paused. "Deep down, I know that she hates my father, but she didn't say much about him. She fears him. But enough of my family. Can we please talk about something else?"

He stopped in the middle of the sidewalk, "You're right," he said sensing that she was becoming uncomfortable. "We've been wandering around a while now, and this festival looks amazing, but other than these two mugs of beer in our hands, we really haven't done anything yet."

"What did you have in mind?"

"Ladies choice," he said, glancing about, "we can do a drinking game," he joked as he pointed to a table full of people playing cards and drinking.

"I don't think that was really part of the festival. It looks like those people just sat at a table and started playing," she said giving him a light push.

He pointed further down the street, "I think I see some magicians down there. Surely you don't think magic is blasphemous?"

She smiled remembering the time Greg had tried to show her a magic trick with cards and she had initially refused to watch because she was taught that magic was blasphemous. "Oh no, I'm too old for magic, Sir Gregory," she said in a mature tone before cracking a smile.

"Well, at least you know it's a trick now," he said. He continued to look about the streets, "Oi, what about that man over there," he said pointing down a side street, "looks like he's got all sorts of paintings and such. Want to look at his art?"

"If I like anything, do you have enough money to buy it? Or can you only afford a magic trick?" she said raising her brow.

"I might have enough money for a painting. Depends on how good he is," Greg winked.

They headed toward the side street of paintings when Sofia noticed some familiar faces. She held up her arm, stopping Greg from walking down the street. "Is that who I think it is?" she smirked as she nodded her head in the direction of Sam and Belle.

"Looks like he finally asked to escort her about."

They watched the pair as they looked at the paintings. Belle tapped Sam on the shoulder, pointing to a painting, she hopped up and down on her feet. Without a word Sam handed over some money to the artist, and Belle picked up the painting, beaming.

"Well, surely if Sam can afford to buy a painting from this artist, you can," Sofia joked.

"We don't even know how good he is yet. Besides Princess, I'd be willing to bet that I could paint you something far more artistic than anything that bloke did," he boasted with a huge grin.

"That I'd like to see."

"You saw my room in Buckingham Palace. I painted all the work in there, you know that."

"So you've painted all sorts of things for Alex's homestead but nothing for me yet?" she teased.

"Do you really want anything from that artist?" he asked.

"Well, let's take a look."

They walked down the alleyway, the cobblestones were not well kept and Sofia had to mind her heel. She observed the pictures, and the artist watching her keenly. There were paintings of different streets and buildings in Edinburgh.

"Do you have any paintings of Holyrood House?" she asked the man.

He tilted his hat up, "I think I still might. He shuffled about, looking through the different canvases. "I just sold one moments ago, but I'm sure I have another."

"Where you from mate?" Greg asked, realizing he wasn't Scottish.

"I've lived all over. I was born in Italy, grew up in England."

"Sorry, I'm just having a hard time placing your accent," Greg said.

"Get it all the time. My folks and I moved about quite a bit," the man said as he continued sorting through his work. "I do have a lovely painting of a horse and carriage next to Holyrood House. Painted it a few weeks ago."

"Is Holyrood House in the background?" she asked.

"Yes," he admitted.

"I was more interested in the residence itself," she said. "Thanks though."

She took Greg's arm and the two went further down the alley. Once they were out of earshot, he spoke, "He seemed like a nice bloke, you didn't like any of the paintings?"

"He's nice," she agreed. "But it was difficult to see anything. The light from the lamppost was dim so I couldn't get a good look at much. Besides, if I couldn't have a painting of Holyrood House by itself, then I'd prefer something a little more risqué."

"Really?" Greg said with interest, "Why?"

"Well," she began "there were so many artists that used to come to Madrid. My father has a large collection. But mostly everything he has looks similar."

"He likes classical art?" asked Greg unenthused.

"Oh yes, and renaissance or baroque style. Anything that looks like a Leonardo or Michelangelo he's fond of. Anything with a religious theme, too."

"What about romanticism? Like what about Goya? Does he like Nude Maja?"

She burst out laughing "No. My father doesn't like romanticism that much. Thinks the artists are going too far with that; not following the rules of art. But we had artists bring in collections of art that were nudes. They would visit the palace hoping father might be interested."

"But he rejected them all?" he asked as they turned the corner and went down the next street.

"Absolutely. My father would never have had such debauchery under his roof," she said, a coy expression on her face.

"But …" he began with a suggestive grin, "did my little Princess do something she shouldn't?"

"Are you kidding? My father would kill me. But he wouldn't kill Carlos," she hinted.

"What does that mean?" he asked eagerly, anticipating what her answer might be.

"Oh, what's that over there?" she said seeing some dancers hopping about on a stage.

"What do you mean what's that over there? You were in the middle of telling me something, go on."

"But what are they doing?" she said pointing to the crowd. "Is that a dancing competition?"

"Yes. Highland dancing competition," he said dismissively. "Now you were telling me a story."

"No I wasn't," she blushed, pushing on towards the dancers. "I want to join that dance competition."

"Sorry, no," he guffawed. "I'm not helping you with that until I hear about what Carlos did. Did he buy some naughty art?"

"I'm not telling you a thing until you dance with me in that competition," she said glancing at the scene. "Are we supposed to wear those kilts? Do they give you one?"

"I think you have to bring your own," he said, looking at the dancers.

"Humph! So, I can't compete then," she pouted.

He looked at all the dancers. They were all wearing kilts, "To hell with that. We'll dance anyway." He grabbed her hand and they ran toward the competition. Greg asked one of the spectators staring up at the stage, "Oi, can anyone join the competition?"

"If ya know tha dances," the gentleman said.

"What about the kilts? Do we need to get some, or does someone provide them?"

"Ha! Tha English always share personal things like kilts?" the man asked giving Greg a strange look.

"Look, I would like to get the lady a kilt so she can join the competition," Greg replied gesturing to Sofia. The man glanced over at her.

"There be a vender ov'r there selling them!" he said pointing across from them, shaking his head. "Ya tha' cheap lad?"

Sofia tittered behind her fingers.

"Right, thanks," Greg said abashed.

They headed back across the street to the vendor.

"I'd like to get two kilts, one for myself and one for the lady," Greg said to the merchant.

"Just kilts lad? I think there's a whole outfit, ya need. What'd ya expect tha lady to wear on 'er chest?" he asked aghast.

Sofia went scarlet in embarrassment.

"Well, I guess I'll get her the whole outfit then," Greg said.

"You and her will be needing brogues too then, laddie?" asked the merchant.

"Brogues?" Greg repeated.

"Shoes," the man said.

"Fine," Greg nodded. "How much for an outfit for her and a kilt and shoes for myself?"

"Ya don't want tha sporran?" the man asked.

Greg rolled his eyes as he fumbled to take out some money, "Seriously, I'm English I don't know these Scottish and Gaelic words."

"The pouch that rests on ya nob."

"Yes, yes I'll get the sporran," Greg said hastily, wondering if Sofia knew what the Scottish slang for penis was. He handed the money to the vendor. "Where can we get dressed?" he asked.

"I dunno. I'm just tryin' to sell tha stuff," the man huffed as he counted Greg's money.

"We can't expect her to get dressed in the street," Greg said.

The vendor looked about annoyed, "You can get dressed behind there," he said gesturing behind him.

"Behind the curtain?" Greg asked in astonishment. He wasn't sure Sofia would want to get dressed there.

"Either tha' or the alley," the vendor said shrugging his shoulders.

Greg turned to her and shrugged, "We can go back to Holyrood House if you want."

"It'll take us an hour to go there, get dressed, and come back," she said shaking her head. "By then it'll be over. The lampposts aren't that strong behind the curtain."

"All right, I'll keep watch while you get dressed."

She went behind the vendor's set up and got dressed as quickly and discreetly as she could. Greg kept an eye down the street. People passed by, but didn't suspect a thing. She came out.

"Now ya look like a Scot," the vendor said grinning at Sofia.

Greg nodded in agreement, "You look quite lovely in a kilt."

After Greg changed, they headed toward the competition.

"Now you were telling me about some risqué paintings, Princess," Greg said eagerly. The only reason why he had bought the outfits was for the chance to hear the rest of the story she had been telling.

Sofia didn't respond but kept walking towards the competition. Greg kept up with her, looking for another opportunity to get her to share. Once they reached the stage, she looked up at the dancers.

"Are you going to be able to dance with them?" he asked as they watched a group of women dancing in a circle.

"Dancing isn't hard. I'll watch them for a few minutes, then, I'll join."

"You have no idea at all how to do this dance?" he asked.

"Do you?'

"No, but I thought you might have had some training with it. Isn't that what they teach princesses?"

She giggled, "I was taught traditional ballroom dancing. I don't think my father would ever approve of me dancing like this."

She watched in awe as the girls bounced about on their toes.

"No, he wouldn't like the way their skirts are swaying. Too suggestive."

"That reminds me, there was a little story you were telling me a few moments ago. Now what was it," he said smiling from ear to ear, "your father didn't approve of risqué nudes and rejected any pieces that had anything suggestive or nude."

"Oh I think I understand the dance now," she said as she climbed up on the stage joining the circle of women.

"Come now," he sighed as he watched Sofia dance with the other ladies. He knew by the smirk on her face as she glanced over at him that there was an erotic ending to that story and he wanted to hear it. All the dancers were women, but he didn't care. He hopped onto the stage and began to dance with them. The crowd cheered and laughed at Greg.

"Lad, ya be dancin' the ladies dance," a man next to the stage called out.

"Always wanted to learn," Greg said skipping nimbly over to Sofia, who was trying not to laugh at him.

The rest of the girls tittered and whispered to one another.

"Sir Gregory, I believe this dance is just for the ladies," Sofia chortled as she switched feet and began skipping again.

"Oh, I know," he said breathlessly, "but you said you'd tell me what Carlos did."

"I think it's pretty obvious."

"Carlos started his own collection?" Greg asked.

"Yes."

"And my little Princess found it?"

She didn't think he'd figure that part out. "If you must know, yes," she said.

He beamed, "How did you find them? Where?"

They continued dancing as she began to recount the story. "One day, I was in my brother's apartments. A footman had told me Carlos wanted to talk to me and was in his room, so I went. When I first got there, I couldn't find him. So, I went to his drawing room and to his desk to write him a note."

Greg laughed, 'And there were nudes in his desk?"

"Loads of small paintings. But they were unlike anything I had ever seen. I mean, they were quite graphic. I didn't recognize the style either. But then I started recognizing the people in them."

His jaw dropped, "You must be joking."

"Hardly, all sorts of women and men from the court."

"Men too?"

"I had no clue how he got them or where he got them from," she giggled.

"There'd only one person in the Spanish Court that I'd take an interest in seeing nude. But something tells me I wouldn't find her in that stack of his." He stopped dancing and pulled her close to him, kissing her passionately in front of everyone.

She kissed him back, then pulled away. "Greg," she whimpered, "You shouldn't do that. It's not proper in a crowd like this."

"Then where should we be go? This scandalous talk is having me want to steal away a moment with you."

They gazed longingly at one another. They didn't know when this dream would end. Deep down, both of them felt it was a season, much like Romeo and Juliet, their houses were divided. It would only be a matter of time before one or the pair of them would pay the price. Every opportunity for a stolen kiss couldn't be ignored. He scooped her up, "If it is improper here, I'll carry you back to Holyrood House." He began to climb down the stairs of the stage with her cradled in his arms.

She pressed her mouth against him as he did. He carried her past the vendor they had bought the kilts from.

"I want you now," he growled.

She looked about, "The lampposts don't light the alleyways well," she said in a sultry voice.

He considered her for a moment, surprised at what she was suggesting. "No, they don't," he said and headed toward the dark corridor. It was narrow. Perhaps a shortcut people might take to get from one street to the next. But it was twisted and dangerous to navigate through the dark. Greg's eyes followed the scant light that settled on the brick walls until it went pitch black.

She giggled, "Greg, I can hardly see a thing."

"Neither can I. I suppose we found the perfect spot, haven't we?" He set her on her feet and she held onto him unsteadily, nearly falling over. He caught her, pulling her up against the brick wall behind her.

"Easy there, Princess."

She couldn't see anything, so she held her hands out in front of her, trying to find him, "Ow, that's my eye," he grimaced.

"Sorry."

"You don't think anyone will come down here, do you?" she asked.

"That's the beauty of kilts, Princess. We can have our fun, then drop our skirts. No one will know."

She tittered, and he closed in on her, pressing his warm lips against her neck and nibbled his way up to her jaw. She held his face, her soft hand spurring him on. Wrapped in his affections, her pulse quickened with the smell of his breath and the soft caresses of his lips.

"Princess," he grunted between kisses, "you are so beautiful. I have to have you now."

The sweet taste of her skin combined with the muffled noises from her throat inflamed him. His hands slid up and down her sides appreciating her feminine form. His mouth dropped kisses about her neck and nested on the slope of it where he knew she was most sensitive. Her body gave a sharp quiver, and he pushed his hips to hers.

Spurred on by her excitement of having him be so intimate with her in such a public place, she felt the dampness between her thighs and knew she was ready for him. She wrapped her leg around his; rubbing her calve up and down his, her eagerness to have him inside her at a fever pitch.

But he avoided the raw, animalistic instinct to claim her; he ached to see her nude, to appreciate her glowing skin, and the valleys and peaks of her curves. It was impossible in the alleyway; the only way to remedy it would be to touch what he couldn't see. His lips descended on hers as his hands loosened the laces of her corset. He slid his hands between her skin and the corset and explored the hardened peaks, gently pinching. She threaded her fingers into his hair, gently pulling, her mouth moving along with his in a frenzied whirlwind. His kisses trailed to her chin, her neck, then her clavicle, where he lined her the hollow with soft pecks. He moved lower, kissing and nibbling her breasts. She could no longer withstand it. The desire within her roared like wildfire, capable of destroying anything within its path. She didn't care of the costs to be with him; should they be found, reputation and Spain be damned. She loved him. Her back arched, and she gasped, "Now…now. Please."

He moved his hand lower, and it rose along the silky soft inner skin of her thigh. She shuddered as his fingers came closer. He rested his thumb flat against the pearl and moved it subtly. Her toes curled under the smooth slight motion. Losing self-control, she yelped, gripping onto his large arms. He repeated the motion as her moans growing louder; he covered her mouth with his, hushing her sound.

The thrumming of her lips was more than he could bear. He backed her into the wall and lifted up her kilt, and she felt the brisk air on her flesh. It sent a flutter through her until she felt him, hard and warm. It soothed the chill, and he guided himself into her velvet. They fell into tempo, both of them pecking and panting with every stroke. Nothing was more erotic than this, knowing they were steps away from being caught, but each refusing to stop.

The kilts between them gathered, the heat intensified. Consciousness of their surroundings was lost; the cold brick wall, the hollering from a distance. If there were footsteps nearby, they would have fallen away from the world they were in. Sweet words fell from his lips as she felt him crumbling, "Beautiful, Princess….my God, I'd do anything for you…I love you." Her muscles shut tightly around him, and she collapsed onto his shoulder, moans of ecstasy escaping her lips. This incensed him, and he groaned, eliciting his essence into her.

She held to him as he settled her onto her feet. She wasn't able to hold her own weight. After several minutes, Sofia let go of him and tightened the laces to her corset. She looked up, "Run."

Greg hadn't heard her as he adjusted his kilt and sporran. Then, he heard several footsteps and Spanish voices not far from them.

"Run."

"Bloody hell. We need to move," he said, turning to her.

But she was already gone, sprinting down the alleyway.

Greg took off after her. He could see her silhouette making it to the end of the alleyway, back to the street. He tried calling out to her, "OI! Cinderella! It's not midnight yet!"

But she didn't turn back. When he made it to the street, he frantically looked about for her among the crowd but couldn't spot her.

It was then Greg felt a tapping on his back. He turned to face two tall men with dark black hair. They were Spaniards, but didn't appear to be armed. Nonetheless, Greg firmly gripped the dagger hidden in his coat.

"Are you Sir Gregory Umbridge?" one asked.

Greg glanced back into the crowd. Instinct told him that Sofia was long gone, she must have heard their voices, too. Greg surveyed the man's hands. The soldier was holding an envelope in his hand that had a wax seal.

"Yes," Greg said. "How can I be of service?"

"By order of his Majesty, King Fernando of Spain, I have been sent to deliver you a letter."

Greg let go of his dagger and took the letter from the man and shoved it in his coat pocket. He gripped his dagger beneath his coat again, preparing for the worst as the men continued to scowl at him.

"Thank you for the letter gentlemen," Greg nodded. "You can leave now."

"The King wanted to be sure that you read it," said the man that had handed him the letter.

"Assure him that I did," he responded curtly.

"King Fernando also insisted that you answer immediately."

Greg lifted his brow, released his dagger and pulled the letter out of his pocket.

SIR GREGORY UMBRIDGE,

That you've been given such a dignified title as Sir was a ridiculous decision by your foolish King Henceforth, I won't address you as such. Umbridge, send back my daughter with my messenger or suffer the consequences.

My son, Prince Carlos has told me what a rogue you can be. I know that you may not do as I command, but I will be down in a few short weeks, after Spain conquers England. If you don't release Sofia we will invade Edinburgh Castle. You will be publicly tortured and I'll place your head on a stake and post it in front of Edinburgh Castle for all to see. No English or Scotsman will question Spain's authority.

His Majesty, King Fernando of Spain

GREG LOOKED up from the paper at the messengers, "The King is looking for an immediate response? I don't have his daughter any longer," he lied as he shoved the letter into the man's chest. "Sofia has run off."

"King Fernando demanded that you be a man and explain yourself in a letter, Sir. He instructed me not to leave Edinburgh until you did so."

"Well then," he sighed looking up at Edinburgh Castle. "I suppose I'll need to make a quick stop at the castle to get some paper and a quill."

He looked up at the castle, unsure of how the men in Edinburgh Castle would react if he tried barging in. He had gotten to know a few that had worked there. But it seemed that King Fernando was assuming that he was staying with Sofia in the castle, not Holyrood House. If the Spanish came to attack, it would be to his advantage that they attack the castle, not Holyrood House.

"No need, Sir Gregory," said the messenger pulling stationary from his coat pocket. "I have it here."

"Then it seems all I need is a place to sit," said Greg. He spotted some people sitting at a table eating haggis with several candles in the middle. He sat down next to them, the messenger following in his wake. He stared at the candlelight for a few minutes before he put the quill to paper.

Your Majesty, King Fernando of Spain ...

He etched with his quill, and the rest quickly flowed. He wrote several lies and then finished the letter, signing his name before taking out another piece of paper. He copied the letter he had just written onto the paper. The messenger tapped him on the shoulder.

"Are you writing the letter twice, Sir Gregory?"

"Yes. I'd like to remember what I wrote," he said casually.

He scrawled it again, then took one of them and placed it an envelope. He took one of the candles from the table and tipped it and it dropped some wax to seal it. He pressed the end of his dagger, which had his insignia imprinted to it, against the wax as it dried.

"That should do it," he said handing it to the Spaniards. The messengers took the letter and took to the streets. Greg picked up the copy of the letter and continued scrawling on it. When he finished, he waxed it then stamped it with the end of his dagger.

Immediately after, Greg went to find Sam. He couldn't trust McFadden to deliver the letter promptly. Sam was the only other man in town he could ask and trust.

He walked about the festivities looking about for Sam or Sofia. He knew there was a good chance she had run back to Holyrood House. As he walked, he looked down side streets. He passed a games table with a magician doing card tricks and he spotted Sam with Belle. She looked bright-eyed as the magician pulled a card from his sleeve.

"Is this your card, Miss?"

She giggled and clapped her hands.

"SAM!" Greg called, breaking through the crowd.

Sam's eyes met Greg's. Sam beamed and waved Greg over.

"Sam," Greg said nearly out of breath when he reached him. "I need you to do a favour for me."

"Certainly. Where's Miss Sofia? Would you like me and Belle to find her?" Sam offered.

"No, actually. I think I know where to find her. I have an important message for King Alexander. I need you to ride to Windsor to give it to him."

Sam opened his mouth to speak but then noticed that Belle, who was no longer paying attention to the magician, listening to Greg and Sam with a confused look on her face.

"I'm not sure I could find my way," Sam said.

"I'll give you a compass and a map, it's not that hard to navigate."

Sam looked over tenderly at Belle and frowned.

"If you'd like you can take Belle with you for company," Greg offered realizing the reason Sam wasn't keen on leaving.

Sam's eyes widened, "Would that be all right? I mean-"

"If you take one of the carriages and fill it with supplies for your journey I'm sure it would be fine," Greg assured. "But I need you to get there as soon as you possibly can. The King needs to read what is in this letter as soon as possible.

Belle looked between the two of them, trying to understand what was happening.

"Where's Sofia? Maybe she can explain this all to her," Greg said exasperated.

"I'll try to explain to her, Sir Gregory."

Sam looked at Belle and showed her the letter. He put his hand to his chest,

"Belle," he began enunciating, "I must go to Windsor."

"Windsor?" she said, "You go?"

"Yes. For King Alexander," he said waving the letter.

She nodded in understanding.

Greg shook his head, "You go with Sam, Belle," Greg said pointing at Sam.

"I go?"

"Yes. Go with Sam."

"But, Miss Sofia?" Belle asked with a worried look.

"Don't worry," Greg said nodding, "go."

Sam took her arm, "Let's go, Belle," he said and the three of them headed back for Holyrood House.

* * *

"SOFIA!" Greg yelled as he entered Holyrood House, "SOFIA!"

Belle and Sam followed in his wake, but he turned to them. "I'll find Sofia, start packing for your journey," he ordered.

"Yes, Sir Gregory," Sam said bowing. He took Belle by the hand as he flashed the letter to her, "Go Windsor?" she asked timidly.

"Yes, now," Sam said.

Greg made his way to the King's Bedchambers, but when he arrived, she wasn't there. He went to the closet, then back into the Great Gallery. Then it dawned on him. He took off down the Great Gallery and through the Queen's Lobby.

He ran up to Mary Queen of Scot's Chambers, to her bedroom. He pulled back the tapestry that hung on the wall. He remembered when they were given a tour, they were shown a hidden dining room just off the Queen's Bedchamber. He pushed the wooden panel back.

Sofia sat at the table looking out the window, her eyes bloodshot from crying. He thought of the time she had told him that she used to be locked in an old run down tower with rats and birds if she had misbehaved.

She turned to face him, 'You're all right! Thank God!" she ran over and embraced him "Sorry I ran off like that."

"You knew those men, didn't you?" he asked.

"One of them was one of my father's advisors. If he saw me, I know he would have dragged me back with him."

"What about me, Princess?"

"If you were seen with me, I'm sure he would have slit your throat. I told you to run," she said quietly. Another tear escaped and stung her eye. She had cried so hard worrying about Greg.

"That man wasn't leaving until he spoke with me," Greg said. "He gave me a letter from your father."

"Was it for me?"

"No. It was for me," he said.

"I suppose he's demanding that you send me back?" she said, her voice shaking.

"Yes."

"I'm so sorry. I'll- I'll-" she began to sob. She knew she needed to go back to spare his life.

"You're not going back Sofia," he said as he lowered her down onto one of the dining room chairs. He sat next to her, rubbing her back, "Your home is here with me."

"But he'll come," she said fearfully. "He'll kill you if you try to keep me. My father has an army of men he could send here." She rested her head on the table and sniffled into her arms.

"Alex has some men here, too. Not many, just enough to look after the castle," he said slowly. "Your father said he is going to attack Windsor and London first. He said so in his letter. If he succeeds, we'll go on the run."

"Where will we go?" she squeaked, lifting her head up.

"Does it matter where? As long as we are together?" he said taking her hand.

She shook her head and wiped away her tears.

He pressed a kiss on her head and brushed back her hair, "It wouldn't bother you living the rest of your life as a commoner, would it?" he asked.

"If I were with you, it wouldn't."

GUEST AT CURFEW

*I*t had been a long week for Alex. He had been trying to have a secret meeting, but it was almost impossible. Sir Ashton Giles had to be sure that it was private and that no one would ever find out that the meeting had occurred. It wasn't easy to arrange; Sir Ashton cancelled a meeting of the House of Lords to clear Alex's schedule. The biggest challenge of all was getting Alex's guest through the castle. A disguise was needed.

Alex paced nervously in his father's old drawing room. He was unsure about what he was about to do. It wasn't often that he was unsure of himself. Perhaps it was guilt; he had never had gone behind Madeline's back. He never imagined he would. He sat down at a large desk, deciding that his pacing would make him appear weak.

Sir Ashton Giles entered, a man standing next to him in the Windsor uniform and a wig of long brown hair.

"Thank you, Sir Ashton. Be sure to lock the doors as you leave," Alex said.

He nodded and left the room shutting the double doors around him.

The man looked around the room. There were several large Rubens paintings of different monarchs as well as some oriental pieces of furniture, black and lacquered. "This room hasn't changed much since your father ruled. The walls were green then, too. I've heard you don't use these apartments?"

Alex raised his brow, "No I don't, your Grace. The King's Apartments are located in the Round Tower now."

There was a long silence as the Duke observed the organ clock, his eyes following its complex mechanisms. Alex was uncertain what to do. It didn't seem Walt wanted to talk.

"You weren't one to bow or refer to my father as 'your Majesty', were you?" Alex asked.

He chuckled, "No."

"Why?"

"Does Greg Umbridge call you 'your Majesty'?"

"In jest," Alex smiled. "Take off the wig and have a seat, Walt."

The Duke hesitated for a moment before he pulled the wig off his head.

"I hope that Sir Ashton made it clear," Alex continued. "I have no ill will toward you, your Grace."

"Forgive me, but we both know your Queen feels differently. I'm in a cell for a reason. I don't believe this ridiculous accusation. You know I didn't give my ship to Susanna."

"Why wouldn't you?" Alex said, "You have never really made it clear where you stand politically. I could never tell whether you favoured myself or Bathory."

"I never cared for the politics of court. For the most part, I stay out of it, unless I have something to gain. I have nothing to gain by helping Susanna out. If I gave that woman that ship, I would get nothing in return. Possibly some enemies. I believe most of Lord Bathory's followers have either been killed for the cause of making him King or have given up. Susanna has angered many Lords over the years. I don't think many want to see her take the throne."

There was another long silence. Finally, Alex approached the subject he'd been wanting to talk about for months. "There are things you and I need to discuss. There's been something weighing on my mind. I've visited Swan Manor ... a few times now. During

Madeline's trial for the title, and a few times since ... I've searched about."

The Duke sighed, his face went pale. He began tapping his fingers on the desk. "Always bright, even as a boy. You know, then?"

"I've known for some time now."

"How did you find out? People have been looking for years. You happen to go there a few times and manage to figure it out?"

Alex shuffled in his chair, a chill crawling up his spine.

"I'm glad you haven't said anything," Alex said. "I don't ever want Madeline to know."

The Duke looked away for the moment, his eyes glassy, "No one can know," he said slowly. "I've tried to destroy it."

"I'm sure you have."

"Does Sir Gregory know?" he asked, looking intensely into Alex's eyes.

"No."

"Will you tell him?"

"This? This, I intend to take this to the grave with me," Alex said shortly.

"Good," he said, feeling relieved. "So, you won't hang me for what I did?"

"No, Walt. To be honest, I would have done the same. But, I wish you would leave. This upcoming war has been a distraction, but as soon as it's over, Madeline will turn her attentions to you. I love her, you know."

"You'd have me killed then," he nodded knowingly.

"I'd prefer you left the country. I thought I made that clear last time we met."

"That's asking too much."

"No it isn't," Alex said stern. "Go back to Tahiti. My father told me you had many adventures there. Said you wouldn't stop talking about it for years."

"I have no desire to go there again, Alex."

"I heard you had quite interesting experiences there," Alex said suggestively.

"I won't go there, your Majesty."

"If you stay here, you stay here knowing that I'll behead you. I'm giving you an out, Walt. If I were you, I'd take advantage. I think we'd both agree that a man would do anything to protect the woman he loved. If that means killing you, I'll do it."

The Duke of Axford looked back at the ornamental clock. He knew Alex wasn't going to leave that room without hearing an answer that he would be satisfied with. If he didn't tell Alex what he wanted to hear, he would never leave Curfew Tower and would eventually be sentenced to death. Lying was the only way the Duke would be allowed to leave. He'd be on borrowed time, but it was better than being behind bars.

"I suppose I'll make my way to America then," he said casually. "Won't be under the rule of a king over there."

Alex chuckled, "Am I so bad?"

"No. Your father was more demanding. But that's the hardship of being the King's right-hand man. How is Sir Gregory?"

"Having himself quite the time from what I understand," said Alex.

"Do you believe what everyone is saying? That he's been throwing party after party these past few weeks?"

"Well, they always say there is a half-truth to every rumour," he said smirking. "I'm sure he's more than having parties. By now, I wouldn't be surprised if Holyrood House was nothing but rubbish ... if not the whole town."

"He's always been an amazing companion to you, though. As crazy as that boy is, I've got to admit, he's likeable."

"I miss him."

There was another silence as Duke Axford tapped his fingers on the desk. He and Alex were the only two that knew what happened the night the Swans had died. It made Walt anxious. He felt uncomfortable that Alex knew. He wondered what Alex planned to do about the situation.

"Swan Manor. What will you do with the evidence?" Walt asked.

"I think I've found a way to destroy it, without anyone suspecting a thing."

"You have?" the Duke said in disbelief. He knew Alex was intelligent, but he had been trying to figure out how to do the same thing for twenty years. People were always curious about the Swans and watched for any odd happenings at the manor. His attempts were all in vain. Most plans he had thought of had too many complications to work, or would have people highly suspicious again.

"What are you going to do?" Walt asked, curious if Alex had really solved the problem.

"I took Madeline there. Twice now," Alex said not answering his question.

"Why?" he said his jaw dropping.

"After seeing the diaries, she was quite distraught. Obsessively reading everything Elizabeth wrote. I had to take her there to bring her some closure. She sprained her ankle the first time. The ground was soft. The foundations aren't so strong anymore," Alex said with a dark expression.

The Duke's eyes widened and he opened his mouth to speak, but his lip trembled as they stared at one another before Alex continued. "Don't worry. She's been in the manor too, but she couldn't bear to look in the parlour. I don't think she noticed anything odd. There isn't much time, there are a few items there I could work with to get rid of the evidence."

"There are?" the Duke said in shock.

"Yes. I'll have to do it soon, too. Otherwise, I think the evidence might end up revealing itself. I'm sure all the people in the kingdom would be outraged if they knew. I'm sure Madeline would leave me."

"Just how do you intend to do this? Your country needs you more than ever now. It's about to be under attack. I'm surprised they haven't come yet. After all that has happened, I'm sure Spain won't be kind." The Duke stood up and began to pace about, "You must be at the end of your tether."

"Well, I guess I'll have to tie a knot and hang on then," Alex said calmly.

The Duke shook his head, knowing he couldn't do much to help, "I guess I'll be going then."

"Sorry Walt, but I can't allow you to walk out of here. It would be quite upsetting to Madeline. I'll have Sir Ashton Giles arrange an escape for you from Curfew Tower at an opportune time."

"When might that be?"

"Not long from now."

"Is Sir Ashton waiting for me outside this room?"

"Yes," Alex said curtly.

"He's going to take me back to Curfew then?"

"Yes."

"Perhaps you are more demanding than your father," said the Duke raising his brow.

"If you were in my position with the love of your life, I'm sure you'd demand the same."

AN EXTRA ADVISOR

S usanna looked in a full-length mirror, Queen Isabelle stood next to her smiling in delight.

"You look so lovely," the Queen said, "I wore a red wedding dress, too."

Susanna wanted to throw up. Since she and Carlos announced they wanted to get married, the Queen had been flitting about her, trying to help her with the arrangements. Susanna had been trying to spend time with her, but being with her was getting on Susanna's nerves.

The Queen never stopped talking. Before then, Susanna thought the Queen was either mute or forgot when and how to speak. Out of the presence of King Fernando and other men, she talked non-stop. Even her ladies in waiting found it irritating. When the Queen was with them, the ladies barely said a word. Susanna figured that this was because every time someone responded to the Queen, she would start rambling. Either it was a long, boring story about her childhood or something recently purchased for the castle.

"Yes, the red dress I wore was designed in France," she said to Susanna. "The designer was very well-known at the time. I can't remember his name now. It's hard to find quality dresses like that these days. Now there are these light fabric, empire dresses. No big, large cages. Oh, they were a pity to wear, but they looked marvelous …"

She continued to prattle on. It was getting more annoying by the second. Susanna had heard of the popular phrase, 'made my blood boil', but just thought it was a figure of speech. As she looked down at her skin, she could see her arms turn red. Red. That reminded Susanna of someone and a wicked smirk came upon her face.

"Your Majesty, do you think Princess Sofia would have worn a red dress?" she asked innocently. "I've noticed an awful lot of red in her apartments."

Isabelle stopped adjusting her dress, and the rest of the ladies stopped what they were doing. Isabelle pulled away and sat down on an ottoman behind Susanna, putting her hand to her mouth. Susanna watched her in the reflection of the mirror. The Queen let out an audible whimper, then broke down in tears.

The ladies stood and watched her, but none of them approached her. They waited. In a short time, the Queen pulled herself together, before approaching Susanna again.

"So do you think this will be the dress?" Queen Isabelle asked.

Susanna was speechless. She had never seen such an odd display of emotion. But it made sense. She wondered if the ladies in waiting reported to King Fernando on the Queen's behaviour. Susanna got the feeling that certain behaviours weren't tolerated, even when he wasn't present. She realized there was a reason she only talked about her childhood and objects; they were the only safe things to speak of.

"Ladies, leave," Susanna ordered sternly, "and shut the door on your way out."

Though the women should have taken their orders from the Queen, they left, shutting the doors behind them.

"Do you miss Sofia?" Susanna asked.

"Terribly," she whispered, her eyes shifting about the room.

"Are you not allowed to speak of her?"

The Queen didn't respond.

"It's all right. Don't answer. I know. I imagine King Fernando doesn't want you ... worrying yourself over her," Susanna said knowing she needed to tread carefully.

Queen Isabelle nodded, pulling out a handkerchief, she wiped away a few tears that fell from her face.

"Have I gotten you in trouble with the King for speaking about Sofia?"

She hesitated, "I'm not sure."

"Do you like the presence of your ladies?" Susanna asked. "They don't seem to have much to say."

"Many of the ladies are just trying to gain favour in court," Isabelle admitted. "Make good connections and find a good husband."

Susanna sat down on the ottoman. "Sit next to me," she said patting the seat. "Why keep these ladies?" Susanna asked as Isabelle sat. "They come and go, don't they?"

"Yes. But that's court life," Isabelle said.

"Be honest. Do you like any of them?"

"I never really get to know them, they come and go."

"Who chooses your company? King Fernando?"

"Yes."

That didn't surprise her. Most of the women were fairly young and attractive. Something told her they were often in King Fernando's company.

"You miss Sofia. What do you miss most about her being away from home?"

"She was my only lady that didn't come and go. The only one I could talk to."

"She kept your secrets from the King?"

"Yes. Mind you, King Fernando he ... he ..." she stopped.

But she didn't have to answer. It was obvious the King interrogated his own daughter about what her mother did and talked about when he wasn't around.

"Was she successful? Could she keep your secrets?"

"Sometimes, yes. Depended on how determined Fernando was to know the truth."

It seemed that Sofia was the only person Isabelle opened up to.

Now that Sofia was gone; Isabelle hadn't been able to express herself freely in months.

"If we talk," Susanna began, "I don't think it's a good idea to allow the King to know. I will not be threatened by him. I'll invite the ladies back in, so this doesn't look suspicious."

Susanna went to the door and invited the ladies back in. They looked at the pair of them strangely. She knew that all of them were dying to tell King Fernando about what had just happened. They needed to be taken care of.

The women entered and sat down, some with smug looks on their faces as they eyed Susanna and Isabelle.

Susanna walked over to the full-length mirror and continued looking at her dress.

"I think I quite like this dress," said Susanna. "Now your Majesty, you said you had worn red dress? This is a bit bold, but do you think you might have some jewellery I could borrow to go with it?"

"Yes. They are in my apartments," Isabelle said as she gestured some of the ladies to go with her to her private apartments.

"Actually, your Majesty, could the ladies stay here? I would like to practice the wedding march and need them to help me with that."

Isabelle narrowed her eyes, but proceeded to her apartments, leaving Susanna with all the ladies.

"You," Susanna said, pointing at one of the ladies, "shut that door."

The woman obeyed her.

"All of you sit," she ordered, glaring at them. They did what Susanna said, looking at one another sceptically. "It's easy to see what is happening here, Queen Isabelle talks about the same boring things. She has difficulty talking about her own daughter. It's clear that all of you report on the Queen's behaviour to King Fernando."

They all sat silent, smiling at one another. Some were even chuckling. To them, this English woman didn't know her place.

"I'm sure you sleep with the King for favours too," Susanna continued. Their smiles disappeared. "Listen carefully, I'm not the Queen of Spain, but I am the future Queen of England. Spain will not achieve ruling England if Prince Carlos and I do not marry."

One spoke up, 'I don't think the King will allow Carlos to marry you if he finds out that you are trying to have secret communications with the Queen."

Susanna walked up to the lady and smacked her so hard across the face, she fell to the floor. Susanna then turned and picked up a candelabra on a nearby table with lit candles and threw it at her, the flames just missing her dress. "Next time I won't miss, you stupid girl! And don't be a fool! King Fernando wants England for his son and his descendants. That's more important to him than if the Queen and I communicate."

All the ladies looked up in fear, knowing Susanna's words were true.

"Here's the new rule," Susanna continued her teeth clenched. "You can mess with the King all you like ladies. But you don't mess with me. If any of you tell the King anything, if I even suspect one of you did, I swear to you, when I become Queen of England, I will have my men hunt you down and torture you. Every last one of you. They will drag you from your beds in the middle of the night and do things to you so horrendous you'll wish for death, just before they burn you alive."

Some of the ladies began to cry. "As for you," she said directing herself to the girl on the floor. "I may do that to you, anyway. Depends on how generous I feel once I become Queen. So, you'd better thank God for every breath I allow you to have."

All the ladies looked down to their laps, discreetly wiping their tears away, their fear making them immovable. They had never felt more frightened or threatened in their lives.

* * *

ALEX LAY on a couch in the Crimson Drawing Room at Windsor staring wide-eyed out the window, clutching a letter in his hand. His face pale, he dug his fingers into one of the pillows next to him.

"Damn it, Greg!" he screeched, chucking the pillow across the room. Madeline walked in the red satin and gold tassels of the pillow brushed against her feet. He looked up, "Sorry, dolcezza."

She picked the pillow up from the parquet floor. He looked away. She could see him trying to hide his emotions as he turned his head. She had never seen him like this.

He looked tired and concerned.

"What's wrong Alex?" she asked sitting next to him. She put the pillow on her lap and guided him back so his head was on the pillow.

"Greg," he said softly. "I think he's just put his neck in a noose."

"What did he do?"

He handed her the letter and she began to read.

Alex,

The King of Spain was so humble to write me and tell me that he plans to conquer England. It sounds as though he is going to invade both Windsor and London. Of course, he warned me to release Sofia, or he would have my head. I'm sure he'd kill me either way, so I wrote the following letter back to him:

It's funny that you think my title as 'Sir' is unfitting. I've always found your title as 'King' to be unfitting too. Although, you don't have the charisma to back up the title, I bore you no ill will.

In fact, I'd like to thank you for leaving your precious Sofia in England. She was a bit of a shrew at first, but I feel I've tamed her.

Yes, our relationship has changed quite a bit since you last saw her. I'd write the nature of our relationship here, however I'm not sure that it is acceptable to write such details.

I know that you and I have had our differences. But if you saw how happy I can make your little girl, I'm sure you'd feel there was no better man for her.

Traditionally, a man asks for the permission of the father to marry his daughter. But I haven't the time to make the trek out to Spain. Therefore, I've decided to marry her the first Sunday of November. You are welcome to join our festivities, so long as you don't bring an army, weapons, or a stake.

Your future son-in-law,

Sir Greg Umbrage, commoner

· · ·

SORRY ALEX, I hope this doesn't confuse things with whatever you have planned as a counter-attack. Any of your bright ideas would be very much appreciated. Just send them back with Sam.

Hope you're both well,

Greg

"DEAR GOD," Madeline said breathlessly, "has he lost his mind? Is he really going to marry Sofia?"

Alex hesitated to answer, "I'm not sure. He does love her, I think."

"Does this ruin what you had planned?" she asked worriedly.

"Not exactly. But King Fernando is a loose cannon. When that man gets this letter, he might forego Windsor and London," Alex said.

"I doubt that. Surely it would be wiser to conquer England first."

"Greg has insulted King Fernando beyond measure. King Fernando will want him dead," Alex sighed.

Madeline shook her head, "Maybe. But maybe this isn't such a bad thing. Perhaps Greg has bought you some time, Alex."

"How?" Alex asked cocking his brow.

"Well, it takes longer to get to Edinburgh. If King Fernando tries attacking there first, he'll be spotted and that will give you lots of time to organize a counter-attack."

"I don't think he'll do that," Alex said rubbing her belly. "If anything Greg has lost us time. After reading that letter, King Fernando will want to get on a boat as soon as he possibly can. If he leaves in the next week, my men will be ill-equipped."

"I guess it depends then. What kind of man is King Fernando?" Madeline said thoughtfully tapping her finger to her chin. "If he wants to be well-prepared and have a victory, he may decide he needs a few extra days to plan."

"I'm sure he knows he'll have an advantage if he leaves sooner rather than later," Alex countered.

Madeline furrowed her brows in confusion. She glided her fingers through Alex's soft black hair, and kissed him, "Why hasn't King Fernando come yet, then? He has had an advantage for some time.

You've had time these past few weeks to rethink and change the battle plans several times. You thought Fernando would attack weeks ago. But we haven't gone into hiding because Fernando's ships haven't been spotted. If it's to his advantage to come here sooner, then why isn't he here now?"

"He never came sooner because we had both his heir and his daughter. But now, that his son has arrived home, I – I" Alex stopped. "I'm not really sure."

"Maybe he's waiting for more men?" Madeline hypothesized. "Does Spain have any allies that would fight alongside him?"

"None nearby. I don't think any other European country would attack England. He might have tried to send for men from his colonies."

"That's why they haven't attacked then. Fernando is waiting to collect a bigger army."

"Possibly. It would be a foolish thing to do," Alex said. "It would take weeks if not months to get to his men to come back from Spanish colonies."

"Most of the men that attacked with Bathory were from the Spanish army. Do you think the battle either killed or imprisoned most of his men, and now he doesn't have enough to attack?"

"I'm not sure," Alex admitted, "but even if it was a huge loss to him, even half his army could overthrow Windsor with a strategic plan."

"But they didn't last time they were here. I think Fernando wants a certain victory," Madeline concluded. "Losing the first battle looked foolish of him. There is no room for error if he invades again."

"Hmm," Alex murmured as his hand circled her belly again, trying to find reason in it all. "But he must know that we have fewer men here. Now would be the best time, his best opportunity is when I have fewer men."

She shook her head, "Once bitten, twice scared. Last time he came here, he lost. He lost under a surprise attack, and you had fewer men then too. That's a humiliating loss. He won't leave Spain unless he is certain he can take England. If he plans to attack both Windsor and London at once, he will need more men."

"Some of my Lords and Colonels have theorized that he would do a double-attack," Alex said thoughtfully. "It makes sense. He has delayed this much longer than I would have imagined. What do you think of Greg then? You don't think Fernando would be foolish enough to try a triple-attack?"

She laughed, "We've been lucky so far, I'm not sure we are so lucky that he'd do that."

"He might change his plans, though."

"Yes, if he receives Greg's letter and wants to attack Edinburgh, the only thing he could do is split his men further. I doubt he would have enough men to do that, though. Or, he may wait longer and come up with a new plan."

"Makes sense," Alex said, his eyes transfixed on her as his hand rubbed her belly.

"Oh," she said in surprise, smiling, "the baby kicked."

"Really?" he said excitedly.

"Yes. I think I know why. Baby agrees with me."

He laughed. "So maybe Greg's letter is a good thing," he said slowly in thought. "King Fernando will do one of two things; he'll decide to attack London and Windsor as soon as he can, then destroy Edinburgh after."

"Or he'll decide to wait a little longer and attack all three," said Madeline. "There is one other option though, Alex. If Fernando decides to go earlier, he might abandon attacking London and overthrow Windsor and Edinburgh, then invade London later. Are you going to have to change the battle plans again?"

"Yes," Alex admitted. "There will definitely be a double-attack of some sort. I need to go find Sir Ashton Giles and reorganize our plans. Sorry, Madeline." He pecked her on the cheek and rushed out of the room. She could hear him ordering a footman to find Sir Ashton along with some others and left.

In a half-hour, Alex had all his advisors, Lords, and Colonels in his military quarters. Sir Ashton set up some maps on a table before them.

"I know I've called this meeting suddenly," Alex began, drawing the men's attention, "but I just received some important information that will change our plans."

"Your Majesty," Sir Ashton started, "should we wait for Colonels Evans and Roberts?"

"We will fill them in when they arrive," Alex said. "Lord Davis, will you set up our original battle plan, please?"

"Certainly your Majesty," he said bowing his head slightly. He picked up the miniature ships and men and began to place them according to the original plan.

"I've received a letter from Sir Gregory," Alex went on. "It appears that King Fernando knows that Greg has Princess Sofia and has given him a warning to send Sofia back or he will torture and kill him."

There was silence in the room.

"Did he send her back?" asked Sir Ashton Giles.

"No," said Alex.

"I think Greg knows that we can still use her as a bargaining chip," Lord Davis said.

Sir Ashton laughed, "Bargaining chip? Sir Gregory fancies that woman. Don't think he wants us to use her as a pawn."

The rest of the men nodded in agreement. Alex looked away in embarrassment knowing he could never use Sofia as bait. Colonels Evans and Roberts entered, Sir Ashton stood next to them and began whispering what Alex had said to them.

"Right," said Alex and continued, "King Fernando doesn't know that. It seems Fernando think Greg has kidnapped her against her will."

"Are we going to use that to our advantage?" Lord Davis asked.

"Possibly. You see, Greg Umbridge wrote King Fernando, explaining how, ahem, familiar he has gotten with his daughter."

All the men raised their brows in shock.

"Is he mad?" Colonel Evans interjected. "I'm surprised King Fernando has waited this long to attack us. I suspected the delay because he cared for the well-being of his daughter."

"I don't believe he cares much for Sofia," said Alex placing his hands on the edge of the table before him, looking down at the original battle plan. "I think that Fernando held off at first because of Prince Carlos, but now is the time to invade and he hasn't. But he's not worried about Princess Sofia; if he were, he'd either strike a deal, or he would have invaded Edinburgh."

"Do you think he feels he's not ready?" Colonel Roberts asked.

"Yes. I think the battle in Windsor with Lord Bathory really shook him. It was a surprise attack, they had more men and we still won."

A new maid came in with a cart of tea, "Sir Ashton, should I serve tea now?" she whispered to him in a heavy Dutch accent.

"Certainly. Start with his Majesty of course."

She moved the cart to the side and began preparing the tray for Alex.

"Anyway, I think the reason why the King hasn't attacked is because he wants a certain victory," Alex said. "In fact, Fernando wrote to Greg explaining that he will attack Windsor and Buckingham Palace at once and then go to Edinburgh."

"I'm guessing Miss Susanna Bathory must have plans to marry Prince Carlos soon," Colonel Roberts said.

"It would ensure that no one would question their authority. King Fernando's future grandson would be England's rightful heir," confirmed Alex.

The new maid came around to Alex and set down his tray of tea, preparing the honey in it. Sir Ashton Giles quickly took a sip.

"Seems fine, your Majesty," he said as he passed the cup to Alex.

"Now," Alex continued. "Our original plan was to try to get as many men as we could from Europe to the north coast of France, then London and Windsor by Dutch ships within the next two weeks."

"They'd be here in hours once they departed," said Colonel Evans.

"Yes, but now that Greg has done this, there is the possibility of the King striking Edinburgh instead. Sir Gregory may have bought us some time. You see, if King Fernando attacks this week, there is a strong chance he would win. But I think once King Fernando receives the letter from Sir Gregory, he is going to change his plan, and it may take a few days to reorganize a new one. I've seen the letter Greg wrote to the King. Trust me, he will be enraged by what he has written." He paused for a moment. "Sir Gregory has told King Fernando that he intends to marry his daughter the first Sunday of November."

"Greg Umbridge wants to get married?" Colonel Evans asked in disbelief.

"It looks like that is the situation. But King Fernando knows if he defeated London and Windsor before going to Edinburgh, it would give Greg an opportunity to marry Sofia, then flee."

"If he isn't doing it already," Lord Davis chuckled.

"King Fernando knows that Greg won't flee Edinburgh unless England is defeated. I'm not sure Fernando can afford to do a triple-attack, it would be foolish. But he won't leave Edinburgh and Greg to chance, either. He will go after him somehow. It's personal."

"But what if King Fernando doesn't? We can't gamble the future of the crown on how vengeful King Fernando may or may not be. There is no time to send men to Edinburgh. Most of the men should be in Windsor and London," Colonel Evans reminded them.

"True," admitted Alex. "But we are going to have to change the plans to suit both situations. If he does a double or triple attack, we need to be ready."

"What did you have in mind, your Majesty?" Colonel Evans asked.

"Once the Spanish ships are spotted in the English Channel," Alex began, "Madeline and I will leave to go to an undisclosed location. Hopefully, they do attack next week. By then, our men will have made it to Northern France and the Netherlands and will have departed for London and Windsor. If the Spanish don't attack London and head for Edinburgh instead, we can have those ships follow the Spaniards from behind and attack." He sighed looking at the dismal number of ships, "We wouldn't have many ships to attack the Spanish fleet, but it's better we do. Edinburgh doesn't have much of a defence." He took several ships demonstrating the idea. He massaged his temples, there weren't many ships off the coast of Europe. He needed more. He turned to the new maid, noticing her tall and blonde features, much like Aletta.

"Are you Dutch, Miss-?"

"Miss de Wit, your Majesty," she said curtsying.

"You don't think the Dutch would mind us borrowing some of their ships to go to battle, do you Miss de Wit?" Alex chuckled.

"Certainly not, your Majesty," Miss de Wit said setting the final tray down. "As long as the English give back whatever ships they take … and more."

Alex grinned.

"The Dutch have always been good allies," Lord Davis reassured him. "I'm sure they won't mind this last minute decision."

"Good."

Sir Ashton raised his brow, "I'm not sure the Dutch would have enough men to help us in an attack."

"No. I'm not expecting the Dutch to go to war for us," said Alex. But we need to make our defence plan stronger. More ships mean we can divide the men to where they are needed."

They discussed several ideas over the next hour. By the time it was over, Alex felt assured. Hopefully, Greg's letter would delay the attack by three or four days.

THE ARRANGED MARRIAGE

*S*usanna looked into the palace chapel. Though it was small, it was very decorative with Michelangelo inspired paintings and gold moulding on the walls. Any space on the wall that didn't have a painting had a green marble pillar or a slate of marble. There were ivory cherubs and angels, chandeliers, arches, domes and beautiful windows. And a life-sized crucifix at the altar. She never pictured herself marrying in a Catholic ceremony. But when in Rome ... well, in this case, Madrid. Though the chapel was lovely, she hated everything about the whole affair; her wedding in England would be different from this.

The lack of nobles bothered her most. She would have thought Fernando and Carlos would have wanted a more public occasion. There were only twenty-five people there. As she peeked down the aisle, she could see Señor Astucia standing in one of the pews. As usual, he looked handsome, towering above everyone around him. She could only picture herself crawling on top of him. Too bad she couldn't. It must have been annoying for Sofia to have a brother with a gorgeous friend.

King Fernando and Queen Isabelle entered, and everyone bowed and curtsied as the pair walked past. Soon the ceremony would begin, and Susanna would be saying her vows. Queen Isabelle's ladies in waiting were her bridesmaids; she turned to one of them, "You, get me something to drink."

"Now my lady?" her bridesmaid asked stunned. "The ceremony is about to start."

Susanna said nothing but gave her a deadpan expression. The girl quickly left, hoping she wouldn't be punished for leaving; she didn't know if she had enough time to get Susanna a drink before the ceremony started.

But Susanna didn't care. To her, each lady looked identical to the next. She doubted anyone would notice one of them missing.

Prince Carlos followed the priest up the aisle. It was then that Susanna noticed her; a woman sitting just behind Señor Astucia was staring longingly at Carlos. For a moment, Carlos's eyes met hers. So, this was 'court'. Susanna put her hands on her hips in disgust. Susanna had been expecting some competition, but 'court' was short and stocky with a round, chubby face. Her hair was pinned in doll-like curls, some of which were clearly fake. Either this girl was willing to do anything between the sheets, or Carlos needed his eyes checked.

"Here you are, my lady."

Susanna turned around. The bridesmaid she had sent came back, out of breath. "What is it?" Susanna asked, taking a sniff as she swirled it in the glass.

"Brandy," said the girl.

"Well, at least you're good for something," Susanna drank it in one gulp and handed the glass back to her.

"Right then," Susanna said, quickly feeling the effect of the alcohol, "let's get this over with."

The ladies lined up, and Susanna stood behind them. She could hear the organ begin to play along with some violins a Spanish-style tune. She stuck out her tongue and rolled her eyes. They would probably play a traditional Spanish song for her entrance too. She waited as the girls began to move down the aisle. It was a short aisle, and it didn't take the girls long to get to their pew.

As they went up, Susanna glared at 'court'. Girls like her annoyed

Susanna; she seemed unconfident and insecure. 'Court' sat with a sad look on her face as she checked herself in a small compact mirror she had. She observed her hair, making sure every strand was in place, then looked longingly at Carlos again. She had a mousy look, much like Queen Isabelle. "Argh!" Susanna said under her breath in disgust, "pathetic."

Handel's Wedding March began to play. A German composer. Not English, but a respectable song. Susanna began to walk up. Though everyone had turned to face the aisle, she noticed how 'court' continued to stare at Carlos. Her eyes were full of emotion. He tried not to look, but Susanna noticed how his gaze dropped from her to 'court'. He glanced at her for only a split second, then glued his eyes onto Susanna again. Señor Astucia stood in front of 'court', and like everyone else was looking at Susanna as she made her grand entrance. Good thing he was so tall, as Susanna passed by 'court' she leaned her head behind Señor Astucia's large stature and spat on the front of 'court's' dress.

Seeing the spit on her dress, 'court' glared at Carlos in shock. His jaw dropped. Surely other people noticed what Susanna had just done. But strangely, the music continued, and she made her way to the altar.

"What was that about?" he whispered, unable to contain himself.

"One of those ridiculous ladies-in-waiting gave me some brandy. Tasted funny. I could barely stand it," she whispered back.

"Brandy?" he said in a daze.

"Yes, better I spit it on an ugly girl that hasn't any hope, than you," she said softly and smiled at him.

Carlos was speechless. Susanna casually handed her bouquet to one of the ladies, then quickly locked elbows with Carlos, and the two of them turned to the priest.

The mass was said in Spanish. Susanna was made to practice with the ladies her lines in Spanish. Not that she needed to. But from time to time would pretend to say the wrong word.

After the 'I do's', there was a small reception in the Royal Dining Room. The dinner was disappointing. Susanna kept reminding herself that once she was crowned Queen of England, she and

Carlos would do this again. Properly. She'd invite all the nobles of Spain as well. They clearly needed a lesson on how to celebrate such occasions in style. Carlos had explained that because of the upcoming war and Napoleon's fall, it would be poor manners to have a lavish party. But to Susanna, that made no sense. In her opinion, the people deserved to enjoy themselves for a night, regardless of cost.

As the night went on, people were brought into the Room of Columns. It was a small ballroom but served its purpose. She and Carlos danced and though she didn't enjoy his arms wrapped around her, it was comical to see 'court' twisting her handkerchief in her hands as she watched. "Who is that ugly girl that keeps staring at us?" Susanna asked, pretending not to know.

"What?" Carlos said astounded by her choice of words.

"I'd like to apologize to her for earlier, I mean, I'm a little embarrassed about spitting on her dress."

"You want to apologize?" he asked eyeing her suspiciously.

"Why wouldn't I? I intended it to go on the floor, but her skirt was so big."

"That's Señor Menendo's daughter, Señorita Esmeralda."

"That's a lovely name," Susanna said trying to sound polite. But forever in Susanna's mind she'd be referred to as 'short court'. When they finished their dance, Susanna made her way over to her.

As soon as Esmeralda saw her approaching she immediately started a conversation with the woman standing next to her. It was obvious she didn't want to talk.

But Susanna didn't care; she interrupted in English. "His Highness tells me you are Señorita Esmeralda, Señor Menendo's daughter," Susanna began.

Esmeralda stopped conversing with the lady next to her and curtsied to Susanna. Unable to make eye contact, she quietly said, "Congratulations on your marriage."

"I must apologize," Susanna continued, chuckling. "One of the ladies gave me something awful to drink before I walked up the aisle. I couldn't swallow it, or spit it on my soon-to-be husband. Sorry, but

195

I'm sure you'll forgive me. The Prince has told me that you're good friends."

Esmeralda nodded, "Of course. All is forgiven," she said softly. "Oh Señor Astucia," she said in relief, as he came from behind Susanna. "How are you doing? I've been meaning to speak to you."

"I would Señorita Esmeralda, but I came to ask her Highness if she would dance with me," Señor Astucia said.

"Her Highness? I suppose I am now," Susanna giggled, feigning modesty. "I think Señorita Esmeralda forgot, just as I did. She congratulated me on my wedding, but forgot to call me 'your Highness.'"

"I'm sorry, your Highness," Esmeralda said quickly.

But Susanna paid no attention, directing herself to Señor Astucia, she smiled, "I'll take you up on your invitation," she held out her hand, and he escorted her to the dance floor.

"Do you waltz, your Highness?"

"I can," she said seductively.

"Will you waltz with me?"

It was a daring thing to ask. The most intimate of all dances. She should have waltzed with Carlos. But waltzing with Señor Astucia sounded much more enticing.

"I'll waltz with you," Susanna said. "But you don't think anyone in court will see it as improper?"

"Oh no. I know you're very proper in England, but we are more relaxed here." He put his hand on the small of her back and began leading. "Are you enjoying the festivities?" he asked.

Up until this point she hadn't, but she could not tell him that, "It's all been like a dream so far," she lied.

"Really? I thought the English liked their pageantry."

She blushed, his accent saying the word 'pageantry' was alluring. She gazed dreamily at him. It was tempting to pull him into another room.

"So you don't mind that it wasn't a huge party?" he said.

"I do enjoy a little more decoration and people," she admitted.

"Maybe when you get to England, you can celebrate in your way."

"Will you celebrate with me?" she asked batting her eyelashes.

"If that's what her Highness wants, I'll be ... how do the English say ... delighted."

She went weak in the knees. She couldn't think of a time a man had made her feel that way. There was something about him. She had been with plenty of gorgeous men, but none made her feel comfortable. She got the feeling she could tell him how she truly felt about Spanish culture, King Fernando and Prince Carlos and he wouldn't judge her for it. She wondered if he could be as open with her. "Are you and Carlos very close?" she asked.

"I am one of his advisors, as you know. We've known each other since we were teenagers."

"So you've been around the royal family for quite some time?"

"More than ten years now."

"So what do you think of them?"

Stunned, he opened his mouth to speak, then stopped. "Does it matter what I think? I'm a friend to Prince Carlos -"

She giggled, flirtatiously, "No, no. Señor Astucia. I asked you a question. It seems you are trying to avoid it. That's rather rude."

"I'm not trying to avoid it," he said making his excuses. "I'm just surprised that you want my opinion."

"We'll start with the member of the royal family that isn't here. Princess Sofia, what is she like?"

He chuckled, "Very sweet. A bit odd."

"Yes. I sensed that the first night she was at court in England. It seemed as though she never really knew what to do or say."

"She never liked large crowds of people," Señor Astucia said nodding. "I think being in a place where she doesn't know anyone would be scary for her."

She laughed, "What about you, do you like large crowds?"

"I like large crowds, except for one thing."

"What?" she asked.

"Being in a large crowd when you want to spend your time with just one person can be frustrating," he said his eyes piercing hers.

"Yes," she said softly. "What about Queen Isabelle? Does she like crowds?"

"I'm afraid I don't know. The Queen is very quiet."

"Why do you think that is?"

"I think we both know the answer to that."

He turned her about, as she questioned him again, "What do you think of his Majesty?"

"Don't I get to ask you any questions?" he asked, grinning with hooded eyes.

"I asked first."

"You've asked plenty of questions. What do you think of his Highness?"

"That's too bold," she said giving a nervous laugh.

"So is asking me all the questions you have."

She said nothing. It was clear that Señor Astucia did not like King Fernando, but didn't want to be overheard by someone else; no more than she wanted people to know what she really thought of Carlos.

"Speaking of his Highness, where did he go?" she said, trying to change the subject.

He looked over her shoulder, "I talked to him just before we started dancing. I'm sure he hasn't gone far."

But she didn't need to go searching. Obviously, Carlos was somewhere else in the palace, talking to Esmeralda.

"Can I ask one more question, Señor Astucia?"

"Not until you can answer the one I asked."

She paused, "Our marriage is exactly how I had always pictured my marriage to be."

He gave her a double-take, confused by her answer. "You thought your marriage would be like this?" he asked dumbfounded.

"Yes. So, tell me about Señorita Esmeralda."

"Señorita Esmeralda? I thought you wanted to know-"

"I don't care what you think of Carlos or his Majesty," she said her eyes narrowing. "I'm more interested in knowing how close his Highness is to Señorita Esmeralda."

"They've known each other for a long time," he said trying to be casual.

"I didn't ask how long they've known each other Señor Astucia, I asked how close they are."

"You're quite intelligent, your Highness. You helped Prince Carlos escape when the King's men had failed. The Queen's ladies-in-waiting seem to obey you, which is unusual. They typically concern themselves with what the men of this palace think. You've also managed to fool everyone here into thinking that you barely know Spanish."

Her simpleton smile turned into the fear of a small child getting caught doing something they shouldn't.

He cupped her jaw gently, "I'm intelligent too," he said huskily in his thick accent. "You don't speak at dinner because you're busy listening. You understand more than you're willing to admit. You can speak Spanish." He released her jaw, placing his hand on the small of her back. "You know how close they are Susanna. You don't need to ask," he said simply.

They continued dancing in silence moving about the room. When the song ended, he bowed, "A pleasure as always your Highness," he turned to walk away, but she called him back.

"My Lord?"

"Yes?"

"Does his Highness know I speak Spanish too?" she asked softly.

"He used to suspect that you did, but now he seems to think you're not bright enough."

Señor Astucia walked away, not giving her a chance to respond. He was right about everything he had said about her. He knew what she knew; wherever Carlos was, Esmeralda was with him.

It didn't bother her, but it was confusing. *While I was traveling with Carlos, he seemed interested in me. He seemed to want a relationship with me. Why did he try if he is in love with Esmeralda?*

MIDNIGHT ESCAPE

*"Y*ou want to leave now?" Madeline said exasperated, as she rose from her bed at Frogmore. "Alex, why didn't you tell me that us leaving at any moment was part of the plan?"

It was the early hours of morning and Alex had just woke her up and explained to her that they needed to leave.

"I'm sorry," he said apologetically. "But leaving unexpectedly was part of the plan. Sir Ashton arranged it that way. I'm so sorry. I didn't tell you because I knew you would want to tell the girls. Keeping a secret is hard. I didn't want to put the stress on you and the baby."

"Why tonight? Why now?"

"Sir Ashton has just received information that Carlos and Susanna have plans to get married as soon as possible, and that Spain intends to lead an attack days after the ceremony. They could be on their way this minute. I suppose Greg's letter didn't have the effect we had hoped for."

She frowned, "Where are we going?"

"I'm still not sure. Sir Ashton didn't say when he came in. He just said to pack our things and meet him outside."

"How long will we be gone?"

He sighed, "I'm not really sure dolcezza, but we can't stay here."

She got out of her bed and headed to her closet, Alex followed her with a trunk.

"Just put your things in here with mine," he said as he pulled things out of her drawers and shoved them in. She turned and tried folding them in neatly.

"Dolcezza, we don't have time for that. Just drop your clothes in."

She folded her arms and began to cry, tears streaming down her cheeks in frustration. "ALEX!" she wailed throwing her clothes to the floor. He stopped what he was doing. It was understandable that she was upset. He wrapped his arms around her.

"I'm sorry. I'm so sorry." He allowed her to cry onto his chest, feeling his shirt become wet with her tears. "I know this isn't easy, especially when you're pregnant."

She whimpered, he rubbed her back for a few minutes. He leaned to his side and picked up a piece of clothing. "You want me to fold it?"

She nodded. He almost wanted to laugh, but somehow he knew he would regret it if he did. She picked up some of her clothes and folded them along with him, placing them in the trunk.

They folded and packed the rest of Madeline's clothing in silence before Sir Ashton came into the closet.

"Your Majesties, I'm sorry, would you like some help?"

"It's fine Ashton, we are almost finished anyway," Alex said.

Sir Ashton watched as they filled the trunk and could sense that he had come in at a sensitive time. He left and came back with Mr. Barry.

"Mr. Barry and I will help take your trunks down, your Majesties," he said.

"Do you know where we are going, Sir Ashton?" Alex asked.

"Yes. Once Mr. Barry and I have packed your luggage onto the carriage outside, I'll let you know."

As the men grabbed the trunks and packed the coach, Alex wrapped his arm around Madeline and rocked her for a few minutes. Though he said nothing it was comforting, and she hated parting from his embrace when Sir Ashton came back.

"Everything is ready, your Majesties," Sir Ashton said bowing.

"Let's go," Alex said, as he softly guided her by the small of her back. He led her out of her apartments and down the stairs and out of Frogmore. On the driveway, there was a coach waiting. The coach was packed and it seemed that Mr. Barry had left Sir Ashton to take care of the rest of the arrangements.

"Again, my apologies for waking you both so early, your Majesties," Sir Ashton said. "This coach is going to take you to a place just outside of London, from there you're going to take a railway to another location, then take a carriage to Warwick Castle."

"A railway?" Alex repeated.

"Yes," Sir Ashton confirmed. "It will be a faster and smoother ride for her Majesty."

"Thanks Ashton," said Alex. He helped Madeline into the carriage and followed her in. He leaned out the threshold to speak to Sir Ashton.

"Continue meetings with the Colonels and Lords concerning our plans. Have one last meeting with the House of Lords. Don't forget to take care of those odd ends I mentioned, too."

"Yes, your Majesty," Sir Ashton said nodding.

"Also, do me a favour and write Greg. Don't tell him what the plans are. But let him know that we have a plan."

"Of course," Sir Ashton said, shutting the carriage door and going back into Frogmore, then Mr. Barry emerged from the house and came to the carriage window.

"Now, your Majesties," Mr. Barry said bowing, "Sir Ashton will not disclose to me where you're going, but I'm going to take you to the railway. From there you'll be taken to another location."

Alex nodded, "Very good, Mr. Barry."

Mr. Barry got into the driver's seat and took the reins.

But curious eyes peered at the carriage from behind a nearby brush. As Sir Ashton walked back into Frogmore, the slender figure came out from her hiding place watching the carriage leave.

"Warwick Castle?" she murmured. It wasn't too far; she could take her horse and be there by midday. It would be difficult to ride in the dark. She sighed. "Alex needs me though," she said justifying her plan to herself. "Besides the roads are clearly marked. I just need to make sure I find all the signs." She ran back into a nearby forest to find her horse.

* * *

MADELINE CUDDLED up to Alex as they rode through the night, "I'm tired," she whimpered.

"I know. Try to rest," he said running his fingers through her silky tresses.

"You don't think we'll have to move to other places when the Spanish attack?"

"It depends if Sir Ashton suspects that our location is compromised, then we'll have to leave."

"Do you think some people are still loyal to Lord Bathory and would help King Fernando?"

"Possibly. Who knows, some of them may be loyal to Susanna as well. She managed to free Prince Carlos, destroy some of our semaphores, and sail back to Spain. Someone must have helped her."

He clasped his hand in hers and squeezed.

"Will we go to another royal residence?" she asked.

"Well, we haven't figured that part out yet," he sighed. "We can't stay for too long once the Spanish invade. We only want them to chase us to Warwick Castle. Once we get word that they're headed towards Warwickshire, we'll find another safe spot."

"Will we go back to Windsor?" she asked.

"If the English army has secured the town and the castle, then we will head back to Windsor."

"Alex, that's dangerous. How can we safely get back to Windsor, if there are Spanish people swarming Windsor?"

"I know. It's all in the timing, I'm afraid. Sir Ashton plans to secure a safe route for our return."

She rested her head on his lap, and he continued to comb her hair with his fingers.

"I'm not really worried though, Madeline," he lied. "We can lead them in another direction. If we have to go separate ways, we'll do that. Not many subjects know what you look like. Neither do the Spanish."

"I'm not leaving you, Alex," she whispered.

"For the baby, you will."

She said nothing. Alex turned his attention to the view out the window. The moonlight shone across Frogmore pond, its light shimmering on each ripple in the water. A part of him wondered if he'd ever see it again.

He knew that no matter what happened, she would be stubborn. If he ordered her to leave him or separate, she wouldn't listen. If he sent her away in another carriage, she'd risk everything to get back to him. As they rode, he knew that while he had a fairly good defence and counter-attack plan, he had not considered that Madeline's emotions might hinder the outcome of the plan. He knew there would be a point in which they would have to separate. He shuddered at the thought, he might have to fool her in some way; he might have to trick her into believing he did something she wouldn't forgive him for. An action that would make her want to leave him.

* * *

GREG WRAPPED his arm around Sofia as she slept in the crook of his shoulder. It had been a long night before, and the two of them had slept in. It was almost midday. Since the festival, Sofia hadn't been herself. The past few weeks, she had been paranoid, sometimes quivering in fear; any sudden sounds or movements startled her and she was often surveying her surroundings. He would sometimes find her on her own too, staring out the window toward the sea. It seemed as though she was expecting her father to come any minute.

Greg tried to ignore the behaviour. He thought in a few days she would relax and realize that King Fernando wasn't coming as soon as she had thought. But the paranoia didn't stop. She kept asking questions about what was keeping Sam and Belle. He had expected them to come back any day now. He also imagined that by this point, the King had most likely received the letter.

Sofia had asked all sorts of questions about the letter King Fernando had sent. But he didn't want to tell her that King Fernando had threatened to torture and kill him. She would want to leave and go into hiding. He knew Alex would send a message back with Sam and Belle, so Greg didn't want to leave. He was sure there would be some kind of instruction for him.

There was a sudden rumble outside. Thunder roared from several miles away. Sofia popped her head up and ran to the window in the buff, and looked outside.

"What was that?" she said frantically looking out the window.

"It's just thunder, Sofia. Look at the clouds about the hills, and Arthur's Seat," he said calmly.

"Are you sure?" she asked glancing towards the old dormant volcano.

"Absolutely," he smiled. "Come back to bed, Princess."

She glared out the window, "But it sounded like a canon."

"It wasn't. I saw lightening."

"This time in the morning?"

"Weather's a fickle thing here."

Her eyes were still looking off, expecting another roar. He waited. She needed to see it, to know for certain. Finally, another boom came from the clouds and she let out a deep breath in relief.

"Come back to bed, Princess," he said patting the spot next to him. She walked back ruefully and pulled the covers over her. Bending her knees, she wrapped her arms around her legs and rested her head on her knees.

"You said you sent Sam and Belle to give Alex a letter. What did you tell him?" she asked.

"Nothing much, just told him how things are going around here."

"Stop keeping things from me, Greg," she said with annoyance in her tone. "I know it was something urgent. Why else would you send Belle and Sam? It must have been important. Just after my father's advisor speaks to you, you send Sam and Belle away with a letter? Tell me what happened," she demanded.

"I received a letter from your father. He demanded that I send you back."

"Yes, yes," she said impatient, "I know that, but was there more that you're not telling me?"

"He threatened me."

"What?!" she cried in fear. "Did he say when he is coming?"

"He said that after he defeated Alex, he would come to Edinburgh and kill me. I told his messenger that you had run off and I didn't know where you were."

"Oh," she nodded. "I suppose you think my father will believe that?"

He chuckled, "I know he won't. I wrote him a letter for his advisor to give him."

She was afraid to ask, but she had to know, "What did you say, Greg?"

"I told him that you and I are getting along quite well."

"How well?"

"He knows that we've, uh, gotten familiar."

"WHAT?" she shrieked. "You told him that we – dear God, what were you thinking?"

"I thought since he has a plan to come down here and kill me, I might as well take advantage of the opportunity to tell him what an arse he is."

"You called him an arse?" she said, her mouth hung open.

"Something like that," Greg said uncomfortably, preparing himself for her reaction.

"YOU CAN'T BE SERIOUS?" she bellowed.

"It makes no difference if I try to be kind now," he said sitting up. "I kidnapped his daughter."

"I would have gone back," she said tearfully.

"He'd kill me either way. I'd rather die a happy man with you by my side than know that I sent you back to him. Admit it, your father makes you miserable. He's a terrible person."

She was about to object, but stopped. Everything Greg said was true.

"You have a lot on your mind you know," Greg said, "but there's something I need you to do, should your father come into the city."

"What's that?"

"I have no intentions of giving you up Sofia, not even in death. I don't believe your father is going to leave you unpunished should he capture you. Whatever the future brings, don't go back to Spain. If your father takes my life, you are better here than there."

The truth cut like a blunt blade, hacking into flesh. It was something she had always known, but had hoped Greg would never say. She never wanted their love story to end in such tragedy, but she knew he wouldn't allow her back into the clutches of her father, and if Sofia didn't do as Greg asked, his effort to make her life a better one would be in vain. Greg would rather Fernando take his life than take Sofia back to Spain. Tears streamed down her cheeks and she turned to him, her voice cracking, "Greg Umbridge, I've never known anyone as selfless and loving as you."

He rubbed circles into her back. "Don't worry, if the worst happens, Alex will keep you. He will hide you. He'd do it for me."

WARWICK CASTLE

*B*y late morning, Madeline and Alex had arrived in Warwick Castle. The castle was gothic style but much smaller than Windsor. When they arrived, their driver escorted them up a large set of stairs and into the main hall.

"I'll go get Mr. Canterbury," the driver said, leaving Madeline and Alex alone in the hall.

Madeline walked around the hall. The walls were stone with arched doorways and large displays of swords, spears and antler racks. There were suits of armour lining the perimeter of the room. The floors were tan and crème harlequin. Medieval chandeliers hanging from the timber beamed ceiling gave off a dim light which gave the room a cosy feeling.

"It's gorgeous here. How come we've never been to this castle?" she asked, turning to Alex.

"It doesn't belong to the crown," he said simply. "It used to. But a century or so ago it was given to Lord Davis's family."

"Does he know that we are here?"

"Yes. Only he and Sir Ashton know. None of the servants will know who we are. The servants and the driver think we are relatives of the Davises."

"So I'm Lady Davis?"

"That's right."

Madeline continued to look about the room, touching the chain mail and cold steel of the armour until the driver and Mr. Canterbury entered through one of the arched doorways.

"Good morning Lord and Lady Davis. My name is Mr. Canterbury. Your uncle told me of your visit. Welcome to Warwick Castle. If there is anything you need, please don't hesitate to ask me or anyone on the staff here for assistance."

"Thank you, Mr. Canterbury," said Alex. "It's been a long ride, I'm sure that my wife's delicate condition may require her to rest."

Madeline gave Alex a look, "I may be pregnant Lord Davis, but I think a tour of the castle will be fine before I rest."

Mr. Canterbury sniggered.

"Whatever pleases the Lady," Alex smiled.

"Right this way, follow me," Mr. Canterbury said.

He took them into the next room which was a great hall with black and white harlequin floors and huge arches across the ceiling. The stone walls were filled with swords and game antlers. It reminded her a little of the Weaponry Room in Windsor, except there were full suits of armour all about the room.

"As I'm sure you know, your uncle is quite the collector of war antiquities."

"Yes," said Alex looking about. She noted that even he was amazed at Lord Davis' collection. He walked closer towards a rather large set of armour. His eyes widened.

"Is this Edward Longshanks' armour?" Alex asked as he approached a chain mail piece that was clearly built for a very tall man. Madeline recognized a lion on the shield and the traditional red and gold colours.

"Yes, it is my Lord," said Mr. Canterbury, "very astute."

Alex stood staring at the armour as Mr. Canterbury moved down the hall. Madeline whispered behind him, "You think that should be yours, don't you?"

"Well, it is part of royal history," he said beneath his breath.

"Don't you have enough priceless treasures?" she whispered.

"I do," he said staring into her eyes. He took her hand and they followed Mr. Canterbury out into the corridor.

Fortunately, the tour wasn't too long. Though the castle was clearly full of rich history, Mr. Canterbury didn't delve into it, nor did he share any humorous anecdotes. Madeline was grateful, as much as she was interested in hearing more about the castle, it didn't take long before her feet began to swell.

He didn't go through every room either, but the castle did have some unique rooms. There was an old chapel with a floor-to-ceiling arched stained glass window filled with all sorts of colours. There was also a cedar drawing room with cedar wood walls. It was small, but felt cosy. There were several large gold framed paintings in the room with some of the most realistic looking faces she had ever seen. The dining room had white walls with gold wainscoting and oversized paintings filling the room along with gold painted statues and candelabras on a marble-top buffet. The dining table itself was a simple long mahogany table that sat sixteen.

There were plenty of bedrooms and drawing rooms. There was even a music room with a harp she could play. But the most fascinating room was Lady Davis' room, where Madeline and Alex were staying. It had a large antique four poster bed, the tallest she had ever seen; the top of the bed nearly touching the ceiling. It had huge red and gold silk drapery. There was antique furniture about the room and colourful tapestries hanging from every wall. She looked above the white marble fireplace and saw a painting of a stern looking woman.

"My," Madeline said looking about the room, "this room is quite something."

"Yes," Mr. Canterbury admitted, "everything in the room is well over a hundred years old. Even the tapestries. Lady Davis wanted to keep the theme of the room in antique style in honour of Queen Anne."

"Queen Anne?" Alex repeated. "Is that her above the mantle?"

"Yes, my Lord, the bed there is also hers. It was left here just over a century ago."

"How did that happen?" Alex asked curiously.

"Well, the Queen was supposed to visit here, so they sent the bed from Windsor to prepare for her coming. Unfortunately, she never made it, so it never left."

Madeline laughed loudly, noticing the expression of shock on Alex's face.

"Is everything all right my Lady?" Mr. Canterbury asked, stunned by her abrupt laughter.

"Just fine," she said, "but I should really get my rest, Mr. Canterbury."

Mr. Canterbury left and Madeline continued to giggle at Alex's dumbfounded expression.

"Are you all right, your Majesty?" she teased. "I guess there are so many royal artefacts, your residences couldn't house them all."

"I know. I don't mind. It's just, I was under the impression that anything royal and historical was in my residences. If Lord Davis has this kind of history in a residence he rarely visits, it makes me wonder what other interesting pieces other nobles might have that I don't know about."

THE ROYAL ARMOURY

$\mathcal{J}$t was the night before the Spanish army were to depart from Madrid to invade England. Susanna glared around in disgust. All the court was in attendance for a ball. There were plenty of drinks, an assortment of delicacies, and several groups of musicians spread throughout several staterooms, all of which were decorated. The Room of Columns had red festoons hanging from the pillars and a group of flamenco dancers (some of them were also ladies-in-waiting) danced in the centre of the room. They swayed to the rhythm of the music, the material of their dresses swishing with their movements. King Fernando put more money into these festivities than her and Carlos's wedding.

The attack plan had finally been decided. King Fernando was taking his men up the English Channel towards London. They planned to break free the men from the Tower of London and then take the city. If Alex happened to be in Buckingham Palace, he'd most likely escape, but King Fernando didn't think it would be long before the men tracked him down.

Carlos was taking the rest of the men to Brighton, a small town on the south coast of England. From there, they would trek to Windsor, take the town, then head into the castle.

They were going to continue with the plan of invading the tunnels. After much convincing from Carlos, King Fernando felt the men could invade Windsor Castle more easily using the tunnels. She was going to make more suggestions to Carlos, but she didn't care to.

When she first arrived in Madrid, she couldn't wait to wage war on England and succeed where her father had failed. But as time passed, she became more annoyed with Fernando and Carlos. It was hard to imagine ruling England with Carlos at her side; she couldn't care less about how the war turned out. If anything, she would have been pleased if neither of them lived. She would still have Spain. There was still the matter of Queen Isabelle, but she doubted the weak woman would present much of a problem for her. Since the day she tried on her wedding dress and put the ladies in their place, Susanna had become Isabelle's confidant. It was unlikely that Isabelle would try to run the country without her.

Susanna was taken out of her reverie as Señor Astucia ogled her from across the room. She casually walked over to him. A grin came across his face, "Are you enjoying the party your Highness?"

"Quite," she lied. "Tell me something, have you seen my husband? It seems that he's disappeared again."

Arsenio looked away. They both knew the answer to the question, and he hated that she asked it.

"Perhaps you can help me go search for him," she joked.

"I'm sure that-"

She took his hand and discreetly grazed her fingers over his hand.

"Come with me," she said in a heavy tone.

He pressed his lips together, and looked down into her lustful eyes, "I think I might know where he went."

He locked arms with her and began to escort her out of the room, heading toward Sofia's apartments.

"Your Highness!" A footman called behind her in Spanish racing toward the pair. She and Señor Astucia turned about to face him.

"That is no way to address royalty," Señor Astucia said in Spanish, "yelping across the room like an animal."

"Forgive me," he bowed, "but his Majesty wishes to see Prince

Carlos immediately. It's important. I thought he would be with you, Princess."

"It's quite all right, Señor Astucia," she said an evil smirk on her face. "This man is only following the orders of the King." She released herself from Señor Astucia's grip. "I know where the Prince is. I'll go get him myself."

She rushed out and headed to Carlos's apartments. She was surprised that the footman hadn't thought of searching his private apartments first. But it was possible he may have mistaken Señor Astucia for Carlos.

There were several guards just outside Carlos's doors. But Susanna didn't stop to address them, she threw open the doors, between them and walked into his drawing room. "Your Highness," they called several times after her, but she didn't turn to glance. She ran towards his bedchamber door, and they began to chase after her. She burst through the door, and the laughter that filled the air between the lovers dropped.

Esmeralda pulled the covers to her neck and the guards stopped at the bedchamber door. Carlos gawked at Susanna, his eyes wild like hunted prey.

Susanna walked over to the bed and traced her finger along the wood at its footboard, wearing a crafty smile, "Your father is looking for you, Carlos. He says it's important."

Carlos froze, unsure of what to do.

"Don't be so modest Carlos," Susanna said. "There's nothing you have that I haven't seen."

Esmeralda's eyes narrowed. Though her English wasn't strong, she understood what that meant. Carlos got out of the bed and began to put his clothes back on. The two women watched, as he dressed hurriedly. "All right, let's go," he said walking toward the door. But Susanna didn't follow. "Aren't you coming?" he said staring at Susanna. "No. Your father doesn't want to see me. He hasn't much use for what I have to say. Why would I go?"

"Leave the room, Susanna," he ordered.

"I could leave the room now. But what difference does it make if I leave now? You're leaving us both in Madrid. If I don't deal with Esmeralda now, I'll deal with her once you leave," she said grinning innocently.

"No. You. Won t," he said waving his finger at her.

She laughed wickedly, "Just how are you going to stop me?"

"If you do anything to her, I swear to you, you'll be dead before you set foot in England again."

He said nothing else and walked out. A few moments later, Susanna could hear him berating the guards. When it was silent again, she looked at Esmeralda.

"I will deal with you, Esmeralda."

"No," she said assured, her glare locked on Susanna. "If you do, he will kill you."

"*If* Carlos makes it back to Spain. Pray that he does. King Alexander is quite brilliant. I'm sure you heard what he did in Ireland when he was just thirteen."

Esmeralda swallowed hard as she pulled at the covers.

CARLOS FOUND his father in the Royal Armoury, surrounded by his advisors, Señors, and Coronels. Fernando's face was a deep purple, and he was cursing and yelling in Spanish as he slammed his fist onto the map of England.

"I want that rogue dead! Forget London! Carlos can still go to Windsor. I want Edinburgh! I want Greg Umbridge to experience the most horrid way to die ever recorded in history!"

The King looked up, noting Carlos's presence. Carlos walked over to him and Fernando shoved Greg's letter to Carlos's chest. Carlos took the letter and began reading, his jaw dropping further the more he read. Carlos hated Greg before for capturing him and humiliating him in front of his men. "He must be lying. Sofia would never be with that scoundrel," Carlos said his eyes bulging in disbelief.

Several more people of the court entered, hearing the commotion. King Fernando looked to Señor Menendo. "Get them out. Have everyone go to the Throne Room. Announce that we will no longer be leaving in the morning. Let the men know that we will be heading to Edinburgh, not London."

Señor Menendo left, escorting the people out of the room as he went.

"What?" Carlos said.

"These plans must be changed. I am going to Edinburgh instead. London does not need to be defeated. Once you've found King Alexander and have killed him, England is ours."

"How many men will you be taking?" Carlos asked.

"We will decide that in the next few days."

All the Coronels and Lords looked from the plans on the map and stared in shock at Fernando.

"Your Majesty," began Señor Astucia, "would it not be risky to give King Alexander more time? I fear his men might reach London very soon if they haven't already."

"That's why it is a brilliant plan, Astucia. The English will send their men to London, but our men will be heading to Edinburgh. Both the King and Umbridge will be crushed."

There was dissension among the men as they began uttering their frustrations beneath their breaths.

"WHAT?" King Fernando boomed. "Do any of you think it's right that Umbridge has defiled my daughter and thinks he has the right to marry her without my permission?"

One of the Coronels stepped forward, "Your Majesty, there is no doubt that what Greg Umbridge has done is unspeakably rude and crass, but we shouldn't give King Alexander more time. I've heard that his men are organizing themselves and have already started to head back to England."

"Impossible!" Fernando barked. "Even if it were true, there is no way he could get those men organized to protect both Windsor and Edinburgh. You watch! He will be foolish. All those men will head straight for London, then Windsor. Edinburgh will be easily defeated. Then I will take my men back to London and Carlos can advance with his men from Windsor. It's perfect. We'll take London from the east and the west."

"It is a good plan," Carlos said, trying to placate his father, "but I just worry that a change of plans so impulsively, may not be wise."

"I agree with Prince Carlos," Señor Astucia said. "Defeating Edinburgh does not do anything in your campaign to take England. It may anger the Scots."

"Bah!" Fernando dismissed. "The Scots will do nothing. Once they understand that Spain is taking the British Empire, they will back down."

The meeting went on for hours. Several of the Coronels and Lords tried to persuade King Fernando to go back to the previous plan. But Fernando only grew more irate, mentioning how insulting Greg Umbridge had been. Finally, Prince Carlos dared to say something everyone was thinking but hadn't the audacity to say, "Father, is it possible that Sofia may *want* to marry Greg Umbridge?"

SMACK!

For the first time, King Fernando struck his son publicly. The sting of the King's backhand hurt, but Carlos managed to keep himself composed.

"If Sofia dares marry that man or even wishes to, I'll disown her," Fernando said through gritted teeth. "HELL, I'LL KILL HER!" he roared before he stomped out of the room.

* * *

THE ROYAL ARMOURY in Madrid Palace was impressive. As Susanna walked down the long hall filled with statues of full-armoured horses and knights lined up along both sides, of her. She noticed that each set of armour came from different ages, from medieval times to the present. Reading some of the plaques next to the statues, Susanna realized that some of the armour belonged to former Spanish kings and princes. As she continued to walk toward the battle plan that stood on a table in the middle of the room, she observed the marble harlequin floors, the tapestries on the walls and the large displays of swords and shields. Although Alex's Royal Armoury had lots of diversity with weaponry from across the world and historical pieces, the Spanish armoury was a still a site to been seen. She was surprised she had never heard of people speak of it. She stopped and glimpsed at the map and small model ships and military.

She wasn't supposed to be in there. If King Fernando or Carlos caught her, she was certain that she'd have to pay for it in some way. But she didn't care, she wasn't going to obey them. Women like Queen Isabelle did that, and she lived in fear. Susanna would never allow that for herself.

As she looked at the plan, she was a little confused; the miniatures were in their finishing positions, so she didn't know what the steps were to the plan.

"You shouldn't be here, your Highness" a deep voice echoed across the room.

She turned to see Señor Astucia, standing next to one of the entry ways.

"True. But I doubt you would tell the King," she said, lightly touching the hillocks of her breasts. "You wouldn't want to see me punished, would you?'

He sauntered next to her, "No I wouldn't. But I do see an opportunity. What will you do for me?"

"Do for you?" she said looking up at him innocently.

"Yes. You don't want me to tell King Fernando, so what would you do to – how do the English say- 'keep mum'?"

"I'm surprised Señor Astucia. I thought it was clear the other night that I was going to give you something you wanted," she said coyly.

"I was very disappointed to see you go. I was frustrated to be dragged in here to change the plans."

"Don't think I wasn't disappointed myself."

"I don't wish to wait much longer," he said taking her hand and kissing it softly, "You're going to have to do something for me. Otherwise, I might have to run to tell his Majesty."

"No one tells me what to do, Señor Astucia," she said firmly.

He leered at her. He loved a challenge.

"Rather than being a snitch, why don't you tell me what the plan is?" she said pointing to the miniatures. "Prince Carlos isn't willing to share."

"I will if you can give me something I want. Now."

"What is it you want?"

"A kiss."

"Here? Now?" she scoffed.

"Yes."

She moved toward him, giving him a soft, slow, warm kiss on the lips. He rocked her in his arms.

"Mm, more," he said his eyes closed.

"I believe you need to tell me of the plans, Señor Astucia," she purred.

He pursed his lips and turned to the map of England. He placed all the miniatures in their beginning positions.

"Prince Carlos will leave earlier. He will take his ships, reach Brighton and then trek to Windsor. It will take a few days or so. King Fernando will then leave Santander with his fleet. As they pass Brighton, the King will make certain that all is going well with the invasion. If so, our men will raise a red flag. If not, a white one. If they raise the white flag, King Fernando, and his men will arrive as back-up. If not, he will continue to Edinburgh.

King Fernando suspects that if the English do arrive in England, they'll arrive in London first, then head to Windsor. They won't care about Sir Gregory. Once he finishes Edinburgh, which shouldn't take more than a day, he'll return to London and head to Windsor, to help Prince Carlos. If he needs any."

She tapped her finger on the map. England. She was about to allow her own country to be invaded by another empire. But as she surveyed the map, she wondered aloud, "Why is there only a map of England? The English army is in Europe. When you military men sit and discuss such things, don't you discuss where your enemy will be?"

"There's no need for a map of all of Europe," he said, "the battle-ground will be England. King Alexander will try to protect his strong-holds first, starting with London because it's the closest."

Then she knew. Spain wasn't going to win. Alex was the type of man that looked at the bigger picture. It was narrow-minded to assume that England was the only battling ground.

"What has his Majesty done to protect his motherland?" she asked. "I mean what of Madrid?"

"King Fernando has considered it. But because of England's battle with Napoleon, King Alex's resources are low. If the English have all their men walk over all that terrain, it will only exhaust them. King Fernando only laughs at whatever feeble attempt the English might have. They really don't have much to attack with."

"Don't underestimate the English," she said.

"Every empire falls. King Fernando believes it is England's time."

"If England falls, it won't be under King Alexander's rule," she said certain.

"I thought you hated your King," he said, curiously.

"I do. But I can't deny he is brilliant. He's the type of man that can look at things from so many angles."

"So, it's not a good plan?" he asked intrigued.

"I didn't say that. It seems flawless. It's just-"

"What?"

"I look at this plan and it's good, but it's not enough," she said picking up one of the miniature ships. "King Alexander thinks differently. He's not going to do something you expect. He's going to do something you don't think of."

"What makes you say that? England's ships are located throughout the English Empire. His men are scattered about Europe. He hasn't enough time to organize a good defence."

"I think of it this way Arsenio; my father always had fairly good plans, too. But it didn't matter, Alex was always a few steps ahead."

"Are you giving me a warning your Highness?" he said his eyes piercing hers.

But she continued in a serious tone, "If I am, it doesn't matter. If you were to tell King Fernando what I've told you, he wouldn't pay any attention."

"No, he wouldn't. He is still fuming over Greg Umbridge."

She snickered. She had often considered Greg Umbridge a clown, a man that sponged from Alex. But in a strange way, she wanted to thank him. She had never hated anyone more than King Fernando. Ironically, a man she looked down on, did her a favour.

"What did he say in that letter?" she asked her eyes bright.

"He mentioned how much Sofia enjoys being with him ... and how familiar they've become. He also announced that he was going to marry Sofia."

Her jaw dropped. Sir Gregory was known for crossing the line. But all his drunk buffoonery, dancing after every gambling win, and destruction of the homes and royal residences he had been in, seemed nothing compared to this.

"That's shocking," she said, putting her fingers to her mouth, "even for Greg Umbridge."

"I've told you everything you need to know, your Highness," he said pulling her hand away from her lips, he kissed her again.

"Are you not worried, your King or your friend the Prince might walk in here?" she asked raising her brow.

"Believe me, they are busy," he said. "I checked before following you here."

He continued kissing her, backing her in between two large steel horses. She tripped to the floor.

"Oh!" she said as she landed on her bottom.

"Sorry, your Highness." he said casually, crawling on the floor toward her. He slowly moved his hand on her ankles sliding it up her calf. Just then, someone entered the room.

"Señor Astucia, what are you doing on the floor?" Susanna could hear Carlos say in Spanish.

Calmly, Señor Astucia rose, extending his hand out to her. She took it and pulled herself to her feet.

"Her Highness fell," said Señor Astucia. "She tripped on the floor and I was going to help her get up. But then I tripped on her shoe."

The Prince walked across the large room and stood next to them.

"I never knew you were clumsy, Susanna," he said with suspicion.

"There is the rare occasion," she admitted.

"What are you doing here? You know you shouldn't be in here," Carlos said glaring at her.

"Señor Astucia was just telling me the same thing," she lied.

Carlos grinned, self-assured, "My father and I have talked Susanna. We feel that once we have conquered Windsor, you will need to be immediately escorted back to England to have your coronation."

"Of course, but who will escort me there? I want someone that speaks English. I refuse to travel with any frustration."

"I'm not going to free any of those English men we brought here if that's what you are asking," he said annoyed.

"A peasant man as an escort for me?" she laughed. "I hardly think that's suitable for royalty."

Carlos nodded in agreement.

"If you'd like your Highness, I can take her," Señor Astucia offered. He leaned over to Carlos whispering something in Spanish she couldn't understand.

Carlos nodded again, "Yes, that's what I was afraid of. Wouldn't want a repeat of that kind of behaviour."

Susanna scowled at them both. Obviously, they were talking about her promiscuity on the journey to Madrid.

"I'll send a messenger when Windsor has fallen," Carlos said patting Arsenio's shoulder. He turned to Susanna, "You'd better be ready. I don't want to wait longer than necessary. Order one of the servants to pack your things before the end of today."

"Yes, Carlos," she said.

"Leave, Susanna. You don't belong in here," Carlos said firmly.

She was about to object, but she knew it was useless. She exited but kept close to the door trying to overhear their conversation. But it was too difficult. The Royal Armoury was large, and they were speaking in hushed voices. She heard only a few words.

The two of them left through another door. She walked to her apartments in fear. Señor Astucia's behaviour was complicated. She didn't know if he was genuinely interested in her, or if she had just been set up by them both.

MISS HAMPTON

"So what do you think so far?" Alex asked Madeline as they walked through the streets of Warwick in simple clothing. "It's quaint here," she said looking about.

They had been in Warwick a few days, but hadn't left Warwick Castle. The trip to the castle had exhausted her. Though riding the railway had been fascinating, the baby kept her awake, with its soft kicks. She had spent the past few days resting. Alex didn't seem to mind. He had already had several private meetings, most of them were held in the castle. But there were several held late at night. Typically, the meetings were in the afternoon and he would be gone for several hours. She never asked about what was discussed. Whenever he came back, he seemed tired. She was getting the feeling that discussing possible attack plans and guessing when and how the Spanish would strike was intolerable.

When Madeline wasn't resting, she wandered about the castle. Though the castle was under guard, there weren't many servants inside. When they first arrived, both she and Alex were given personal servants, but Alex dismissed his saying that with all the meetings he had, there wouldn't be much of a point of being waited upon. Madeline had considered doing the same. Her servant was far too young and for some reason, reminded her of Sissy. Like Sissy, Lily was scared and timid. Though Madeline tried to be warm, Lily often fumbled about, dropping and breaking things while trying to help Madeline in the morning.

Overall, the servants were lazy, scared, or daring. While walking about, Madeline had found several items in odd places. In the guest bedroom, she had found a hairpiece on the rug. In the dining room, she found a hand fan on one of the chairs, and then one day while reading in the library she saw a dirty handkerchief on a side table. Either the servants weren't consistently cleaning the rooms as often as they should, or they were borrowing Lady Davis's things without returning them in their proper place.

Madeline had mentioned it to Alex, but he didn't seem to think much of it, "Well, they are understaffed," he dismissed.

"A hand fan sitting on a chair in the dining room?" asked Madeline in disbelief. "I would think someone would have noticed it while clearing the table. Seems a bit odd."

His lips curved, "Are you worried Lily is going to start borrowing your things?"

She pressed her lips together trying not to laugh. It was hard to imagine. Lily was full of fear just touching her belongings.

"Could be worse dolcezza, she could be stealing your things," he teased.

"Right," she said sheepishly.

Since they hadn't done much together over the first few days, Alex had suggested they take a walk and have afternoon tea in Warwick. It was good to get away from the castle. Though it was a nice place to stay, Madeline was beginning to feel cabin fever.

Warwick was a charming town. It reminded her of Windsor, but with fewer people. There weren't as many shops, but she had no need to go shopping. Before leaving, a new wardrobe had been brought in for her. She was no longer wearing tight corsets – she was too pregnant for that. She had been given new dresses that were flexible for her growing body. She still had chemise and empire waisted dresses. But now they were accompanied by stays that held up her chest with her breasts peaking out. Fine silk aprons covered her breasts and tucked into the stay. She admired the comfort of it. Her clothing was still fashionable, comparable to a woman that wasn't pregnant; but now it adapted with her changing body.

Alex held her around her waist as they walked.

"Remember the first time we went to the King's Head?" he reminisced. "No one knew who we were? This is even better. If anyone recognizes us, it will be someone from court."

"Yes," she said, "but wouldn't Sir Ashton have sent a few people to keep an eye on us?"

"Probably," he said casually. "But they won't bother us. They are probably keeping watch on the castle and anything suspicious happening in the town."

"If you saw any of them in the street, do you think you would know who they are?"

He snickered, "I think I might have an idea. But that's the price you pay when you have an advisor as thorough as Sir Ashton is."

"Are there spies in Spain?"

"Of course. They were sent weeks ago, but most of the intelligence they bring back isn't newsworthy. King Fernando keeps the meetings about invading England exclusive. We sent several men there. They've been unable to give much information, except for the arrival of Susanna and her marriage to Prince Carlos, but we were expecting they'd marry."

They came across a tea house, not far from the castle. It was an old Tudor style home, but its large wood timber frame and white walls looked unweathered. It was at a fork in the road, and patrons sat outside on a small patio drinking and chatting.

"This looks like a lovely little tea house," she said grinning.

"Would you like to have tea here? Do you need to rest?" he asked concerned.

"I'm not tired, but if we are going out for tea, why not here?"

"All right."

There was another place he had wanted to take her. It had been a while since he and Madeline made love. With everything that had been happening, she had been distant. He knew it was nothing personal. Like him, she had a lot on her mind. But unlike her, he was craving a night to make love to her. He wondered if it was because she was getting bigger that maybe she didn't feel as attractive. He had heard about women feeling this way while pregnant. But he couldn't understand why. He had never found himself more attracted to her. She glowed while pregnant, her smile seemed sweeter and her green eyes twinkled in a way they never had before.

They walked into the tea house and a server greeted them, "Welcome," he said bowing, "have a seat wherever you can find space."

Alex looked around, almost every table was taken. All that was left was a small table by the window, its wooden chairs teetering on the stone floor.

"I don't think that will do," Alex said to the server.

"I'm sure it will be fine," Madeline insisted.

"I'm not letting you sit there," Alex said beneath his breath. "I want you to be comfortable."

"We do have some private tea rooms upstairs," suggested the server, "there are several couches."

"That will do," Alex said.

"It does cost extra to have a private room," the server said.

"That's fine," Alex replied.

"Excellent. Follow me," the server said as he turned and began walking to the back of the tea house.

They came to a steep staircase and the server began climbing up the steps.

"Ladies first," said Alex, gesturing her to go ahead. "Make sure you hold on to the balustrade."

Alex followed them up the stairs and into a room at the end of the hall.

"It's a little large for two, but it is quite comfortable," the server said.

The room had several couches and chairs with small tables between them. There was a fireplace on the other side of the room and the server began to light it along with several candelabras. Alex and Madeline sat down on a large couch.

"There are some menus on the table right in front of you," the man said. "Feel free to take a look, my name is Mr. Turner if you need anything."

"Are you very hungry?" Alex asked Madeline as he perused the menu.

Madeline nodded, she was famished.

"We'll have your afternoon tea plates with Earl Grey tea," said Alex.

"Certainly, Sir," he said.

When Mr. Turner finished lighting the room, he gave Alex a bell.

"If you need anything, just give this a ring, Sir."

Alex took it into his hand, "Thank you Mr. Turner, but once we have a tea and snacks, I doubt we'll be needing anything else."

"I understand Sir," Mr. Turner said before giving a small bow and exiting.

Alex leaned his back against the arm of the couch as Madeline rested on his chest. He wrapped his arm around her.

"That walk was much more exhausting than I thought it would be," she said.

"Could you imagine having the table by the window," he laughed.

"No, thanks, this is much more cosy."

He placed his hand on her thigh, "I'm glad you think so."

She looked down at his hand. Somehow she got the feeling he was feeling frisky, but she put the thought out of her mind. She doubted he found her attractive now; he was just being affectionate.

He looked down at her biting his lip. The cut of her dress was low and revealed an ample amount of cleavage. It also fit her snugly. It was at that moment he noticed that she wasn't wearing a corset. Her nipples poked out through the thin material. He exhaled. The fact that Mr. Turner would return any minute was becoming an annoyance. He pecked her softly on the head, putting his fingers through her soft black hair pinned in soft curls.

She raised her head looking up at him curiously. His lips caught hers and she cupped his face surrendering to him. "Uhh," she murmured as he tweaked her nipple through the muslin.

He pulled back piercing her eyes with his own, "I want you now," he whispered.

"Alex," she tittered, "this is hardly-"

He began nibbling around her ears, she could hear a creaking in the hallway and the doorknob turn. She jolted up just before Mr. Turner entered the room with a cart. Alex glared at him.

"Here are your afternoon tea trays and your tea," Mr. Turner said as he pushed the cart over to them. He placed the tiered plates on the sofa table in front of them, along with some milk and sugar. Madeline noticed there was no honey.

"Is there anything else I can get you? We also have some other flavour jams."

"That will do," Alex said in a curt tone.

"We have some honey as well," he offered.

"No. Everything is fine," Alex said quickly.

"The scones are warm," Mr. Turner continued not catching the hint, "but I wasn't sure if you preferred butter or cream."

"What we'd prefer is our privacy," Alex said in an irritated tone.

Madeline glanced at Alex in shock; it wasn't like him to talk that way to anyone.

"Let me help you to the door, Mr. Turner," Alex said as he got up.

Mr. Turner looked up from the tea trays confused, "That's not necessary, Sir."

"No. It is."

Madeline watched as Alex walked to the door with Mr. Turner. They spoke in hushed tones and then Alex shook Mr. Turner's hand. She was certain she had seen a gold sovereign in the shake. Beaming, Mr. Turner left shutting the door behind him.

Alex turned to Madeline, his familiar devilish grin on his face. She picked up a petit four from one of the trays. *Not possible. He has done daring things before, but for some reason, I always felt safe. Though we never had anyone walk in on us in the castle, I always took comfort in the fact that I know the guards and servants would be professional and discreet if they found out. This is different. A bunch of strangers are downstairs and if anyone heard us, I will later have to walk through the crowd with him.*

He looked lasciviously at her.

"I'm pregnant and hungry," Madeline said sternly.

"That's fine," he said softly. "Eat."

She took a bite out of her petit four, her eyes glued to him.

He sauntered over, his eyes not leaving her body. She was beginning to feel like prey. He sat next to her, as she finished her petit four.

"Are you tired too?" he asked.

She nodded at him as she watched him suspiciously. He grabbed several pillows and stacked them behind her against the armrest.

"Relax then," he said, gently guiding her towards the pillows. She sat propped up against them, and he lifted her legs and placed them across his lap. He slowly pulled each of her shoes off. She hesitated, wondering if he was about to try to seduce her in the teashop. She thought better of it – him trying to woo her in such a public place was ridiculous.

"Alex …"

"Here," he said, leaning forward, grabbing a petit four and putting bringing it to her mouth. She bit down and took it in her hand. His hands moved to her calves, and he began massaging.

"Aren't you hungry?" she asked.

"Yes," he said, his eyes on her body, "starving."

Wrong question to ask. Perhaps he did have intentions. She had to distract him. If they started anything, she'd moan, and she couldn't imagine the embarrassment of being overheard in a teahouse.

"The fire is too hotcan you tend to it?" she asked. *That will keep him busy.*

"You're hot?" he said huskily, continuing to massage her stems.

She sighed. She wanted him. Desperately. His sultry smile and sleek muscles were hard to ignore. But hearing the muffled sound of the patrons below them, she knew one of them had to be the voice of reason.

"Yes, it's warm in here," she said and finished her petit four.

"Mm," he said casually as he leaned toward her. She took in his familiar smell, the hint of sandalwood, and his natural musk. The fire and the food were of no concern to him. He wanted her.

His mouth held to the crescent of hers, and she squeezed her eyes shut, resolving not to let it go further than this. His warm lips were soft, and as his fingers slid down the nape of her neck, she felt herself melting, her mouth loosening. She surrendered, her fingers threading through his lush black hair. His lips retreated from hers, "If it's too hot for you, we can loosen your aprons."

She glanced down at the silk scarf material at her chest. All he needed to do was pull it, and her breasts would be exposed.

"I know you must be tired," he said, trying to be considerate of her delicate state. "But you needn't do anything. I'll nurture you from here."

He hovered over her, his large arms on either side of her. She gripped onto his broad shoulders, his head dipped down, and he kissed her tenderly, his mouth moving across her face. The gentle flurry gave her a sense of warmth in her belly, her face going flush. He nuzzled his nose to hers, then edged her jaw with sweet soft pecks. A small gasp escaped her throat. She cupped his face, and her lips sparred with his.

"I can't promise I will be quiet," she said between broken kisses.

"You needn't promise anything. Your sound is more glorious than music."

She tittered. Was he not going to think of the customers downstairs? Clearly not. He took small samples of her neck, his mouth brushing lightly across her skin.

He loosened the apron and slipped between the silky fabric, fondling her breast. She let out a deep sigh, rousing with desire. He was the morning sun, and she a flower that opened when the light beckoned her. He swiftly tugged the silk apron, baring them both. He grunted at the sight of her, appreciating the glow of her skin contrasting with the hardened swollen peaks. He felt a tightness in his trousers but reminded himself that he had promised only to nurture her. His fingertips grazed the pink buds, and she arched her back, her body beckoning for more. He enveloped the bud in his mouth, and she moaned faintly. She bit her lower lips, and her fingernails dug into his shoulders. He held his mouth to her, tantalizing and teasing, prompting her to wriggle beneath him, aching to moan. He smiled on the inside, watching her writhe. He relished her when her good sense told her no, but her heart and body told her yes.

He sank a hand between them, not taking his lips off her supple breast, and gathered her skirts to her belly. The briskness of the air made her shiver slightly. He released her from his mouth, his eyes penetrating hers. He crawled lower, his head between her thighs, his hair grazing across the flesh in her thighs. She shuddered, his fingers and mouth making contact.

He teased and stroked, taking his time, being careful, attentive to all her movements and responses. She fell into a gentle whirlwind of delight, like a leaf that a fall wind had carried off, dancing, circling about. It was dizzying. He was the wind, conducting her highs and lows until he finally brought her to her precipice. Involuntarily, she cried out loudly then held her hand over her mouth. He kept the onslaught, and she ground her teeth, and several tears squeezed from her eyes, aching as she focused all her energy on not making a sound. It was near impossible, but a delicious pain coursed through her, and she fell away, gasping for air.

When he was certain she had more than she could bear, he rose from her and placed the skirts back over her legs. She yawned, her vision of him somewhat blurred. He said nothing but casually rubbed her calves beneath the muslin fabric.

She woke up sometime later, confused, "Alex, how long have we been here?"

He looked at the time, "You been sleeping the past half-hour. Are you hungry?"

She raised her brow. "Shouldn't we be leaving? I'm sure other patrons would use this space."

"Don't be silly, Madeline. For once, we have time to ourselves without worrying what or who might call." He got up and walked toward the fireplace and threw in a couple of logs.

She took a blanket and covered her torso as he took a couple of scones from the tray, cut them in half, and smeared whipped cream onto them.

He put it on a plate and passed it to her, "Here you are," he said as she took it. He sat down next to her and watched her as she took a bite.

"Aren't you going to have some too?" she asked, gesturing to the other scone sitting on the table in front of them.

He shook his head, "Not right now." He looked down at her feet, "Your little feet are swollen, it looks like they could use a little attention." He sat down on the couch, resting her feet on his lap and began to massage them.

"I thought you were done with all the special attention," she said as she took another bite of her scone.

His mouth curled, "I just think you deserve a chance to relax. You've been busy creating the next heir to the English empire."

As she nestled her head back into the pillows, eating her scone, he continued to massage each foot. She glimpsed up at the ceiling, noting the large wood beams above her and sighed. She could feel his large hands taking hold of her calves, massaging her tired muscles.

"How do you think Greg and Sofia are getting on?" she asked.

"One could only guess with those two."

"Why do you say that?"

"Well, Greg usually does whatever he feels like. But I've noticed with Sofia he makes exceptions."

"So the Princess gets her way?"

He laughed, "Not entirely. While they were at Windsor Castle, Sofia would make exceptions for him, too. Personally, I always had a feeling that she had admired Greg's attitude. I think she wishes she could be more like him."

"How do you think they will deal with King Fernando?" she asked concerned.

"Lord only knows. Greg fears nothing. I doubt he spends much time thinking about Fernando." His hands move up from her calves to her thighs.

She sighed, her muscles relaxing. It was so sweet of Alex to look after her like this, "What do you think Greg spends his time thinking about?"

"What every man thinks about when he's with the woman he loves," he said gazing at her.

"What's that?" she asked innocently, shutting her eyes.

"Anticipating the next time he can take care of her, and hold her in his arms."

They cuddled and chatted for some time as they listened to the patrons come and go. But she was still wary of leaving.

"I'm afraid of going down there," she admitted. "I'm sure someone heard something."

He chuckled, "It bothers you that much?"

She gave him a look, "Right. You can go down there with big smiles and it's nothing shameful for you. You're a man. You're bragging. If I go down there I'll get people giving me an evil eye."

"Would you like to go down separately? I can have the server, Mr. Turner, escort you out?"

"Mr. Turner?" she guffawed. "Won't everyone think I was with him?"

"I doubt that. He's been busy scurrying about, serving everyone. I'll go now. I'll tell Mr. Turner to escort you out. While I do, you can freshen up."

He grabbed a small tart from one of the plates and ate it. "I'll make sure he knocks before he enters," he said, giving her a kiss on the cheek before walking out the door.

Madeline looked about the room for a mirror. Her reflection was dishevelled. She desperately needed to redo her hair, and wished there were a comb. She fussed with it using her fingers and some water Mr. Turner had brought up. She put on her shoes, then went to the window and peered at the people below sitting at the tables outside. She could see Alex leaning over, talking to a woman sitting at a table. The woman was wearing a blue two toned striped dress and had blonde hair. Madeline couldn't see much else to identify her. As she watched him talk to her, the woman kicked her feet and giggled pressing her hand to his arm. But he didn't remove it. Madeline cocked her brow, she wasn't sure if she could wait for Mr. Turner to escort her down. She went to the door.

KNOCK, KNOCK.

"Mr. Turner is that you?" Madeline said as she placed her hand on the doorknob.

"Yes."

She opened the door and without a word, took his arm.

"How was everything?" he asked.

"Fine. But I really need to get going," she said as she pulled on his arm. He trailed behind her down the hall.

When they got to the stairwell, he stepped in front of her.

"I can see you're in a hurry, but I do think it would be wise to let me go first." She looked down at her belly, it poked out a little, but she didn't realize that people noticed. After he led her down the steps, she scurried out, looking for the woman and Alex, but he had already crossed the street and was waiting for her on the other side. She hesitated looking around for the woman. Alex waved his hand, motioning her to come over. As she slowly crossed the street, her eyes continued darting about looking for the woman.

When she reached the other side, she spotted her further down the street – it was Miss Hampton.

WINNING FAVOUR

*S*usanna sat in Sofia's Drawing Room, tapping her fingers on the writing desk. The last few nights she had been doing a lot of thinking. Prince Carlos and King Fernando had left the night before to the Spanish coast. They departed with two thousand men; King Fernando would take eight hundred with him to Edinburgh, after Carlos and his men had secured safe passage through the countryside to Windsor.

But over the past several days, Susanna knew how the war would progress; Alex was going to let them in. Just like he had when her father tried to invade Windsor Castle months ago. He'd have some kind of trap set for them. England knew the Spanish were coming. They had known for months now. Yet the Royal Navy and English countryside seemed quiet, too quiet.

With all the Spanish spies that were in the English countryside as well as Windsor and London, nothing of consequence had been reported since she and Carlos had come to Madrid. A couple hundred English men were securing each town, but Buckingham Palace nor Windsor Castle were preparing for a huge battle. Strangely, the only thing mentioned was some changes to Curfew Tower. Susanna had imagined that was because of her entry into the tunnels and Carlos's escape.

It was too easy, and because of that, she knew something wasn't right. The night they had left and Carlos had said his goodbye, a part of her questioned if she was sending him to his death. Not that she cared. Even if they took England, King Fernando would always be a thorn in her side that she would need to get rid of.

It left her with a lot to think about. *If Carlos doesn't return and King Fernando does, what would become of me? What would I do? If Spain is defeated and they return, it wouldn't be a good life for me. Both King Fernando and Prince Carlos would try to control every aspect of my life. They already are. In time, my life would start to resemble Queen Isabelle's.*

If the King returned alone, Susanna would have to kill him. If it were just Carlos, she would have to tolerate him having an affair with 'short court' Esmeralda. She could go outside the marriage as well, but she would have to be careful. Carlos was the jealous type and though she knew he wouldn't punish her as severely as King Fernando would, there would be hell to pay.

But what if neither returns? Would I be banished from court? Spain and Queen Isabelle had no strong loyalties to her. If the Spanish were bitter about a loss to England, she might end up being hated by the people. She had never thought of this happening.

When she had first conceived the idea to free Carlos and try to get the Spanish to join her campaign to usurp the English throne, she had been too idealistic. She thought that she would be able to gain the court and Spain's favour when they had found out that she had heroically rescued their Prince. She thought the nobles would be vying to meet her.

King Fernando had robbed her of a good reputation with the court and subjects. If they knew what risks she had taken, they would have accepted her as their Princess. But, to them, she was just an English woman that Prince Carlos had taken home as a prize, as though she were the spoils of war. Prince Carlos became the celebrated hero at the homecoming; the people weren't fascinated or intrigued by her at all. They barely knew her. Looking back at it now, she knew why King

Fernando wouldn't give into any of her requests. It was more than having no respect for the English or women. He feared her being popular with the people because it threatened his power.

She sighed as the possibilities circled about in her mind. She had gotten herself into a no-win situation. *If Fernando and Carlos come back, they would make my life difficult. But if they don't, the Spanish wouldn't want me around.* She knew her future in Spain depended on how the people felt about her. If they liked her, they would take her in as one of their own. If they hardly knew or cared for her, she'd be banished.

She had to do something that would make her popular with the nobles. Lavish parties were something most nobles favoured. However, most would consider it odd that she would want to party when her husband was at war. She stood up and began pacing about in thought.

"What do the Spanish want?" she asked herself, "What could I do that neither the King nor Carlos could punish me for?"

There was no easy answer. The only thing she could think of doing was befriending Queen Isabelle. Sofia's absence had been awful for the Queen. She no longer had a true friend or anyone to confide in. Filling the void would be easy, but would it be worth it? She doubted the Queen would do much to defend her. On the other hand, Susanna might be able to get the Queen's help in gaining favour with the Spanish nobles.

Susanna rolled her eyes; the Queen had no influence over the nobles. It was unlikely that the friendship would do much for Susanna. But at this point, winning the Queen's favour was all Susanna had.

* * *

SINCE THEIR TIME in the tea house and seeing Alex talk to Miss Hampton, Madeline had tried to bring it up to Alex but was uncomfortable. She wondered why she saw Miss Hampton there. It didn't seem like a coincidence. What would Miss Hampton be doing in Warwickshire?

Seeing Miss Hampton made Madeline think a lot about the odd ends she had found around Warwick Castle. She began to questioned if the hairpiece she had found on the bedroom floor and the hand fan she saw by the dining room table belonged to Miss Hampton.

She sighed, feeling ashamed for questioning if Alex was secretly seeing Miss Hampton. If he was, it would also explain the handkerchief she had found in her bedroom closet at Frogmore weeks earlier. She never had figured out who it belonged to.

All this time she had thought that the Duke of Axford was lurking about Frogmore, but maybe it had been Miss Hampton all along. Madeline was brought out of her reverie as Alex walked into the drawing room.

"Hello, dolcezza," he said and kissed her on the forehead.

"How was the meeting?" she asked.

"Spanish ships have been spotted. In a few short days, they'll be in Windsor or London."

He sighed as he slumped onto the couch next to her.

"Are the men prepared?" she asked biting her lip.

"As prepared as they can be until reinforcements come. The plans will change depending on how the Spanish attack."

Madeline nodded, feeling horrible. Though the country was about to be attacked, all she could think about was Miss Hampton. She needed to stop thinking about it and confront Alex. She breathed unsteadily, "Um, the other day outside the tea house I saw Miss Hampton ... do you know what she is doing in town?"

"Miss Hampton?" he said looking away.

"Yes, you were speaking to her."

He raised his brows, looking confused, "I was speaking to someone, but it wasn't Miss Hampton. I imagine she's at court in Windsor or London now."

"That wasn't Miss Hampton?" Madeline asked in disbelief.

"No, we do have spies and messengers in town. The lady I was speaking to was relaying a message to me."

"What was it?"

"The time and place when I'll be meeting Sir Ashton next."

"That woman looked like she could be her twin," Madeline said suspiciously.

His lips curved. "Hardly."

They sat in silence, she hated to think that he would lie to her. As long as she had known him, he'd never done anything to make her feel that she couldn't trust him. She tried to change the subject.

"How many spies and messengers are in town?" she asked.

"There are several," he said as he pulled her closely to him. She rested her head on his hard chest.

"How much do they know? Do they know where we are staying?"

"Yes. But each of them only knows so much. They don't all know details of where we would go if Warwick were attacked."

"Do any of them know I'm pregnant?" she asked, concerned.

"You are showing a little you know," he said rubbing her belly. "I'm sure a few of them may have suspicions if they've seen you. If Sir Ashton had to tell them, they would know not to speak of it."

"Do you think anyone in town recognizes you?"

"Most of the subjects have never seen you or me closely. I've never stayed in Warwick, so I doubt it."

"You know, if we have spies, I'm sure the Spanish do, too," she said uneasily.

"I know. We've identified most of them. Most are in Windsor and some are around London."

"But none are here?" she asked surprised.

"No, we don't believe so."

He didn't like having these kinds of conversations with her. He knew that she had never considered that Spanish spies were already in Windsor until this moment. They had been for weeks before they had left. They were everywhere in the country. He could see the fear on her face, he was beginning to wish he hadn't said anything.

"Do you think that Spanish spies have found out that I'm pregnant?" she asked, her her mind wandering to the mysterious handkerchiefs and hand fan she had found.

"Madeline, don't worry. I'm sure no one knows," he said reassuringly.

She bit her lip. "Alex, I think I have something to tell you."

Madeline proceeded to tell Alex about the hand fan and handkerchiefs she had found at the castle and Frogmore. He sat in thought for a moment before finally speaking.

"If there were a spy, indeed we would have been attacked by now. Any spy that was able to come into the castle would have killed me. It's possible that the items belong to one of the servants."

"What if it doesn't? The intruder would know both our location and the fact that I'm pregnant."

He could see the fear on her face and wanted to calm her, "The information that you, the Queen, is pregnant would only be known by those we have told, unless you believe someone you've told would divulge that information."

"There is that possibility," she said with a pained expression.

He shook his head. "I know Doctor Sheffield and Sir Ashton haven't told anyone. Greg may have told Sofia, but that news isn't something they would share since they are trying not to draw attention to themselves. Why? Do you think one of the ladies may have said something?"

She paused, "I told them not to, of course. I don't think Marie or Martha would."

"And Sissy?"

"I honestly haven't seen much of her recently," she admitted. "She keeps heading out to London to visit a friend."

He held his breath, trying not to react. If he grew fearful, she would worry even more, "Do you know anything about her friend?" he said remaining calm.

"Not really," she sighed. "Sissy has told me that she really wants to come to a court party to meet me."

He bit his lip and closed his eyes, "Madeline, be honest. Do you think Sissy said something to this girl?"

"It's possible," she said, her voice cracking. "Sissy may have told her thinking she could trust her. Oh god." Madeline began to cry realizing that Sissy's friend could be a Spanish spy.

"We could send someone to speak to this friend," Alex said. "If we did it today-"

"There's no need for that." Deep down Madeline already knew, and so did he. He held her, rocking her gently.

Sissy was naïve and trusted others too quickly. As Madeline wept, she thought of all the times Lady Watson duped Sissy. One occasion specifically stood out. For months, Lady Watson would give Sissy a grocery list and some money and order her to go to town to get food. Each time Lady Watson would intentionally give her less money than what she needed. It left Sissy with a choice; buy the rest of the list with her own money, or go home and be whipped for not getting all the items on the list. Fearing the pain, she always bought the rest of the items. When she came back to Watson Manor, she would bring receipts, but Lady Watson never paid her back. Lady Watson would tell Sissy she'd give it back in her weekly pay. Sissy believed she would for some time. Then Madeline pointed out that she was the only person sent to town who got short changed.

"Her friend's name is Delilah," Madeline said.

"Delilah? That couldn't be her real name? Or is it a joke?" Alex said furrowing his brow.

"Why?"

"It's a biblical name. Ever heard the story of Samson and Delilah?"

"Sorry your Majesty," she smiled faintly, "my father wasn't very religious and Lady Watson never had many books. The ones she did have were about tea etiquette and how to run a household of servants."

"Do you know much about the Bible?" he asked.

"I was given a testament by Mr. Sheffield when I was younger. I read it."

Curiosity struck him. It was strange that with no formal education Madeline had learned to read.

"How is it you learned to read? I mean, you served afternoon tea and I thought you might know some words, but you've read the gospels? How did you learn?"

"Tsk. That's the only favour my father ever did for me. He took me to the theatre and the actors would act out the play onstage and I would follow a copy of the script. Eventually, my father had me study lines with him."

"Ah," he nodded. "We will have to send word to Sir Ashton to find Delilah and question her then."

"So who is Delilah? What's in a name?" Madeline asked intrigued.

"It's the name of a woman who betrayed a man named Samson. It's a beautiful name but because of the story, not many people name their daughters Delilah."

"Are we going to have to leave Warwick?"

"Possibly. I'll talk to Sir Ashton about all this. But don't worry, everything will be all right."

He took her into his arms and guided her head to his chest, again. She loved when he did this; let her sleep to the sound of his heart beating in his chest. The rhythmic sound was peaceful and she closed her eyes, feeling safe.

He stared up at the ceiling and slowly exhaled. This wasn't good. He had no idea who Delilah was, nor did he have time to find out. He didn't want to scare Madeline or make her feel guilty, but they could no longer stay in Warwickshire. He had to hide her somewhere else. Worst of all, they needed to be separated.

DEPARTURE

*S*tanding next to the ships' bow, Carlos inhaled the sea air. They had landed on the coast of England several miles from the small town of Brighton. The beach was pleasant and magnificent; it went on for miles, and the sand was soft with hardly any pebbles in it. England will be a beautiful addition to the Spanish Empire, he thought haughtily. He heard the seagulls squawking above him but nothing else. Taking the beachfront of the countryside was hardly an effort. The people of Brighton saw the ships and quickly went into their homes. He had seen some townspeople lighting a pyre as they came to shore; King Alexander would soon receive word that they had arrived. But that didn't matter. The English knew they were coming, but without many men, there wouldn't be a counter-attack.

Carlos held his binoculars up and surveyed the rolling hills of the English countryside. It was clear. Not a single man could be seen for miles. He doubted that there would be. The King probably had his men stationed closest to his own location for protection.

"What orders would you like me to give the men, your Highness?" Señor Menendo asked in his native tongue, bowing his head.

"I don't think we have much to be concerned with here," Carlos responded. "We'll sleep on the ships and beaches tonight. I don't want the men entering Windsor tired. Tomorrow, we'll take the horses from Brighton and any others we find on our way to Windsor. I doubt these peasant folks will have much to say. You might as well fly the flag now. Father can head to Edinburgh and kill Sir Gregory."

"How many men to guard the ships?" Señor Menendo continued.

Carlos chuckled. "Most of the men will come with me. No Englishman is going to take these ships when their King is about to be attacked. Besides, where would they take them? London? We won't be needing many men for the task. Twenty should be enough."

Señor Menendo nodded, "I'll see to it, your Highness. I'll find some men that are reliable."

"There's no need for that, really. Just grab any of them. If they are under attack, they can use the canons on the ships. As I said, those ships are useless to the English anyway."

"But we will need them to send the men back to Spain, won't we your Highness?" Señor Menendo said cocking his head to the side.

"When we are finished with England, this will be Spain. Part of the Spanish Empire."

Señor Menendo smirked, "True."

* * *

"I THOUGHT it would be a nice getaway for the both of us," Alex grinned as he and Madeline rode inside a coach. "I know you're worried about that Delilah character. But I talked to Sir Ashton this morning, and we've got it all figured out."

She smiled faintly, hearing the clip-clops of the horse and the wheels turning upon the cobblestone streets.

"So where are you taking me?" she asked softly.

He grinned, "Oh, there's a spa here in town called the Royal Pump Rooms. It just opened and has been very popular. Being called the Royal Pump Rooms, I thought it was fitting we go."

She blushed, "Is it like the one in Bath?"

"Well, I've reserved the place just for us for the day if that's what you mean."

She nodded, knowingly.

"They have different types of baths too. Salt baths, mud baths, and an herbal infused one. There are also several treatments you can have done on your skin. I figured it would be nice to have a little fun. I mean, we've both been under lots of stress," he winked.

When they arrived, Madeline went to the women's changing room and then headed to the shower, thinking that Alex would join her for some fun, but he never came.

She sat down on a wood stool and began to wash with a sponge and surveyed the room. When she had gone to the ancient spa in Bath, she had felt like she was living in a different time; the stone and the decor was from another time or renovated to look like ancient Greece. The Royal Pump Rooms was European styled, the tiling done around the shower room was intricate and colourful.

She scrubbed her body once and soon found herself doing it again getting between her toes and behind her ears. She had expected Alex to come in by now and seduce her, but he hadn't. She continued to wash, waiting, but she was beginning to grow impatient. *Maybe he is in his shower room waiting for me?*

She threw down her sponge, turned off the water, and went into the next room. It was a huge square room filled with several baths and pools of water. There were windows at the tops of the walls, letting some sunlight into the room. Despite the humidity, she could smell a hint of lavender and assumed that one of the pools was infused with the scent.

"Took you long enough," he said, his head just above the water in one of the hot, steaming pools.

"I thought you would have come to escort me in," she teased, "you came into the ladies' showers last time."

"Ah, so you thought I'd be up to my old tricks again?" he grinned.

"Usually, you are."

Their tryst in the tea house had made her eager to have him again, even though she wasn't feeling confident about how she looked naked nowadays. She wasn't fond of looking at her swollen feet and her round belly.

"Do you like it, dolcezza?" he asked as he climbed up some stairs and out of the hot pool, revealing more of his body with each step.

"Like what?" she said staring at his chiseled abs.

"The spa."

"It's lovely. Why don't we go into this tub?" she asked, walking over to another hot tub with swirls of steam rising above its water. The tub itself was encased in planks of wood. It looked to be the hottest one in the room.

"Ah, ah, ah," he said holding up his hand. "You really haven't been reading much about pregnancy, have you?"

"Why? What's wrong with me taking a bath?"

He smiled, "You can take a bath in warm water, but not scorching hot like that."

"Was this a test to see how much I know about being pregnant?" she asked, tilting her head.

"No. Even if you had read it, there's always the chance you'd forgotten," he said as he cupped her face and gave her a kiss on her temple.

"Can I go in cold water?"

"Yes."

"Probably better for me, anyway. I've been feeling so hot lately."

They walked together to a very small tub made of stone, it was above the ground like the wooden tub, but there were small steep steps to climb to get in.

"I'm not so sure that's safe," she said wearily.

"I'll walk behind you," he offered, "just be sure to hold the rail."

She went up the steps, him following immediately behind her. Once she reached the top, she looked down at some steps submerged in water.

"What if I slip?" she asked fearfully.

"Sit on your bottom on the step you are on. I'll get into the tub and help you in."

She took his hand and lowered herself down onto the step. He turned and went back down the steps and attempted to climb over the side of the tub to get in. He looked awkward doing it, and she giggled as she watched him try to straddle the edge of the tub.

"Alex, you are treating the side of this tub as if it were a horse!"

"Better that than you slipping and falling."

As he said this, he fell in, his whole body submerged in the cool water before he resurfaced.

"Are you all right?" she asked, feeling terrible that she had laughed.

"I'm fine," he said, slicking his thick black hair with his hands. He went to the top of the steps and helped her into the tub.

She placed her foot on the first step, sinking her skin into the water. It was nice and cool, and she continued down the steps with him. Once she was inside the tub, Alex settled her onto one of the seats.

"Relaxing?" he asked.

"It feels amazing," she said, a cool tingling sensation dancing on her skin. He sat next to her, enjoying the extreme from his hot skin to the cold bath. He sighed and began to slowly weave through the tresses of her hair. "You know, I've never had the privilege of getting away from court life like this," he said. "I've never been made this unavailable to my court and advisors."

"And how do you like it?" she asked, curious of what his answer would be.

"It's not what I thought it would be," he said thoughtfully, "I always thought that being a noble would be much more casual. I thought some of the servants at the castle would be friendlier and easier to talk to, but they are not. I feel like some of them resent me. Why is that?"

Madeline laughed, "Some servants do resent their masters. I mean, think about it; anyone of noble privilege didn't work hard to get to where they are, they got handed the world, and they look down on everyone else."

"I'm not looking down on any of them," he said, confused.

"I know. But as far as servants are concerned, you having them polish the dirt off your shoes and lay out your clothes is snobby."

He wrapped his arm around her, "Why is it so different with

royalty? One of the servants rolled his eyes this morning when I requested him to get another pair of shoes from the closet. I've asked my valets that plenty of times without them thinking anything of it."

She lay her head on his chest, "People respect royalty. Being royal has a lot of responsibility. It's a stressful place to be in; you have to be sure that your people are happy. When you're a noble you don't have that kind of pressure; you're born into privilege and responsible for no one but yourself. Lady Watson is one of the most self-absorbed people I've ever met."

A naughty smile grew on his face, "What about Princess Sofia? She certainly had some firm opinions about privilege."

"Her actions didn't say that, though," Madeline observed thoughtfully. " When I think about all the excursions the four of us went on, whenever Greg said a joke, she would usually giggle and blush."

"Yes, I noticed that, too. I think it was difficult for her to recognize her feelings for him at first. It must have been scary when you have a father like King Fernando."

Alex was right. Though the two of them had their trysts, their fear of being caught was for the sake of his title and what was expected of him. There would be no one to lecture them, and their fear was that Alex would lose the respect of his peers, thereby making Bathory's chances of usurping the throne far greater. Sofia, on the other hand, had her father and all of Spain to answer to. Marriage to Greg offered the country no political gain. Madeline shuddered at the thought of what kind of confrontation Sofia would have with her father in due course.

Alex noted her shivering, "Are you cold?"

"No, I was just thinking of how awful it would be to be a princess."

Alex nodded, "Strange with all the fairytales written of princesses that the reality of being one is quite scary. All princesses are pawns to their fathers."

"And queens?"

"Last I checked, queens were the most powerful players on the chessboard," he said as he stood up. "I'm not sure about you, but I'm getting a little cold myself. I think I'll take another dip in the hot bath." He gave her a soft peck on the cheek then climbed up the stairs.

She watched him as he got out, beads of water sliding down his skin. She missed the heat of that body. Alex was becoming more aware of her need for space. He didn't try to initiate too much; he knew she was often tired. But there were times like these, where she'd watch him in his masculine perfection and desire just a sip, a taste of what she knew to be heavenly.

He turned, "Do you plan to stay, or would you like some help out?"

"I'll get out of this one now," she rose, and he went back to take her hand. Descending down the stairs, she stumbled and fell into him, her hand slipping along his abs and lower.

Alex stabled her quickly to her feet, but her hand was immovable.

"Do you want.. ?" he asked, almost hesitantly.

She said nothing and dropped her hand, slightly embarrassed. She couldn't imagine him wanting the sight of her. But his words only made her cool skin become flush. He gazed down at her glowing skin. Light shone off her delicate curves, and the edges of her figure were illuminated. He sighed. Her beauty could drive a man to madness.

"Perhaps we should have a seat on the bench," he offered.

He assisted her to a large nearby bench, and she lowered herself onto the seat. He sat next to her and grazed the slope of her back, settling his hand on the small dimples between her hips. "How have you been feeling, dolcezza?"

She sighed heavily, "I've been well."

He softly kissed her shoulder and her neck, "Not tired?"

"No."

She felt the familiar heat that emanated from her and warmed her limbs. Using his weight, he guided her back onto the bench, his mouth dancing across her clavicle. She loved his attention, but she doubted her body could give him much pleasure.

There was a tentative expression on her face.

"What are you thinking?" he asked, his hand sliding across her abdomen down to the crevice of her thigh.

"Just…just… if I can…" she trailed off. His hand. His fingers. She gasped. She wanted him to touch her and much more. But it wasn't fitting for a woman to want a man at this point in her pregnancy. She was more than showing now, and desires like hers were seen as unholy.

"I want to," she shamefully admitted, her eyes darting from his. "But I'm not sure...such thoughts might be seen as wicked."

He chuckled, "Don't forget, dolcezza, I'm a king. Kings are thought to be ordained by God himself."

She smiled.

"Things may be a bit different now, but we can adjust," he promised. "Let me know what feels right."

She sighed, her delicate flesh giving way to him, his touch gentle. She closed her eyes, "That...feels...." Her moans and mutters answered what felt right, and he keenly obliged her, using every part of his being to pleasure her. The heat of it was disorienting, but through the fog, she felt his rough cheek bristle against her thigh, then his mouth consumed her. Her legs quivered like a leaf moments away from falling from a tree branch.

"Alex," she said his name breathily. A cry echoed through the chamber, and he released her.

Inflamed by her sounds and the sight of her, he kneeled on the bench, taking her legs into his arms, his hands softly massaging her thighs. Her eyes shot open, the brush of his manhood alerting her.

"I thought perhaps you wouldn't want to," she said, surprised.

"You must be joking," he said, the back on his hand caressing her belly, her stomach, then her face. His thumb pressed against her bottom lip, "So precious. So beautiful...this bump says you're mine alone."

His words rendered her speechless. He broke through her insecurities, her uncertainty of her shape, and sealed his lips to hers. They quenched their thirst for each other in kisses, inhaling the scent of lavender about them, and her muscles drew him in.

The tightness and warmth enclosed around him, cradling him as he gently rocked forward. The sensation was heightened, and it took every inch of his being to control the urge to take her quickly. Every stroke produced a murmur, and he knew it wouldn't take much to bring her to bliss She pierced his biceps, her lips wrangling his. A flurry of short gasps and cries surround them as wave after wave came crashing through her. His body called for him to relent and pour himself into her, but he held firmly to the bench beneath them, determined to satiate her. There was nothing more he desired in the world.

She became breathless and her eyes welled, unable to keep up with the onslaught. At last, he abated, a frisson pulsing through his body as she watched the features of his face contort to pleasure. She held his face, lowering it to hers for one final kiss.

He held himself inside her for some time, showering her skin with soft caresses and kisses. In her rapturous fog, she heard him whisper, "These past few weeks, I've been aching to have you. I don't think I've ever been more attracted to you than I am now." She smiled, glad he had the courage to convince her to take the plunge.

Later, they cuddled in one of the lukewarm herbal baths, breathing in the heavenly scent, "This has been absolutely lovely," she said smiling as she nuzzled to his chest, "I'm glad we did it. But I think my skin is starting to look like a prune."

"Well, we've been here for some time," he said, combing her hair through his fingers.

"Yes, as much as I don't want this to end, we should get going."

"Why don't you get a treatment?" he suggested, his hand stroking hers.

She smiled, "I think I already got my treatment. Besides, I'm too pregnant to get a massage."

"Oh no. If anyone's giving you a massage, it will be me," he said, rubbing her shoulders. "But if you want to take advantage of the other kind of services here, they have an ancient Egyptian facial. All the noblewomen have raved about it for years."

"What will you do?"

"I'll get dressed and wait for you."

"You don't mind?"

"Not at all." He scooped her up in his arms and carried her back to the changing room. He got dressed and gave her a soft kiss on the lips.

"See you soon," he nuzzled his nose into her neck, and patted her tummy, "I love you both." He pecked her cheek and walked out.

She got ready and headed out the change room. As she walked out, a lady approached her.

"Hello, my Lady, my name is Miss Christie. Your husband was telling me that you wanted an Ancient Egyptian facial?'

"Yes, um where did he go?"

"He's just waiting in the lobby, Ma'am. Come this way, we do our facials over here."

The room she led her to had several windows revealing a picturesque garden outside. There were several chaises lounges about the room. Each had one arm on one side that sat higher than the other. She could hear some birds chirping outside. She grinned, it would be great to take her friends here sometime.

"Just sit here, Ma'am," Miss Christie said touching one of the chaises.

Madeline lay down, her back stretching across the high arm.

"Just put your head back Ma'am," Miss Christie said as she placed a white towel behind her head.

Madeline closed her eyes, leaning her head back.

"So, uh, what exactly is in the mask?" Madeline asked trying to make a little conversation.

"Oh," said Miss Christie, somewhat surprised, her wealthy clients usually had no more than two words to say to her. "There's Greek yogurt, honey, and some sandalwood oil. But before we start, would you like some tea or water?"

"Hm. Water would be nice."

"We have cucumber or lemon. Which do you prefer?"

"Cucumber, please."

She could hear Miss Christie pour a glass and set it on a small table next to her. She drank as she sat on the chaise, listening to Miss Christie preparing the ingredients in a glass bowl, the spoon tapping the sides. She took a sip of the water and set it back on the table.

"I know you were just in the baths Ma'am, but I'm going to start today with putting a warm cloth on your face."

Madeline tilted her head upwards and Miss Christie wrapped her face with the cloth. She sat there under the warmth of the cloth, listening to Miss Christie move about the room, preparing the treatment as the birds chirped outside. It was heaven, intimacy with the man she loved and a facial. Soon Miss Christie took off the cloth.

"First, I'm going to cleanse your skin with an exfoliating tonic. They didn't use this in Egypt, but it is homemade from Provence, France."

Madeline grinned. Compared to a year and a half ago, her life had changed drastically. There was a time she was applying French crèmes and cosmetics on Princess Sofia and Lady Watson. But Lady Watson always wanted Madeline to be stingy with the product. When it came from France, it was expensive and Lady Watson wanted it to last.

She could feel a cool tingle as Miss Christie slathered it onto her face with a brush. The bristles were soft and tickled a little. Once the tonic was applied, Miss Christie took a warm, wet sponge and began buffing her skin in a circular motion, removing the product. It smelled fantastic. It reminded her of the first time she smelled rosewater in Alex's hair.

"What is in the tonic you're using?" she asked.

"It's a mixture of different essential oils."

"It smells lovely. Is it possible to buy some?"

"Well, I don't know Ma'am, I'll have to ask. We don't usually sell it. I'm not sure how much it would be."

Afterwards, there was another tonic, then finally the mask. It was relaxing. Madeline could feel her baby rhythmically kick her stomach. She rubbed her belly in response.

Miss Christie took another warm towel and as she wiped the Egyptian mixture off, she explained more about it. "This mixture has been used for centuries. The sandalwood oil isn't easy to get, but it's worth it. It evens out the tone of your skin and leaves it glowing." When the treatment was finished, Miss Christie sprayed her face with a soft mist. "If you'd like we could do a makeup application, Ma'am."

The idea was enticing, but Madeline didn't want to keep Alex waiting too long. "That should be fine," Madeline said. "Could you find out if I could buy what you used today?"

"Certainly. I'll escort you to the lobby, and then I'll find out."

As they descended down the staircase, Madeline looked about for Alex. But there was only one man, Sir Ashton. She gave him a puzzled expression, her eyes shifting about. Sir Ashton bowed, "No need to worry my, uh, Lady, your husband was just given word of a meeting."

"Without telling me or saying goodbye?" she said disappointedly.

Miss Christie looked uncomfortable, "I'll go see if I can get you those bottles."

"No need," Madeline said. "I'll come back for them another time."

Miss Christie curtsied and left the lobby.

"Ashton," Madeline began firmly, "Where is my husband? It isn't like him to leave me without telling me."

"Come outside to the carriage," he said, then lowered his voice to a whisper, "it wouldn't be wise to discuss personal matters here."

They made a quick exit and Sir Ashton helped her into the carriage outside. The coachmen took off as soon as he closed the carriage door.

"What's going on?" asked Madeline mystified.

"I'm sorry your Majesty, we've just received word that the Spanish are on the coast near Brighton. They are headed this way."

"Where is Alex?" she said her eyes widening.

"He has left to attend to matters concerning the situation."

"Make it plain," Madeline said sternly, "what is he doing?"

"His Majesty has given me orders to take you to a new location."

"Will he be there when we arrive?"

"No."

"Where did he go?" she said frustration in her voice. But she already knew. He was heading back to Windsor to fight.

* * *

Alex stared out into the English countryside. The scenery passing him quickly, the driver speeding down the dirt paths as fast as the horses could take them. The blonde woman sitting across from him staring at him wantonly, "Was it hard to get away?" she asked.

He sighed, "It was unexpected, so it wasn't easy, Miss Hampton. How is your godfather? Is he enjoying his newly awarded freedom?"

She looked out the window, "I haven't seen him. I think he's left the country."

"I know you well enough to know when you're lying to me," he said shortly.

"I'm really not sure where he is," she said as she began to play with strands of her blonde hair.

"If you see him, tell him I can't spare him if he's caught. If he stays here in England, he's playing with fire. I mean, there are 'wanted' signs all about the towns."

"Does the Queen know he's escaped?"

Alex gave a dark look, "I've tried to tell her. But I don't think now is the time."

She stopped playing with her hair, "What are you going to tell her if someone else tells her?"

He buried his face in his hands, "I guess I'll have to think up another excuse."

"Ah, so you've been telling her lots of lies?" she said brusquely. "That's not surprising."

"Madeline saw you the other day at the tea shop. What was I supposed to do?"

She pursed her lips.

OWNER OF THE HOUSE

*O*ver the past couple of days, Susanna Bathory had been flitting about Madrid Palace, trying to be friendly to Queen Isabelle, visiting nobles, and being kinder to the ladies in waiting. She had taken to pretending to learn Spanish, asking others how to pronounce words and saying short broken sentences. It was unlikely that it would help her situation, but she felt she had to try. At this point, she was unsure of her fate. She was scared. The outcome of the war with Britain didn't matter; she would be forced to be a broken woman like Queen Isabelle or forced into exile by the Spanish people. If the Spanish lost the war, they wouldn't want to house an English woman.

She was beginning to have regrets. Her mind began to question things she never had before. She didn't agree with how Alex ruled his kingdom; his ignorance of privilege and desire to encourage an educated middle-class repulsed her. Sir Ashton Giles, a man that was once a slave was his closest advisor and like a father to him. Their relationship was strange to her. Greg Umbridge, most likely the rudest commoner in England, was his best friend. Then there was the fact that Alex had hopelessly fallen in love with his servant, married her, and made her the Queen of England.

Not much of what Alex did made any sense to her. But many things her father Lord Bathory did, didn't make much sense either.

Lord Bathory had the ambition to be a king, but no experience. He had never proved himself to have leadership skills though he had been given plenty of opportunities to do so. After King Charles had Alex, he grew bitter; losing his place in line to the throne was all he thought about. He was full of resentment. For years, he made snide comments during the House of Lords meetings, and soon his loyalty to King Charles was put into question. That's when he lost his title as Prince.

Despite losing his royal title, her father didn't stop. Nor did he try to make a political reputation that the people respected. Instead, he began plotting. Eventually, this led to the murder of King Charles, and though nothing was proven, he was still unable to secure the crown. Even as a boy, the people favoured Alex. By thirteen, Alex proved himself a leader during the Irish Uprisings, a hero and a legend overnight. If her father were wise, he wouldn't have targeted the royal family. He would have gained power through relationships. Or used all the wars England had been involved in to become a legend himself. But she now knew her father had been foolish; he had expected the crown to be handed to him without any effort. He expected this because of his belief in privilege.

Along with everything her father lost, Susanna kept losing too. Not only titles but the trust of other families at court. Some families did support her father and wanted an England for the privileged. But over time, that group dwindled.

Alex's philosophies and way of ruling were disagreeable to her. But there were several things she had to admit; Alex was an extraordinary ruler. Though she hated Greg Umbridge, she admired his bravery in his words to King Fernando. The contents of the letter were supposed to remain a secret, but what he did was so outrageous, she had heard nobles whispering about it at court. She couldn't help but crack a smile when they did. She doubted anyone humiliated King Fernando more than him.

When she thought of the things she had done in the past few months, she knew she was making the same mistakes her father had made. Plotting and seeking the crown he did not deserve never got her father anywhere. It had put her in a hole. She felt that there was no way out of this situation, and a part of her begrudged him for it. Since the men had voyaged to England, she had spent all her time thinking about what she could do to make things better for herself. Killing Carlos and Fernando seemed like the obvious solution, but deep down she knew her life wouldn't be much better. There was only one thing that she fancied thinking about any more. Señor Astucia. He had been at the castle every day, attending to some of Carlos's duties. He'd wink at her whenever they crossed paths. She wanted to play with him. But there was a problem with that too. If the court found out, she would lose their respect.

* * *

"McFADDEN, I need you to help me with this," Greg said, standing on a ladder, holding a red festoon. "I expected that Sam and Belle would be back by now, but I can't wait any longer. I've wanted to do this for a while now."

Greg had been busy decorating the Great Gallery, trying to prepare for a fun filled evening, a Spanish themed party for Sofia. He had gone to some lengths to find girls that could flamenco dance and someone to cook traditional Spanish tapas and drinks.

McFadden raised his brow, "Why don'tcha stop being such a cheap arse? Get some folks in 'ere get them to decorate your party." He pulled out a flask from his belt and took a swig.

"Stop that," Greg said, descending the ladder and pulling the flask away. "I need you to help me with all of this."

"Where is tha' Lady anyway?"

"I sent her out for the afternoon," Greg said cheerfully.

"Where did ya send her to? She could 'ave helped us."

"I had some of the noble ladies in town take her shopping. Besides, this is supposed to be a surprise for her."

McFadden looked around the room, "Ya' don't got much going for ya, lad. Yer decorating is shat."

Greg observed the room glumly. He knew McFadden was right. If he were at Buckingham Palace or Windsor putting this together would have been much easier. He had never been so grateful for the help at both residences, he began to feel guilty for all the times he trashed the rooms in the castle. It was a lesson in humility, but it couldn't have come at a worse time. He wanted the party to be perfect for Sofia.

He was unsure of everything he had planned so far. When he and Alex took lessons together languages wasn't his favourite. He could scarcely remember much of the Spanish language or culture. There were only two subjects he did well in, art and music. He had no idea if his decor celebrated the Spanish culture. There were some red festoons hanging on the walls, but between them hung a bunch of mythical paintings of Scottish lore and kings. It didn't feel very Spanish.

There was also another problem. Decorating the Great Gallery was going to take several days. He needed to think up other ideas to keep Sofia busy. He also needed to keep her away from entering the room.

"These pictures are crap with ya theme laddie," said McFadden taking another swig from his flask. "Looks like facking Christmas."

He hated to admit it, but McFadden was right. The red festoons placed against the pale green walls looked festive. There was also the gold and white painted crown moulding on the ceiling.

"You're right, mate. It looks like a Scottish Christmas with a bunch of kings," Greg said feeling defeated.

"If tha walls were yello' it'd be like a Spanish flag."

It gave Greg and idea, "Get some yellow material. We'll cover these walls and paintings with the yellow material."

"That'd be crap!" McFadden laughed. "A bunch of material hanging from all tha walls. If you be doin' tha', you might as well throw the party in a tent."

"While you hang all the yellow material, I'm going to paint a few masterpieces," said Greg encouraged by his vision.

"Wha? Does tha' mean I gotta hang it on me own?"

"Yes, McFadden. Get lazy on me and I'll send you back to Alex."

"Fine, ya bastard. But where ya gonna find all the canvas for tha paintin's?"

"I'll find something."

McFadden looked at him sympathetically. There was nothing in Holyrood House but the walls themselves to paint. He was beginning to sense that what Greg had planned was no ordinary party. He had something special planned for Sofia. It had to be perfect.

"Lemme go to town lad," he said gently, "see if I can get some help."

"Really? How do I know you're not just trying to get out of helping me?"

He put his hand on his shoulder, "You can count on me, lad."

As he turned to leave, something told Greg he could.

* * *

MADELINE PACED about the foyer of a small residence Sir Ashton had taken her to. It was a lovely home, but she doubted it was owned by Lord Davis. It had a large mahogany staircase that winded up several stories to a dome window in the ceiling.

"Where are we?" Madeline asked angrily. She couldn't believe Alex had ordered this separation. But every question she had asked so far Sir Ashton had avoided giving answers, and she knew it was on Alex's orders.

"You can tell me who owns this place, Sir Ashton," she demanded.

"I'm sorry your Majesty, I really am. The King told me to take you here and tell you that you will stay here until the war is over. But that is the only thing I could tell you."

"So he's gone back to Windsor?" she said trying to read the expression on his face.

He didn't confirm her suspicions.

"The fact that you won't answer is a 'yes,'" she concluded. "What is he doing in Windsor? They are about to attack there. It's him that they will try to kill."

"You must understand, his Majesty is truly a man of honour," he said in a sympathetic tone. "He would fight for his country like any other English soldier."

"What about his family? He does realize he has one, doesn't he?" she said her eyes welling up. She knew it was a selfish thought, but she had never been more livid with Alex. If something happened to him, she wasn't sure what she would do.

"Lord Walsh is here to look after you," said Sir Ashton trying not to cave in to her emotion.

She rolled her eyes, "You can't be serious," she said her voice cracking.

He walked past her stiffly, trying to dismiss her, "Lord Walsh is quite capable, I assure you.'

"Who's home is this?"

"Your Majesty, you're stressed," he said turning to her. "I think it's time you take a nap."

"Excuse me? Like I could sleep at a time like this!"

"His Majesty asked me to make sure that you got some rest. He knew you would be troubled by all of this. You must understand that getting your rest is what's best for you now. You are in a delicate condition."

She had heard that repeatedly from everyone the past few months. The word 'delicate' was annoying her. She sat down on a bench next to the staircase and crossed her arms, pouting.

"I'm not going to sleep," she said shrewdly. "Where is Lord Walsh?"

"He is here."

"Send him to me."

Sir Ashton came back with him several minutes later. Lord Walsh bowed to her, "Your Majesty, I'm glad you were able to make it here safely. You-"

"Lord Walsh," she interrupted, getting up from the bench. "Who's residence is this?"

"Very cunning your Majesty," Lord Walsh said unenthused, "but King Alex has given me the same orders as Sir Ashton."

"Does it belong to the Hampton family!?" she blasted.

Neither of them answered. There was a long uncomfortable silence and Madeline found them unreadable.

"I must be going, I have other duties to attend to," said Sir Ashton. He walked out the front door, leaving the two of them alone. Madeline turned on Lord Walsh, "Are you the only person here?"

"Yes."

"I'm not tired, but I am hungry. Could you make me something?"

"Yes, let's go to the kitchen," Lord Walsh offered.

"Actually, I'm kind of tired, I think I will take a nap."

A puzzled expression came over his face. Her sudden change of attitude was strange. But he had always heard that pregnant women could be moody. He left the room to go to the kitchen.

Madeline looked up at the dome window. Somewhere up that staircase was evidence of the owner of this home. She was going to find out who that owner was.

MY DOLL

King Fernando smiled as they sailed by Brighton. Looking through his telescope, he could see several flags hung high on the ships' masts. He didn't think his son would have any problems getting to Windsor. *It is certain victory. As soon as I defeat Edinburgh, torture and kill Greg Umbridge, I could head to London to secure the capital.* He placed his hands on his hips with a cocky grin. *Once we take England, we will own the seas too. My son will rule over one of the largest empires in history.* He closed his telescope and tossed it to one of the crewmen.

After they had taken England, there would be a few matters that needed to be dealt with. Susanna was one. He could have her killed immediately after the defeat. He and Carlos toyed with having the ship she would take back to London sink. But Carlos and Fernando agreed that it might be too suspicious, and he didn't want to anger the English subjects and possibly start a rebellion.

Fernando knew that his son wasn't content with his English wife, but to secure the English throne, Carlos would have to produce an heir with Susanna. Carlos hated this, but a death during childbirth sounded plausible. The English subjects would have sympathy for Carlos and support the new heir.

Another matter that would have to be taken care of was Sofia. She had weighed heavily on Fernando's mind since he had received the letter from Greg Umbridge. So much of Sofia's fate depended on how much of that letter was true. He questioned how he would ever get the truth of her relationship with Greg. If she had relations, she would most likely lie about it. Over the years in Madrid, there were several times Sofia had lied to protect herself or her mother. Sometimes, even after hours of questioning, Sofia would still insist on the lie she had initially told him. There was no tower with rats or birds he knew of in Edinburgh.

There was only one way he would know if she had fallen in love with the rogue. She would have to watch Greg's torture. If she was pleased, she had probably been taken prisoner and abused by him. But, if she screamed and cried, begging for it to stop, Fernando would want her to be tortured and killed along with him.

* * *

SUSANNA SAT in Sofia's drawing room eating lunch by herself. Most days, she would have eaten with the Queen. But she wasn't in the mood to spend time with anyone. She couldn't get her mind off what was happening in her life. She hadn't left her apartments all day. She was still in her bedclothes, her blonde curls askew about her head, she hadn't moved from the seat she sat in since she ate breakfast.

A young footman stood by the door observing her; he noticed that she hadn't said a word all morning. She just stared into nothingness, but it didn't worry him. He had seen the Queen and Sofia do this from time to time. He didn't quite understand it, but figured it must have been something women just did. Finally around noon, Susanna asked for lunch. But she didn't eat much then, either. She had taken a few small bites of the Spanish fritters that were served earlier and didn't touch her coffee. When lunch was brought in, it was several minutes before she stopped staring and put her spoon into the soup bowl. She had a couple spoonfuls before she accidentally dropped the spoon back into the bowl.

She sighed, resting her face on her fist. For days, she had been thinking up different solutions to whatever her future would be. But deep down, she knew, *There is nothing I could do to win the favour of the people.*

She hadn't heard anything about the progress of the Spanish in England. She had asked Queen Isabelle from time to time if she had heard anything. Usually, she would shrug and say messengers wouldn't come unless something of importance happened. But Susanna doubted that. She had heard things in the corridors of the palace such as Lords mentioning that Carlos had taken Brighton. It was then she realized that King Fernando didn't want his wife's involvement in these kinds of affairs. She and Isabelle would only be told what had happened when it was over.

Begrudgingly, she had tried to befriend some of the ladies in waiting. She imagined that they might have been updated by one of the Lords. But they feared Susanna and often when she entered a room, they would leave.

Then there was Señor Astucia. It was getting more frustrating thinking about him. She had planned on being with him as soon as Prince Carlos and King Fernando had left. But the fear of what might happen if she did, had gotten to her. She watched him from afar now. She knew she couldn't be alone with him. But, she had decided if he made any advances, she'd give in.

She took another spoonful of soup, as the footman nearby watched. She didn't know his name, but she hated his presence. Since the day she was caught in the Royal Armoury, she felt as though she was being watched. It wasn't every hour of the day. But for some unknown reason, a footman had been ordered to keep watch in the Royal Armoury and the drawing room in the apartments she was staying in.

It was obvious that Carlos had ordered them. A look of indignation came across her face. The footman in the Royal Armoury was there because he didn't want her to know about the battle plans or go to any meetings the Lords might have, but the one standing in the room with her now was there because Carlos didn't want her to be unfaithful. Certainly, she had given him reason to think she would be; she had been with quite a few men on the ship. But he was a hypocrite. He could play around with Esmeralda without consequence, but she had to be true to him. She threw her spoon, slapped her hand on the table, and scratched the wood with her fingernails, making marks. The footmen looked at her in shock. "Don't worry Princess, your Prince will return soon," he said in Spanish.

She gave him a look that could kill. "Leave," she said in English.

"Sorry," he continued in Spanish, "but Prince Carlos requested-"

"I don't care what he requested," she replied in fluent Spanish. "I ordered you to leave. He's not here. I am. If you don't do what I ask, I will torture you with any object I can find in this room until you do." Her eyes fell on the flame of a candle in front of her on the table. She sliced her finger through the flame then glared at him.

He stood shocked at her Spanish words but said nothing. He backed out of the room.

She stood up abruptly, knocking the chair beneath her to the floor. *It doesn't matter if Spain wins or loses this war. Either way, I'll have a miserable life. If that's the case, why the hell am I trying to please anybody? I can't believe I'm letting Carlos and Fernando control me from thousands of miles away.*

Then it hit her. A solution. An evil grin came upon her. She was surprised she had never thought of it before. If it was respect she needed, she had to have something of value. Something the people of Spain or King Fernando or Prince Carlos couldn't deny. She could get Arsenio to help her. He could be anywhere in the palace. She tapped her fingers to her lips. She was going to have to find him on her own if this was going to work. He was probably outside somewhere in the gardens having lunch or in the Royal Armoury. She looked down at her bedclothes. She needed to get changed and look her best.

She charged out of the room and into the bedchamber. As she entered, she stopped in surprise. Arsenio was there. Sitting on a red velvet chair, he casually pulled his finger through some gold fringes hanging on a red lampshade on a table next to him.

"I've been waiting for you, Susanna," he said softly.

Her cheeks dimpled, "I've been looking for you."

"Come here."

Normally, she'd never followed the orders of someone beneath her. Had he been anyone else, she would have put him in his place. But, she knew why he was there, and she'd didn't want to sour the mood. Not when they had both been desiring each other for weeks. Having sex with him right now was exactly what she wanted and needed to do. Though she looked like she just rolled out of bed, she walked over to him. Timidly, she sat on his lap, and he put his arms around her hips. She felt small in his embrace. He looked deeply into her blue eyes, "You remind me of a doll my sister had. The only blonde-haired doll she had." He put his thick fingers through her messy waves, tracing the back of her neck. Heat emanated to her core.

"Did you play with the doll?" she asked softly.

"I stole the doll," he grinned.

"What happened to her?"

"She's sitting on my lap," he teased. He grasped her hair between his fingers tightly, 'Kiss me.'

She entwined some fingers into his glossy black hair, her eyes filled with desire. She leaned toward him and pressed her mouth to his.

Pulling her closer, he moved his lips about hers with purpose. She closed her eyes, surrendering to the moment. But she knew that if she were to get pregnant with Arsenio's baby, he'd have to be agreeable to the circumstances. She pulled away, "Arsenio, I need something from you."

He stared at her through hooded eyes, "Believe me, the feeling is mutual."

She smiled slightly. "What do you think will come of me if Carlos comes back."

He went silent. He knew nothing good would come of Carlos' return. But he also doubted there would be a return. King Alexander wasn't someone to be trifled with. Arsenio had thought Fernando and Carlos insane to go on with their mission. His breath hitched, then he finally answered. "It's not that I don't have faith in my King, but I have my doubts that this will be a successful mission."

"So, you don't believe they will return home?"

"Fernando might," he admitted. "Carlos is too foolish and impulsive. If he returns, it'd be by some miracle."

Susanna was relieved by his words. She dug further, "If Fernando comes back, or not, what do you think will come of me?"

He paused. He couldn't imagine that Fernando would lend some compassion or consideration toward Susanna should he return. Seeing that she was of no use, he'd banish her from the castle unless she was the mother to an heir. Then it dawned on Arsenio what Susanna was asking of him. He looked into her large blue pools that pleaded with him.

"Should you be pregnant – with Carlos' child – I'd imagine King Fernando would keep you. If Carlos doesn't return, the King will need an heir."

Susanna nodded. Arsenio's hand grazed across the back laces of Susanna's stay, "Well then, I shall then consider myself a lucky man to be at service to you. But if we do this your Highness, you won't make any commands of me. When we do this, we do it my way. Understand? You're *my* dolly to play with."

SEARCH FOR EVIDENCE

*S*ir Ashton Giles looked up to Alex as he gaped out a castle window, watching the Spanish army invade the streets of Windsor.

Alex sighed, "You're sure the town has been evacuated?" he asked as he watched some Spaniards set flame to some of the buildings.

"Don't worry your Majesty, we sent out messengers before your arrival. They had a day to get their belongings and go to London."

"The walls are secured, too?"

"Yes. The crooked house is too."

"As well as all the other entrances to the tunnels?"

"The one in Frogmore was left unguarded."

Alex shrugged, "I suppose it doesn't matter."

"We've just received word that King Fernando has passed Brighton and is on his way to Edinburgh."

He smiled, "Excellent. Did Carlos leave many to guard his ships?"

"It appears not your Majesty. Just twenty men."

"Good. Our men in the Netherlands know of the plans then?"

"Yes, Lord Davis told me they are well prepared. When King Fernando passes London, they will chase after them."

"Hopefully, there will be enough ships to take them," Alex said screwing his lips together.

Sir Ashton patted his back, "It's a brilliant plan Alex, I'm sure all will go well."

"Where is Miss Hampton? She's not in the castle, is she?" he asked raising his brow. He had hoped he would not have to see her again.

"No, we managed to get her to a safe place," Ashton reassured him.

Alex paused, "How is Madeline?" Sir Ashton hesitated, opening his mouth to speak, but Alex stopped him. "She's angry with me, isn't she?" he said feeling a twinge of guilt.

"She's not happy, your Majesty."

He sighed, "Did she ask many questions?"

"Plenty. She wanted to know who owned the residence she's staying at."

"Please God, tell me you didn't say."

"Of course not, your Majesty. But don't forget, she is … resourceful."

Alex knew he was right. Madeline wouldn't waste time, she was a daring enough woman to try to look for answers, no matter what she was told.

"Please tell me you took out any evidence that might point to the owner."

"Yes, Lord Walsh and I searched every room top to bottom. It hasn't been visited in years, so there really wasn't much to take out."

He tapped the windowsill in front of him, looking at Windsor ablaze.

"You don't think she suspects anything about Miss Hampton?" he asked.

"No, I don't think she has thought much of it. Not since you told her that it wasn't her."

"I suppose we should get in our positions then. Carlos will soon be reaching our walls."

"Yes, your Majesty."

* * *

MADELINE WASTED no time in searching the house. She neglected to take a nap and began her hunt at the top of floor and worked her way down. The place was dusty. It felt as if it had been abandoned for years.

Every floor had five or six rooms. Most of the rooms on each floor had been emptied except for one; strangely, each floor had one room full of furniture, covered with sheets. The rooms on the first floor and the bedrooms she and Lord Walsh slept in on the third floor, were the only rooms that were set up for guests. She was on the second floor, in the room with all the sheet-covered furniture.

She hadn't found anything that would hint to whom the owner was. All the drawers, dressers, and tables were emptied. Every now and again she would find a chest, some of which were locked. Whenever that happened, she'd take a knife and screw off the hinges. A skill she acquired while living at the Watsons.

Most times she couldn't find anything in the chests. Just old newspapers and books. Both English and French. Did Miss Hampton have French lineage? Something told her the home belonged to the Hampton family. *Why else wouldn't they tell me?*

She was in the middle of breaking into another old chest when she could hear Lord Walsh on the stairs, each step creaking as he ascended.

"Your Majesty," he called out in the politest tone.

She quickly hid under some sheets. Then she stopped and uncovered herself. She wasn't a servant girl stealing any more. She was a Queen snooping, and he couldn't order her to stop.

She stood up, "I'm in here, Lord Walsh," she called.

He entered the room and bowed, "What are you doing here?"

"Nothing that concerns you," she said quickly. "Why? Have you come to check on me?"

"I have just finished making you something to eat and was wondering where you were," he said uncomfortably twiddling his thumbs. "It's a little lonely downstairs and we are the only two people here."

"Oh, well I'm just searching through this home," she said casually. "Curious who might own it."

"I'm not sure that is a wise idea. The King doesn't want you to know."

"That's his position," she dismissed. "It's not mine. Now, come over here and help me open this chest."

"But your Majesty," he began uneasily.

"You aren't disobeying my husband if you come over here and help me open this chest."

"But-"

"But nothing. I just gave you a command. Come here and help me with this chest."

Begrudgingly, he went over to her. She put the knife into the hinges and started to try to take it apart.

He sighed. "Let me," he said.

She moved aside and he broke into the chest, removing the heavy lid. She dove into it. But there wasn't much of anything. Just some fabric, beads, and buttons. She stopped, noticing something peculiar. A swatch of lace was very familiar. She picked it up, and Lord Walsh's jaw dropped. He recognized it, too.

"This is from my wedding dress," she said slowly. She inspected it for a moment then looked back down at the contents in a new way. "Why would anyone keep a chest full of scraps of fabric and buttons?" she asked.

Lord Walsh shrugged.

"And how did some lace from my wedding dress get in here?"

"Not quite sure. But these could just be odd pieces to other garments. That lace could have come from another dress."

She glowered at him, "Really, Lord Walsh? That's the best you got? I think Miss Hampton likes to have little keepsakes from Alex's life. Wouldn't you say?"

He pursed his lips, "Perhaps. But maybe we shouldn't be too quick to make conclusions." He lifted the lid and rested it back on top of the trunk.

"You're right," she said coyly. She walked about pulling more sheets off more furniture. "I'm sure there is something in here that can give us a clearer picture."

A panic-stricken look came across his face. Pulling off the covers, she had revealed a dresser, a writing desk, and some chairs. "Let's take a look, shall we?" she said and began opening the dresser drawers.

Empty.

Empty.

Empty.

Empty.

She turned on him.

He ignored her glare.

"Makes sense. Nothing. Just like everything else around here!" she said throwing her arms into the air in frustration. "But there's still other places to look."

She opened the writing desk drawers and ruffled the papers within them searching. Then she saw a familiar face. Her own. It was on the front of The Society Pages. She cocked an eyebrow. She was surrounded by all sorts of people, a glass of wine in her hand. Something about the drawing seemed off. Everyone surrounding her was wearing outdated clothing. So was she. She read the headline.

DUKE OF AXFORD FINDS HIS AMOUR

IT WAS her mother in the drawing underneath the horrid headline. Madeline imagined that they were referring to her having been raised in France. Madeline shook her head. Beneath, she read a small caption,

THE DUKE OF AXFORD has finally found love with the elegant and charming Miss Swan. The wedding is expected to be the social event of the season, if not, the year.

. . .

SHE GLARED at the younger version of the Duke of Axford, clenching the paper in her hand. There were happy expressions on everyone's faces. But the Duke was more than happy, he was exuberant, his eyes fixed on Elizabeth Swan like he had found the most abundant treasure in the world. "Leave me. I'd like to be alone," she said staring at the paper, as she sat down on one of the chairs.

Lord Walsh left and she read the article. It didn't really give much information. They planned to wed on Valentine's Day the next year, which happened to be the night they had met. There were no comments or quotes from anyone. Looking at the drawing, it gave her shivers to think that in a little more than a year later, she would be dead, killed by the man standing next to her.

It made her sick. She stood up and pulled the chair up to the writing desk and sat down again. There was a stack of Society Pages in the drawers. She pulled them out and began to leaf through them.

Her mother was in it. Almost weekly. Reports were on superficial kinds of things; parties she was at, other socialites that were there, and what the ladies were wearing. Nothing substantial was quoted by anyone.

Shuffling through them, she finally came across one that piqued her interest. Amongst a group of adults, including her mother, was an adorable black haired little boy. Alex. He looked to be around three or four years old. He held his hand behind his back, a perfect gentleman. He looked adorable, but serious. She touched her belly, the idea of having a baby boy brought a smile to her face.

She looked around for Greg. He wasn't there. It was hard to imagine that there was a time Greg wasn't in Alex's life.

She spent a couple of hours reading through the rest of The Society Pages. She came across several more articles with Alex in them. It was mostly just gossip. Nothing of real importance or interest was ever mentioned.

* * *

AT THE EDGES of the town Carlos looked through a pair of binoculars at Windsor Castle. Many buildings and homes were up in flames. Some of the squadrons had reached the tall walls and were beginning to set up their cannons. The English barely had a defence. Men were lining the battlements shooting arrows and pistols. But no one was defending the town.

With an air of confidence, Carlos lowered his binoculars, "Tsk, England thinks their King is a military genius?"

Señor Menendo pushed through the men crowded around Carlos. "Your Highness! Your Highness!" he called in Spanish, out of breath as he bowed. "Some of the men have reported that they heard Sir Ashton Giles order some men to take King Alexander to safety through the tunnels."

"Excellent. I imagine that if we take down the walls with our cannons, King Alexander will have some cannons to fire back when we invade the castle grounds. It's time we take to the tunnels. All the squads are near the passage entranceways?"

"Yes, your Highness."

"Send half the men into the tunnels to look for him."

"What would *you* like to do your Highness?"

"I think I'll take to the tunnels," he smiled. "You see, my wife seemed to think that King Alexander would be impossible to defeat. This is the feeblest attempt at a defence I've ever seen. The only thing he has done is evacuated this town! This will be a memorable day in Spanish history. I want to be the one to drive my sword through him."

"King Carlos the Great," Señor Menendo said grinning.

"Perhaps. I'd like to go through the Frogmore tunnel. By the time we reach the castle, I'm sure someone will have the King subdued and waiting for me. Give each company of men strict orders that I will make the kill."

Señor Menendo nodded.

* * *

ALEX TREMBLED UNDERGROUND in a small chamber, its walls made of iron. He sighed. He wanted this to be over with. In his opinion, Carlos was slow to action. He'd been waiting down in there for some time now. He held his ear to one of the iron walls that encased him. Nothing.

He exhaled slowly. As soon as he heard the Spanish arrive, he'd still have to wait.

* * *

CARLOS MADE his way to Frogmore and led his men through the tunnels.

"This is the easiest victory in the history of mankind," he said confidently, as he led his men deeper into the channel. They were a long way off from Frogmore now. He smiled haughtily; with all his men invading the castle from all the tunnels entrances and passages, it was the ultimate surprise attack.

With these thoughts in his mind, he began to race down the dark passage. He and his descendants would be royalty of many nations. Then he slowed down, hearing voices speaking in Spanish ahead of him. It was odd. The night he escaped with Susanna she had told him that not many of the tunnels were attached. He turned to the Coronel next to him, "Do you hear those voices?" he asked.

The Coronel nodded.

"I thought this passage led directly into the castle grounds," said Carlos.

"It should."

Carlos ran towards the other men and the Coronel ran alongside him. But something in the air smelled awful, "What is that under our feet?"

As he said it, they had rushed into a large open area in the passage. Carlos surveyed the area with his torch. Many tunnel passages seemed to lead to the area. He saw the rest of the men from the other squadrons begin to fill the large space, looking about in confusion.

"Your Highness," began the Colonel, "I think it's straw beneath us. Perhaps it gets muddy down here from time to time."

"Certainly is a lot of straw," Carlos said moving toward the centre of the space. He looked about disbelieving. He'd never been in a place the size of this. It could have been half the size of the town.

ALEX HELD his breath hearing the voices on the other side of the small iron encasement. He sighed. He didn't want to do it. All that there was left was to open the small vent in the iron encasing, drop a match and head up the stairs and back into the castle.

But it was difficult. It reminded him of when he was a thirteen-year-old boy, hearing the pain and screaming of the Irish men suffering from the belladonna. He bit his lip. He never wanted to go through an experience like that again. He hated the blood of so many on his hands.

But Alex knew he had to do it. He couldn't ask another man to do this. It was his brainchild to remodel the tunnels to make one large cavernous room and inflame the squadrons that entered. To ask someone else to do the act of lighting the flame felt cowardly. He heard the voices and the words 'your Highness' in Spanish tongue. Prince Carlos was there. He had to do it now. There would be no rest if he didn't. Nothing could be negotiated with King Fernando or Prince Carlos at this point. If he didn't do this, he'd put his country, himself, Madeline and his unborn baby at risk. He felt beads of sweat at his brow and let out a deep breath.

CARLOS BENT DOWN and inspected the floor, "Straw? Why straw?"

He looked up, seeing a small flame floating in mid-air drop to the floor. The straw ignited into an inferno. In that second, Carlos realized that the report of the changes and work being done on Curfew Tower to make it safe were false. Men had gone into the tower to change the layout of the tunnels. He'd either die by flame or by smoke.

"Run!" he cried, heading back. He knew it was unlikely, but Frogmore was a few miles away. The best air would be there. Though the English army had probably covered all the exits, he'd take his chances. Frogmore had a hidden entrance in the garden, it would take time for the smoke to reach that far. He might find a weak spot amongst the cobblestone and dig his way out.

Rentering the castle, Alex closed and locked the door behind him. Lord Davis and Colonel Evans bowed, their expressions solemn.

"It's done. The straw quickly became a blaze," Alex said, trying to hold back emotion. "It may take some time before they've all died."

Colonel Evans nodded, "I doubt that it will take very long, Sire. All the men will try to run for the exits, but we've set them aflame as well."

"That wasn't part of the plan," Alex said.

"We know your Majesty, but it's our country to fight for too," Lord Davis said. "It cannot be left on the shoulders of one man to bear the weight of such a burden."

Alex knew he couldn't argue this. For a moment down in the iron room, he had hesitated. He wasn't sure he could do it.

"Around how many Spanish military are still fighting above ground?" he asked.

"There are several squadrons," Colonel Evans reported.

"I don't want another one of my men dying when this battle has been settled," Alex said, "this entire thing has been nonsense."

Lord Davis and Colonel Evans nodded their heads in understanding.

"We can't make an announcement of Prince Carlos's death until we know for certain, your Majesty," Colonel Evans reminded him.

"I know," Alex said regretfully.

"The battle must continue until the men figure it out and retreat," Lord Davis commented.

"But the question is, where will these men retreat to? We're stealing their ships in Brighton," Alex reminded them.

UNEXPECTED PROPOSAL

*G*reg looked around the Great Gallery, with his hands on his hips he teetered on his feet proudly. He once helped Sir Ashton and Lord Walsh with designing Alex's eighteenth birthday party. He had done several paintings for different times in Alex's life, but he wasn't as pleased with that series than he was with what he had accomplished in the past few days.

His collection of paintings hung around the room. Because he had little time, he used bigger canvases. He found working with smaller ones too time consuming when a mistake was made. It had been an exhausting few days. He barely got much sleep and was giving Sofia several different excuses to sneak away for hours. The most believable lie was that McFadden had gone into town and needed to be found to tend to Holyrood House.

To keep Sofia out of the Great Gallery, McFadden told her that renovations were being done on the room to paint and replace several of the paintings that had been damaged.

Greg invited all of Edinburgh. He knew the Great Gallery couldn't hold them all, but he didn't want to leave anyone out. Though he didn't know every person in town by name, they had all been so welcoming of him and Sofia. *Besides, mostly everyone came to all the parties anyway, why not invite them to this one?*

* * *

SOFIA SAT in the Morning Drawing Room. She had just arrived back at Holyrood House after going into town searching for Greg. He'd been acting so strange lately, and it scared her. She took her shawl off her shoulders and flopped onto the settee and glanced at the mythical stories on it. She knew what they all meant now, but as fun as it was to learn about, it was trivial now.

Fear had consumed her. Belle and Sam hadn't returned yet, and she could feel it in her bones that her father was coming. Worst of all, it seemed Greg was abandoning her, too. He had been acting very odd. He was rarely around Holyrood House, and always seemed concerned with what McFadden was doing.

She understood why he was distancing himself, and a part of her welcomed it. There was no doubt in her mind that Greg would be a dead man when her father arrived. She had begged Greg to flee Edinburgh upon her father's arrival, but he had refused. She had toyed with the idea when her father attacked, she could try to negotiate a deal; she would go back to Spain, on the condition that Greg could live. Though she would have nothing to live for in Spain, but Greg could go on to live a happy life.

She was stunned at herself. She hadn't known until that moment how much she loved Greg; she was willing to sacrifice her own happiness so that he could live. Even if that meant him being happy with someone else. She couldn't imagine a world without Greg. Or, maybe she didn't want to. His love had brought her to life in ways she had never imagined. A world without Greg would leave her with a cold, dead heart.

Besides, if Greg lived, there was hope that they could be reunited in the future. It could be years, and though he might be married someone else with children, it would still be good to see him again. A tear trickled down her face and she gasped, trying to hold back her whimpers. It was hard to accept that the dream she was living would soon end.

She felt a lump in her throat and swallowed hard. In the next few days she would have to find a way to convince Greg to leave her. She couldn't bear watching what punishment King Fernando would have in store for him. Deep down, she knew her father wouldn't compromise. Fernando would make her watch Greg's punishment. He made her watch when he punished her mother.

If Sofia had to, she'd tell Greg she no longer loved him. Anything to be able to imagine all the happy times they had together for the rest of her days; not to see his final moments of torture and death at the hands of her father. Blinded by tears she wept, soaking the material of the settee.

* * *

AFTER SEVERAL HOURS, the battle in Windsor had finally finished. Though Alex had very few men, once the Spanish learned that more than half their men had died underground, including the Prince of their country, it was demoralizing. The decision to burn parts of Windsor also backfired. It soon became impossible for the men to make formations or organize an attack on the castle without debris falling about them as building after building caught fire. As more men died, some of the men began to flee. Soon, they hadn't enough men to carry an invasion and retreated.

After it had ended, Alex and his team of advisors met in the Throne Room. Alex looked about and noticed something amiss, "Where is Sir Ashton?"

"He hasn't returned since he left the castle to instruct the men by the tunnels," Lord Winthrop said.

"Sir Ashton- he-," Alex stopped, collecting himself. "That was hours ago. Have you not sent someone to look for him?"

"Yes, your Majesty. We sent several men," Lord Davis answered, "they haven't reported back to us yet. It's possible he has gone to retrieve the Queen. He did mention that he wanted to reach Warwick as soon as he could because he knew she was distraught."

He nodded in understanding, "What is the status of our men?"

"We haven't gotten a report on casualties yet," said Colonel Evans. "Right now the men are trying to put out the fires in the town."

"Has Prince Carlos been located?" Alex asked.

"Yes. His body was found in the tunnels near Frogmore," Colonel Evans reported.

"All right and what of King Fernando? Do we know where he is located?"

"Yes. He and his ships were spotted passing London."

"Good. Are our men ready in Brighton?"

"They are on their way," Lord Davis answered.

* * *

Sofia woke up to sounds in the room next to her. It sounded as if Greg or McFadden let in a bunch of townspeople. She rubbed her eyes. It wasn't her intention to fall asleep, but after exhausting herself crying, she had drifted off. It was then she heard a familiar voice.

"Has no one seen her? I thought she came back to Holyrood House?" Greg said almost frantic.

"Do ya want me to search Edinburgh?" McFadden said half joking.

"Most of Edinburgh is here," Greg pointed out, "no one has seen her."

"She's probably sleepin' in the King's Bedchambers."

Greg opened the door and Sofia looked up at him and McFadden standing in the threshold.

"Why is most of Edinburgh here?" she asked. "Are you throwing another party?"

"I hope that's all right," he said timidly.

She looked down at her clothes. She wasn't wearing anything special, but a simple red empire dress that she had put on earlier that day. She eyed Greg up and down, "Is this some kind of special occasion? Why are you all dressed up?" she asked noting him wearing a black coat and white cravat. He looked so dapper. She felt she looked almost plain in comparison. "I'm going to get dressed," she said as she rose up. "Even McFadden looks more formal than I do."

"'Eh lass, I always be lookin' nicer than you," he chuckled.

She howled with laughter. Greg didn't. He looked apprehensive, fiddling with the buttons on the sleeve of his coat. She'd never seen him look like that before. She bit her lip. Maybe he was planning to leave Edinburgh, he just hadn't told her. Knowing him, he'd want to have one last party before she went back to Spain and he went into hiding.

"You look a little pale. Is something wrong?" she asked noticing Greg's face.

He shook his head awkwardly. McFadden grinned as he patted him on the back, "Ya do look a bit peckish, ya bastard."

"What's the party for anyway?" Sofia asked.

"We have parties often. There's never really been a reason," Greg said nervously.

"Why are you all dressed up then?" she said looking at him up and down.

"Uh, well I …"

"You're leaving Edinburgh, aren't you," she said, her voice becoming quiet and soft, "I suppose this will be our last party before my father comes?"

Greg was taken aback, "You think I'm leaving?"

"Aren't you? You've been ignoring me these past few days."

He pressed his lips together, "I just thought we could make the best of things tonight. I don't know when your father is coming. But I noticed you've been a bit down since those messengers had come here. So I threw this party for you, as a surprise to get your mind off things."

She chuckled, "You threw a party and thought that would surprise me?"

"It's a party *for you*."

"For me?" she said, blushing. No one had thrown her a party before, not even her parents. Of course, celebrations were always thrown in Carlos's honour. Occasions like her birthday were always a private affair. A select few were invited for dinner and the guest list was King Fernando's closest advisors. She grew a little emotional, "Then I'll get a new dress," she said happily turning to go to the King's Bedchambers.

"You look perfect," he said earnestly. "Besides, everyone is waiting to see you," he took her hand. "You don't want to keep our guests waiting, do you?"

She nodded though she really wanted to primp herself before seeing anyone.

"Ya look lovely lass," McFadden reassured her, noticing the uncertainty on her face. Locking elbows, Greg escorted her into the Evening Drawing Room. The room was full of people from the town, the room went silent and all the guests had huge grins on their faces.

"They are all looking at us," she said beneath her breath as they walked through the room.

"Of course, they are," he said, "tonight's party is for you."

Room after room they walked into, each one was full of the townspeople and some of the guests would follow them into the next room. Once they got to the Queen's Lobby, she turned to him.

"Did these people have a few drinks before coming?" she whispered to him.

"I suppose," he said. "Why?"

"Quite a few of them are following us," she said looking about unsure.

He put his hand on the door to the Great Gallery.

"I thought there were going to be renovations on the room, Greg. Don't tell me you let people in there. They'll just ruin it again."

She heard some chuckling from the people around her.

"There were no renovations … just decorations," Greg said smiling.

He opened the door, and she could see the Great Gallery had been transformed. The walls were covered in yellow with red festoons hanging, flowing down the yellow material to the floor. Between the red festoons, there were paintings with a style she somewhat recognized. There was silence in the room as she looked about. The paintings were exquisite; full of colour and movement but had an abstract kind of feel to them as she tried to make out the scenes.

One was of Holyrood House. It was a gorgeous piece. Greg stood in the middle of the room as everyone stood about, staring at her.

"Do you like it? Do any of the paintings look familiar?"

"That's Holyrood House," she said. She could hear some snickers around her. Then she noticed two people in the painting standing outside the residence. They were small, but she could see that one of them was a man, the other a woman wearing red.

"Is that us?" she asked Greg.

He beamed, answering her question. She looked at the next large painting next to it. It was her, smiling and dancing, and him playing the fiddle. "That was at Windsor Castle. When I was taken on a tour of the-" She stopped mid-sentence questioning if the guests knew her identity as the princess of Spain. But no one had bowed. Either they knew she was a princess and understood she didn't want all the pleasantries, or they just didn't care.

"Yes, that was when the King and I gave you a tour of the castle," Greg finished. "Wasn't the King a horrible musician?"

Everyone laughed. *They know. They probably figured out who I am ages ago. But my identity is a trifling matter to them. The Scottish laugh at their King.* It is part of their culture, she supposed. They hadn't seen their King in decades.

Another was her, peering through something with a coy smile. She recognized the room and realized what it was. Her, spying on him in the morning. She tried not to laugh, only she and he knew what that painting was about.

There were other paintings. Him, holding her hand as she touched Evie the falcon at Frogmore, the English countryside and the carriage they had taken to Edinburgh. Her, sitting silently by a window reading Scottish myth lore. Them dancing at the festival. She laughed there was even one of her scolding him in the crooked house.

She observed the last painting and cocked her head. Alex was standing in front of his throne, a startled look on his face. Next to

Alex she was unconscious in Greg's arms. She opened her mouth to speak, but noticing her expression, Greg beat her to it.

"Remember when you thought it was Alex that caught you when you first met him and fainted?"

She nodded smiling, "But you caught me."

"I will always catch you."

He got down on one knee, she gasped slapping her hands over her mouth. Her eyes began to well up, "Sofia, will you be my Princess forever?"

She gaped as he held out a gold ring with a gigantic ruby with a heart shaped cut. She had no clue where he had gotten it, but she didn't care. She stood stunned, unable to say anything.

"Will you marry me?" he asked softly.

She was still speechless, wondering when they'd marry. Her father could come any time now. The crowd watched in anticipation. Greg looked up worriedly.

"Wha' the hell lass? Will ya marry tha King's bastard's arse or not?" McFadden blurted out.

"Yes," she squeaked, her head bobbing up and down. She put out her hand and he placed the ring on her finger and stood up.

"How are we going to do this?" she whispered.

"Well," he said hesitantly, thinking she knew. "I thought we could do it now."

"Now?" she repeated in disbelief.

"What'd ya think he had in mind?" McFadden laughed. "Yer father could be here any day now."

She pulled Greg aside and said in a hushed voice, "If my father is to be here any day, then maybe we shouldn't get married. Maybe you should leave Edinburgh. Go into hiding."

"Without you? No," he said waving his arm. "I'd rather die a happily married man than leave you. I'm not a coward."

She melted. She knew he meant it. There was no point in arguing with him.

"How can we do this now? I think we would need a church?" she said

"There's an abbey in Holyrood House. McFadden never took us to it because it's in ruins, but we've decorated it, and it looks lovely."

"Lovely if you like the rugged kind of look," said a voice from the crowd. Sofia turned. It was Sam, he was holding hands with Belle. She hadn't even noticed them there. They were both smiling widely. More questions began to run through her mind.

"Let's forget about everything else," Greg said reading her thoughts. "Let's do what makes us happy."

She nodded her head up and down in agreement, beaming. It made sense. Their time together would soon come to an end. She didn't want to have any regrets.

"Com' on everybody, she gonna marry 'im!" McFadden yelled merrily as he rushed to a door that led outside.

"There's a priest outside in the abbey," Greg said.

"You managed to get a Catholic priest to do a ceremony here?" she said in surprise.

"I figured that would be what you wanted."

"Is the abbey a Catholic one?"

"It had Catholic roots. Actually, Mary Queen of Scots got married in there. At least, that's what McFadden was telling me." He took her hand and they went out the door in the Great Gallery that led outside, their guests at their heels, cheering.

She immediately spotted the Gothic style abbey as soon as they went out. She could tell by the old stones and wreckage around them, that not much of the original structure was there. The nave was the only thing left, but had no roof. Though she couldn't quite see inside, it looked romantic. Huge bronze bowls of flames hung in all the stone arch windows.

"Wow. It looks beautiful Greg," she said excitedly.

"I'm glad you think so. The ceiling caved in a few centuries back, so we'll be wed under the stars."

They walked in and she looked about. There were already some people inside and the rest of the guests filed in behind them. The inside of the abbey was unlike anything she had ever seen. Along with the large bronze bowls in the windows, there were wrought iron candelabras about lighting the old ruins. The stones had turned a tinge of green along with moss growing between the crevices of the stones. Red and gold silk was wrapped about the pillars and a long red carpet extended to the front of the nave.

Belle came to her and offered Sofia a bouquet of red roses.

"Merci, Belle," Sofia said taking the bouquet.

"Bon chance," Belle said.

Sam smiled at them both. "Best of luck to you both!" He took Belle's arm and escorted her into the crowd. Sofia looked outside the abbey, there were tons more people lined out the door, all with huge smiling faces as they stood on their tiptoes, peering in at them.

She looked up at the stars and then at Greg. She never would have pictured this as her wedding; marrying a man she loved, not someone her father ordered her to marry.

She looked at Greg, with tears in her eyes.

"Shall we?" he asked offering his arm.

"Yes," she said grinning, taking his arm.

They walked down the red carpet, the townspeople people surrounding them. Where the carpet ended stood the priest. He had greying hair and wore a thick pair of glasses.

Once they reached the front, they turned towards one another and the priest began the mass.

But his accent was so heavy; neither of them could understand what he was saying. Greg stared at him, unsure of how it would go. He questioned if maybe he was speaking a different language in his heavy Scottish accent.

'Are you understanding any of this?' he mouthed to Sofia.

She shrugged, her eyes alit in the candlelight. McFadden stood near them in the crowd, he nudged Sam, "I don' think they know wha' Father McLaglen is sayin.'"

"What is he saying?" Sam asked.

"Don' tell me ya don' know."

Though only McFadden understood what father was saying, the service went on until Father McLaglen said, "Rungs?" and held out his hand.

Sofia took off her ring and placed it in his hand, realizing she had nothing to give Greg. Feeling a little embarrassed, she looked down at the other rings on her hands. But they were all feminine and not likely to fit his fingers. Nonetheless, she began fiddling, trying to pull a silver ring with some small sapphires off her middle finger.

McFadden stepped forward stopping her. "'Ere ya go, lass," he said, taking his own gold ring off his finger.

It was a magnificent ring. Intricate Celtic designs were etched around a thick gold band. She took it, smiling. McFadden stepped back. She wanted to giggle, she wasn't expecting McFadden to stand up for her.

Father McLaglen began to cite the traditional vows, expecting Sofia to repeat them. Everyone in the crowd sniggered, seeing the look of confusion on Sofia's face, though, they hardly understood him, either.

McFadden stepped forward again and began to whisper the words to Sofia and she repeated them. Placing the ring on Greg's finger, they gazed at one another. Despite everything that was happening in their lives, it felt right.

McFadden then walked behind Greg and delivered a special set of vows, "I, tha King bastard's arse …"

Greg bit his bottom lip trying to contain himself, "I, Greg Umbridge,"

"Take tha lass," McFadden said.

"Take you, Sofia,"

"Ta be yer stupid husband."

"I'll just say the rest myself," he whispered in frustration. He continued, "I Greg Umbridge take you, Sofia, to be my beautiful wife," he paused and looked deeply into her chocolaty eyes, "te amo Sofia, I always have, and I always will."

"Ohh, Greg," she gushed softly at his Spanish profession of love. She gazed down as he placed the heart shape ruby ring on her finger.

Father McLaglen continued, mumbling more words to the couple then paused, staring at Sofia.

"Oh, um, I do," Sofia said quickly.

Father repeated what he said, then looked at Greg.

"I do," he said.

"Ya me kess da breed," said Father McLaglen.

They were the only words anyone understood, Greg leaned down toward her and took her in his arms dipping her as he kissed her, his tongue massaging hers. The guests laughed, clapped, and cheered. He lifted her back to her feet, slowly parting his lips from hers.

"Greg," she objected, playfully pushing his shoulder.

"I don't want everyone forgetting our wedding ... or our kiss," he said.

She looked around, she had never seen or heard of a wedding like this one. "I don't think anyone will forget this."

* * *

GREG PROPPED himself on the pillows. Though he had gotten a letter and a package from Alex the day before, he hadn't gotten a chance to read the letter. Just as he was looking for Sofia to propose, Belle and Sam had arrived. Anxious, Greg opened the package but didn't read the letter. He found the letter now, sealed in wax on his bedside table when he woke up as Sofia slept soundlessly next to him.

He watched her a moment, then her eyes began to flutter and she yawned, "What's that?" she asked sleepily.

"It's a letter from Alex," he said showing his seal on the back.

"Open it," she said, hastily curling up to him.

He ripped it open and began reading aloud.

GREG,

I'm sorry I didn't write earlier, but I didn't want to send you a letter without letting you know what the plan is. I imagine that by the time you receive this, our battle with the Spaniards in Windsor will have ended. It's been reported that Prince Carlos has just arrived in Brighton. I expect to be seeing his army within the next day.

Regardless of the outcome, we expect that King Fernando will head to

Edinburgh. I'm hoping to send you some reinforcements. If the men come, you can be rest assured that we managed to defeat Prince Carlos. If my men don't make it, and you see King Fernando's ships, then you and Sofia MUST escape. I have arranged a safe house for you in Lake District. Once you arrive, look for Lord Davis. From there, a navy ship will take you both to a colony of your choice. You'll be financially provided for, so don't worry about taking more than the clothes on your back.

I should also mention that if my ships reach King Fernando's in time, I cannot guarantee his life will be spared. I will order my men to only capture him if possible. The same goes for Prince Carlos, but this is war and there are no guarantees. Please explain to Sofia that I'm sorry. It is not my intention to make her life difficult. Though I'm sure, she despises me after all that I've dragged her through since she arrived in England.

I've given your friends Sam and Belle something you won from the Duke of Axford several years ago. I'm sure you've thought of it quite a bit lately. Perfect for someone who loves red.

I miss you, and wish I were there with you,

Alex

THERE WAS A SILENCE BETWEEN THEM. Neither knew what to say. Though she hated and feared her father, a small part of her felt bitter toward Alex. "Be honest Greg. You know him best. Even if Alex had the opportunity, he wouldn't spare my brother nor my father."

"He did once," Greg said cautiously. "Remember the first time they invaded England? Alex captured Carlos, he could have had him killed then. He could have attacked Spain immediately afterward. I'm guessing he never planned anything because of you."

She folded her arms and shook her head defiantly, "The only reason why Alex never attacked Spain was because he didn't have the men to attack."

"Possibly. But your father should have cut his losses. He wants this empire for Spain. Should Alex just let him take it?"

She crawled to the other side of the bed. He sighed and edged next to her. Turning away she began to whimper.

He grasped her soft brown curls. "He's a king," Greg reasoned, "he has to make those kinds of difficult decisions."

She knew Greg was right, but she felt sick with guilt.

"Don't forget, Alex never used you as a bargaining chip. He never used your life to threaten your father."

"I know," she said, "but I feel like I'm betraying my family and my country."

"Better that than your heart. If your father were to find us, you and I could never be together."

She rolled around and cuddled back up to him. The truth hurt.

"Well, we don't know what could happen," he said softly. "Your father hasn't arrived here yet. If Carlos doesn't capture Windsor, he might have a change of heart and head back to Spain."

BOOM! CRASH! BOOM!

They heard a thunderous roar coming from outside and both of them rushed to the window. In the distance, they could see a large fleet of ships on the water firing at Edinburgh.

HIDDEN TEARS

*I*t was a strange sound. Madeline had never heard anything like it. As she crept down the stairs, it became louder. She was sure it was coming from the parlour. Someone was crying. As she entered, she saw Lord Walsh, sitting with a drink in front of him, sniffling into a handkerchief.

It was odd to see Lord Walsh so emotional. She stood paralyzed, unsure of what to do. He felt her presence and looked up. He shifted in his seat, "Your Majesty," he stood up abruptly and bowed, quickly wiping his face. "I wasn't expecting you."

"I'm sorry," she said though she wasn't sure what she was apologizing for. "I just ... are you all right Lord Walsh?"

He sat back down, unsure of what to say to her.

"A good friend–" he began, his voice cracking. "Our good friend ..." He put his head in his hands.

"Who?" she asked, rushing over to his side, kneeling next to him. "What has happened? Is Alex all right?"

"Oh yes, his Majesty, he's fine."

"Is the battle over? Who is it you're talking about?"

"The battle is won ... but Sir Ashton ..." he put his face into his hands again.

She paused, confused by Lord Walsh's emotions about Sir Ashton Giles. She rose from the floor and sat next to him. She didn't know they were close. Often times, she felt that they were at odds with one another, sometimes they bickered like an old married couple. She watched him, as he wept and rubbed his back. Her heart was broken, too. Sir Ashton was a good man. A wise one. She knew that Alex wouldn't be the kind of man he was if not for Sir Ashton Giles. He raised Alex as if he were his own, taught him how to respect and care for his subjects. He was more than a trusted advisor. He was Alex's father. She couldn't imagine how Alex was feeling now. She shed a tear.

"Someone, some coward killed him," he sobbed. "Stabbed him in the back."

"Was Alex there?" she asked in a choked voice.

"No."

She was confused. Usually, Sir Ashton would be by Alex's side in a situation like this.

"There was a plan," Lord Walsh went on through his tears. "While they said they were making renovations on Curfew Tower, they were using the tower to enter the tunnels. They redesigned the tunnels so that they all led to one large room. The tunnels and room were full of straw; the Spanish were barricaded inside and the straw was set aflame."

She didn't have to ask. She already knew. Something told her Alex had set the fire.

"Sir Ashton went to several of the tunnels' exits to confirm that Prince Carlos was dead ..." he stuttered through sobs. "Then, then ... some coward came, and stabbed him."

She looked outside. She could see a carriage outside waiting on the street. Ben Caston was standing next to the carriage talking to the driver. "I suppose Mr. Caston has told you of all of this?" she said. "When did he arrive?"

"Around an hour ago," he admitted.

She would have asked him why he hadn't informed her immediately. But it was obvious, she had never seen a man so distraught. She stood up and walked over to the window. "I'll have Mr. Caston and the driver pack your and my things," she said.

"Thank you," he whispered feebly. Since Ben Caston had told him, he had been unable to do anything.

* * *

SUSANNA AND ARSENIO had been unable to keep away from one another. Neither of them had heard anything concerning the war in the past week. But they hardly noticed or cared.

Every evening, after dinner and chatting to Queen Isabelle in the Queen's Apartments, Susanna would go back to her bedchamber, a huge grin on her face. Arsenio was always there, waiting for her.

He'd stay the night and seduce her again in the morning. Normally, she didn't like being dominated, but from him, she loved it. He knew when to take charge. Outside the bedroom, he still referred to her as her Royal Highness and was respectful.

In fact, the dynamic of the court had completely changed since Prince Carlos and King Fernando and several of the Lords went off to war. Being Prince Carlos's closest friend and being given the responsibility of looking after Susanna, the court held Señor Astucia in high esteem. Whenever he spoke, other nobles listened.

Unlike Prince Carlos and King Fernando, Arsenio gave Susanna an opportunity to give her opinion publicly, too. He never interrupted her when she spoke of religion or politics. The atmosphere was different; Queen Isabelle spoke during last night's dinner. It wasn't anything much, but she spoke a little of Scottish culture. It was obvious that Sofia was on her mind.

Inside the bedroom, there was no talk of politics, religion, or anyone at court. As soon as Susanna walked in, without words their bodies were pressed up against one another, tearing off each other's clothes.

He seemed to have a fetish for her blonde hair. No matter what the ladies had done with her hair in the morning, every night he would take out all the pins and hair ornaments and comb her hair with his fingers. He was also demanding. He knew what he wanted and didn't like to be denied. He hadn't proposed anything she would object to, but once she had tried to say, 'No' to see his reaction. She was curious about what he would do.

"Spread your legs, Susanna," he mumbled one night, as he nipped at her thighs.

"Not tonight, Arsenio."

"What? Not tonight?"

"I'm not really in the mood."

"Not in the mood?" he repeated seductively.

"No," she said simply.

"I want to eat what is between your legs, so what would put you in the mood?"

"I just want sex."

He chuckled. "Then we have a problem," he whispered his accent heavy.

"How is that?"

"I won't be ready for sex until I get what I want."

"I doubt that, Arsenio," she said wrapping her hand around him. "You seem ready to me."

He shook his head. "Ah, ah," he said pulling her hand away. "I'm not ready until I know you're ready. You won't let me touch you there, so how will I know?"

She smiled and parted her legs, "You can touch me," she said guiding his hand.

He massaged her and slipped his finger inside her.

"Uh," she murmured, as he pushed inside her at a steady pace. "Mmm, Arsenio, huh." She leaned toward him kissing him on the lips.

He kissed her back, his lips tugging at her bottom lip. He grasped her blonde waves between his fingers, then withdrew his finger.

She pouted, she was enjoying his prowess.

"Susanna, I want to taste you," he said plainly. "I won't be satisfied until I do. Neither will you." He pulled her head toward him roughly, his mouth next to her ear, "Don't refuse something I know you like."

. . .

SHE HADN'T SEEN him since that morning. Usually at this time, she would be with Queen Isabelle, doing some embroidery or having tea, but not today. Queen Isabelle had wanted time alone to pray a novena in the chapel. Susanna didn't mind. It was beginning to get cooler and the day was a beautiful one; she wanted to take advantage before colder fall days arrived.

She hadn't bothered to discover the grounds around Madrid Palace since arriving. It was kind of nice to be able to do so on her own. She had wandered through a hedge maze before sitting on the edge of a large pool with a fountain at its centre. She looked at her reflection in the water. The past few weeks had been exactly what she had needed. She hoped it would last longer, and was dreading the news of the war. She had mulled it over countless times. *It was possible that Alex would be able to defeat Carlos's men but Greg Umbridge was hopeless. Probably dead. He had nothing to defend Edinburgh.*

Clink. Clink.

She glanced up from the water and saw Arsenio standing next to her. He held a bottle of wine and two wine glasses.

"Out here, all alone Susanna?" he asked.

"Mmm."

He sat next to her, on the ledge placing the glasses between them. "Do you like red wine?"

"Where is it from?"

"Italy," he said grinning. "I thought we could drink in honour of him."

She squinted her eyes, "In honour of whom?"

"Correct me if I'm wrong, but his Majesty of England is also Italian?"

Her cheeks went pink, "Some of the noble girls at court used to call him the 'Italian Stallion.'"

"Really? Why was that?" he joked as he opened the bottle.

"I'm sure you could imagine why," she sighed. "It was embarrassing to hear that sort of thing about family."

"I'm sure he knew a few things about you too that he wished he didn't," he said as he poured her a glass and set it next to her.

"So why are we drinking to him? I suppose he's dead?" she said softly.

"Just the opposite. He's defeated Prince Carlos."

She went silent. She didn't want Carlos to come back, but she had never imagined that Arsenio felt the same. They were friends, or so she thought. "Is Prince Carlos *dead?*" she asked, her eyes bulging.

"Yes," he said simply pouring a glass.

"We are celebrating-" she stopped. "Do you care for his Highness at all? I mean, he was your best friend, wasn't he?"

"Does a man bed his best friend's wife? No." He handed her the glass sitting next to her, taking the other for himself. But she put hers down.

"What is it?" he asked. "I thought you would be happy. Do you want England so badly that you'd tolerate King Fernando and Prince Carlos to have it?"

"No. It's not that. I suppose I knew Carlos was heading to his death. You're right. I haven't been looking forward to them returning. Even if they took England, I'm sure I'd have no say in how it was ruled."

"Then what is it?" he asked puzzled.

"I didn't think you felt the same way about King Fernando and Prince Carlos as I do. Does everyone at court feel that way about them?"

"Well," he began, "I don't think they know every detail of the royal family. But living in the castle for as long as I have I can honestly say I have no respect for this family."

"Why did you stay so long?" she asked cocking her head in confusion.

"It wasn't my choice. Prince Carlos preferred me as his advisor."

"Oh."

"The only good thing that ever came of me being here was King Fernando rewarding me with some land and a manor."

She pursed her lips, "You have no respect for anyone in this family? Not the Queen or Princess Sofia?"

"The only person in this family that I would feel sorry for is

Princess Sofia. If the Queen were wise, she would have sent her to live at another royal residence. What Sofia was put through was awful."

"Why didn't she? I mean Queen Isabelle does care for Sofia, why didn't she send her away?"

"She's a selfish woman. I understand that you probably think she had no choices, that King Fernando has firm control over her. You're right. He does. But there were opportunities for Queen Isabelle to send her daughter elsewhere to be educated. She never took them. She kept Sofia around for herself. The Princess paid for that selfishness."

It wasn't often Susanna felt sorry for other people, but she couldn't help but to think that Sofia grew up in misery. She had only had to tolerate them for a few weeks.

"Don't you think we are celebrating a little early? King Fernando could still return."

"Tell me Susanna, if King Fernando were to kill Sir Gregory, would King Alexander let it go or would he destroy him?"

* * *

Greg grasped Sofia's hand tightly, and the two took off through Holyrood House. As he pulled her along, he could hear her sobbing. He ignored it. He had to get them both out of there.

"I don't want to leave the people here," she cried. "The Scottish have nothing to do with this! I've come to love the people of Edinburgh! They're all lovely people that accepted us and came to our parties!"

He said nothing but continued to run, dragging her along through the drawing rooms and Throne Room before they came to the staircase and ran out the door closest to the carriages. She tripped on the skirts of her dress onto the grass, and he turned to pick her up.

"Greg, the letter. Alex's letter. They'll find it. They will know where we've gone."

"Forget that. It could be weeks before they find it, Sofia. They think we are staying in Edinburgh Castle! We can't waste time."

"Do you think Windsor has been taken?" she asked fearfully.

"I don't know," he said in a panic.

He opened the carriage door, "Get in!"

"Where are we going to go? What about Belle, Sam and McFadden?" she cried as she rushed into the carriage.

"I'm sure McFadden-"

The boom of cannons suddenly echoed around them. The ships were aiming for the homes along the shore, they both covered their ears as the thunderous sound reverberated around them.

"GREG," she shouted trying to speak over the sound of the cannons.

"THERE'S NO TIME!" He slammed the door shut and jumped into the driver's seat.

It was so loud outside; she didn't hear the horses begin to move, but flew to the opposite side of the coach as it lurched forward. "GREG!" she screamed as she fell to the other side.

He didn't hear her, as he drove recklessly into the street. He had no idea of what direction to take to get to Lake District, where Alex had directed him where to go. As they darted through the town, he saw everyone in the streets running in all directions. "OUT OF THE WAY," he yelled as the cannons struck again. He had no clue what direction to head in. He had no compass and his sense of direction wasn't very good. When he and Alex went hunting it was always Alex that knew how to find their way back to the horses. Even Alex's horse Princess had a better sense of direction than him. "SOFIA! SOFIA!" he bellowed over the chaos.

Certain she had heard her name, she slid the small window open and poked her head out.

"WHICH WAY IS NORTH, PRINCESS?"

* * *

THE RIDE back to Windsor felt awkward. For the most part, it was quiet. Though Ben Caston had tried on a few occasions to start a conversation, Lord Walsh had a frozen look of devastation that was hard to ignore. He sat staring into nothing, his eyes bloodshot, hardly blinking. He held a handkerchief and was wringing it with both his hands. He held and twisted so tightly that Madeline noticed that his hands were fleshy red.

"I'm sorry, your Majesty about Sir Ashton Giles's passing," began Ben. "He was a very good man."

"He was," Madeline agreed. "How has Alex been with all of this?"

"Honestly, I don't know. Mr. Tinney had sent me as soon as he heard word of his death. He said that King Alexander ordered that you come home immediately."

"Well, Alex did love Sir Ashton. He was always there for him."

"A great loss for all of England, your Majesty."

"Quite," Madeline nodded in agreement.

Lord Walsh let out a small gasp and quickly held the handkerchief to his mouth.

"I must admit though; I found it surprising that King Alexander wants to hold a party," said Ben.

"A party?" she repeated.

Lord Walsh sighed and put his hands on his face.

"Yes. Didn't Lord Walsh tell you?" asked Ben giving him a funny look.

"I'm sorry, your Majesty. I think I forgot to tell you," he whispered quietly.

"That's fine, Lord Walsh," Madeline consoled. "It's hard to celebrate a victory over the Spaniards when we've lost someone dear to us all."

"That's not exactly what his Majesty had in mind," said Ben.

"How? What do you mean?"

"The King feels it's time that the country shares in your joy. Congratulations," he said smiling.

"What about Sir Ashton's funeral?" asked Lord Walsh dolefully. "The country should be in mourning."

"His Majesty insisted on a state funeral," said Ben. "He's planning the party because he knows that when all the subjects see the Queen, there will already be suspicion."

She looked down at her swelling belly, "It is getting more difficult to hide," she admitted.

Lord Walsh said nothing during the rest of the trip home. Ben tried his best to keep Madeline entertained. But it wasn't easy. He was trying to keep things light and cheerful, though there was hardly any good news to speak of. Many parts of Windsor had been burned to the ground. Some townspeople were staying with relatives in other parts of England. He tried to change the subject to the upcoming party. Ben didn't want to speak about the battle, but Madeline still had questions, "How are Martha, Sissy and Marie?"

"Oh, all is well with them. They've gone back to Frogmore," he paused, "though this Delilah character has seemed to have gone missing these past few weeks. Since searching for her, no one has been able to find her."

Madeline's ears perked, "Delilah has gone missing? Did Sissy have much to say about what she was like?"

"Yes. She had been entertaining some Lords living in London. They were questioned, but it seems as though she disappeared."

"Now that the Spanish have been defeated in Windsor, maybe she is trying to find a way home," Madeline said, quite sure Delilah was a Spanish spy.

He chuckled, "That won't be easy. Brighto-"

CRACK!

They hit a bump and Madeline closed her eyes tightly, throwing her arms up, trying to protect herself and the baby. She flew to the side of the seat and grasped the ledge of the window. The carriage came to an abrupt stop.

When she opened her eyes, she could see Ben Caston rubbing his head.

"Your Majesty, are you all right?" Lord Walsh asked as he went to assist her.

"I'm fine," she said holding her belly. Ben opened the door and stepped out shutting the door behind him.

"What the bloody hell?" he yelled at the driver. "I asked you to go slowly. The Queen is with child."

"I tried to," Madeline could overhear the driver making his excuses sheepishly, "I understand how important it is-"

"Do you? The wheel is cracked and broken. What happened!?"

"There was a rock in the road Mr. Caston, covered with dirt. I didn't see it."

Lord Walsh and Madeline exchanged looks. This wasn't good. They were out in the middle of nowhere. Someone would have to walk several miles to reach a town and bring someone to get a wheel and replace it. She sighed. It could be hours before they moved again. It would be dark, and they would need food.

Lord Walsh slouched in his bench seat which was something she had never seen before. She could understand his urge to be home. He was having a rough time with the ride itself. It was obvious he was down, lost in his emotions.

Ben went on complaining to the driver for several more minutes before he came back inside.

"Here's the situation," he said stiffly. "Our driver hit a large rock. It has damaged the wheel and we will need a new one to replace it."

"How far is the closest town?" asked Madeline.

"Several miles, but it's quite small," Ben said. "I'm not sure we can find someone to give us a spare wheel or carriage."

"What about Sir Ashton Giles's funeral," Lord Walsh piped up. "When will that be?"

"Tomorrow. We may not be back by then, though."

Lord Walsh went pale, "But we must make it back. The King will be devastated that his wife could not be there to support him in a time like this. The kingdom and all the subjects will question where the Queen is."

"We will have to send a messenger to explain why," said Ben in a practical tone. "The Queen is not fit to be riding a horse all the way back if that's what you're suggesting."

"I'll go then," Lord Walsh said immediately. "I will ride and deliver the message to the King. I would hate for him to worry."

"I'm not sure that is a good idea," Ben said. "The Queen needs someone to wait upon her. We can't leave her here at the carriage."

Lord Walsh's eyes welled up, Madeline spoke quickly. "No it's fine Mr. Caston," she said. "I wouldn't want the King to worry about my whereabouts."

"But how will we do this your Majesty? The driver and I will have to go to the nearest village; it will take both of us to bring the wheel back."

"Never mind that," said Madeline. "If one of you goes, I'm sure you will find one of the villagers to assist you."

"You will trust a complete stranger with such a task?" he asked in disbelief.

"No. I trust the common English countryman," she said confidently.

Ben nodded, "I'll send the driver to the village then."

He exited the carriage, leaving Lord Walsh and Madeline alone.

"Well, you best be on your way then," Madeline said. "Be sure to let Alex know that I am fine."

"I'll have another carriage sent out here, just to be sure," he said, his eyes roving about. "Thank you," he said his lips quivering. He bowed before leaving.

* * *

GREG AND SOFIA were several miles outside of Edinburgh. Though it looked small behind them, they could still hear the thunderous booms of the cannons and clouds of smoke beginning to cloud above it.

But as he looked out to the sea, his jaw dropped. He could see another small fleet of ships behind the Spanish ships. He pulled the reins, and the horses came to a halt. He didn't recognize the new ships. They were not English, nor did they have a country flag flying on the masts. They could be pirates. He bit his lip fearing King Fernando had made an allegiance with pirates sailing around Spain.

Sofia hopped out, seeing his confused expression.

"What is it, Greg? Why have we stopped?" she asked.

He pointed out to the sea, "Do you see those ships?"

She climbed up the steps and sat next to him on the driver's seat.

Putting her hand above her brow, she looked out onto the water squinting.

"Do you recognize them?" he asked.

She was taken aback. She had never seen ships like those. They seemed to move quickly. "I don't know. But they are fast."

"Would your father befriend pirates?"

Fear came over her. "I don't know," she said slowly. "I suppose. He has used them before. Many years ago, he made an agreement with some to-" She stopped. "No. Pirates wouldn't help my father; he didn't fulfil his end of the bargain all those years ago."

"They never sought revenge?" Greg asked curiously.

"It was a small crew of pirates; my father had them executed."

"Who do you think they might be?" said Greg as he continued to stare out into the horizon.

"It's possible they could be pirates," she said. "But do you know any pirates that would have that many ships?" There were quite a few ships. About half as many as King Fernando had.

"Neither one is attacking the other," he noted. "Whoever they are, I think they may have come to conquer Edinburgh, too."

CORONEL HERNANDEZ RUSHED up the stair on the deck, looking for King Fernando, who was watching through his telescope.

"This is too easy," he said in his native tongue, tossing the telescope to Coronel Hernandez as he approached him. "We will have this town by the late afternoon."

"Your Majesty," Coronel Hernandez began breathlessly, "I've just received word from some of the men that there is a small fleet of ships coming from behind us."

"Is there? Are they English?"

"We don't know. There is no identification on their masts. But they are fast moving ships."

King Fernando snatched the telescope back from him and peered through it. Behind several of his ships, he could make out a smaller fleet racing through the fog.

"Tsk. Nothing to fear. Those are just Dutch ships. Quick ones. But that's hardly a fleet. If they had any interest in this, they would be in Windsor, defending King Alexander. Look at that," he pointed. "They are beginning to turn their ships east. Maybe they are headed for some trade in Denmark or Norway." He gave Coronel Hernandez the telescope. "Leave them be. My only concern is Greg Umbridge."

"Wow," Greg said sadly seeing several more Spanish ships behind the Dutch ones.

"Those Spanish ships behind those unknown ships must be Carlos' fleet," Sofia said horrified.

"So you are the face that launched a thousand ships," he said, smiling weakly.

Sofia shed a tear, "I'm sorry Greg," she said softly. "Alex- Wait a minute …" She stopped and squinted her eyes again. "Those unknown ships are hoisting something up their masts."

"Your Majesty," yelled Coronel Hernandez, looking through the telescope at the Dutch ships. "Those Dutch ships are flying the British flag!"

"What?" Fernando's voiced boomed. He looked behind at the Dutch ships.

"But look at that! My Carlos is coming from behind," he said confidently. "We can fire from both sides of them. Organize the men. We'll get those ships down."

"If those Dutch ships are really *our* Royal Navy, I feel sorry for them," said Greg biting his lip. "Your brother's ships are going to attack those English ships. They have no chance of staying afloat being where they are."

"That makes no sense," she said with an air of certainty. "Carlos would need those men to hold down Windsor. Those ships aren't firing at the British ones either."

He nodded, "O! You're right. It looks like those Spanish ships are getting in formation with the English ones ... My, what is going on?"

BOOM! BOOM!

KING FERNANDO HOWLED, "What is happening Why are my ships attacking ... MY SHIPS?"

Two cannon balls had hit a ship behind them. Coronel Hernandez knew he was supposed to answer to the King, but he didn't know what to say. A horrendous suspicion came over him. He knew that though the ships flew a Spanish flag, it was a ruse. It was a masterful counter-attack. The English had stolen the Spanish ships from Brighton and with the help of the Dutch, were attacking King Fernando and his fleet. Unfortunately, for Fernando his ships were all facing north, giving them few cannons to strike back with. All of the English ships were now facing east, each one of them able to utilize half a dozen or more cannons.

They all began to fire at once.

SOFIA AND GREG could hear the booms from the ships as the cannon balls whizzed between the ships. Not many came from her father's ships, and already, some were going down. She watched with a solemn expression. She climbed down from the carriage and walked towards the beach half a mile from them.

Greg followed her onto the beach, unsure of what to say. They stood in silence as they watched the battle unfold in front of them. They could faintly hear screams.

.   .   .

"DIRECT EACH SHIP TO HEAD EAST!" bellowed King Fernando over the bedlam. But no one heard him. All the men on every ship scrambled about in different directions, trying to avoid the cannon-balls. As the missiles hit the ships, debris and pieces of the ships flew into the air.

Some of the ships slowly began to turn to defend, but were unable to do so without suffering several shots of the cannons. One by one, the ships began to sink, as the English kept up the assault, firing the cannons from each ship in succession.

SOFIA COULDN'T TAKE her eyes off the water, as the Spanish ships failed to get into an effective formation and more went down.

"What's that?" she asked pointing. It looked as though something was aflame on one of the English ships. Then, the flames went flying through the air. It was a massive ball headed directly for the half-sunken ships. Another one flew across the water, hitting another half sunken ship.

"I think they built a kind of catapult for the ships," Greg said awkwardly answering her.

"RETREAT!" King Fernando shouted. But again, no one heard him. Smoke from the half-sunken ships around him began to fill the air.

He raced across to the deck, as fast as his large frame could carry him, repeating 'retreat'. He coughed several times, as the smoke from the other ships filled his lungs.

"THIS SHIP WILL BURN IF WE DON'T MOVE! DIRECT THE SHIP NORTH AND RETREAT!"

THE SHIPS WERE BEGINNING to go down quickly, now. The English began to form a half-moon formation around the remaining Spanish ships. There was no clear direction for the Spanish ships to head but north. But it was useless. The English ships remained virtually untouched. Whatever direction any Spanish ship would head, the English with the fast Dutch ships would immediately be tailing them.

Many of the ships were now aflame. Some flaming ships had crashed into others while other ships in flames began to explode from the gunpowder below deck. As some of them began to explode, they doomed the ships around them.

After an hour or so, the water grew quiet, and Sofia slumped down into the sand watching.

They could hear the cheers coming from the English ships, and Greg slowly sat next to her, unsure of what to do or say. The ships then began to set sail back toward London, but one stray one headed toward Edinburgh.

Greg knew that the ship was intended for him and Sofia. So did she.

"I'm sorry Sofia," he said putting his arm around her. "I think that ship is going to Edinburgh to find us. To see that we are safe. What do you want to do?"

He honestly had no idea what she would want. If she wanted to stay with him still or if she'd want to go into hiding. She sat in deep thought, then finally admitted, "It was either him or you. One of you would die. My father wouldn't go on in life without having your head."

"Do you hate me?" he asked. "Do you hate Alex?"

She took a deep breath. "I love you, Greg Umbridge, I could never hate you. That's impossible."

"And Alex?"

"Alex did something for me today, which I would never want you to do for me."

"Kill your father?"

"Yes. It would eventually have come to that. I'm glad you weren't in a position where you had to defend your life. If my father killed you, I'm sure he'd have me witness your death."

He cringed, "Why do you think he'd do that?"

"Control. To teach me a lesson. My father would kill you but he would never care if I was safe afterward. He'd never worry how it would affect me."

"No, he wouldn't," he said affirming her belief. "I'm sorry that Alex killed your father. But," he sighed and held her hand, "he's not just sending that ship to see that I'm safe. He's sending it for you, too."

"I don't think that is the case," she said folding her arms. "He wants you back with him. He'll expect you-"

"He won't expect anything," he said to her reassuringly. "Alex has always told me I could leave the castle whenever I wished. I have a wife now. He knows that."

"Then why take us from Edinburgh? Hasn't it become our home? If we go back to Windsor, where will we stay? I don't want to stay in the castle with him."

"I know. But I think he just wants us to visit. If you're that uncomfortable staying there, we can stay somewhere else. When everything is settled, we can head back to Edinburgh."

She picked up some sand and let it fall between her fingers, "I want you to promise me we won't stay long," she said. "It will be so awkward to be there. I don't want to be in front of the English court – I – I-" She began to cry, "I'll feel like a traitor to my own country."

"We won't visit court," he said firmly. "No matter what kind of invitation Alex extends, I promise I'll refuse it. If you would like, I'll take you back to Spain. I suppose you are the heir to that throne now."

She had never considered that. She was now Queen of Spain. There was still her mother, waiting in Madrid Palace. She would now be the Queen Mother.

"I don't want to be Queen of Spain," Sofia said firmly. "Not living like a royal these past few months has been the happiest time of my life."

"And your mother?"

Sofia felt unconcerned about Queen Isabelle. All the years of abuse that her father had put her through, her mother did nothing. She felt sad, but going back to Spain would only complicate things. She wouldn't want to be the Queen. She wouldn't want to spend the rest of her life there, either. "I don't wish to see her now. Maybe in time, I'll feel different."

"So," he said still trying to figure her out, "what exactly do you want?"

"I want you. I want Holyrood House," she said. "Alex should give it to me as a wedding gift."

Greg laughed. The truth was, he didn't know how Alex would react to her request. Handing a residence to another royal might be considered acceptable.

* * *

MADELINE AND BEN had already been waiting several hours for the driver to come back with a villager and a replacement wheel. While waiting in the carriage, Madeline talked to Ben. An odd kind of conversation. Once he got talking, he couldn't stop. It was surprising that he had become one of Alex's valet's. She wouldn't have imagined Alex choosing to have such an opinionated person around. He was also quite gossipy. She had remembered Marie once telling her that Alex's valets would sell information about the King and his schedule.

"You know," he began casually. "I think I had known about you and King Alexander before most people did."

She was shocked that he was so forthright.

"Really?" she chuckled. "Why is that?"

"Jack, Richard and I knew there was a lady. We figured there had to be one. There seemed to be a spring in his step. Whenever he found a woman he was really interested in, his demeanour would suddenly change."

Miss Hampton sprung to Madeline's mind. "How many times would you say he had changed like that?" she asked curiously.

He smiled, "Oh there were several times before. Miss Haskin, Miss Cavendish and his music tutor, Miss Embry. Though, she was much older. It's not a wonder he had such a love for music. Of course, there was Miss Hampton."

Obviously, Ben didn't know how insensitive he was being. It was as though he thought she already knew of Alex's former loves. She wondered if she should keep up the conversation, or politely point out that it was best she didn't know. But she wanted to know, "There were others, though. Others he didn't care as much for?" she pressed.

He chuckled, "Oh yes. Plenty. I think that Miss Pye thought she was the love of his life. He hardly ever mentioned her. Then there were all the ladies of the French court that would pay a visit to England. Lady Brasson would come by to visit England for several weeks. Then it would turn into several months."

It was a lot to take. But Madeline kept an even expression. She wanted to know about his feelings for Miss Hampton. She laughed, "I didn't know she made excuses," she lied, making it sound as though she knew who Lady Brasson was. She continued, "I've noticed that Miss Hampton still seems quite interested in him. She gawks at him a lot."

"Well, that makes sense. After all those two had been through together."

She paused, "Been through? What have they been through?"

It was at that moment Ben realized that Alex hadn't gone into much detail about the women of his past. Ben had thought at the very least Alex had mentioned them, or that they had come up in conversation. It was strange to him that she didn't know anything about Miss Hampton. He supposed he had given her more information than Alex had ever intended. "I don't know all that much," he said cringing.

"You know more than I know, Ben."

"I'm sure there are things you don't want to know," he said uneasily.

"Tell me. What was their relationship like?"

He swallowed hard.

"Don't make me order you to tell me," Madeline said. "I will if I have to."

"Well, this is a fine position to be in," he said sheepishly. "Either I'm in a bad way with the King or the Queen."

He was right, but she didn't care. "If you don't tell me Ben, I may have to ask him myself. If he questions why, I'll say I talked to you."

He looked fearful.

"But," she continued. "If you tell me, I'll never tell him where I got any of my information from."

He sighed, "It was a relationship that had a lot of ups and downs."

"When did they meet?"

"Oh, they've known each other practically their entire lives. The Duke of Axford is her godfather, so they were introduced to each other quite young. Before I came to work for the monarchy."

"Do you know if he met her before Sir Gregory?"

"Possibly. They've known each other since they were kids."

"You said it was full of lots of ups and downs. What kinds of ups and downs?"

"I think she knew he liked to chase after her, so she'd play games. She'd have him court her for weeks; then she'd start becoming interested in another bloke. Mind you, he did the same kind of thing, seeing other girls."

"How long did this go on for?"

"Years. Greg found it annoying. Greg thought she was head over heels in love with Alex but played these games to keep Alex interested."

"What do you think?"

"I think they were in love at one point. But because of the way they treated each other, eventually, they grew irritated with each other."

She thought of the first night she had met him. The first night she had seen them together. She remembered how Miss Hampton teased – almost taunted him. It was a game. Their interaction was her gaining control.

"Do you think they got tired of one another?" she asked.

"I don't know. For a long time, we all thought that they'd outgrow being the way they were."

"When do you think it ended?"

"I think she's still in love with him."

She didn't want to ask how Alex felt about Miss Hampton, so she decided to change the subject. "So, she's the Duke of Axford's goddaughter? What is her relationship with him like?"

"I'm willing to bet that she knows where the Duke has escaped to. It's been a while now, I'm sure he's been in contact with her. The Duke was never really close to many, but always had a soft spot for Miss Hampton."

She was speechless. She had no idea that the Duke had escaped. Once again Ben spoke too soon. She wanted more information but knew she would have to act casual.

"Being away in Warwick Castle, worrying about the battle with the Spanish, I've lost track of time. How many days has it been since he escaped?"

"Days? More like weeks. I think it was just a few days after you left Frogmore, wasn't it?"

"Mmm," she said, her blood beginning to boil, though she wouldn't let it show. Alex had to have been informed of this immediately after it had happened. It disgusted her that he was keeping a secret from her. She felt betrayed. It seemed Alex was trying to free the Duke. Or maybe he was just pleasing Miss Hampton? There was no doubt in her mind that it was Miss Hampton she had seen in the tea shop in Warwick. The place she had stayed in was the Hampton's homestead. There had been few times in Madeline's life where she grew so angry that she couldn't contain herself. Living the way she had before she had met Alex had made her skin like steel. But as she sat there, Ben noticed her shaking, "Are you all right?" he asked concerned. "Is it all this waiting?"

"Be honest with me Mr. Caston," she said harshly, "is his Majesty with Miss Hampton right now?"

"I – I," he began stuttering. He wasn't sure what to say. He knew that Miss Hampton had gone back to Windsor Castle with Alex. He wasn't sure if she was with him at the present. He didn't want to tell her that he had taken a carriage back with Miss Hampton. If there was something going on between the two, he didn't know. But, even if he did, he didn't want to tell Madeline.

"IS HE BEING UNFAITHFUL?" she erupted.

"Not sure, your Majesty," he said weakly.

"AARRRGGHHHH!" she cried out, pounding her fists into the

314

bench. She threw the door open and stepped out. Ben went after her, following behind as she stomped on the dirt road.

"Your Majesty, what are you doing? Where are you going?" he asked afraid.

"Our driver is taking far too long. I'm sure I could take one of these horses and ride back. Alex has some explaining to do."

"Uh, your Majesty with all respect, do you think that wise? You are with child."

"I'll do what I please."

"I'm not sure that the King has been unfaithful! If he has been, there's nothing you can do about it at this moment. Please reconsider this, your Majesty."

She stopped, turned around and wagged her finger in his face, "He's lying to me! Why wouldn't he tell me about the Duke of Axford escaping? Why would he spend so much time with Miss Hampton? He's had all sorts of private meetings over the past couple of weeks. I've found some odd things around Warwick Castle. I thought it may have been a spy. But no, he's been seeing her! That house I was in. It was hers, wasn't it?"

"Honestly, that house does not belong to the Hampton family. That much I do know your Majesty," said Ben shakily.

"Free this horse," she said pointing to the strongest looking one. "I'll ride this one back."

"Please don't do this," he begged. "A ride that long isn't good for you. You're in a delicate state."

"That's a royal command untie the horse."

He followed the order, slowly separating the horse from the others, he continued to try to dissuade her, "If not for your health, you should think of your baby. I know you're angry, but could you live with that regret?"

She felt a soft kick in her stomach and a tear fell from her cheek. She nearly collapsed in the dirt, but Ben caught her and gently settled her to the ground. She kicked her feet in frustration. He sat next to her. She began to wail, uncontrollably.

He was uncertain of what to do. If he touched her, even patted her

315

on the back, it could be seen as inappropriate. He took out a handkerchief and offered it to her.

She took it, and wiped her eyes, looking away from him in embarrassment. Off in the distance, she could see the driver with another man coming toward them.

* * *

AFTER THE FUNERAL, Lord Walsh accompanied Alex in the carriage back to Windsor Castle. Neither of them said much. Once they reached Windsor Castle, Lord Walsh asked if he wanted some company for afternoon tea. Though Alex wanted to be alone with his thoughts, he knew that Lord Walsh needed company. They had tea in the Green Drawing Room, sitting next to the mantle.

"It is beginning to get draughty, don't you think your Majesty?" Lord Walsh said. "Perhaps I should request that the servants begin to get the fires in the castle going."

It was late October, cool, but there was no reason to begin lighting the fireplaces. Alex didn't want to insult Lord Walsh; the man was already in a frantic state. He sat across from Alex, twisting his handkerchief tightly in his hands, his bottom lip trembling. It was an awkward situation. Alex knew that Lord Walsh wanted to talk about Sir Ashton.

"It was a beautiful day today," Alex began.

"Yes, the state funeral was a good choice, your Majesty. He was truly a patriot of England."

"He was more than a patriot to me," Alex said softly.

Lord Walsh nodded, "Your father picked a very good advisor."

"No. Perhaps I shouldn't say this, but my father picked someone who ended up taking his place. Sir Ashton was always nearby. I can't say the same for either of my parents."

"You will miss him dearly then."

"Yes. Nothing around here will ever be the same."

"No, nothing," Lord Walsh paused. "I'm sorry for asking, your Majesty, but he was, uh, a good friend to me. Do you know anything about what exactly happened? Do you have any idea who the perpetrator was?"

"I have a number of men investigating, but they haven't reported back to me yet."

"He was an amazing man. Came from such humble beginnings and managed to earn the respect of kings and nobles," Lord Walsh said as he began to loosen his grip on his handkerchief.

"Mmm. True. I never knew a wiser man. He taught me so much about life."

"He had a wealth of knowledge. He will be hard to replace," Lord Walsh said.

"He's irreplaceable," said Alex as he tapped the side of his tea cup with his finger.

"Well, he died a truly rich man. Other than your father, I've never seen a funeral with so many people," Lord Walsh commented.

Alex nodded, "I would agree, but I have a feeling that Sir Ashton would disagree with the idea that he was rich when he passed away."

"Really?" Lord Walsh said with interest. "What would make you think he wasn't a rich man? He had the respect of everyone in the kingdom."

Alex stretched his feet up on the couch and kicked off his shoes, "I remember when I was still just a boy, there used to be a gardener at Windsor Castle. You may remember him, Mr. Morris."

"Oh yes," Lord Walsh smiled, making himself comfortable along with Alex, he released the handkerchief and rested his arm on a pillow. "Yes, he was a lovely man. Often brought his children and grandchildren in the spring to help with planting, isn't that right?"

"Greg and I loved chatting with him. Always a happy fellow, he'd get excited about the simpler things in life. When the first sprouts of spring would come, he would pull Greg and I aside to show us. He loved the conservatory at Frogmore, too. He knew a lot about nature."

"As I recall he had a great sense of humour, too."

"Oh yes," Alex nodded. "He used to play some great jokes on the people around Windsor and Frogmore. Then, he passed away. I was only seven, but I had a dog that had died earlier that year, so I understood that he wouldn't come back."

"He wasn't that old, was he?" Lord Walsh said.

"Mr. Morris? No. I was quite upset about that. For some reason, I felt sorry for Mr. Morris. I thought he had missed out. But Sir Ashton didn't think so. He told me that Mr. Morris was the richest man he knew."

"Really?" Lord Walsh asked. "How so?"

"Everyone Mr. Morris knew, loved him. His parents loved him, his siblings, his children, his grandchildren and his wife, his in-laws. He was surrounded by love throughout his life. Days before he passed, he was surrounded by the people who loved him. Very few people have that much love in their lives, Lord Walsh."

"I don't know your Majesty. Sir Ashton died a highly respected man by all those who knew him."

"Yes. But the people that mattered most to him were not always by his side."

Lord Walsh wished he could correct Alex, but he couldn't. His eyes welled up.

Alex continued, "Hardly any man has that much love surrounding him through his life. Think hard. Imagine one person you know like Mr. Morris."

Lord Walsh sat in thought, then snapped his fingers, "Perhaps Sir Gregory."

"Closest you may come. But he hasn't had children or grandchildren. Not to mention the fact that his in-laws are not crazy about him."

"In-laws?" Lord Walsh said in surprise.

"I'm imagining by now Sir Gregory has married Princess Sofia," Alex chuckled answering his thoughts.

Lord Walsh shook his head with a grin. He doubted the King or Queen of Spain were impressed by this.

"Do you think that they are safe?" Lord Walsh asked.

"I have a feeling that they are. Greg wouldn't be foolish enough to stick around."

"It's a shame that he couldn't be here for Sir Ashton's funeral."

"It won't be easy news to tell him," Alex admitted. "If the English defeat the Spanish, I have sent a ship and some men to find Greg and Sofia and bring them home. After we have the baby announcement party, I would like to have a party for them. Would you be up to the task?"

"Certainly, your Majesty."

"Excellent."

"Speaking of which, is everything ready for the announcement party?"

"Invitations should be sent out tomorrow."

"Good. After all that has happened, it would be nice to celebrate."

THEIR CONVERSATION WAS INTERRUPTED as Madeline stormed into the room, Ben Caston at her heels.

"Madeline," Alex exclaimed as he got to his feet with a huge smile on his face. "Lord Walsh told me what happened." Alex dashed over to hug her, but she put up her arms to stop him.

"Lord Walsh, Mr. Caston, please leave," she said in a surly tone. "I would like to speak to my husband alone." The two exchanged worried looks as they headed toward the doors. "Close the doors behind you," she said curtly, her eyes boring into him.

Once they were alone, Alex ignored her glare and tried to put his arms around her again, "Are you all right, Madeline? God, I'm sorry, I know that must have been hard."

She pushed him away. "What must have been hard? The fact that you abandoned me to risk your life? You didn't even say 'goodbye.'"

"I -I" he stuttered, trying to explain.

"Oh, wait. Maybe you're sorry because you left me in a strange place, most likely owned by the Hampton family. How was your trip back with her, anyway? Did you think I wouldn't find out?" she said, her voice rising.

"I can explain all of this," he said hoping he could calm her down. But her hands were clenched into fists.

319

"You can start with telling me why you decided to not tell me that the Duke of Axford escaped Curfew Tower. Or was he let out?"

Alex became speechless, unsure of how she could know that he had ordered Sir Ashton to free him.

"I suppose Miss Hampton couldn't bear to see her godfather locked up," she yelled pushing his chest, "and you couldn't deny her his freedom."

"What?" he said utterly confused. "You think I've been seeing her?"

"Aren't you? All these private meetings? All the odd things I've found around Frogmore and Warwick Castle. Do you care to explain? Maybe she was the one who tore my room apart at Frogmore!"

"Madeline, don't be ridiculous," he said putting his hands to his temples massaging them.

"Ridiculous?" she squeaked. "You're the one keeping secrets! Now you expect me to believe that you aren't seeing Miss Hampton? Ben told me about you and her. I didn't know you were in love with her. By the sounds of it, you two courted quite a bit over the years."

"It's in the past."

"And in all the time we've been together, you've never mentioned how close you two had been! She was a big part of your past! Blast! You've known each other since you were children, Alex!"

"When I'm with you, I'm not thinking of her, nor do I care to talk about her," he said trying to approach her again.

"Why should I believe that now?" she said stepping back from him. "After all you've been keeping from me, I'd be daft to trust what you're saying!" She burst into tears, then stormed out of the room.

LOVE AND WAR

Greg gazed at Sofia longingly. Since coming on aboard the ship, she was a little down and had hardly spoken a word. When they had first boarded, Captain Keswick gave up his living quarters for them, explaining that it wouldn't be appropriate for the royalty of Spain to stay in an unsuitable apartment.

Sofia sat at the Captain's desk. It was a large piece of solid mahogany, with carvings of topless mermaids etched into each of the corners. Though Sofia was glum, she knew it hadn't much to do with her family; she was concerned about what the future would hold. If they couldn't live in Edinburgh, it would be an adjustment for her to go to London or Windsor.

Greg tried to brighten her spirits, "You know this could be something like a honeymoon," he said as he hopped onto the bed with its blue and white silk sheets. "This cabin is lovely. How many people get to set sail after their wedding? It's romantic."

Sofia grinned, "So, being on this vessel full with the English Royal Navy is romantic?"

"Hardly I suppose," he said surveying his surroundings, "but this is a stunning room."

She looked out the gallery of windows. It did have a kind of charm.

The sun was setting, and the water shimmered. The blue and white silk decor on the solid wood panels made it a cosy place.

"That is the most beautiful sunset I've ever seen," he said, gesturing to the windows.

"Yes," she admitted, "this probably is the nicest room on the ship."

"I doubt the crew's barracks are anything like this." He gave a weak smile, "I'm sure the best wines and liquors are in this room, too. Would you like to drink with me?"

She nodded. He began to open up some cabinets, and pulled out a few wine glasses and set them next to her.

"What would you like red or white? Oi, there's some Bordeaux wine in here!"

"Oooh, I like Bordeaux," she said clapping her hands, looking over at him.

He picked up the bottle, "A little light, think there may only be half a glass. He walked over and poured her what was left.

"You can have it," she said.

"No, Princess, we drink together, remember? Besides, I'm sure there's more on the ship; perhaps we should get something to eat, too. Why don't you sit here with your wine and enjoy the view? I'll get us some more Bordeaux and something to eat."

"All right," she said, "Oooh, and see if there's any fresh seafood."

"Certainly."

He turned on his heel and left.

She sat watching the water gleam as it moved. Alone, she exhaled slowly, there was so much pent-up emotion built inside her, she felt as if she were about to burst. She had her freedom and the man she loved. She had never dared dream that she wouldn't have to answer to her father or her brother. A grin came across her face. She had wanted to do it since she saw the ships go down. Her eyes glistened with tears of joy. "Gracias ... gracias ..." she said to no one in particular. All she knew was she was grateful.

She lifted her half glass of Bordeaux, raised it to the sunset, laughed then drank.

Sometime later, Greg came back to the room and she howled at the sight of him. He was wearing some old ratty clothes, a bandana around his forehead and had a couple of bottles in his hands.

"What are you wearing? You look like a pirate!"

"I know!" he said excitedly. "I ran into some blokes that were telling me that this ship used to be Captain James Cook's!"

"Who?" she asked.

"You don't know who Captain James Cook is?" Greg said shocked. "Thought you would have learned that in your history lessons."

"You think my father wanted me educated on British History?" she said shaking her head.

"Right. He was an explorer. Lived about forty years ago. He went all over the world mapping different territories and documenting the kinds of species and plants he saw when he sailed. Guessing he may have come across a few pirates at some point."

"Those clothes don't look very old, Greg," she said pointing at them.

He shrugged, "Well, I'm not really sure when the pirates came about. But I also found out what kind of food is on the ship. They had quite a few different types of fish. They even had some shellfish and crab. Of course, I made sure that you and I would get a lovely dinner. I found the stash of booze, took a few bottles and offered some Bordeaux to the chef."

She shook her head as her face lit up; getting dressed as a pirate while wining and dining her. It was obvious he had gone all around the ship trying to find something to lighten her mood.

"Thank you," she said blushing.

"My pleasure. We'll have to wait a bit for the food. It'll take a while for it to be prepared."

"So why the pirate costume?"

"Just thought it would be fun. Do you like me as a pirate?" he asked, standing in profile.

She did. Though she was embarrassed to say so. He looked rugged, his hair a mess and his shirt worn loosely, she could see his hard chest through the material. He looked dangerous and sexy.

"You're more of a clown to me," she lied.

"So you married a clown?" He walked over to the desk, grabbed a couple wine glasses and headed over to the dining table, "Let's have a drink together, Princess."

She looked down at his trousers. They hung on him loosely and he wore a sash to hold them up. She pictured loosening the sash and the trousers falling to the floor. She doubted he had much on underneath. She bit her lip, thinking of the time she and Greg travelled to Edinburgh and he shackled her to the spokes of the carriage wheel. She liked being his captive.

"Princesses don't usually keep pirates as company," she said softly.

"No," he said noticing the way her eyes drank him in, staring at his crotch. He put the wine bottle down and went over to her. Lifting her chin with his finger, his eyes penetrated hers, "Princesses don't usually spend their time with pirates. But, this isn't Spain or England. You're on the water," he said huskily, "You're on my boat and you will do what I say."

She bit her lip trying to contain her anticipation, he obviously knew that she wanted to play. "A lady of my status wouldn't listen to a thief like you," she said feigning dismissiveness as she stood up. "You're just going to have to deal with that," she whispered into his ear.

"Now Princess, you don't want me to get tired of you," he said shaking his finger at her. "You're in my cabin for a reason. If you can't be a good girl and take off your clothes, I'll just send you down to the sleeping quarters. I'm sure my crew would love to tear that pretty dress off you."

"I would never dream of being with a man like you," she said through grit teeth.

"You will after I'm finished with you."

They stared at each other hard. He waited for her to try to run for the door. She slowly moved across the room, but he followed her every step.

"You walk through that door, and I'll leave you to my crewmen. Trust me; they would love to have a taste of a fine woman like you."

She darted for the door, but he caught her in his arms. Squealing and kicking, he dragged her over to the canopy bed and tossed her onto it. She scrambled about the sheets feigning to get away, but the bed was tucked in the corner of the room. Only one side of the bed was open, and he was blocking it; the other three sides had solid wood panels.

"Nowhere to go, Princess?"

"I'll find a way out," she said in a sultry tone.

"No, you won't. You don't want to." He grabbed both of her thighs at once and pulled her down. She landed on her bottom.

"Mmm, Greg," she giggled as he nibbled her neck.

"Princess, I'm the Captain of this ship. You'll do as I say."

He came, pawing at her like a pirate ruffian. He tore at her dress, pulling at the buttons. They ricocheted off the bed and rolled onto the floor. She pulled at the sash around his waist, and his trousers slipped down his legs. She sighed at the sight of him, and he was ready for her. "You think this will be good enough for a princess?" she said tauntingly as she stroked him.

"You seem to approve. You can't keep your hands to yourself."

He held her head at her nape, gazing at her as if she were a precious treasure he'd just found. Her amethyst globes stared back at him, the tension between them growing. He was moments away from ravaging her but save for this, the desire in her eyes. There was nothing more arousing to him than seeing that covetous look in her, and he'd sometimes pause before delighting in her to enjoy the insatiable look, which was almost equal to his.

"Since we will be sailing for a while," she began breathlessly, "you can take your time."

"I intend to."

He pulled her dress down her legs, and she loosened her stay. He pulled it away, revealing her curvaceous form. He skimmed his hands up and down her sides, her skin tingling like fire under his touch. She reached out, grasped his shirt, and tore; buttons popped off and scattered across the floor. Greg's eyes widened. She smirked, "You did ruin my dress."

"Go on," he said, incited by her initiation.

Now he was hers, and she felt more daring. She tugged hard on his shirt, and their lips crashed together, their lips a whirling force of passion. His musky scent mixed with the salty sea smell delighted her senses. Her hands roved through his hair and onto his broad shoulders. An aching roared inside her; she knew the dance of their lips and pawing at one another wouldn't last long.

He gripped her bottom, pulling her toward him. She felt her intimate flesh next to his and gently nibbled his bottom lip. His fingers slipped between her thighs, delving into the soft, damp curls. Her body gave a shudder, but she had wanted control. Her hand slipped down between them, taking a firm grasp. His eyes bulged open, a gasp escaped his mouth, and his eyes became slits.

"I want you laying on this bed," she said, giving a slight pull, as she leaned back. He climbed onto the bed, and she guided him onto his back. She straddled over him, the hard mast beneath her. He held the curves of her hips, as the warmth sheathed around him, he exhaled, shuddering. The vision of her was enticing; she was seconds away from gratifying herself upon him, and sight of it could send him over. But he held on – it would be arduous but delicious.

She took charge, tormenting him as she slid up and down, her muscles constricting, inviting him in. Instinctively, she found the motion that satisfied her best, and the air filled with her moans and thumps of the bed with every descent. She fell apart on him once, muzzling her sharp cries by crashing her lips to his. Though she was enjoying herself, she had not quite felt her need abated. She stared down at him, noting a mischievous expression on his face. He was holding back, letting the intensity of it grow as she did all the movement.

"Please," she begged.

"If we hold out a little longer, I swear you'll see stars, Princess."

"I swear to you, I nearly do. Please."

He considered her lovingly, admiring the sweetness of her pout. He tucked a strand of her disheveled hair behind her ear.

"I really do have a hard time telling you 'no.'"

She held him, and he powered through her, like a ship slicing through waves, redirecting them. His efforts were so much more direct than her own, reaching her depths harder and at a quicker pace. Her body responded, twitching. He was right. She felt dizzy, her mind in a fog. Heat surged through her, and her breath became shallow. She whimpered, pounding down on his hard chest with her fist, unable to stop the force shattering her apart. She cried out, almost screaming.

As promised, he took his time and spoiled her again and again. What had begun in the daylight had finished at dusk, with the pairs' glistening flesh bound to one another's. He huffed and puffed as she lined the edges of muscles on his chest with her fingertips.

"I'm so tired," she said lazily.

"What about the food?" he asked. "We haven't eaten for hours. Are you more tired or hungry?"

"Tired."

"We'll eat later then," he said, yawning, and the two drifted off to sleep.

* * *

MADELINE HAD DONE her best to ignore Alex over the next few days. She locked herself in her room at Frogmore, and would only let Martha, Marie, or Sissy visit.

Feeling the tension, the girls tried not to talk about the situation. Though they knew exactly what the quarrel was about – as Ben Caston had told several people at Windsor Castle – they decided to say nothing.

Hurt by what Alex had done, Madeline scolded herself for marrying a king. Powerful men always lied and cheated on their wives.

Everyday he'd come knocking at her door and try to speak to her from outside. She hardly responded to anything he said. She'd either tell him to leave or give him the silent treatment. "You know dolcezza, if you just let me inside, I'm sure we could sort this all out."

Silence.

"I was only with Miss Hampton because a messenger in Warwick was needed. She was a messenger, that's all."

"There were plenty of other people you could have chosen. Why her?"

He didn't know what to say. The truth was a long story and it would hurt. "Please let me in," he begged.

"Not for anything."

He paced back and forth for a while. "I missed you. I hated that I couldn't say goodbye to you after our stay at the spa."

"For all you knew that could have been our final goodbye, Alex. If something happened to you, she would have been the last woman you were with. Wouldn't she?"

"Madeline let me in," he said brushing his hand down the panels. "I know you're angry, but I …" He stopped, questioning if he should suggest it. He was getting desperate. It killed him that she was hurt. Seeing her again was what kept him going. He wanted her. "I promise if you let me in, I'll do anything you ask to make you feel better."

Her jaw dropped. *Is he trying to bribe me with intimacy?* She walked over to the door and tried to peek through the crack. The thought of having him for a couple of hours, at her will was enticing to her, and he knew it.

He sensed her near and she could see him smile devilishly.

"Anything you want, dolcezza. Deep down, you know I wasn't unfaithful to you."

She put her hand on the knob, then dropped it. She couldn't allow him to seduce her so easily, "Are you serious? Why would I want to be with you?"

"I never cheated on you with Miss Hampton," he said sternly. "I kept things from you, yes, but only because I wanted to protect you. I love you." He stormed off down the hall and Madeline sank down to the floor, a sense of guilt coming over her.

She didn't have any evidence that he had been with Miss Hampton. No one had seen anything. She knew he and Miss Hampton were over. But his strange behaviour made her wonder if there was something more sinister at play. *What is he protecting me from? Why isn't he telling me the truth?*

An hour later, Madeline had all three of her friends in her drawing room, the doors locked. Martha, Marie, and Sissy entered with some tea and treats thinking they would be there to listen. But it seemed more like Madeline wanted to interrogate them. "Sorry, but there is no time for tea," Madeline said firmly as she set the pot aside. The three exchanged worried looks. "All of you have spent the last few weeks and months here at Frogmore and at Windsor Castle. Have you noticed anything odd about Alex?" Madeline asked pacing in front of the three as they sat on the couch.

"How do you mean?" Martha asked cautiously.

"Well, who have you been seeing him spend his time with?"

The ladies all looked at one another, each hoping the other would speak up.

"Should I separate you all?" Madeline said her look severe.

"Is that necessary? Do you think we would lie to you?" Marie asked, with a sympathetic expression.

"Ah. But you know something," Madeline said, wagging her finger.

"Yes, we've noticed some odd things," Marie said looking up at Madeline worried. "But I'm not sure it has anything to do with Miss Hampton."

"What have you seen? You've seen some odd behaviour, haven't you?"

Martha sighed. "There's a rumour going around that his Majesty met with the Duke of Axford privately before the Duke escaped."

"What!?" Madeline said, staring in shock.

"We don't know what it was about," Sissy chimed in. "I mean, he could have been demanding a confession."

"I doubt that Sissy," Marie shook her head. "He had the Duke wear a disguise just so he could meet him."

"Where did you hear this?" Madeline asked flabbergasted.

"Harold. He had duties in Curfew Tower that day. Sir Ashton Giles came and got him."

"What about Miss Hampton?"

"Well, Alex has been meeting with her. Very private though."

Embarrassed Madeline asked, "Has anyone heard things, uh, sounds coming from the rooms they are in?"

"I heard them yelling at one another once," Martha offered.

"Yes, but Harold told me they used to do a lot of that when they saw each other," Marie said.

"I don't think anyone thinks there is anything going on there, Mad," Sissy said absent-mindedly, "I mean, your Majesty."

Madeline guffawed, "Never mind pleasantries, Sissy. What do you think these meetings are about?"

"Not sure," Sissy shrugged. "I wouldn't be surprised if there was a lot of talk about plans for the battle with Spain."

"Maybe it has to do with the other odd thing some servants have noticed," Marie said a light going off in her head.

"What? What odd thing?" Madeline pressed.

"Harold told me that a few people have seen him go back to Frogmore and Windsor Castle a frightful mess," Marie confessed taping her finger to her lips. "It has happened several times now."

"A mess?" Madeline asked, fearing his clothes looked dishevelled from a romp with Miss Hampton.

"He's left a few times during the night, apparently," Marie continued. "A couple weeks before you left to go to Warwick Castle, I saw him come home to Frogmore with a dirty face. His clothes were covered in mud."

Madeline stared in wonderment. Alex had excused himself late at night, telling her he had secret meetings to go to concerning the war. But he had never had late night meetings while they stayed in Warwickshire. He had been going somewhere near Windsor Castle and Frogmore.

"Where do you think he may have gone?" Madeline asked.

"No clue," Marie said. "But it sounds doubtful that he was with Miss Hampton. These days she spends most of her time at court in London."

"I think the King has been at it again since he has come back," Sissy pipped up. "My friend Delilah had said she had seen the King walking nearby the King's Head covered in dirt. It was shortly before you came back, Madeline. Delilah wanted to know if I knew anything about it."

Madeline paused. She had completely forgotten about Delilah.

"I thought that no one could find her? I thought your friend had gone missing."

"Oh she's come back now," Sissy nodded. "She had gone away for several weeks. It was short notice for her. One of the Lords had whisked her away to the countryside," her voice squeaked in delight.

"Some of Alex's advisors wanted to have a few words with her," Madeline said, a little frustrated. "You know the crown has been suspicious of her Sissy. Why didn't you have her meet with one of Alex's advisors?"

"There's really no need. She wanted to know if she could attend the party tomorrow night. You can question her then. I'm certain she's no spy, Mad."

"Sissy, I'm not sure we should have someone at our party that Alex nor I know anything about," Madeline said.

Marie giggled, "I doubt Delilah has anything to do with the Spanish if that's what you're thinking, Mad. If she were involved with them, wouldn't she be running off to Spain? They lost."

"Good point, Marie," Madeline said biting her fingernails, but she still had her doubts.

Sissy looked at her pleadingly, "Please Mad, I'm sure Delilah will be no trouble. If she were, she would have done something by now, I'm sure."

"That's fine, Sissy," Madeline said uneasily. "You only have a day to get a messenger to your friend. Why don't you go talk to Mr. Barry?"

Sissy excused herself, curtsying, a big smile on her face as she left the room. After she had left, Madeline turned to the other ladies. "I don't know who this Delilah character is, but to me, she sounds a little too cunning. What do you think?"

Marie chuckled again, "Are you serious, Madeline? Are you paranoid about everything and everyone? What do you think she's done?

Just because the King is acting a little strange, does that mean everyone can't be trusted?"

"Actually, I agree with Madeline," Martha said. "I mean, I've heard that the King has gone out at night a few times too, coming home at the most ungodly hours. How is it that Delilah has seen him? What is she doing out on the street so late at night?"

"Well," began Marie blushing. "I think we all know that she's the type of lady that gets paid for her time."

"True," Martha said. "But most subjects could not spot the King looking dirty. Knowing King Alexander, he probably wore a disguise. Whoever Delilah is, seems to know a thing or two about him."

* * *

SUSANNA HADN'T BEEN FEELING WELL over the past week. She had plenty of headaches and thrown up a few times. Not that this bothered her. It was a sign she'd been waiting and hoping for. Staying tucked under her sheets with a bucket next to the bed was a small price to pay. She had been pregnant before. Several times. She always went through the same signs around the second or third week. The first time she was pregnant, she went to see a doctor thinking she had some kind of illness. Now whenever she threw up and had a number of migraines for a week or so, and missed her period, she knew she was pregnant.

There was no doubt in her mind that it was Arsenio's child. She and Carlos never consummated their marriage after they wed; they had been together only once. If she was as far along as she thought she was, she must have conceived after Carlos and Fernando had left. It was perfect timing.

Of course, there would be a few that would doubt Carlos was the father. She and Arsenio had been spending a lot of time together. Queen Isabelle seemed to be oblivious to this. The Queen had warmed to her over the past few weeks, but if someone suggested that Susanna had been cheating, it might end the trust she had worked so hard to gain. Susanna didn't know what to expect from

Queen Isabelle. Initially, when several of the Lords broke the news that the Spanish had been defeated in Windsor, she collapsed on the floor and cried. But later in the day, before dinner, she seemed to be fine again. Since that day, Isabelle had never mentioned Prince Carlos again.

Susanna and Arsenio suspected the same thing; Queen Isabelle wasn't sorrowful about losing her son. If the Spanish won the war, her life wouldn't change for the better. If anything, King Fernando would become more paranoid of her behaviour. Carlos's death gave the Queen reason to hope. If King Fernando was defeated, it meant that she would no longer live in fear. She could finally be free of her prison. But it was apparent that the Queen still missed Sofia.

However, if King Fernando brought her back, he'd use the two women as pawns again. Arsenio had told Susanna that King Fernando used to hurt his wife to discipline his daughter and vice-versa. Though Isabelle often left her daughter to be punished, Arsenio believed that Isabelle loved Sofia more than anyone. If the King didn't return, the next time the Queen saw Sofia, they wouldn't have to worry any longer about what they did or said.

One of the ladies in waiting entered the room. "Uggh!" Susanna moaned rolling over in her bed. "I am royalty! What in the bloody hell are you doing barging into my room like this? What is the meaning of this?"

The lady looked at her dumbfounded. "I'm sorry, your Highness," she said awkwardly in her heavy Spanish accent. She curtsied. "The Queen has asked for you."

"I'm not well. I'm sure the Queen has heard."

"It's important. It's about the, the …" she got lost trying to think of the word.

"War?" Susanna said quickly.

"Yes. That's it, your Highness, it's about the war."

Susanna pulled off her covers. She stood in the middle of the room and spread her arms.

"Dress me, please."

"What would you like, your Highness?"

"An afternoon dress would be fine. I have plans to come back here."

"I'll find something easy to wear."

After getting dressed, Susanna was escorted down to the Throne Room. Queen Isabelle sat on the throne. Señor Astucia was there, along with the rest of the ladies in waiting and some Lords. Susanna did a curtsy to the Queen, "Forgive me, your Majesty," she said in Spanish as she curtsied, "I haven't been well."

Queen Isabelle nodded.

A man Susanna had never seen before stepped forward and the conversation continued in Spanish tongue, "Her Majesty felt that it would be best that I deliver this news. His Majesty, King Fernando of Spain, has died in the North Sea. Though he fought well and was brave even in his final moments, the English were sneaky. They borrowed some Dutch ships and attacked. They also commandeered Prince Carlos's ships from Brighton and attacked with those as well. The English are not the gentlemen they claim to be."

No one spoke, all eyes fell on Susanna. She looked down to her feet.

"Excuse me," Señor Astucia piped up. "I don't think it's appropriate to insult the English when her Highness, Princess Susanna, is English."

"We have lost Prince Carlos, King Fernando and possibly Princess Sofia to them. I have no shame in saying what I said," said the Lord. "I think her Majesty, Queen Isabelle, should consider sending this impostor back to England."

"You make it sound as though she planned the attack," Señor Astucia said accusingly. "It was her husband that died. Her opportunity to be the next Queen of England was also lost."

The messenger grew nervous at his words, "I never said that she had a part in it, but-"

"It doesn't matter what you think," Señor Astucia said cutting him off. "It is Queen Isabelle's decision to make." He turned to Queen Isabelle and bowed his head, "Your Majesty, would you prefer Princess Susanna to stay here in Spain?"

Everyone looked to the Queen, but Susanna could see the weakness in her. Like a timid deer, her mouth hung open. Queen Isabelle never spoke on these kinds of matters. Susanna stepped forward and curtsied, "I can't leave," she whimpered dramatically, "I think I may be with child … the future heir to the Spanish crown." She threw her hands to her face and pretended to cry.

Silence and tension filled the room. But Señor Astucia spoke up, "We cannot send away the future heir of the Spanish throne," he said simply. "Are you sure that you are pregnant, Princess?"

"I'm not certain," Susanna admitted. Pulling her hands away from her eyes, she sniffled, "but there have been several signs."

"That settles it," Señor Astucia said. "Princess Susanna stays here in Spain, for as long as Queen Isabelle would prefer her to stay."

"Queen Isabelle, what will you do if Princess is not pregnant?" the messenger asked.

"Enough bombarding the Queen with these types of questions," said Señor Astucia angrily. "She has just heard the news that she has lost her husband. You're nagging her about the Princess is insensitive. What needs to be done is a proper funeral for the country to mourn the deaths of two great leaders. Her Majesty has had a difficult month. I think that she, as well as the Princess, need time alone."

"Thank … you, Lord . . Astucia," Susanna mumbled, feigning to choke on her words. She wiped her eyes, "I do believe I need time alone, though. I miss Prince Carlos. Your Majesty," Susanna curtsied to Queen Isabelle, who nodded and she left the room.

Most women in Susanna's position would be fearful, but she wasn't. King Fernando and Prince Carlos were dead; leaving Spain to go to another country with nothing was better than a lifetime with them.

When she reached her room, she stripped off her dress and crawled back into her bed, wearing just her stay. She sighed looking down at the bucket.

KNOCK, KNOCK

She rolled her eyes, "Spaniards." She sighed, "Come in."

Señor Astucia walked in, "Sorry, if I'm disturbing you."

"Arsenio," she shifted in her bed so that she was sitting up. It was then she realized that she had left without speaking to him.

"Is it true? Are you pregnant?" he asked.

"I'm fairly certain," she said softly.

He sauntered next to her, brushing his hand across the bedcovers, anxiously, "You believe Prince Carlos got you pregnant?"

She swallowed hard. He knew just as she did, that the chances that it was Carlos's were slim. She and Arsenio had been at one another for weeks, taking every opportunity they could. She glanced about the room, uncertain if she should speak her suspicions. He could feel that she was uncomfortable saying it aloud.

"Do you think you got pregnant just after you wed? Before Prince Carlos left?" he asked, his eyes penetrating hers. It was obvious Arsenio knew that she and Carlos never consummated their marriage.

"If I am pregnant, I'm quite sure it happened after we wed," she said giving him a toothy grin. "It must have been the wedding night."

He chuckled. The night of their wedding, Prince Carlos had spent the night with Esmeralda. "Oh yes, it must have been *that* night."

They stared at one another for a long moment. She could sense from his cheeky chagrin that Arsenio didn't mind her saying that his child was Carlos's.

"I'm sure the heir will be a strong one," he said confidently.

"As long as the child is raised well," she said touching his hand.

"I'll see to it. The baby will be educated by Spain's finest tutors. I'm sure that is what Carlos would have wanted."

"Thank you," she whispered.

"You can show me how grateful you are later," he grunted back. "I should be leaving. Now that most of Carlos and Fernando's advisors have died in battle, I need to ask the Queen of how we shall go about finding replacements."

"I think she may feel the need to have other ladies in waiting," Susanna said. "I have noticed that many of them are quite young and inexperienced. I doubt she has ever found much of what they have to say entertaining."

"I'll remind the Queen," he pursed his lips as a thought came to him. "I suppose you wouldn't like Esmeralda Menendo around either."

"Absolutely not," she said folding her arms.

"I would prefer that you don't do anything to her, Susanna," Arsenio said firmly.

"Why not? She slept with my husband."

"It would look bad on you to do so. Leave her be. If you try to do something to her, I'm sure she'd start making claims that you were also sleeping with other men. I don't doubt that Carlos told her that," he warned.

She pouted, "She can't prove anything."

"You will do yourself, me, and the baby a favour. You will start nothing with her," he said with a stern look on his face.

"I don't think you understand. If I allow Miss Short Court to-"

"Short Court?" he interrupted, guffawing. "Is that what you call her?"

"The night I came here Carlos asked you about how 'court' was doing. But he didn't mean the nobles. He meant her. She's short and stalky, too. So, that's what I call her."

"Are all pretty girls that petty?" he asked disgusted by her attitude. "I mean, you're talking about her looks, something she can't change. Are you jealous that Carlos loved her, despite her not being that beautiful?"

"I'm not petty because I'm pretty," Susanna corrected. "She wronged me. She had plans of cheating with my husband before I married him."

"So, that means you're going to insult her for her looks?"

"Why can't I? Just because I'm pretty, I must be nice too? Esmeralda isn't. I could speak about what an evil, manipulative little rat she is. But I thought that was obvious by what she had done."

"You had no plans to be true to Carlos, either. Admit that," he said pointedly.

"Esmeralda didn't know that. It's funny when an attractive woman decides to seek revenge on a woman like Esmeralda, everyone thinks she is a wicked witch. A sharp personality to match her sharp face?"

"I didn't say that."

"No, but I haven't done a bloody thing to her. You defend her position because you think she's not pretty. Like everyone else, you think 'poor Esmeralda'," Susanna's tone became sarcastic, "she's so hideous she could never get another man like Carlos. She'll never get an opportunity to have one of the most powerful men in the kingdom again. Princess Susanna should forgive Esmeralda's indiscretion."

"Well, she probably won't get a powerful man like Carlos again," Arsenio shrugged.

Susanna shook her head. "Let me tell you something, Arsenio. Women like her, women with no looks but charm exist in every court. With her skills of manipulation, she will quickly move on to the next man she feels is powerful and rich enough to give her the things she wants. Carlos had no respect for her. But that doesn't matter to her. If she married Carlos, she'd let him sleep with every woman that caught his eye. She'd act oblivious to it, as long as she had her status and lifestyle. Carlos never loved her. She was just willing to play along with that kind of charade. Women like her sicken me."

Arsenio laughed.

"I'm serious," she went on, "don't underestimate her. Defending her makes you as easy to manipulate as Carlos. She would do anything to get what she wanted. Even sleep with a man on his wedding night."

He sat on the bed next to her. Susanna was right. Though Esmeralda was not attractive, for as long as he had known her, she was always on the arm of some rich and powerful man.

"I don't defend her or what she did," he said, "you're right. What she did was wrong. But it hurts me to see that you care so much of what happens to her. It makes me think that you had feelings for Carlos."

"No. I just don't want her influencing any men of importance again. I want her gone."

"Are you afraid she might have some influence over me?" he asked teasingly, rubbing her thigh.

She didn't answer but shyly looked away.

"It would look bad on you if you were to try to punish her," he said, trying to regain her attention. "The court would not approve of you. She grew up in this court. She has connections."

"What should I do?" she said turning to him.

"Invite her to court parties and in time, when the baby comes and the court favours you, invite her less and less."

She thought on this, "What if she begins to tell people that she doesn't believe the baby is Carlos's?"

"If she does that, I'll take care of her." Arsenio leaned in and kissed her on the forehead. "The royal family of Spain isn't the only family with secrets."

"Oh really," she smiled sultrily.

"But let us not be naughty, until we have to," he murmured.

Though she wasn't feeling well, she pulled him toward her, giving him a weak, gentle kiss.

"Get your rest," he said softly.

She sank down into the pillows.

He pulled the covers over her and pecked her on the forehead. He walked toward the door, but before he reached for the handle, he turned to her, his demeanour changed. He spoke aloud as if they were advisor and Princess again. "Oh, one more thing, your Highness. I hope what was said about the English being sneaky didn't offend you. I think having lost the war, some of the Lords are a little bitter. Even I have to admit, the English defence plan was nearly flawless."

"It's war. Battles are won by doing the unexpected," she yawned. "Even if it's sneaky. Someone should remind them that war isn't about pleasantries."

He laughed, "True. I believe the English have a saying; 'All is fair in love and war'?"

She nodded. He smirked and then left.

SILENT TREATMENT

*D*espite not speaking to Alex, Madeline knew she had to make an appearance at their party that evening. She didn't understand why he had decided to have the baby announcement so quickly after Sir Ashton's passing. But as she looked down at her swelling belly that morning, she knew her next public appearance *was* the announcement. Rumours that she was pregnant were probably circulating. She felt sorry she couldn't be at the funeral, so earlier that day Marie accompanied her to visit Sir Ashton's grave. Madeline ordered Marie to have Howard come along, too.

To Marie, Madeline insisting that Howard go with them to the site was odd. But Madeline convinced her that Harold would be there for her protection.

"We have no idea if there are still Spanish spies lurking about Windsor," Madeline said as the three rode along in the carriage.

"Have you seen his Majesty today?" Marie asked.

"He came earlier this morning," Madeline said awkwardly.

"Did you talk to him?"

"I promised him I would come to tonight's party. Other than that, we discussed nothing." She immediately tried to change the subject.

"Now Harold, you are working in Windsor Castle right now, aren't you?"

"Yes," he smiled.

"He's moved up to an important part of the castle," said Marie beaming. "He's guarding the King's Apartments! Didn't his Majesty tell you?"

Harold chuckled, "His Majesty doesn't decide things like that. Mr. Tinney and Sir Ashton did. He was a good man, Sir Ashton."

"Yes," Madeline nodded. "He had a way with people. He was the type of man that respected everyone and was trustworthy."

"I don't think England has ever seen such a great advisor," Marie said.

When they arrived at the cemetery, Harold assisted Madeline and Marie out of the carriage and the three began to make their way toward his gravestone, with Harold leading the way. It wasn't hard to spot, there were piles of flowers and arrangements lying about his memorial.

"Oh, blast!" Madeline said as they came up to Sir Ashton's resting place. "I forgot. I picked a bouquet of flowers in the garden earlier today. I left it in the back of the carriage. You wouldn't mind getting it for me, Marie?"

"I'll go," Harold offered.

Madeline laughed, "I'm afraid it's quite a delicate bouquet. Marie is wearing gloves. I'd prefer she gets them."

Marie stomped back to the carriage, annoyed. She looked over her shoulder. Madeline had been acting so crotchety since she had come back from Warwickshire, and paranoid. It was obvious that she was going to ask Harold for a favour. Madeline had never asked Harold to come along to shop or for any other outings before. Madeline also didn't order Marie about. Whatever she wanted to talk to Harold about, she didn't want Marie there.

Madeline stood next to Harold looking into the grey clouds. It had rained earlier that day and the grass beneath her feet was wet. Once she was certain that Marie was out of earshot she spoke, "Don't look at me while I speak to you. But we must make this quick. Marie will be back shortly."

Harold folded his hands uncomfortably, "What is it, your Majesty?"

"I need you to do something for me. No one must know about it. Not even Marie. I have a special assignment for you."

He hesitated to speak, he didn't like keeping things from Marie.

"I know I'm asking you a lot," Madeline went on. "The reason I don't want you to tell Marie is because she won't like what I have in mind."

"What is it you would like me to do?" he asked cautiously. He had a feeling that he wouldn't want to do what Madeline was going to request.

"I want to know what my husband is up to. Strange things have happened since we got married. I've come home to Frogmore to my room torn apart and mud footprints all over the place. Every place we both stay in has personal items like hand fans, handkerchiefs, and hair combs lying around. None of which are mine."

"So you would like me to follow him?" he asked and gave a heavy sigh.

"Yes. I've heard that he has come back to Frogmore and Windsor Castle several times covered in mud and dirt."

"Yes. I heard he did so again last night," Harold admitted, nodding.

"Find out where he is going."

He looked down to his feet, "If he finds out that I am trying to invade his privacy, what do you want me to tell him? I don't want to be tried for treason against the crown."

"Keep your distance. Alex has combat training. He knows when there's a presence in the room with him. Don't go into his apartments if he is there. But make notes of who is in there with him."

"At night when he leaves, how far a distance should I keep?"

She looked over, Marie was beginning to make her way back from the carriage, "If you have the slightest inkling that he knows someone is following. Stop. Continue another time."

"How shall we communicate?" he asked.

"If I go out with Marie into town, expect that I want to see you that evening."

"Yes, your Majesty."

"It may take some time to figure out what he is up to. If you find out that he has been spending time with Miss Hampton, I want you to report to me promptly. Once you find where he is going, I want you to come to see me at Frogmore. I'll tell Mr. Barry I will see you immediately if you come calling."

He bowed his head and they waited in silence as Marie approached. Once she reached them, she handed Madeline the bouquet.

"Here you are," she said slightly out of breath.

"Thank you, Marie." She bent down and placed them next to the other flower arrangements on Sir Ashton's grave. The three stood there in silence, paying their respects. Madeline shed a tear. A part of her felt guilty for doing what she had just done, in Sir Ashton's resting place. She wished he were here. If Sir Ashton were supporting Alex's behaviour, she'd know that she would have nothing to be concerned about. Though Sir Ashton was obligated to Alex, she knew that he would set Alex straight for being deceitful to her.

* * *

"MADELINE! LET ME IN! I'D PREFER THAT WE GO TOGETHER!" Alex yelled, pounding on Madeline's bedchamber door.

"I'm not ready yet," she murmured, slightly intimidated. He had never yelled at her like that before.

"I'll wait," he said through gritted teeth.

"I may be a while."

"This needs to stop, Madeline. I told you I was sorry."

"What are you saying? You think because you've said 'sorry', I need to forget the fact that you didn't tell me that the Duke is free? If Miss Hampton was only helping with the Spanish, then why didn't you tell me that day we were in the tea house, it was her? You lied. Then you abandoned me and went back to Windsor Castle with her."

He let out a deep breath, "You won't accompany me to Windsor Castle tonight, will you?"

"No," she said sharply. "I'll attend the party, but I refuse to take a carriage with you and stand next to you and play the dutiful wife."

"Please, dolcezza," he begged.

"Stop Alex. Leave without me, or I won't go."

He couldn't believe her. He had never seen her be so stubborn. He walked down the corridor, shaking his head. Tonight was going to be an awkward night. If she publicly gave him the cold shoulder at the party, rumours would be flying.

Though Madeline had been cold and unfeeling toward him, she cried after he left. She wanted to forgive him but decided to hold out. She wanted the truth and she wanted to hear it from him. If Harold came back to her telling her something she didn't want to hear, Alex would be sorry.

Alex and Madeline arrived at Windsor Castle separately. Though Madeline had hoped to be able to ignore Alex, Mr. Tinney immediately escorted her to the Garter Throne Room, where she was taken behind a curtain, to the thrones. She saw Alex sitting upon his throne and stiffly sat in hers next to him. She focused on the curtain in front of them knowing that their guests were on the other side. Mr. Tinney left and Alex glanced sideways at her, "We need to do this together, Madeline. Everyone here knows there will be an announcement tonight. If I were to do this alone-"

"I'm not putting on a show for everyone," she said getting up, "I'm leaving."

He stood up and pulled her close to him and pressed his lips against hers.

She tried to push him off, but he overpowered her, clutching his arms around her tightly. The curtain pulled back, and there they were; him, his hand entangled in her hair and her clutching his arms trying to push him off.

Mr. Tinney announced their presence, awkwardly stumbling as he noticed the pair. "Their Majesties ... King Alexander and his Consort, Queen Madeline.

Though Madeline tried to pull away, Alex firmly held her hand to his side squeezing tightly, "If not for me, then for our unborn child. Do not humiliate this child by causing a scene," Alex said beneath his breath.

Madeline stopped resisting, embarrassed by what she had nearly done. She hated to admit it, but he was right.

"My beautiful wife Madeline and I have an announcement," Alex said loudly to the crowd. Everyone in the room looked captivated, "We are proud to announce that this upcoming winter, we are expecting a child. A future prince or princess."

The guests applauded and cheered uproariously, and Madeline couldn't help but smile as she felt a little kick at her abdomen.

Mr. Tinney continued by inviting the guests to enjoy the party and food. When he finished, Madeline discreetly released Alex's hand and wandered off into the crowd looking for her friends. Alex watched her, still longing to speak to her.

Ben Caston stood next to Alex's side, "Your Majesty, is everything all right?"

Alex gave Ben a dead stare. "What the hell did you say to the Queen? She hasn't spoken to me in days," Alex fumed.

Ben shuffled about on his feet, "She asked all sorts of questions on our way back to Windsor. She demanded that I tell her the truth about you and Miss Hampton."

He rolled his eyes. "You held nothing back?"

"I thought she knew how-"

"Ben, use your head. Why would I tell Madeline about my past relationships? Especially Miss Hampton?"

"She was suspicious," he said shrugging "She didn't understand why you refused to tell her who owned the residence she had stayed in after you left."

"Did you tell her?" he said his eyes wild with fear.

"No."

Madeline watched Alex as he talked with Ben. It was obvious Alex was angry. His face grew redder by the second and soon he stormed off leaving Ben pale-faced. She felt terrible for putting Ben in the position she had. She approached him, "Ben, what did his Majesty say to you?"

He sighed as he bowed, "He's not happy with me. He made that very plain."

Her eyes wandered over to Alex, who was standing across the room talking to some nobles.

"Why don't you just forgive him?" Ben asked.

"If he would tell me why he's been keeping things from me, and why he's spending time with Miss Hampton, I would consider forgiving him. But he won't tell me the truth."

"Have you ever considered that maybe the truth would hurt you?" asked Ben. "Maybe given your delicate state, he doesn't think it would be wise to tell you anything that might upset you."

Madeline had never thought of that. But if he was protecting her from something, why was Miss Hampton so involved? She looked over in Alex's direction but he was gone. She moved about the room trying to look for him. But as she made her way through the crowd, several people stopped to congratulate her.

Sissy came from behind and curtsied, "Congratulations, your Majesty."

"Thank you, Sissy," said Madeline awkwardly. It was still strange to see Sissy curtsy and call her 'your Majesty'.

"My friend Delilah is here," Sissy said as she rose from her curtsy. "She's excited to meet you."

"Oh, where is she?" Madeline asked looking around.

"She's awfully shy right now," she chuckled. "Actually, I have never seen her like this. She asked me to escort you to her."

"She entertains nobles," said Madeline in disbelief. "Why is she nervous about seeing me?"

Sissy gave a wide grin and shrugged, "You are the Queen now. It's not every day she meets a queen."

"I suppose."

"She's outside in the courtyard."

"In the courtyard?" Madeline repeated.

"Yes, she said, "she was feeling a little peaky and needed to get some fresh air."

Sissy cut through the crowd, and Madeline followed several feet behind, receiving congratulations as she went. Finally, the pair reached outside. Surprisingly, there were several people already there. The lights from the lanterns were dim, but she could see Alex talking to a woman.

"Oh, she's over there," Sissy said pointing across the yard to the other side. Delilah was standing next to one of the pillars, in the shadows. Madeline couldn't make out many details, but she could feel Delilah's eyes watching her.

Sissy linked arms with Madeline and began to take her in Delilah's direction. But Madeline couldn't keep her eyes off Alex. He hadn't noticed her. He was preoccupied speaking to whoever it was that stood next to him in the shadowy light. Then she realized who it was, it was Miss Hampton. She brushed back Alex's hair between her fingers and pulled him toward her planting her lips on his.

Madeline came to a halt and Sissy turned, seeing her friend's face contorted in anger. "What is it?" she asked. Her eyes followed Madeline's, and she saw Miss Hampton pressing her lips against Alex as if she owned him. Sissy bit her lip as Madeline stormed away from her, heading in his direction.

Seething, Madeline's hands clenched into fists as she glared at the two. She felt naïve for thinking that Alex may have had other reasons to be spending time with Miss Hampton. Now the truth was out. She didn't know who she wanted to punch first. But then he pulled away from her embrace. He was saying something to her, but Madeline couldn't make it out. He turned on his heel and headed for the Throne Room. Madeline darted toward the door, following him inside.

There were several people loitering about, but he passed by them and walked into the King's Drawing Room.

She chased after him, as she reached the threshold, she saw him move into the next room, King Charles' Bedchambers, Alex's father's old unused apartments.

She bit her lip, looking about. She decided to wait by the door.

What if he has given Miss Hampton instructions to meet him inside the bedchamber? If I wait, I might be able to catch them.

She waited a few minutes looking for Miss Hampton to walk through the King's Drawing Room. But she didn't. *Miss Hampton must have taken a different route,* she thought. She ran across the King's Drawing Room to the bedchamber door, threw it open and looked around. Her jaw dropped. The bed was no longer there. The room was filled with the guests' coats. Alex was sitting on a large ottoman in the middle.

His face in his hands, he looked up. "Madeline," he said surprised, "were you following me?"

She crossed her arms, "What are you doing in here?"

He stood up and walked over to her, wrapping his arms around her waist. "It's hard to celebrate this when you're ignoring me. It's hard to do anything knowing that you don't trust me."

"Why should I? I saw you kissing her, Alex."

He sighed, "What you saw was *her* kissing *me.*"

"Why?"

"She still has feelings for me."

Her lips trembled, "How do you feel about her?"

"I don't think of her any more. I haven't thought of her since I met you." He pulled Madeline closely to him, "Do you really think I would throw what we have away?" His crystal eyes were piercing hers. "When I first saw you, you were just a fantasy to me. I didn't think we had a chance. I thought the night I saw you at the Watsons would be the only night I'd ever see you. I left that place with a broken heart."

She cracked a smile, "You're a king you know, you shouldn't have had any problems getting a slave girl."

"Didn't I?" he said lifting her chin. She began to feel weak in the knees. "We've gone through a lot to get what we have."

He rubbed her belly and placed his hand on the small of her back. His mouth pressed to hers, telling her without words that she was the only woman he would ever love.

"Mm," she whimpered and put her hands on his cheeks. It was true: he had risked his title, his reputation, and his life to be with her.

She felt ashamed for forgetting that so quickly and assuming the worst.

"There will never be anyone for me but you," he whispered. "If we lived in a different world, came from different cultures, and spoke different languages, we would have found one another. Neither you nor I would feel complete until we did." Just then, he felt a soft kick at her belly, "Baby agrees."

His eyes drank hers in like wine, he held her chin, and he melded his lips to hers. Madeline felt her body melt like chocolate, surrendering to his touch. Her chest was now thrumming. She weaved her fingers into his hair and clenched the softness, their mouths dancing.

He pulled away; his thumb grazed her jawline. She could see his mind at work, questioning what was appropriate for a woman at her stage of pregnancy. He slipped his large arm beneath her knees and her shoulders and lifted her off the ground. For the first time in months, she felt small, and she basked in his touch. He carried her to the ottoman he had been sitting on and lowered her onto the seat. The pair shoved the coats that had been lying across the ottoman onto the floor.

He stood above her and tore off his clothes, his eyes piercing hers. He threw them about without a care, his only concern satiating his need. She watched with an unreadable expression on her face. "I know I shouldn't, Madeline," he confessed, an expression of guilt on his face. "But I can't help myself. If this isn't something you want now, I understand."

SHE ROLLED FORWARD and lifted her skirts up to her belly, exposing herself. The unreadable face had become one of wanton desire, and he wanted to fulfil her urges.

"You are too good to me," he said huskily.

He dropped to his knees and poured his efforts and affections into her. She became entangled in his fervour, and she wondered who enjoyed it more. She fell into an abyss, and soon the pressure and intensity became too much. She was aware of every nerve ending and grasped his thick black locks, crying out. He fell back, rubbing her thighs gently.

"Thank you, dolcezza."

He rose from the floor and hovered over her. Tracing her clavicle bone, he sought the courage to ask her. He longed to be inside her, to have her close to him in the most intimate way. She had been furious with him, and he longed to know that she no longer begrudged him. He hoped she recognized that despite the emotional anguish he put her through, he had done it for them. Had he stayed with her, he'd endanger her life.

"More, please," she said, reading his thoughts.

"Madeline, that may not be–"

"I want you to. I need you, Alex," she said, smiling tenderly and grazing his cheek with her finger.

He pressed his body to hers, and the heat of him sent a rush of excitement through her. She felt him, and her body uncoiled in response, inviting him in. An intensity overtook them. Their eyes penetrating, they both knew both had longed for the other. Their quarrel wasn't something either of them wanted, but given the circumstances, unavoidable. They had both, in their hearts, wanted a resolution, and now it had finally come. His muscles flexed, and he bucked forward, a torrent of pleasure cascading out of him. She rose from the ottoman with her lips clamped to his, tasting the delicious noise reverberating from him. Her hands at his chest, she felt his heavy heartbeat battering against his ribcage. Her breath became short. Uttering a sharp cry, she surrendered to him, grasping his shoulders as she did.

THUMP.

They stared at one another, perplexed. "What was that?" Madeline asked.

Alex turned and searched through the coats on his knees.

"What was it, Alex?" she repeated.

He didn't respond. Observing the solemn look on his face, she rose from the ottoman. His eyes were unblinking, near tears. She followed his line of sight to what he was staring at on the floor. A dagger.

"Alex," she whispered in fear.

He picked the dagger up and rolled it between his hands, "This dagger fell out of one of the coats... I think this is the blade that killed Sir Ashton."

"What makes you say that?" she said staring down at it.

"There was a mark on the side of his temple. He suffered a blow to the head before being stabbed. The mark left an imprint of a cross." He tilted the dagger. At the stub of the handle, there was a cross. "We aren't safe," he said his voice sounding anxious. "Both of us need to leave. Now."

"Don't you want to find out who the killer is? There's only a dozen coats on the ottoman."

"It would be difficult to figure out which coat it fell out of, Madeline."

"Even so, if we knew the owners of all the coats, in time, you could figure it out," she suggested.

He nodded, "We'll do that. But there's just one problem."

"What?"

"This party started over an hour ago. I don't know what the killer has done or where they are. They could be hiding somewhere in the castle. They have no intentions of coming in here again to get their coat. There's so many weapons in this place, the Guard Chambers, the Grand Entrance, and the Weaponry Room. Plenty of displays all about. I'm not sure what the safest route to take out of here is. Nor am I sure of who can be trusted. Everyone here is a trusted noble or a friend."

"Not everyone," Madeline confessed.

"What?"

"Well, Sissy wanted to invite her friend, Delilah," Madeline admitted, though she felt foolish. "I was curious about her. I thought if I met her, we would-"

"You wanted to meet her?" Alex said stumbling over his words.

"I didn't think she was a Spanish spy," she said defensively. "I mean, if she were, wouldn't she have fled by now?"

"Madeline, Spanish spy or not, she is a suspicious character. Did you meet her?"

"No. Sissy was about to introduce her to me, but then I saw Miss Hampton kiss you."

Shivers came over him, "Was Delilah outside in the courtyard?"

"Yes, I didn't see her, though. She was standing around the cloisters. It was too dark to see her face."

He stood up and began collecting their clothes on the floor. She could see he was puzzled, unsure what the best course of action would be. He dropped the clothes onto the ottoman and began dressing himself. "I can't leave you here alone," he said decisively as he buttoned his trousers. There are several doors to this room, but I'm unsure of which to take. There's a chance Delilah may be waiting outside one of them."

"I'm sure you could handle her."

"Possibly. But if she has a pistol pointed at me, I may not."

"You think she could be waiting outside the door?" she said her head turning in the direction of the door she entered.

"There's a good chance. Whoever she is, she came with the intent to kill."

He stopped and she could see the wheels turning in his head, "Wait, you said she was in the courtyard, around the cloisters?" he asked.

"Yes."

"Why do you think she didn't come after me? I mean, she could have come from behind me and killed me then. But she was concerned with meeting you."

Madeline's eyes shifted about, "Why would she be after me?"

"I think I know who Delilah is," he said shutting his eyes. "Did you see any part of her? Her clothes?"

"I only saw blonde hair. She was thin. I didn't see much more than that."

"Hm. I think it's Tilly. I suppose she's gone back to her blonde hair."

"You've got to be kidding. Sissy knows Tilly," Madeline said.

"Does she? Has she ever met her?"

Madeline held her breath. Sissy had never seen Tilly Smith. Madeline had only given the girls descriptions of her. But when she described Tilly, her hair had been black.

"The only person that might know would be Marie," said Madeline thoughtfully. "If she's ever worked with Tilly in Windsor Castle."

"Tilly never worked at other residences," Alex said, "there's a small chance she's met her."

Fear came over Madeline. *If Marie has met Tilly and ran into her at the party, would her life be in danger too?*

"Do you think Tilly killed Sir Ashton?" she asked making the connection between the dagger and the impression on Sir Ashton.

He tapped his lip in thought, "Yes."

"But why?"

"It makes sense. Sir Ashton was around the Frogmore passage to Windsor Castle at the time of his death. If he ran into her, there's a good chance that he either caught her trying to break into Frogmore or the castle through the passages."

She shuddered.

"Actually, come to think of it, if she had been around Frogmore, she's probably the one that tore apart your room, dolcezza."

"Why?"

He was certain he knew. Tilly wanted Elizabeth's diaries. Somehow the sneaky rat had found out the secret of the Swans or had come close to figuring it out. He shook his head trying to focus, "We have to find a way to get you and the girls out of here safely," he said.

"What about you?"

"I have to stay. If she believes I'm still here, she will think you are here too. I'd rather she think that, and wander the castle."

"Where will I go?" Madeline said frightened. "I don't think Frogmore is safe anymore."

He nodded in agreement, "We'll think of something."

She got up and dressed herself, as he paced about in thought. He looked about the room at all the coat racks.

"Help me find a gentleman's hat and a long coat," he said.

She helped him rummage through the racks and found a Wellington style top hat.

"I've got a coat," he said, tapping her on the shoulder.

"Here's a hat," she said.

He put the coat on her. It was a few sizes too large and went to the floor.

"I'm wearing this?" she said aghast. "It's far too big, won't that look suspicious?"

"Yes, it might," he said putting the hat on her head, he began tucking her hair beneath it. "But Tilly expects to see you in a queen's attire. This coat will hide your belly. Let's get you out of here. I'll escort you outside and order some of the footmen to retrieve the ladies and find Tilly."

"Where do you want us to go?" she asked.

"I haven't figured that part out yet. I may have to have you go back to Buckingham Palace."

"London?"

"I can't think of a safer place right now. I got a report earlier today that Edinburgh was protected. That could mean Greg and Sofia are safe and heading back to London."

Madeline pursed her lips. A lot had happened since she had last seen Sofia; both Sofia's brother and father had been defeated by Alex's armies, and she and Alex had gotten married. She looked down to the floor, noticing her belly and bit her lip.

"It will be fine, dolcezza. If Sofia still had issues with anything, she wouldn't be with Greg. She wouldn't have married him."

Her jaw dropped, "Sofia married Greg?"

"I would have told you earlier, but you and I haven't been on speaking terms," he said curtly.

She rolled her eyes at her immature behaviour, understanding what he was trying to say, "What about you? Are you going to follow in another carriage?"

"I'll have to take care of things here."

"Alex, no. You should be coming too," her lips trembling. "I can't take being away from you anymore." She began to gasp, unable to hold back, she sobbed.

"It shouldn't take too long, Madeline," he said wiping her cheek. "Tilly Smith is a threat. She killed Sir Ashton, she needs to be taken care of." He had walked over to the door leading to the King's Drawing Room before he glanced back at her, "I'll give instruction to the first guard or footman I see. You stay here. Lock the door. I'll come back to take you to a carriage."

"How will I know it's you?"

"Wait by the door," he whispered. "I'll slip one of my rings beneath it."

SLY SUSPECT

*S*ofia yawned, her mouth wide. It had been a long journey to Buckingham Palace. As soon as they entered, Greg was pulled aside by some of the guards to speak to some of the head butlers and housekeepers.

Seeing how exhausted Sofia was, he excused her and she went to his room. She hadn't really thought of what to wear. She found a white chemise made of muslin. It was a little large, and a very thin fabric. But it looked to be the most comfortable thing in his closet, she crawled into the bed, leaving a candle lit on the bedside table. She fell into a deep sleep, until an hour or so later, when Greg entered, with a solemn expression on his face, "I didn't think you'd come here," he said when he opened the door and she rose from the sound.

"Why wouldn't I?" she said sleepily, letting out a yawn.

"I don't know. Was it hard for you to find?"

"No, one of the servants directed me here. It's not like your room at Windsor."

"No, Alex allowed me to decorate the room in Windsor with my paintings. Sir Ashton didn't think it was very proper to do so," he said looking sad, rubbing the nape of his neck.

"What's wrong?" she asked noticing his glum demeanour.

"Sir Ashton ... he was murdered during the battle."

"I'm sorry," she said. Though she'd heard Greg say that Sir Ashton was a father to Alex, she knew that he had also been a father to Greg.

He slumped onto the bed, his lips trembled, "I didn't get to say goodbye or attend his funeral. It hurts." He paused and looked over at Sofia sympathetically, "Are you angry with Alex or me? I mean, your father and your brother. You never got to say 'goodbye.'"

"I'm not angry with you. I've told you that." She crawled next to him and rested her head on his shoulder, putting her arms around him. "I'm not sure what final words I would have had with them," she said quietly. "If you and Sir Ashton had spent his last moments together, I know it would be moments full of love. If I were to spend final moments with my father or brother, I doubt there would be words of love."

"What about Alex? Won't you find it strange to live in England after all that has happened?"

"I'd like to go back to Edinburgh," she said, her expression pleading.

He understood her feelings, but he didn't wish to go back. What made Edinburgh wonderful to him were the people and he could always go back and visit them. He could also invite them down to London or Windsor.

But London and Windsor were the homes of the people he cared for most. Alex, his friends at court, and his family nearby in Aylesbury Vale. Though he hardly saw his sisters and parents now, if he and Sofia moved to Edinburgh, he'd only ever see them every few years. His older sisters were all married and starting their own families in London and the countryside. Though visiting their humble homes was not all that exciting, he didn't want to leave. Moving to Edinburgh would be difficult for his sisters, too. They already felt hurt that he spent so much time in London and Windsor with Alex. "What is it you don't like about London and Windsor?" he asked.

"Really?" she said her face full of sarcasm. "I can't imagine being here now. I don't think the court here fancies me much. I don't want to be living around Alex and Madeline's happiness. Everyone will always question how I feel about everything that goes on in their lives. I'm sure there will be people who think I'm jealous."

"But you're not jealous, Princess. In time, they will see that and whatever gossip is floating about will die down."

"How long will that take? No, I'd rather we stay in Edinburgh," she pouted and crossed her arms.

He no longer knew what to say. If he told her that he didn't wish to go back to Edinburgh, it would most likely start an argument. He had told her they would go back, but he didn't think she would want it to be their permanent residence. "I think we are getting ahead of ourselves," he said. "It's too late to be discussing this, we should get to sleep."

They cuddled next to one another, and Greg blew out the candle.

* * *

IT WAS the early hours of the morning when Madeline arrived at Buckingham Palace. She couldn't sleep a wink during the trip. She could only think of Alex and Tilly.

When she had arrived, it was a shock to everyone there. Upon her arrival, the servants and guards of Buckingham Palace scurried about, making sure that everything and everyone were presentable. As she entered Buckingham Palace's entrance, she could hear each of her footsteps echo across the floor and wished she could sneak inside. She wasn't appropriately dressed for royalty. Just like the first time she had entered Buckingham Palace with Sir Ashton, she felt uncomfortable. She was happy she wasn't wearing the white dress that had barely covered her ankles, but the large black clunky coat and hat she had on was just as humiliating. She wished she could bashfully put her head down and not make eye contact with anyone there. But she was royalty now, and needed to hold her head up high to not show weakness.

Apart from her inappropriate attire, her experience was very different from the first time she walked into Buckingham Palace's entrance. The first time she came, no one was waiting for her and she could admire the large statues in the alcoves, the marble pillars by the staircases, and the gargantuan mahogany lanterns above her. Now, she couldn't so much as glance at them. There was a line-up of heads of house, footmen, and maids waiting to greet her.

"Your Majesty,' said one of the head butlers as he stepped forward out of the line. She surveyed his face, and though she recognized him and saw him walk through the corridors of Buckingham Palace when she worked as a maid, she couldn't remember his name. She stood blankly for a moment, trying to recall what Lord Walsh had taught her to do in such situations. She wished to properly greet him by his name. She gave a curt nod.

"Your Majesty" he continued. "I'm so sorry but we were hardly expecting you. We are immediately preparing the King's Apartments for you. The mistresses chambers are currently undergoing some renovations."

"I understand you were not expecting my presence here today," she said, using speech and a demeanour she knew royalty should use. She took off her hat and casually passed it to one of the housekeepers. "However, circumstances at Windsor have brought me here. His Majesty's apartments will be suitable for the time being, so long as it is adequately prepared with a wardrobe."

"Of course, your Majesty. I will see to it that the apartments are suitable for your needs." He looked in the direction of the servants and several footmen left the room. "Do you have any other requests?"

She looked at him for a moment and she could tell he was hoping she would have some other request. He needed time for her apartments to be prepared for her.

"It has been a long night for me," she said. "I haven't had anything to eat for hours. I'm famished. I would like something to eat if you don't mind."

"Of course," he said beaming. "Anything in particular, your Majesty?"

She smiled, "Zuppa?"

"Ah, the King's favourite soup. Good choice."

He once again turned to the line-up of servants and nodded his head. Several left. "Should we be expecting the King?" he asked.

"He may come in due course. But I don't think you should be expecting him within the next few hours. It may be days if he does come."

He waited a moment and cleared his throat as he looked her up and down.

She got the hint, "I will also need a change of clothing," she said blushing.

"Yes. I will have these ladies assist you," he said as he gestured towards some of the housekeepers.

Madeline looked over at the rest of the servants and spotted a familiar face. A short, stout woman with thick red hair. It took a moment, but she remembered her. Johanna. She had worked with her cleaning the Blue Drawing Room on her first day working at Buckingham Palace. She remembered how Johanna disciplined her for showing up late when she had gotten lost. Johanna made her finish the room and the mantles. Now, Johanna was before her curtsying, hoping that Madeline had forgotten the situation. Madeline wasn't going to be cruel, but she didn't like the idea of Johanna helping her get dressed.

"I do not need so many maids to assist me," Madeline said simply. "I think these two ladies here will be fine." She gestured to two women at the start of the line-up.

"Ladies, follow her Majesty to the King's Apartments and get her some appropriate attire."

Madeline headed towards Alex's apartments, the maids following in her wake.

AFTER GETTING DRESSED and eating lunch, Madeline sat alone in the King's Drawing Room and took in her surroundings. Last time she was there, she was taken with the Grecian statues and the gorgeous painting of the Greek gods in the vaulted ceiling above her. She had hardly glanced at the paintings of the monarchs. Someday there would be an oil painting of her and Alex. It was almost unfathomable considering the last time she had sat in that room – Greg had to sneak her in. Now, she was Queen, pregnant with the King's child. She sat in amazement, *If Alex had not been as resourceful and intelligent as he is, I would not be sitting here. Or maybe it is the grace of God.* Alex had mentioned before that he believed that they were destined to be together. As she sat with her thoughts, her tired body soon drifted off to sleep amongst the pillows on the couches.

Sometime later, she was awakened by Johanna stepping into the room. Her eyes fluttered open and she propped herself up on the pillows. "Your Majesty," Johanna said as she curtsied. "Sorry for the intrusion, but I 'ave been sent here to tell you that your ladies have arrived."

Madeline stared at her, biting her lip. Johanna was Irish and for some reason was trying her damnedest to cover her accent. Perhaps it was because though the war had happened many years ago, many English looked down on the Irish. "I know you're Irish, Johanna. That's fine. You don't have to hide your accent," Madeline said as she looked away in embarrassment.

"Thank ya, ma'am," she said softly. "I'll show 'em in."

She came back minutes later, Marie bounced into the room, "Madeline! I was so worried," she said throwing her arms around her. Sissy and Martha followed Marie in. Martha came in and sat down with Marie, but Sissy remained by the door, staring at her feet.

On the way to Buckingham Palace, Madeline had thought a lot about Sissy and her friendship with Tilly, or 'Delilah'. She questioned how they met, how long they knew each other, and what Sissy shared about her and Alex. But she couldn't help to feel for her friend; Sissy was the naïve, trusting type. She'd never suspect anyone of taking advantage of her. Madeline gazed at her sympathetically, "Sissy, don't feel bad," Madeline said, "Tilly is deranged and determined. If she didn't befriend you, she would have found another way to get behind our walls."

"We tried explaining that to her on the way here," Marie said.

"I still feel horrible about it, Mad," Sissy murmured, her voice cracking. She began to walk toward the couches, putting her face in her hands.

"When and where did you meet Tilly?" asked Madeline.

"I- I- met her one day while I was out in London," she said as a few tears trickled down her cheek. "I stopped into the tea shop on the Strand and she came in." Sissy sat down on the couch across from the ladies.

"I know you feel bad, Sissy," said Madeline trying to relieve her of her guilt. "I know it wasn't your intention that anyone get hurt. No one has gotten hurt."

"Except for Sir Ashton," she said slowly, then began weeping.

Martha approached Sissy and rubbed her back, "What happened to Sir Ashton would have happened whether you befriended her or not."

"That's true," Madeline said. "You didn't set Sir Ashton up. You hadn't seen her in weeks."

"That's true," Sissy said, a weight being lifted from her. "Del- I mean Tilly told me she was entertaining some Lords."

"What other types of things did you and she talk about?" Madeline asked.

"Well, she did have a lot of questions about you and Alex," she said trying to remember their conversations.

"What did she ask?"

She paused in thought, "She wanted to know what you were like. She always asked how you were adjusting to being Queen and how your relationship with Alex was."

"What did you tell her?"

"I did tell her you were pregnant," Sissy said looking shamefully into her lap. "I did tell her that you were often reading your mother's diaries. Actually, she seemed very interested in that."

Marie cocked her head, "Why would she care that Madeline's reading her mother's journals?"

"Well, I did kind of mention that it was taking up a lot of her time," Sissy admitted pressing her lips together. "I said that his Majesty wasn't very fond of that."

"Do you think it was Tilly that ransacked your room at Frogmore?" Marie questioned.

"Probably," Madeline sighed. "But there's more to this. It's strange, isn't it? At first, I had thought that Alex had freed the Duke of Axford to please Miss Hampton, but now I think it was Tilly that helped the Duke escape."

"What?" said Martha in disbelief.

Madeline explained her theory, "When I worked with Tilly in Windsor, she seemed to know more than what the average servant knew. She had often sneaked into Alex's apartments. She rarely was caught. Alex has always been very keen on sensing when there's someone in the room with him. Not so much with Tilly, because she would wait until he was asleep. It makes me wonder if she had the audacity to take the tunnels and secret passages."

"Still," Martha said shaking her head, "what does that have to do with the Duke of Axford? Why would she free him?"

"Someone helped Susanna Bathory to free Prince Carlos from Curfew Tower."

"Didn't Lord Bathory know the secret tunnels?" Martha asked.

"I'm not sure. But even if he knew them and had them mapped out, Alex's men were watching Lord Bathory's residences. Susanna wouldn't have gotten the opportunity to find that information without being caught and brought back to London Tower. Maybe she befriended Tilly."

"I doubt it. Susanna Bathory refuses to befriend anyone of a lower class," Marie reminded her. "But even if she did, that still doesn't explain how, why, or when the Duke of Axford would befriend Tilly."

"It makes sense," Madeline argued. "During the trial, when I brought out my mother's journals to prove my identity, the Duke became frantic. He went on about how it was private information, that no one had the right to look in her journals."

"So, what does that mean?" Martha piped up. "Maybe he genuinely felt that no one should read about her private life."

"I think the real reason why I kept rereading the diaries was because of the way he acted that day," Madeline said. "I truly believed that there would be a hint that would lead to what happened the night she died. I think Tilly sensed it, too. After escaping the carriage that was supposed to bring her to London Tower, I think she befriended the Duke and tried to get the journals for him. Later, when he went to Curfew Tower again, she went into the tunnels and helped him escape."

"It could have happened," Marie conceded with a hint of doubt in her voice. "If they were planning something, why didn't she free him then? He was in Curfew Tower for several weeks afterwards."

"I'm not quite sure. I bet they were biding their time for a reason," Madeline said tapping her finger on her chin. It sounded far-fetched to the ladies, but Madeline felt certain.

"Do you think he went into Windsor Castle during the party last night?" Martha asked.

"There's a possibility," Madeline said. "If only I could talk to Harold. He may have noticed something odd."

"What?" said Marie. "What does Harold have to do with all this?"

Madeline bit her tongue. But it was too late, she would have to confess. She began slowly, "Since Alex has been acting strange, I've, um, asked Harold to keep an eye on him."

Martha rolled her eyes, "That's awful, Madeline. Don't you trust him?"

"I do, but Alex has admitted that there are things going on that he doesn't want me to know about. I know Miss Hampton is involved. But I don't know why or what it's about."

All three of her friends gave her disapproving looks.

"You can't blame me," Madeline reasoned. "He used to court her, and from what Ben Caston told me, she wasn't a lady he casually saw, they were *very* serious."

Martha, Marie, and Sissy dropped their disapproving expressions and began looking at the corners of the room in silence.

"Ah, wait," Madeline said, "all of you already knew that."

"I'm surprised you didn't," Sissy said in earnest awe, "I thought everyone knew. Don't you remember Lady Watson and the ladies she invited over to tea? Once they were done talking about the weather they were always complaining about the women the King spent his time with. She came up quite often."

Madeline thought about it, "Lady Watson griped about everything. When the other ladies dropped by for tea, I didn't pay much attention to the conversations. They were boring. It was nice to have a break and not listen to her whiny voice."

Sissy laughed, "But you never were curious about King Alexander even then?"

She cracked a smile, "Honestly, he sounded like a scoundrel. It sounded like he was with so many girls that he didn't really take any of them seriously."

"He was with quite a few," Marie agreed.

But Madeline didn't want to start talking about how many, "Let's change the subject, I hate thinking of the ladies Alex used to court."

The ladies chuckled.

"If it's any consolation, the only time I can think of that he wasn't with a woman was when you left," Marie explained. "All of Windsor and Buckingham Palace thought it was strange."

Martha nodded, "That's putting it lightly Marie, everyone thought he was going crazy. Like he belonged in an asylum."

"What?" Madeline scoffed.

"Yes, he was doing some odd things," Marie said embarrassed to admit the truth.

Madeline blushed, "Alex had told me he'd gone crazy when I was gone. But I didn't think he meant it literally. What was he doing?"

"I heard he was carrying a vase around with him," Marie chuckled.

"I saw him do it one day," confessed Martha. "I had been asked to lend an extra hand at Windsor. From what some of the guards told me, he would take it with him in different places and just stare at it."

It was hard to believe that someone as calm and collected as Alex would behave in such a manner. As alarming as it was, Madeline was flattered by it. She knew she shouldn't be, but the idea that he couldn't think of anything else but her made her feel extraordinary. He could have any woman he wanted, but he always chose her, even when she wasn't around.

"Did you notice anything else odd?" Madeline pressed.

"I heard from Harold that he would dine in the evening and insist that the chefs bring two plates of each dish," Marie said cautiously. "Of course, one of the plates would return untouched."

"He never really went to court affairs either," Martha continued, "apparently, he would go to events, stay five or ten minutes to talk, then leave. Even Greg Umbridge was concerned."

"And Greg's not one to get worried about much, is he?" Madeline commented.

They all laughed.

"We should get to sleep though," Madeline said as she yawned.

"I'm not tired," Marie admitted. "But I can understand why you would be. You should sleep until late afternoon, you're pregnant and you need your rest."

She looked down and grazed her hands on her stomach, "I suppose we do."

"I'll help you get ready," Martha offered. She helped Madeline up and escorted her into the bedchambers.

Marie and Sissy sat in silence for several minutes before Sissy finally spoke, "I've never felt so awful for anything in my life," began Sissy.

Marie shrugged, "I suppose all of us need to be careful. She could have befriended me too, you know. I wouldn't have thought that someone would befriend us to get closer to them."

"I just wished I paid more attention to the things she said and did. Maybe it wouldn't have come to all of this. Now both the King and Queen are endangered. Same with the baby. I told her Marie," Sissy began sniffling, "I told her about the baby!"

"You can't torture yourself over what could have happened, Sissy," Marie said rubbing circles into her back. "If you focus too much on what happened, you won't keep your wits about you now."

"What does that mean?"

"Well, as guilty as you feel, you're not the only one thinking about all of this. I imagine that wherever Tilly is, she's thinking about this and she's going to be thinking about you, too."

She gasped. Sissy had never considered this, "What do you think Tilly might do now?" she asked frightened.

"Is there anything you care about that she knows about?"

"Not really. We never talked much about me. Both my parents passed on some years ago before I went to the Watsons."

"Hm," said Marie tapping her finger to her lip. "Can you think of anything she told you, that she may fear you telling someone? If she thinks that you have information about her that could ruin her, you have to tell Madeline."

Sissy thought about it, "I'm not sure," she said as a tear fell from her cheek.

Marie sympathized, "Well, any information she told you might be useless anyway. She lied to you about who she was, who knows what other lies she told you. I suppose you can't really believe anything she had said."

The ladies eventually decided to take a nap along with Madeline and slept in some of the guest rooms in Buckingham Palace, but Sissy laid awake for hours staring up at her canopy bed frame and drapes. She thought of every conversation she and Tilly had. Her mind went adrift, reliving her time spent with Tilly. One incident stood out; *Tilly once said she was planning to meet a wealthy man that owns several large estates around London and other parts of the country. It could be the Duke of Axford. He owns many estates. But is there a point in saying anything? Many Lords have estates all around the country.* Thinking in circles, trying to remember any other details that were of importance, gave Sissy a headache. But she couldn't focus on anything else. Stressed that she endangered so many people dear to her, she cried herself to sleep.

* * *

ALEX ALONG WITH MR. TINNEY, Mr. Barry, the valets, and some of the Lords had spent their afternoon in the Crimson Drawing Room. Windsor Castle was in a lockdown. Every entrance and door were closed and locked as the guards searched the grounds. Though he wanted the Lords to go home to their families, many of them insisted on being there. If Tilly Smith was apprehended, the men agreed that they would have an immediate trial on the count of treason.

Lord Walsh sat next to Alex, observing the glazed expression on his face. "You must be quite tired, your Majesty. If you would like, I could go get you a pot of tea."

"That's fine Lord Walsh, but you don't have to get me anything. We are still unsure of how safe it is. When the entire castle has been investigated, we can all leave."

"Where do you plan to go, your Majesty?"

He sighed, "I was just wondering that myself. I would like to be with Madeline, but I'm afraid Miss Smith might follow me if I go to Buckingham Palace."

* * *

TILLY HAD BEEN RUNNING a few miles, but she knew where she was going. She wasn't about to be caught. She'd never gotten herself in so deep, and this time, there was no going back. While at the castle, she noticed the panic in the servants and footman as they scurried about asking if anyone had seen Tilly Smith.

She knew her plot was over. She snuck out of the castle as the guests left and made her way to the only place she knew she could see him again. It could take a few days, but she knew that he would not take Madeline with him there. He only went there alone these days, and the next time he went, she'd take care of things. *He wants to be with me, he just hasn't realized it yet,* she told herself.

Once she reached the nearby forest, she sank to the dirt surrounded by fall leaves. She grabbed several in her hand. *I might have to be here for days,* she thought. She sighed. *The things I do for him. For love. First, I am busy trying to prove to him that Madeline is crazy.* Obviously, Madeline was, her obsession with her mother and the diaries was strange. The whole Swan family was raving mad. Alex had seen to what extent they were. *Why on earth would he continue to be with her? Why would he marry her? Probably for the baby. She doesn't even trust him,* Tilly scowled. *Why would he want to be with her?* She began mumbling to herself trailing off, "If there was no baby, I doubt he would have married her … just need to get rid of her and the baby … I'll lure Madeline Blac here."

"Lure who here?" asked a voice from deeper in the woods. She shot up from the ground, startled.

"Who's there?" she asked, withdrawing a pistol.

"No one you need to fear," the voice said. "I have nothing on me. You're the one with the pistol, why don't you put it down?"

"Not until you show yourself."

He stepped out from the brush, "Come now Miss Smith, I thought you wanted to be friends."

She smiled at him. "I suppose you haven't much use for the Queen either? She wants your head in a noose."

"True," he said walking toward her, he helped her up from the ground, "I was thinking you and I could come to an arrangement."

SIR ASHTON

$\mathcal{M}$adeline awoke later as Martha came in and roused her with a tray of food. "I'm sorry," said Martha, "I thought the baby might be a little hungry and need a snack. I don't think you've eaten much since we left Windsor."

"Actually, Alex had given me some food to take for the journey. But, you're right," she yawned sleepily as she sat up and stretched her arms, "I should get something in me."

Martha pulled a table closely to her bed and set the food down on it.

She chuckled, "I know I'm pregnant Martha, but I'm not lazy. I'll get up."

"I'm thinking you may want to stay in."

She raised her brow, "Why?"

"Well, there is someone that would like to see you," Martha explained. "In fact, he's itching to."

"Alex?" she guessed with a bright grin.

"No, Sir Gregory. He and Princess Sofia are here. No one told us when we arrived, but they arrived here just last night. A few hours before we came."

"Why didn't anyone tell us?" Madeline said disappointed.

"I think now that Sir Ashton is not here, maybe things don't run as smoothly," Martha shrugged.

Madeline nodded. "Well, some of the footmen that were in Alex's apartments seemed to be flustered and embarrassed when I first came into his apartments. I don't think they realized I was the Queen."

"Half-wits," said Martha waving her hand dismissively, "if not for the driver having used to work here as well as Marie, we may never have gotten in."

"Funny thing is, I used to work here," said Madeline. "Marie told me that everyone at Buckingham Palace knew about Alex and I before I ran off."

"You have to admit though it was some time ago. They may not recognize you in pretty clothes. They remember you in a servant's uniform."

"I suppose so. I was wearing a rather large coat when I first arrived," she chuckled. Then she went quiet, "I doubt Princess Sofia wants to see Alex or me."

"You know all the things that had happened to the Princess are hardly your fault," said Martha.

"I know you're right. But I don't think she sees it that way."

"She is married to Sir Gregory now," Martha reasoned, "I would think that means she no longer cares about the King. What happened is in the past now."

While Madeline had slept, Greg Umbridge had followed Marie about which was becoming somewhat annoying to her as she sat amongst old friends in the servants' quarters.

"I don't want to bother her," Greg assured as he sat next to her at one of the long dining tables. "I just want to ask how Alex is doing."

"Sir Gregory, I told you all that I know about his Majesty," Marie said huffily.

"Greg, why don't you leave the poor girl alone," Sofia said, tapping him on the shoulder. "Maybe we should go to the Music Room, I remember Alex once telling me there is a very lovely one here."

"Princess, I don't think you – I mean," he sighed. He knew Sofia didn't want to see Madeline; perhaps he was better busying himself with entertaining her.

He spoke with heavy sarcasm, "Marie, tell her Majesty that once she is feeling up to it, Sofia and I will be happy to see her in the Music Room."

"I don't think you understand, Sir Gregory," Marie explained giving him an evil eye, "or maybe you've forgotten. Her Majesty is with child and last night was a very long night for her." She rose from the table and began making her way out of the servants' quarters. But Greg called to her, "Oi! I understand! But the very least she could do is update me on how my friend is!"

"Greg, let's just go to the Music Room," Sofia said as they watched Marie head off.

"Madeline's been here for hours Sofia, how much longer am I going to have to wait? I've tried to be patient."

"Then going to the Music Room will keep us busy. If she's that exhausted it could be hours before we see her." As she stood up, she took his hand, pulling.

Sofia and Greg played several songs on different instruments in the Music Room, but in time, decided to head back to Greg's apartments for tea. To keep themselves from boredom, Greg took Sofia through the matrix of secret passageways in Buckingham. Though he knew he shouldn't, and the passageways were reserved for Alex, Greg had hoped his shenanigans may result in him having Madeline's company earlier.

It was a long walk, delving between the passageways and cutting through rooms, but they finally arrived in his bedchamber and crept inside from behind a painting. As he turned to close the door, Sofia observed the room. The paintings were not ones he had done; Greg had a distinct style. But they did look amateurish. She had wondered if he had been forced to paint in a style he was unfamiliar with. She furrowed her brow, "Are these your paintings?" she asked. "They don't look like your style.".

"No," he said simply and she could tell he was annoyed that they weren't his.

"Who painted them?"

"My old art tutor. They were a gift to remind me of how fine art should be done. I've always hated them."

It was a series of a bunch of pretty blonde girls playing in the countryside, dancing in an old farmhouse, and eating a simple dinner.

"Why do you keep them then?" she asked.

"Sir Ashton said it would be rude not to accept them considering they are supposed to be a representation of my family."

She looked at the paintings and sadness came over her, "You did it for them, didn't you?"

"Hm?" he said not understanding what she had meant.

"There were a lot of mouths to feed back in Aylesbury Vale, weren't there?" she said softly.

"Yes," he admitted. "Actually, I had to audition to be Alex's play-mate. I thank God he picked me. If he hadn't, I'm not certain what would have happened."

She looked more closely at the paintings and noticed his youngest sister sitting on the floor. She didn't have blonde hair like the rest of them, she had the same wild chocolate brown hair Greg had. But there was something odd, her eyes were staring blankly at some toys in front of her. Sofia glanced at the other paintings and saw the same blank expression on the tiny girl's face.

"Your youngest sister, she's–"

"Different?" he offered.

She nodded embarrassed to ask, "She, uh never seems to smile."

"She smiled," he countered, almost angry. "She didn't smile all the time, but I could make her laugh and smile."

"I suppose your tutor wasn't a good artist then, he couldn't capture the truth," she said seeing his heartbreak.

"I'm sorry Sofia, my sister had a kind of … madness," he said not being able to look her in the eye as he said it.

She looked at him and saw a few tears falling down his cheek. She sensed that his sister was no longer alive.

"What was her name?" she asked softly.

"Sophie."

Her eyes welled up, "She is the real reason you came to court, isn't she?"

"The first day I became his playmate, I told Alex about Sophie. He sent his best doctors to see her the moment I told him, and they saw her quite often for years. They could never figure out what was wrong. When she got older, she started having fits. Eventually, she died of one."

"I'm sorry," she said.

"I'm not," he said, "I'm glad she was a part of my life. Even though it was only for a short time. She was the sweetest person I ever knew. Not a selfish bone in her body. She never felt sorry for herself or her situation, and she was genuinely happy for other people."

"She sounds like she was a light in your life? How come you've never told me about her?"

"She died almost ten years ago now," he said, "and I still have a hard time talking about her. I love my family but visiting them has been difficult."

She grabbed his arm and led him to the couch and they sat down. "I think we should take all these awful paintings down, and someday when you are ready, I think you should paint Sophie as you remember her," she said consolingly, rubbing his shoulders.

He grinned, "I like that idea, but only on one condition."

"And what's that?" she asked grinning.

"We don't just take these paintings down; we tear them apart."

* * *

MADELINE WAITED in the State Dining Room for Sofia and Greg. She had sent one of the footmen to invite them for dinner twenty minutes earlier, but the footman hadn't escorted them back yet. Buckingham Palace was large, so she figured that perhaps that was why it was taking so long. The footman may have had to go all the way to Greg's apartments and that wasn't near where she was.

She surveyed the room as she sat in a cream white empire dress with gold threaded appliqués all over it. Nothing in the room had changed since she had last been there. The red silk drapes and table filled with gold gilt seats were still there, but somehow the atmosphere felt different.

One of the last times she had been in the room was when Alex had randomly decided to have a court dinner. She remembered him sweeping by her in a white coat with gold embroidery. He looked so good, she felt weak in the knees. He still made her feel that way.

Then she understood what had changed. The last time she was in the room she was standing about serving in her maid's uniform. She was longing to be with Alex and she feared that whatever they had going on wouldn't last. She sighed. *After all we have been through together, how could I think that he could cheat on me?* He was keeping a secret, but the more she thought about it, the more she questioned, *Is it for my own protection?*

She wanted to be back with him now. Being at Buckingham Palace knowing that he had to deal with Tilly Smith just after defeating the Spanish made her feel selfish. He had nothing but stress since she had abandoned him. Going crazy after she'd gone, searching for her for months. Then there were the weeks of research, trying to get her a title so he could marry her Then there was the surprise attack from Bathory, Greg and Sofia running off, and the battle with the Spanish. Among other things.

How he had managed to keep so calm through it all? Except when she had taken off. But perhaps that was it. She blushed at the thought. *Am I what keeps him sane?*

Marie and Sissy entered and both curtsied to Madeline, "It'll be a few more minutes. Martha is going to escort them here," Marie said.

The ladies sat down at the other end of the table Madeline was at. "All these chairs," Sissy tittered. "There aren't enough people to fill half of them."

"Never was," said Greg casually as he stepped into the room with Sofia and Martha. "Usually we ate in the smaller dining room. Why aren't we there?"

"I'm not sure," Madeline confessed. "I suppose it's because we-"

She stopped. She had figured that because Sofia was a royal guest, they would eat in the State Dining Room. She looked up curiously,

"Sir Gregory, forgive me, I'm unsure of what you and Alex would normally do for dinner at Buckingham Palace."

"I suppose you wouldn't know that," Greg said. "Don't worry Madeline, it's not a big deal. But since we have all these extra seats, maybe we should invite some company."

"Greg," Sofia piped up, "this isn't Edinburgh."

"I wasn't thinking of inviting the town, just the servants. I mean we can all sit, have dinner and drink in the honour of Sir Ashton."

"That's a nice idea," Sofia said. "If her Majesty doesn't mind, of course."

"Yes, that sounds lovely," Madeline agreed, shocked that Sofia would entertain common folk. But then again, she did marry Greg. "Let's move dinner to the Ball Supper Room. I don't think the entire staff in Buckingham Palace can fit in here."

It took a little more than an hour for most the servants to come down to the Ball Supper Room. It was the most casual affair Buckingham Palace had ever witnessed. As the servants entered the room, many of them carried in dishes of food. Everyone served their friends next to them and all etiquette was ignored. There were not many extravagant dishes given since the party was arranged only an hour earlier.

Madeline began to wonder if she had crossed a line. Now that she had done so, would the servants expect to be as casual as they pleased? She shook her head at her thoughts, *It is too trying to be a traditional queen. I don't have the upbringing of most queens. Why should I question it? These surroundings are most comfortable to me.* She thought of Sir Ashton and realized that perhaps a few words should be said. They had come together to remember him. She nudged Greg's elbow and lowered her voice to a whisper, "Greg, would you like to say a few words in honour of Sir Ashton?" she asked.

"You're giving me the honour?" Greg asked, his heart filling with excitement.

"You knew him better."

Greg stood up and tapped the side of his glass. It hardly echoed across the large room full of boisterous conversation, "Oi …" he called, but the laughter continued, "Oi … OI!"

Everyone quieted and turned to Greg.

"As I'm sure you all know, we've all been graciously invited by her Majesty the Queen to have dinner together in honour of Sir Ashton." Solemn expressions filled the room, but Greg continued, "Sir Ashton was so many things to so many people. He was a head butler, a supervisor, an advisor, a friend. But to his Majesty and I he was like a father." He paused for a moment, "Buckingham Palace has seen many good leaders in its time. But never has it seen a man so likeable that his memory could bring servants and royalty to sit together for a dinner. I know if his Majesty were here, he'd remind us all of something that Sir Ashton used to tell us when we were growing up. 'Any worthwhile person will try to know the heart of everyone they encounter, and see the best in them. Any person that doesn't will never know how wonderful the world they live in can be.'" Greg raised his glass, "To Sir Ashton, James Giles, the most honest and loyal man the monarchy and England has ever seen."

"To Sir Ashton!" everyone cheered and clinked their glasses.

TO WINDSOR

When Windsor had finally been secured, Alex left the Crimson Drawing Room and headed to his apartments in the Round Tower. He had a suspicion that Tilly was still in the castle, or had come back and was wandering the secret passages. At this point, Tilly had one of two choices; either she would flee England, or she would try to beg for a pardon from him. He guessed that she would try the latter.

But, he wasn't going to grant her a pardon. Tilly was not an innocent girl. He had used to think that she wasn't dangerous, just a young girl with a crush. But she was a cold-blooded killer. He doubted that Sir Ashton threatened her in any way. Murdering him wasn't to protect her life or the lives of others; she was deranged. Alex had never shown any interest in her, and yet Tilly seemed to believe that they had a future.

A dark feeling came over him as he realized that Sir Ashton may not have been the first person she had killed to get closer to him. Her infatuation had grown into a dangerous obsession.

He stood up paced about his room alone, trying to feel Tilly's presence. She was so disillusioned, he figured she would convince herself that Alex wanted to see her.

KNOCK, KNOCK

"Your Majesty?" Lord Walsh said in his politest tone. "Could I have a word with you?"

"Mmm, certainly come in," Alex said as his eyes darted about the room. Lord Walsh entered, bowed, and shuffled across the room.

"If you don't mind your Majesty, could we take a seat?" he said gesturing to some chairs.

Alex sat down, "What's on your mind?"

He sat down, "I've been thinking your Majesty, I know you have insisted on staying here while this mess with Miss Smith is sorted out, but I must advise against it."

"Why's that? I don't want to follow Madeline to London. Tilly isn't familiar with my other residences, besides I believe as long as I'm here, Tilly won't leave."

"But, there is a chance that she might go. It is the Queen she is after."

"You don't understand Miss Smith," Alex said. "She wouldn't dare enter another royal residence unless she was certain she could get to Madeline. It took her months to attempt getting into Windsor. She plans things. Going to Buckingham Palace isn't part of her plan, so it's too dangerous. Everyone is looking for her. I suspect that she's gone into hiding someplace nearby."

***

After a fun night of partying with the servants at Buckingham Palace, Madeline woke up feeling a little put out that Alex had missed it all. Knowing that everyone had quite the night, she decided she wouldn't bother anyone for breakfast and just go down to the kitchen and fix herself something. Strangely, she missed doing things for herself. With a plate of crêpes and fruit, she sat alone at a table in the kitchen.

"Old habits die hard?" Greg grinned as he casually entered. He looked rough, his clothes dishevelled and his hair going in all directions, he had just rolled out of bed.

"Sometimes I don't want to bother someone with what I want. I prefer to be alone," she said taking a bite of an orange wedge.

"Is that a hint?"

She chuckled, "No, sorry, that's not what I meant. I just, I guess I know how it feels to serve someone. I don't recall getting up thinking to myself, 'I can't wait to make Lady Watson's breakfast today.'"

He howled, "True. But to be fair, you are a more pleasant person than Lady Watson. I'm sure your ladies don't mind."

A thought ran through her mind, "When you first came here, were you expected to wait upon Alex?"

He pondered what she said for a minute as he put a kettle on the stove. "I think some people of the court thought that was the reason why I was here; a personal assistant or valet to him. I remember being told to hang his coat for him or get him a footstool."

"Really?" Madeline giggled. "What did Alex do?"

"Nothing at first. I don't think he really knew what to do. But to make a point he eventually started doing things on his own. So, if someone demanded that I hang his clothes, he would do it himself."

"Smart. I guess that got the message across."

"Oh yes. King Charles had a problem with it, of course. He addressed Sir Ashton and I about it a few times. To him, Alex doing things for himself as a young royal was humiliating and improper."

"Oh. I always had the impression that King Charles was not a man who thought much of privilege."

"For the most part he didn't," Greg explained, preparing a tray for tea. "But one day when King Charles said that it was improper, Alex said that a man who couldn't do simple things like dressing himself was improper."

She snickered, "Why do you think Alex keeps valets around then?"

"Not sure. Kings have entourages. Maybe it's about image. But I wouldn't be surprised if he does it as a favour to the valets and their families. All his valets come from lower aristocracy." The kettle whistled and he pulled it off the stove. "Speaking of Alex, I was talking to Sofia last night. I know Tilly is a threat right now, but I would like to see him. Did he say if he would come here?"

"He told me before I left that he would come once everything with

Tilly was sorted out. But with Alex, you never really know," she sighed.

* * *

SEVERAL DAYS LATER, Alex had still not come to Buckingham Palace and Madeline was beginning to worry. Greg had often asked her why she believed he had decided to stay in Windsor, but she didn't have any idea.

While sitting in the White Drawing Room, reading books on pregnancy and her mother's diaries, Harold Vallant entered looking around the drawing room in awe. He realized his faux pas and quickly bowed to Madeline, who was sitting on one of the gold silk couches next to the fireplace. "Your Majesty," he said.

Madeline smirked knowingly, "Magnificent room, isn't it?" she said noting his awe.

"Mostly all the royal residences are," he admitted. "Sorry I've never been in all the State Apartments in Buckingham Palace. I've never seen a room of white and gold."

"I remember the first time Marie took me to tour the palace, my mouth hung open the entire time. I had never been in a place more extravagant than the Watsons."

"I've come here on official business," he said gesturing to the couch across from her.

"Have a seat," she said and he sat down.

"You asked me to come and see you as soon as I knew anything," he said removing his Windsor uniform hat.

"You know where he is going?" she said, leaning forward in interest.

"Yes. At least I'm quite sure. I noticed the other night I wasn't the only one following him."

"Who else is?" she said her eyes wild with worry.

"Smaller fellow. Couldn't see his face. He was wearing a cloak. His Majesty has always gone in different directions and backtracked each night. But the fellow following him went directly to Swan Manor.

After following the man, eventually his Majesty did show up at Swan Manor."

"What was he doing there?" she asked horrified.

"I'm not sure. But the fellow on the horse had me worried. I decided that I would keep an eye on him. I hope you understand, I felt that his Majesty needed to be protected.

"Did the man on the horse try to attack?"

"No, but he watched closely for hours and was wise enough to keep his distance. Once his Majesty left, the man on the horse was about to chase after him, but I chased him off."

"Where did the rider go?"

"Into the trees in a wood nearby. I tried to follow him, I'm sorry, it was the earlier hours of morning and there was so much fog. I had no clue what direction he headed in, so I followed his Majesty home at a distance again."

"The rider didn't come back then?" she asked puzzled.

"No."

"Did you tell anyone what you saw?"

"No. I wasn't sure if that is what you would want."

"That's fine. I think it's time I head back to Windsor," she said getting up.

"Are you sure?" Harold asked in concern. "I mean his Majesty only sent you here a few nights ago to keep you safe. I doubt that he would want you to return. Not until all is safe."

"I have a feeling I know who that rider is. We need to go back to Windsor Castle now. Besides Sir Gregory does miss his friend. Get him, Princess Sofia, and the ladies. All of us will head back together."

ALETTA

usanna's morning sickness lasted several more days before she felt better. Arsenio would visit her often to see how she was doing, but he kept visits short to not arouse suspicions about them.

She hadn't had him in days and she did not just want him, she was beginning to need him. He was at the palace quite a bit now, and Queen Isabelle ordered that he stay in the guest apartments while she picked out new ladies in waiting.

Most of the women the Queen chose were around the Queen's age and wives of the most influential Lords at court. Susanna thought it was odd that the Queen wanted women from the higher end of the court. Alex had a habit of picking lower class nobles. She figured the reason why he did it was so that he wouldn't be influenced by the power of the upper court.

She supposed that was the reason why Queen Isabelle chose the more powerful Lords' wives. They could help her make good decisions; thinking for herself wasn't something she was used to doing. There was also another possibility; some of the Lords had died in the war with England. She wondered if she chose these women because they, like her, were widows

All the women had come to present themselves to the Queen during the mornings and afternoons. For some reason, she had chosen Arsenio to help her pick her ladies. Susanna wished she too could have been there to give some advice. But, being sick, the Queen insisted that she shouldn't leave her quarters to do any royal duties. Susanna had left once, to attend memorial services for Fernando and Carlos. Of course, under the eyes of everyone at the court, she demonstrated decorum and manners fitting of a princess, but she had secretly planned to spit on their commemorative statues next time she passed by them in the garden.

Now that she was feeling better, Susanna decided she would try to find Arsenio. She had spent the morning trying to fix herself up. She was still a little pale and though she hadn't anyone to help her, she knew she needed a little colour on her face. So she sat in front of her vanity trying to brighten her face.

After she had finished, she left her apartments. She didn't know when Arsenio would get a free minute, but she wanted to talk to him as soon as he had one.

Now that the war was over, she knew that the Royal Armoury would no longer be under the watch of Carlos's guards or footmen. They may have taken the battle plan apart, but she was still curious. She wandered down there and nearly entered the room when she heard two voices, one yelling in Spanish:

"WHAT? You both have known me for years," a woman's voice wailed. "She doesn't want me as a lady at her court?"

Susanna stood by the door and peeked at the pair.

"Don't take it personally," Arsenio said calmly. "I think she just feels that you are a little young, Esmeralda."

"I thought she liked me," Esmeralda, said stomping her foot.

"She does."

"Maybe you don't?" Esmeralda said putting her hands on her hips, scowling. "I've heard the Queen has an ear for you, Arsenio."

"Hardly. I think without the King or Carlos, she feels lost. She has so many decisions to make."

Esmeralda shook her head with an evil smirk, "I heard a inter-esting rumour about Princess Susanna."

"Really? What is that?"

"She's pregnant. Or at least, that's what she is saying," she said her face filled with anger.

"Yes. A doctor came the other day, and it seems that she may be."

"Whose is it?" she asked her eyes narrowing.

"That's not an appropriate comment to make about the future heir to the throne, Esmeralda," Arsenio warned.

"It's a bastard child. We both know it's not Carlos's."

"Why do you think that?"

"Ha! Carlos told me about all the men she slept with on the voyage here. She sounds like a harlot."

"Men she slept with?" he said curiously as if he had no idea what Esmeralda was talking about. "Who did she sleep with?"

"Carlos didn't tell you?"

"Tell me what?"

"Please, Arsenio," she went on, "Carlos told me. She was playing around with all the crew members on the ship!"

Arsenio laughed in disbelief, "What? He told you that? Strange, he told me otherwise. It seems that Princess Susanna has a distaste for anything less than a prince. Haven't you noticed? She seems to only associate with those at court that are rich and powerful. She hardly remembers names of the lower noble class. I couldn't imagine her touching a common man. Could you?"

Esmeralda paused, feeling uncertain of herself. He sensed it, "You know Esmeralda, Carlos told you a lot of things and they weren't always true. Maybe he told you that to make you feel better about sleeping with him after he wed."

She held her breath. "He told me a few lies," she admitted. "But Susanna's a witch. He told me what a whore she was. That's why he didn't want to consummate the marriage. He only wanted England. If they had won, Princess Susanna's days would have been numbered. I'm sure he told you that."

"Oh Esmeralda," he said a hint of worry in his voice, shaking his head. "Carlos told you that he didn't consummate the marriage? If the Princess is the whore Carlos said she was, why hasn't she been sleeping with all the men in the palace? I mean, if she's willing to sleep with a bunch of common crewmen, why wouldn't she do so when both Carlos and King Fernando were gone?"

"They didn't consummate it. They didn't!"

He shook his head, "They did. He insisted on it the night before he left."

"I don't believe you," she scowled.

"You weren't with him the night before he went to England, were you?" he asked knowingly.

"He was with his men. He felt it would be better for morale if he spent the night with them before the voyage," she said.

He raised his brow, "The Princess is pregnant. From what Carlos told me, Susanna was quite jealous when she saw you two together. I think he spent his last night with her to smooth things over. He told me he felt a little guilty for spending his wedding night with another woman."

She opened her mouth to speak, but stopped, "How do you know we were together that night?"

"The whole court knows, Esmeralda," Arsenio said with a judgemental expression. "And the nobles think less of you for it. There were plenty of people in the palace that night. I know I heard several servants around here talking about it in hushed tones."

Witnessing the panic on Esmeralda's face, Susanna decided to let her presence be known. Arsenio nearly had her convinced, she had to make certain that Esmeralda believed Carlos had lied to her.

"Señor Astucia, I've been looking for you," she said in perfect Spanish. "There are several things we need to discuss."

Esmeralda's mouth hung open in shock, "Princess Susanna, I didn't know you knew Spanish."

"Whatever made you think that?" Arsenio said, looking at her as if she was crazy. "Princess Susanna can speak Spanish fluently."

Perplexed Esmeralda stumbled on her foot, "It's just, his Highness Prince Carlos told me that she only knew a few words."

"I was educated by many tutors," said Susanna stiffly. "My father thought I would be the Queen of England someday, so I was taught several languages."

"Oh," said Esmeralda looking at her feet.

"Señor Astucia, I've been looking all about my apartments. I think one of the servants may have misplaced a letter his Highness wrote me."

"A letter?" repeated Esmeralda.

"Yes, we spent his last night in Madrid together and he made a promise to me that night. The letter was a declaration of his love and promise." She dramatically put her hand to her cheek with a worried look, "I hope it isn't lost, it's the last thing he gave me. His declaration of love for me."

"Really?" she squeaked, swallowing hard.

"Yes," Susanna said earnestly.

Esmeralda frowned, then stormed out of the Royal Armoury.

Once she was gone, Arsenio took Susanna's hand, "You've got more colour in your face," he said in English.

"I'm feeling much better," she said.

"Should we take a walk?"

"Certainly, where would you like to go?"

"I'll give you a proper tour of the palace since no one gave you one when you first came."

"That's all right Arsenio," she said, "I went and discovered it on my own."

"Trust me, you have not seen everything in the palace," he said with a mischievous grin.

"Really? I thought I had."

"No. You haven't. You should know everything that there is to know about the palace. Especially now that it is just you, the Queen, and our future heir," he said gesturing to her middle.

"So where shall we go first?"

"It doesn't really matter. But I do have plans on showing you things that the late King Fernando would object to you seeing."

She grinned wickedly, "Humph, and I thought I would spit on his memorial next time I saw it. This sounds more satisfying."

"Oh, it will be."

Fifteen minutes later, Susanna and Arsenio were in a room she had never been in before; King Fernando's apartments.

"Ugh, are these the King's Apartments?" she asked looking about in disgust. "I hardly want to be here."

"But it's important that you do," said Arsenio, "King Fernando was a very paranoid man, with many secrets. He only let one man clean his room."

She shook her head, "You don't really know anything about the palace that I don't already know, do you?"

"No," he admitted. "But by God, I've been curious. I've been around here for years and Fernando was suspicious of everyone and very particular of his room."

She chuckled, "What do you expect to find in here, Arsenio?"

"Maybe I just take pleasure in the fact that both you and I can uncover his secrets while he turns in his grave."

She laughed, "It seems like you hated him, Arsenio. That's odd. He never treated you poorly, did he?"

"No. But being around them was suffering enough."

He walked about the room to Fernando's writing desk. He pulled the drawers open and she looked over his shoulder as he went through Fernando's personal belongings. Drawer after drawer were full of papers, but nothing of interest.

She wandered over to his night table and rummaged through it. There was a pile of journals dating back several decades. Susanna smiled, "There are quite a few journals in here, Arsenio," she said pulling one out.

Arsenio quickly grabbed it from her hands, "The truth is," he began, "rumours have been going around for years that King Fernando kept information of other nobles in books."

"Why?"

"His obsession with control. Carlos often said that his father liked to treat his Lords like marionettes," he said as he casually flipped through the book.

"That's not surprising," Susanna said rolling her eyes.

"He blackmailed many nobles," Arsenio confessed. "It should be interesting to know what kind of information he knew about them."

They took the journals back to Sofia's apartments and spent the next several hours poring over them. In Susanna's eyes, Fernando was a despicable king. Manipulative and controlling in the extreme, he would often send spies into the nobles' homes posing as servants or guards to discover family secrets, extramarital affairs, sexuality, and sexual preferences. He managed to get some of the nobles to take on favours they didn't want to do, as well as give him land. If he were interested in a man's wife, he would often send them on a mission to a Spanish colony.

Of course, Fernando had a few secrets of his own. There was one journal entry that caught Arsenio's eye, "Susanna," he said, "You may want to hear this." He translated it aloud:

Lord, what have I done? Though I have done many things in my life I do not wish to admit to or talk about, I have slept with many women at court. I never thought it would come back to haunt me. Years ago, I had a daughter with Señor Menendo's wife. Menendo doesn't know the child is not his, but now Carlos has an interest in his daughter.

ARSENIO LOOKED up to see Susanna's reaction. She stood staring into nothing. "And it goes on about his regrets and whether or not he should tell Carlos," Arsenio said passing her the journal.

"You must be joking?" Susanna said taking the journal. "Isn't Esmeralda Señor Menendo's *only* daughter?"

"Yes."

"That would mean-" she stopped, embarrassed to finish her sentence.

"They are half brother and sister, yes."

"Fernando has made my job easy," Susanna said shaking her head. "I was so worried that it would be difficult to find the court's favour as Queen Regent. But any ruler would be better than Fernando."

"So are we keeping these?" Arsenio asked, gesturing to the books.

Susanna thought for a long moment, "I have no intentions of blackmailing the nobles," she said slowly. "In fact, I think we should give back some of the lands and send for some of these Lords to come back from their 'missions'. Privileged nobles should not be treated with such disrespect. On the other hand, I think we should keep the books in case anyone threatens my authority or our little one's parentage," she said touching her belly. "But when I pass, burn these books. They're horrendous."

"What of Esmeralda? Should we tell her of her true parentage?"

"Ugh. I hardly know what to do with that one. What do you think? Should we leave her with her fond memories of Carlos?" she asked cringing.

Arsenio laughed, "I hardly think she really had fond memories. She just wanted a place of power."

"Hm," Susanna said musing, "if she becomes challenging, tell her. But we won't make it public. That's beyond humiliating."

* * *

ONCE THEY ALL arrived at Windsor Castle, Marie, Martha and Sissy went to get settled in the guest rooms while Madeline, Sofia and Greg went to the Green Drawing Room. Mr. Tinney and several servants immediately served them tea.

"We have no idea where his Majesty has gone to," said Mr. Tinney quite embarrassed, as he served each of them tiered plates with scones and desserts. "I've sent every servant and guard in the castle to look for him."

Greg scratched the gold gilt of the arms of his chair, "Bloody hell, I can't stand sitting here waiting. I'm going to go search for him too." Without thinking about the awkward situation he was about to put Madeline and Sofia in, Greg up and left.

Mr. Tinney quickly finished and left, shutting the doors behind him.

Madeline and Sofia glanced at each other briefly. It was an awkward moment. A lot had changed since they had last been together alone. Madeline could only imagine that Sofia hated her; the humiliation Sofia had gone through, failing her country and her family, as well as a broken heart. Madeline wouldn't have blamed Sofia if she never wanted to see her again.

So, it came as a surprise that Sofia broke the tension, "You look much nicer in that dress than your uniform. Good thing you got rid of that old thing."

Madeline spit out her tea, laughing.

"Might need to learn a thing or two about manners," said Sofia giggling.

They looked at one another for a long moment.

"Do you like it?" Sofia asked.

"Like what?"

"Royal life."

Madeline paused for a minute in deep thought, "It's not the perfect dream that I read about in fairytales."

"No, it's not," said Sofia nodding.

Madeline continued, "I mean, it has its perks. But the duties and the expectations. Many things are politics. When I was a servant, I didn't have to go into hiding for fear of my life."

"The expectations are endless. It's as though you're not allowed to have dreams of your own. I'm sure everyone's hoping for a boy?" Sofia said gesturing to Madeline's belly.

Madeline glanced down, "No one has said the words to my face. But Lord Walsh and some servants have said things that suggest having a boy would be better for England."

"Can you live the rest of your life like that?" Sofia asked, sincerely.

"It's not always going to be perfect. I know that. But with Alex by my side, that won't matter. I don't want to imagine life without him. When I tried that, I was miserable. There wasn't a minute I didn't think of him."

"That's how I feel," Sofia said softly.

Madeline's heart sank. Sofia had probably imagined that though being royal would always be hard, having a life with Alex, would be a wonderful one.

"Greg taught me what true happiness is," she continued. "I can't imagine life without him now."

Madeline gaped at the earnest expression on Sofia's face.

Sofia settled her teacup back in her saucer. "That's why I married him," she said. "Do you think Alex is mad that we did it without him? It's sad that we weren't able to attend your wedding. I'm guessing that he's upset Greg got married without him?"

"I wouldn't worry, Sofia. Alex understands. We had to do the same. Sometimes things don't work out the way you expect them to."

"Didn't they?" said Sofia with a smirk of relief. "You got your man, I have mine."

Madeline smiled, "You're right. I suppose everything is as it was meant to be."

"Still, I'm sure Alex has wondered why we hadn't waited."

"Actually, I'm wondering the same now, how did it happen?"

"Greg surprised me with a wedding," she said almost bashfully. "All of Edinburgh was there. He painted all sorts of portraits of moments we had together and places we had gone, then he got down on one knee and proposed."

Madeline gawked at her in amazement. She could never have imagined Greg to be so romantic, the paintings were a surprise, too, "Alex had once told me that Greg was a talented painter, but had given it up. Obviously, someone has inspired him again."

Sofia blushed, and continued, "I said 'yes', then we got married in the abbey there, under the stars."

"Under the stars in an abbey?" Madeline asked confused.

"Yes," she said smiling, "the abbey is an old ruin, the roof is gone."

"That sounds lovely," Madeline said earnestly. She and Alex had an exquisite traditional wedding, but Sofia and Greg had something that was uniquely theirs, "I doubt any Princess in history married in an old ruin under the stars. Now you sound like a fairytale princess marrying her knight in shining armour."

Sofia's face glowed, "Thank you."

"Do you know where you and Greg will stay, now that you're back in London?"

Sofia looked down embarrassed, "I think I'm the first homeless princess in history, too."

Though Sofia was trying to make light of the matter, Madeline didn't laugh. The situation was serious and she knew what it was like to have nothing. "I'm sure that Alex could manage to give Greg and yourself a residence as a wedding gift."

She sighed, folding her hands in her lap uncomfortably. "Greg has suggested the same, but we're doubtful it will happen."

"Why not?"

"When it comes to crown land, politics are always involved. It's not like centuries ago when a king could give land or residences to any man he pleases. Greg has explained that much to me. We hope that because I'm royal, a gift will be seen as acceptable, but I'm not sure."

Madeline cocked her head, "It probably is all right. Extravagant gifts have always been given to royalty."

"Yes. But you're forgetting something, your country was just at war with mine. The nobility of England won't favour a Spanish Princess getting a royal residence as a gift. Even if the Lords know that I am not a spy and have no ill intent, they'll know that the people of England will not approve of it."

"So it's unlikely that the Council of Privileges will allow this?" said Madeline downtrodden.

"If Alex went ahead and did it, he may become unpopular with the people."

Madeline sat in thought, "Alex may not be able to give you a royal residence, but you could still stay in one."

"The people won't see it that way. They will know what the arrangement truly is."

"In time things can change, though. Look at me; I was once thought of as a bastard child and slave. I'm Queen now."

Sofia shook her head, "It's different. The people can relate to someone like you. You're a Cinderella to them."

It was true. Though Madeline didn't read The Society Pages, she knew that she was popular. But other than wearing pretty clothes and being the mysterious daughter of Elizabeth Swan, she hadn't done anything. Sofia was right; the people liked her because she and Alex sounded like a fairytale. "I suppose my marriage does sound like a dream."

"Yes," Sofia nodded. "I was thinking that although Alex can't give us one of his residences, he might consider buying Greg a small home. If it's nothing extravagant, I'm sure the nobility and commoners might overlook it."

It felt wrong. Madeline couldn't understand why she felt it wasn't fair, but it seemed to her that Greg Umbridge deserved more. Throughout his life he had been more than an advisor to Alex; he'd given up his family, risked his life, and was the most trustworthy friend Alex had. He supported Alex in whatever he did, even when it was strenuous to do so.

"You and Greg shouldn't be living in a simple home," said Madeline.

Sofia was surprised, "Why?"

"For all the services Greg has done for the crown, you two deserve better. Alex once told me that throughout history, Kings were always able to favour their most trusted advisors with land and gifts. It's true that the monarch doesn't have the freedom to give away lands or a residence like decades ago. But I was able to take Frogmore without anyone saying a word once I proved myself Elizabeth Swan's daughter. Frogmore wasn't Swan Manor, but when Alex traded the two, no one questioned it. Greg hasn't been able to take advantage because he's a commoner. If he were a noble doing everything he had, I'm sure it Alex could give him a residence and no one would think twice about it."

Sofia looked down glumly knowing that it was true, "So what are you saying?"

"It may take time, but I believe we can help you and Greg have a nice home. We can get Lord Walsh's help. We'll have parties so the court can get to know you. We can have you meet some commoners. In time, the people will warm to you."

"You would go through all that trouble?" Sofia asked surprised.

"Absolutely."

"Thank you."

They sat in silence for a few moments, before Greg rushed in.

"I've talked to everyone. No one has seen him for hours," Greg said breathlessly and plopped himself on the couch next to Sofia.

A worried expression came across Madeline's face and Sofia gave Greg a sharp nudge into his side. "Ow," he said as he looked up and saw Madeline's face.

"Greg," Sofia mumbled beneath her breath.

"No worries. Alex and I used to sneak out quite a bit, Madeline," Greg said trying to make a quick recovery. "I'm sure he'll be back soon. If you'd like I can take a trip down to the King's Head and check to see if he's there."

Madeline knew that he was only trying to reassure her. She knew Greg wouldn't find Alex at the old pub. She casually got up from the couches and walked over to the large doll's house on the other side of the room and began to touch the small miniatures inside it. Her heart was breaking, agonizing over where he could have gone. *Is he visiting Miss Hampton again? Whatever business they had, I pray to God it has really ended.*

"It's fine," Madeline said placatingly. "Alex can handle himself, I'm sure."

She looked into the library and saw a miniature book on the desk. She picked it up and read the cover, 'The Six Swans'. Swan Manor.

"I doubt he's gone far," Greg said. "Believe it or not, there's a few inches of snow on the ground. I'm sure wherever he's gone, he'll be back shortly."

"Right," Madeline said putting the tiny book back into the doll's house. "I shouldn't worry myself with this."

"No, you shouldn't," Sofia agreed. "You're pregnant and you've already had a long ride here. You should get some rest. Greg and I will have the guards continue the search. We'll have Alex go directly to you when we find him."

"Good. I'll just head to bed," Madeline lied.

"I'll escort you," Greg offered.

Sofia gave him an odd look, "She does have the ladies. Let's just get Martha, Sissy, and Marie."

Madeline tried to keep from laughing, "Yes, I think I'd prefer their company. I'll go call on them," she said as she left the room.

Sofia turned on Greg, "Why would you offer to escort her to bed?"

He blushed, "I just thought it would be a good idea. Truthfully, I'm not sure she'd go directly to bed."

She giggled, "Greg don't be ridiculous. I'm sure she's tired. She's pregnant. She wouldn't dare think of leaving the castle. It's cold. There's snow on the ground. Alex would be angry with her and she wouldn't take that risk."

"Mmm," he said with an air of doubt in his voice.

"Don't worry about Madeline," said Sofia confidently. "Besides, I was hoping you would help me search for Aletta. It's been so long since I've seen her. I want to see how she has been, and I would love to tell her all about Holyrood House."

Greg let out a deep sigh, "Sofia, while I was looking for Alex, I spoke to Mr. Tinney. There's no easy way to say this, but Aletta died in the battle that took place in Windsor Castle ... the night we fled."

Sofia's eyes welled up and her lips trembled, "No. No. Are you sure Mr. Tinney is speaking of the same servant?" Sofia cried.

Greg said nothing but gave her a nod and wrapped his arm around her.

"Why would Aletta be killed? She was a maid! Only a coward would kill an unarmed servant!"

She whimpered into Greg's arms, "Before we left ... she was so good to me ... she convinced some maids to get ... me ready ... for the ball."

"Aletta was always sweet," Greg said, rubbing her back.

"She was," Sofia murmured.

There was a long silence as Sofia continued to cry. After some time, she collected herself, "Could you find out from Mr. Tinney where she is buried? I'd like to pay my last respects."

"Of course, Princess."

ESCAPE TO THE MANOR

*fter her conversation with Greg and Sofia, Madeline casually strolled to the apartments for royal guests and other dignitaries. She discreetly went into one of the rooms, opened a chest at the foot of the guest bed and pulled out the mukluks she had gotten as a gift from The Canadas. Some of their wedding gifts she and Alex had received had been stored away in the guest rooms. The mukluks were one of them, as she and Alex would have never have thought they would use them. She grinned raising her brow, his pair of mukluks were gone, too.

She put them on and began fastening them. The first time she saw them, she hardly knew what they were. She had thought they looked ridiculous, and never imagined she'd wear them. Once she put them on, she had a whole new appreciation for them. They were quite nice and comfortable. The beading work was exquisite. She had never noticed it before but there were shimmering white beads making flower appliqués up the sides. She tied them at the top of her calf, then went to find a cloak. She couldn't wear it down the hall, so she neatly tucked it in her dress around her belly, making herself look slightly bigger.

It wouldn't be easy to get out of the castle without being noticed.

Though she knew the tunnels had been changed since she last went inside them, she was sure she could find the manhole in the middle of the street that she and Alex used to use to escape to the King's Head.

She discreetly made her way through the halls, trying to avoid servants. Since the castle offices were in a quieter area of the castle, she didn't see too many people. The few that were about all bowed and curtsied as she passed them. She knew they wouldn't question her directly about what she was doing. If they were suspicious, they'd either run to one of the head butlers or possibly Lord Walsh if he was still around.

She made her way to the office and looked through the desk drawers. The cloak she had stuffed down her dress wasn't very heavy and she needed something heavier. There was nothing. Then she realized something. *Once I leave the tunnel, what would I ride to Swan Manor?* She sighed. *I have to take a carriage. I am too far along to take off with a random horse if I can find one in the streets.* She had to think of a way to get one without getting caught and dragged back to the castle. She also needed a driver. "Aarrggghhh!" she said quietly to herself. *There has to be a way.* She knew that there would be guards keeping watch in the crooked house. But she didn't want anyone unfamiliar to take her.

She had to get going. She couldn't sit around trying to think up the perfect plan. Alex was gone. He was there by now and she wanted to know what he was doing. She would simply have to think up a plan on the way. She quickly wrapped her cloak around herself. Grabbing a candle from the desk, she lit it with a match and put the key in her pocket.

The tunnel wasn't anything like she remembered. It wasn't as damp as it was before. It gave her the creeps knowing that only a couple of weeks ago hundreds of men died inside. She felt sorry for the men that had to clear the ashes and bones from the tunnels.

All she had to do was walk straight she thought. She imagined that the staircase that led up to the manhole was most likely still there. After around ten minutes of walking, she found the staircase and put the key in all the locks. The lid was heavy as she pulled it aside.

"BLAST!" she said to herself and she climbed out carefully. It was strenuous to pull her weight now that she was pregnant. She looked out from the middle of the cobblestone street. The crooked house was nearby, she thought. Maybe she could order one of the guards at the house to get a carriage for her, along with a rider. But it was doubtful that those orders would be followed.

She covered the hole back up, locking it. The streets were abandoned. But that didn't surprise her. Since people had evacuated Windsor during the battle, few people had come back. Repairs were still being made in many parts of the town.

She made her way down the street heading toward the crooked house, hoping that she might find an abandoned horse or carriage. As she walked down the street a man on a horse passed by. It was Harold. She averted her eyes, hoping he wouldn't notice her.

"Your Majesty?" he asked, stopping his horse. He shook his head in disapproval, "I had a feeling I would find you out here."

"Harold, if you think that you're going to convince me to go back to the castle, you're wasting your time," she said sternly.

"I'm no fool. I knew you would want to go to Swan Manor tonight. I thought you might have someone accompany you, maybe Sir Gregory? But when I heard you turned in early, I figured you had plans to go on your own. My guess is at this moment Marie and the ladies are frantic about where you may be."

"This is no business of Sir Gregory's. Nor yours."

"With all due respect, your Majesty, perhaps not. But the streets and the ride there are not safe for any lady. Far less a pregnant queen. How exactly did you plan to get there? You can't take a horse. You're in delicate condition."

"I hate that everyone calls pregnancy a 'delicate' condition," she said cross. "The way people speak of it, you would think I was on my death bed."

"I'll make you an offer your Majesty since I know you're determined to go and you won't heed any good advice."

"You have a lot of audacity," Madeline said shocked at his candour.

"I'd hate to see something terrible happen to you tonight. If you'd like, I could go get Sir Gregory and a carriage and he could take you there."

"There is no guarantee that he would," Madeline said. "I'm willing to bet that he wouldn't allow me to go. He's probably the only one in that castle who would have the courage to stand in my way."

"True," he admitted.

"You can take me," she offered. "If you come with me, you'll be able to protect me from any unsafe situation. It's unlikely Greg would take me. Alex once told me he's petrified of Swan Manor."

He nodded in understanding, "I'll try to get the most comfortable carriage I can find."

"It doesn't have to be anything fancy," she commented. "I don't want anyone to be suspicious of what you are doing. Get a simple, sturdy one."

A few hours later, Madeline and Harold managed to make it to Swan Manor undetected. She got out of the carriage, not waiting for Harold's hand, she stepped onto the ground beneath her.

"I'll keep watch, your Majesty," he said as he climbed down from the driver's seat.

"Don't take this the wrong way Harold, but I'd prefer to wait here for Alex alone."

"Please don't. If something terrible was to happen-"

"Harold, I'll be fine."

"What about the rider I told you about? The suspicious fellow lurking around here. What if they come here?"

"I plan to wait in the carriage. It's deep enough in these bushes, I don't think I'll be seen. I'll just watch. When Alex comes, I'll confront him."

"I wish you wouldn't," he said. "He's not with Miss Hampton if that is what you are thinking."

"It is not what I'm thinking. But he comes home covered in dirt. I'm sorry, but I have a right to know what he's doing. Make your way back to Windsor castle with one of the horses. If Alex returns to the castle and I'm not with him, come out here to search for me."

"But-"

"That's a royal order," she said interrupting him. "Leave."

"Your Majesty, I must advise against this."

"You will do no such thing, Harold," she said angrily. "I ordered you to leave."

Reluctantly, he took one of the horses from the carriage and went on his way. She climbed back in, covering herself with a blanket. It was chilly outside, with an inch or so of snow on the ground. She was glad that she had thought of the mukluks.

She sat waiting for what seemed like hours for Alex. She wondered if she had come too early. But it made sense; from what Harold had told her, he was coming at the most ungodly hours. Then, as she peered back out the window, she saw him. Not Alex. Him. The Duke of Axford. He emerged from some brush across the clearing near the servant's house. Was Alex meeting with him? She felt sick at the thought.

An unimaginable fear crept over every nerve in her body. She prayed to God that he couldn't see the coach. She hid behind the curtain. The man that killed her family was creeping about Swan Manor. She felt faint. *What is going on?* She watched him as he went to the back entry way of the manor and disappeared. Her mouth grew dry. She began to contemplate what she should do. *Is the Duke a threat to Alex? Or are they having private meetings together?*

For some reason, she no longer felt safe. She felt the urge to get out and hide amongst the trees. If the Duke came back and saw the coach, he'd investigate. She took the blanket and crawled outside. She took off deeper into the forest, unable to run very fast, she moved amongst the trees. There had to be a safer place where she could watch what the Duke was doing. Veering to the left, she decided she'd try to make her way towards the front of the manor.

Then she stopped dead in her tracks. Several feet away from her she could see a long black coat and long blonde hair on the ground.

She exhaled unsteadily. She could see a bluish hand, the fingertips grasping at the dirt beneath it. Next to the body, she spotted a dagger with a skull imprinted on the handle. She felt sick. She put her hand over her mouth suppressing a scream. Backing into a tree behind her, she slumped to the ground. It was Tilly Smith. She must have been the rider that Harold told her about. Something told her that the Duke had killed her. Knowing Tilly, she had most likely started poking about Swan Manor once she found out that Alex was visiting. Obviously, the Duke didn't like her presence.

She slowly got to her feet, supporting herself by placing her hands on the tree. She stumbled back. She felt stupid for telling Harold to leave. She darted back towards the carriage. If the Duke were still inside the manor, she'd have time to unleash a horse and slowly ride back to the castle. She walked back, taking her time. She was not sure how loud the crunching of the leaves and the snapping of the sticks were beneath her feet. She knew she was paranoid, but if the Duke had left the manor and noticed something odd, her life would be in danger.

Once she reached the carriage, she looked back at the manor. The Duke was outside on the dilapidated back porch of the manor. He was holding some white things in his arms. Though it was dark, she could hear them drop to the porch floor. It looked like a pile of white sticks. He then turned and went back in.

She held her breath, her thoughts racing. *Are they the remains of my mother and grandparents?* She waited a moment, questioning whether or not she should check it out. But it wasn't safe; she didn't know when he would come back out. On the other hand, if she didn't go over, she would live her life analyzing what she saw. She walked quickly through the long blades of grass, the snow lightly coating them.

It felt wet and cold. The closer she came to the manor, the more cautious she was, ducking her head down, keeping her ears open. She decided that if he came back out, she'd slip down into the grass. But she heard nothing. When she made it to the porch, she glimpsed at the white sticks. It was as she suspected. Bones. Her face went ashen. She gasped unsteadily and bit her fist hard, trying not to cry out. Backing away, she kept her eyes on the doors. When the Duke came out again, she needed to see him before he saw her.

She heard the crinkling of the grass around her as she backed away, and startled herself several times as she stepped on some small rocks embedded in the dirt.

CRACK

It came from the manor. Madeline immediately crouched down, hiding herself in the grass. She heard several more loud sounds before she rose slowly, and peered over the blades. She saw no one, but feared moving an inch. Her heart hammered out of her chest and her body quaked. She scolded herself for being so foolish to come alone, pregnant with no way of defending herself. *What on earth was I thinking? How foolish am I?* she thought as each sound from the manor made her soul shiver. She had never felt fear as inescapable as this; if the Duke saw her, she and her unborn child would be brutally murdered and hidden away like the rest of the Swans. She needed to leave. Now. As hot tears poured from her eyes, she crept away through the grass, sniffling. Finally, she backed into the edge of the forest, not far from her carriage.

But she didn't know what to do; if she took the carriage, she'd have to drive it herself and risk being seen. She also worried about Alex. She wasn't sure that he knew that the Duke was here. *Does he have plans of killing Alex? Is Alex already dead in the manor?* She gulped as the thought tore at her insides.

Then, she heard something and looked away from the house. Off in the distance, a man on a horse was riding through the fog, approaching the clearing. She immediately could tell by the way he carried himself. It was Alex.

Without thinking, Madeline ran toward him. As Alex came closer, she could see he was riding Princess. She stopped. It was strange that he had decided to ride her to Swan Manor. She was such a rare horse, him riding it would give away his identity.

"Madeline?" he called as he came nearer to her. "What the blazes are you doing here?"

She stopped where she was, leaned over and put her hands on her knees. He dismounted from Princess.

"Alex, Alex ..." she said her voice shaking uncontrollably. He went to her, wrapping his arms tightly around her.

"Shh. It's all right," he murmured in her ear. "I'll take care of everything. Tell me what's wrong."

"He's here," she whimpered, her breathing erratic, "it's – he's."

Alex knew whom she was referring to, her pale frame trembling. "The Duke of Axford is here?" he said finishing her sentence. "Dolcezza, I need you to take a drink of water. I think the baby needs it, too. It's not good for you to be like this."

Her eyes widen and she nodded. He took out his canteen and tipped some into her mouth.

"I think he's getting the skeletons. He's looking for a new place," Alex said glancing at the manor. He closed his eyes, still holding her tightly. "Tell me what you saw."

"The Duke ... he came out, from the forest. He has gone into the manor." She was still trembling; he gave her another sip. "He came out with bones. I think that's what I saw. He left them outside on the porch and went back in."

Alex decided to start guessing what happened next. She was having a hard time, between her hard breaths and quivering.

"So you ran back to the forest?"

She nodded. "I saw Tilly Smith, too."

"Tilly Smith?" he said looking about, "where?"

"On the forest floor. Dead."

Alex couldn't imagine how confused she must have been.

"Madeline, I need you to sit down. I need to tell you something."

"What?" she said filled with panic.

"The Duke of Axford didn't kill your mother. I can prove that to you if you need me to. But I need you to sit down first."

404

BONES

Alex guided Madeline back to the carriage and they sat down inside. But Madeline was still quivering in fear. "Maybe you should take a moment to focus on your breathing," he suggested. "I need you to relax first. But I want you to know, you are not in danger right now."

She lay down across the seat, trying to calm herself. She reached out to hold his hand and he took it and squeezed it.

"Deep breaths, Madeline."

She felt safe with him, but water poured from her eyes. Alex watched her, unsure of how to explain what had really happened the night Elizabeth Swan died. He hesitated, trying to find the right words.

"Several months ago, when I was trying to get evidence that you were a Swan, I knew of the journals and tiara. I had found them years ago when Greg and I had come."

She managed to stop her tears and began to listen as Alex continued, "The day I called a break in the House of Lords, I came here during that break to get these things."

"You found her, didn't you?" she said blubbering.

"Yes."

She sighed. There was a part of her that was glad she hadn't found her mother's final resting place. Though she had come thinking that she was meant to find it, after she entered Swan Manor the first time, she knew she would never come back.

"How do you know it wasn't the Duke?"

This was the painful part. The secret that Alex had been keeping from her was one that could destroy her. Alex feared Madeline might leave him because of it. "If I tell you dolcezza, promise me you will never leave me."

She looked into his eyes, they were full of emotion, a tear rolling down his cheek. "Why would I leave you?" she whispered.

"Fear. If people found out, you may find it difficult to be my Queen. You may think it's too shameful."

Her eyes widened, "What happened?"

"Promise me you won't leave me, Madeline," he insisted.

"I-I," she stuttered, "I promise I won't leave you."

"Your grandfather, Lord Swan had a double-life. I think that may have been why your mother left the court and married Isaac Black instead of the Duke. She wanted to protect the Duke's good name."

"What kind of double-life did my grandfather have?" Madeline asked baffled.

He watched her for a moment, it had seemed that she had calmed down, "Do you remember me telling you that Lord Swan was known for releasing his servants?"

"Yes, he helped them start new lives," Madeline said smiling.

"No. He never released them."

A harrowing feeling came over her; her chest clenched, she could barely breathe. "What happened to them?" she mumbled.

"There's a secret chamber under the manor."

"He was killing them?" she gasped holding her hand over her mouth.

He didn't answer but closed his eyes and held her closer.

"What he did doesn't define you, Madeline," he said.

But utter horror overcame her, "Are you sure he killed servants?"

"There are many skeletal remains in the secret chamber."

"How many?"

He hesitated to answer and looked out the carriage window toward the manor.

"Alex," she said firmly, "how many?"

"Many. I'm not sure the number."

"Did my mother know?"

"Yes. I think once she came back to England from France, she eventually figured it out."

"Did he kill her? Did my grandfather kill my mother?" she asked, stumbling over her words.

Alex nodded. Then, the words that were in her mother's journals flashed in her mind, *When I'm dead, I won't be alone, but I'll be free.* Madeline had always thought it was odd that her mother knew she wouldn't die alone.

"What happened that night? I want to know exactly," Madeline insisted.

He didn't want to tell her. It was so grotesque.

"The Duke must have been there," she said, her mouth gaping. "He told you, didn't he?"

"It was mostly guess work for me," Alex said, "but yes, the Duke was there and he confirmed my suspicions."

THE DUKE LOOKED about the clearing. He could see Princess, Alex's horse. *But where is Alex?* "Alex?" he called out. "ALEX?"

He wandered further and further into the clearing. Then, he could hear someone talking and saw a carriage. He slowly pulled out his dagger, "Alex?"

"Walt?" Alex said hearing the older fellow calling his name. He emerged from the carriage, pulling Madeline with him.

"Alex!" he began, "What is she doing here? I thought we agreed that-"

"I've been gone quite a few nights Walt, she got curious." He raised his brow, "How did you find out I was coming here? I was extremely careful."

"Yes, Harold told me that you were. I had him follow you. He had a hard time at first, but then he saw Tilly Smith and followed her here. He saw Princess one night and figured this was where you were going."

"Yes, that Tilly Smith," Walt sneered, "she was snooping about for a few days before I did away with her. I admit I befriended her a short time. She figured things out about the Swans, but thankfully, she hadn't told anyone. I'm sure you know she's been after you, my Queen."

Madeline took a deep breath, holding her hand to her forehead, it was all so overwhelming. She had thought this man was out to kill her. But it seemed as though the Duke of Axford had been suffering the Swan family's dark secret for years.

"What happened the night my mother died?" Madeline asked. "You were there, weren't you?"

"I came too late. I'm sorry for that, Madeline. There's not a day in my life that I don't wish I had gone with her."

"Gone with her?" Madeline repeated confused.

"Your mother came to me the day she passed away. She came with you, actually. She wanted to leave your father."

"So she actually loved you then?" Madeline said in awe.

"Yes, that's what she always told me. When she ran off with your father Isaac, it shocked everyone. Myself most of all. You were just a few months old when she came to me. She never explained that day why she had run off with your father, but she told me that she loved me. She was concerned about you, and she regretted leaving the court life."

"Was I here that night?" she asked, her voice trembling.

"No. I had somewhere to go that afternoon, so your mother left you with a friend in London, Mr. Sheffield."

"Why did she come back here? If she knew what was happening to the servants, why did she come?"

"She knew she couldn't come back to court without apologizing to her parents. I think she was also very concerned for your grandmother. She wasn't quite well."

"I know," she nodded. "Mr. Sheffield told me she tumbled out of a carriage and hit her head on a rock, and she wasn't quite the same after."

"Yes," he said his voice quivering. "I told Elizabeth that I would stop by the manor with her, to convince her parents that I'd forgiven her and still wanted to marry her. Isaac and Elizabeth's marriage wasn't recognized by King Charles." He looked over at the manor with a pained expression, "When I arrived, I knocked several times. All the servants seemed to be gone, so I let myself in and walked into the parlour." He stopped and went flush.

She pulled out her handkerchief and gave it to him.

"Thank you," he said softly as he took it. Trying to gather his composure again. She got the feeling that though it was hard for him, finally sharing what had really happened was also a relief.

"Lord Swan had already killed them both. He was taking them down to the chamber ... I killed him. What he had done. I couldn't bear to see him live. I didn't think of what it would mean afterwards. I just did it. I took his body down to the chamber and locked it up."

Madeline thought on what he had done, "Why didn't you just explain what had really happened? I mean, why did you let so many people think you had done it?"

"This will sound insane to you, but when you love someone you wouldn't be able to bear them to-" he hesitated. "Everyone loved your mother. People thought she was delightful and I didn't want what her father did to tarnish who she was."

Madeline understood what he was trying to say; if everyone knew about what Lord Swan had done, Elizabeth Swan would not be remembered, but her murderous father would have been. Madeline realized how different her life could have been had Walt told the truth. "Thank you," she said, her lip trembling. "I'm sorry I ever thought it was you."

"It's fine, Madeline. Everyone but Alex thinks so too."

She broke into tears at the thought that he had sacrificed so much living with the Swan's horrible secret.

"Why do you keep coming here?" she asked.

"For years, I looked for ways to destroy the crypt so I could destroy the evidence. Because it was owned by the crown, I didn't have to worry about what would happen to it. I knew that if something did, it would be discussed at the House of Lords first."

"Why couldn't you destroy it earlier?" she said glancing over to the manor.

"Coming here so soon after would have been very suspicious," he explained. "For a long time, people were curious about what I did and where I went. By the time everyone stopped visiting and trying to solve what had happened, years had passed. The manor had been torn apart and people scavenged mostly everything. I came by time and time again, but couldn't think of a way to get rid of the evidence without raising suspicion."

She sighed, "That's why you were against me owning it?"

"I was afraid that you might send someone here to demolish it, or have it taken down piece by piece. I had many sleepless nights worrying that what lay in the secret basement would be discovered."

"So that's why you are both here now? You're trying to bury the remains someplace else?"

The Duke glanced away as Alex twisted his wedding ring on his finger, hesitating.

"There were quite a few victims," Alex said softly. "We considered doing that. But even if we did, at some point the remains would be unearthed. We didn't want to take that chance. There was no way of removing them from here without people noticing that something unusual was going on."

"So what is the plan then?" said Madeline aghast.

"His Majesty figured out a fairly smart way," the Duke said nodding at Alex.

"The stones left in the manor from the fireplace, do you remember them when we came here together?"

She nodded, he took her hands. "Walt and I took the stones from inside the kitchen and built a kind of furnace out of the basement."

"What?" she said turning away. "I don't think that's proper at all. It's barbaric."

"Your mother and grandmother won't be there when we burn the remains," Alex said.

"Yes," affirmed Walt, "we've decided that we would take out your mother's and grandmother's remains. We will give them a proper burial elsewhere."

"What about my grandfather?" she asked tilting her head.

"I don't believe he deserves a proper burial," Walt said with disgust in his voice.

But that's not what Madeline believed to be barbaric; she didn't feel that Lord Swan should be with his family or his victims. "But why burn him with the servants? Maybe it's because I was one, I don't think they deserve that, to be laid to rest with their murderer."

"You're right," said Walt decisively. "When I go down there, I'll take out his remains." He turned on his heel and began making his way to the manor.

"You're doing this now?" she said furrowing her brow as she looked at Alex who watched Walt make his way to the manor.

"Well, we had hoped to," Alex said. "Obviously, Walt finished tonight's work sooner than I had expected. We were going to put in the last stones, then take out the remains together."

She watched as the Duke went into the manor but something felt off. "Did you both decide that he would be the one to light it?"

"Yes," he said simply and sat down in the snowy grass. "Sit with me," he said tugging on her skirts. "It's been a long night for you."

She sat next to him, her eyes peeled on the manor. "How long will it take?"

"It takes some time to get down there," he said.

"I don't ever want to go," she admitted. "But what was down there exactly, and how do you get there?"

"In the parlour, do you remember the large cabinet mounted to the wall?" he asked.

"Yes. It was one of the largest cabinets I've ever seen," she said.

"That's the entrance. To be honest, I was surprised that no one had noticed it earlier. But the switch to open it wasn't easy to find."

"Where was it?"

411

"There was a lever inside the cabinet, behind one of the shelves. Once you open it, there's a long narrow staircase, it leads to the basement. Then there are a few corridors and the crypt."

"How many people were down there, Alex?"

"I honestly don't know."

It was obvious to Madeline that he knew. He just didn't want to say. She guessed that there were dozens. She wiped her cheek.

ASHES

he Duke of Axford walked through the basement corridors. He tried not to think about what he was about to do. The crypt had always been a dark, fearful place. Though he and Alex spent hours down there placing each cobblestone individually and he had been there many times before, it still made the hairs on the back of his neck stand on end. But this would be the last time he would ever have to see it. After tonight, he would never have to worry about the Swan's secret becoming public knowledge.

He looked up at his torch. For over twenty years, he'd been trying to find a way to cover the evidence. He had considered fire, but couldn't figure out a way to contain it. Alex was always a resourceful boy, he wished he thought of Alex's idea sooner. He entered the crypt, the walls and floors set with the stones. There were holes above him. Alex had designed it so that there was some ventilation to keep the fire going. He looked down at the bones resting on the floor around his feet and on top of the large pyre he and Alex had made. He wished that there was a more respectable way of doing this. He hoped Madeline wouldn't hate him for what he was about to do. He shut the door to the crypt behind him and dropped the torch to the floor.

"There's smoke," Alex said pointing.

"What if people see it?" Madeline said panicking.

"That's why we decided to do it at night. It's unlikely anyone would come tonight."

"Why's that?"

"It's November first, the night they were killed," Alex explained. "Walt has watched over the years, he told me that no one comes here on this night."

She saw the clouds of smoke drift into the air as an eerie sensation took over her. In the distance, she could see the remains that she had seen the Duke bring outside earlier.

"Perhaps we should get something to put them in," she said pointing over to the bones. She rubbed her neck. "Did you bring anything?"

"No. Actually, I was thinking of getting your mother's hope chest."

"Can we go in together?" she asked.

"Yes, but you can't go up the stairs," he said gesturing to her belly. "It's too dangerous."

"That's all right. I just don't want to wait out here alone," she murmured.

He stood up and extended his hand. She took it and they began to make their way to the manor.

***

Walt lifted his torch around the large man-made cremation furnace he and Alex had built together. Around the room, he had placed buckets of flowers and other keepsakes of Elizabeth's, including her copy of Les Liaisons Dangereuses. He shut himself inside and dropped the torch to the straw filled floor. Immediately, flames surrounded him. As he stepped toward them he felt her presence. He turned and saw a light surrounding her as she held out her hand.

"Tu me manques," Elizabeth said softly.

Without a second thought or fear, Walt approached her and kissed her hand.

"I've missed you," he said moved to tears.

"I've been watching you all these years. You've been so amazing," she said smiling. "I love you. You are the most selfless person I have ever known."

"I love you, too," he said. "You know that's why I'm here, I have to be with you again."

He took her hand and they walked together for the rest of eternity...

I was so engulfed in her, I never felt the burn of the flame.

INNER PEACE

*M*adeline looked fixedly down at the bones. There was only one skull amongst the bones and some scraps of mouldy fabric.

"It looks like there's only one skeleton here," she said. "Did he forget about my grandmother?"

Alex immediately understood, looking up at the cloud of smoke coming from the front of the house. He knelt next to the remains and inspected the bones.

"I don't think that this person is your mother or your grandmother."

Her brow knit, "What do you mean?" She knelt next to him, looking at the bones.

"I don't think these are the remains of a woman, I think that they are Lord Swan's."

She gasped, looking at the smoke, "You don't think he?" her voice cracked.

"I can't believe I didn't figure out he'd do this until now," Alex said shaking his head, as he watched the horrified expression on Madeline's face. "Walt was very particular about what day we do this. To be honest, we could have done this earlier, but Walt insisted on today. Today is All Souls' Day."

"But today is the day to commemorate the lives of the departed not join them, isn't it?" Madeline asked curiously.

"In some other cultures it's known as the Day of the Dead and people believe that the gates of heaven are opened and spirits can reunite with their loved ones," Alex said. He rose to his feet, and helped her up from the ground. He wrapped his arms around her, guiding her head to his shoulder, "Perhaps we should go."

She twisted her lips, "Yes."

"I'll take you to the carriage. Then I'll get Princess."

While Madeline waited in the carriage, she watched the billowing smoke coming from the ground. It looked more like a mist or fog. She watched it as it rose into the night sky, making a soft haze over the moon. Strangely, it was breathtaking. A ghost of a smile was lit her face, her eyes mirroring what she saw above her. Somehow, despite everything, Madeline was at peace.

Sometime later, Alex came and sat next to her and they watched the sky together. As they did, there was a fluttering in her abdomen. They sat in silence until the smoke cleared and the stars reappeared.

The ride home was a quiet one, she didn't think she would, but she fell asleep.

She awoke as Alex carried her into the castle. "We're home?" she asked her eyes slight.

"Yes."

She drifted off to sleep in his arms again.

NEW BEGINNINGS

A few weeks had passed and Christmas was around the corner. Greg and Sofia were still at Windsor Castle. Alex had put forward the motion of giving Holyrood House to Sofia as a wedding gift from one royal to another. However, many objected. Lord Walsh in particular, who felt that because the Spanish throne belonged to Sofia, she should go claim it instead.

"Taking the primary royal residence of Scotland?" Lord Walsh roared in the House of Lords. "If you give that to her, you might as well make her Queen of Scotland as well. Where will his Majesty stay if he decides to visit?"

The rest of the Lords nodded in agreement.

Alex wished he could gift it, but as time passed, Sofia quickly came to know some of the nobles at court, as well as Greg's family. Then, it seemed that Sofia wasn't interested in it any more, "If accepting Holyrood House means that people will suspect me of having political motives of being the Queen of Spain and Scotland, then I'm not sure it's safe to accept," she said one day over dinner.

Alex wanted to ask how long they planned to stay at Windsor. As much as he appreciated Greg's company again, he wasn't sure that staying at the castle or any other royal residence was a good option.

Rumours were flying around the court that Alex would eventually try to give them another one of his royal estates. Though it were only a rumour, it incensed a few of the nobles; there was still some bitter feelings towards Sofia because of the war with the Spaniards. While sitting around the Crimson Drawing Room one afternoon with Greg, Alex finally broached the subject, trying to understand what exactly Greg and Sofia were hoping for.

"I don't know what Sofia wants," Greg said helplessly. "I don't think she knows what she wants. Mostly, I think she wants to feel safe. Right now, I think she feels safest here."

"Really?" Alex said floored. "I thought Madeline and I would make her so uncomfortable she would want to leave."

Greg winked, "Oi, Sofia is happy as long as I'm around."

Just then, Lord Walsh came in with Lord Winthrop at his heels. "Your Majesty," Lord Walsh said bowing. "Lord Winthrop has stopped by to have a few words with Sir Gregory."

Alex raised his brow, "What about?"

"I'm acting as the executor of the Duke of Axford's will," Lord Winthrop explained bowing.

"Sorry?" Greg asked. "What do you mean the executor of the Duke of Axford's will?"

"Sir Gregory, after the Duke passed away, there were many different legal affairs that the Duke asked me to take care of, before releasing the details of his will."

"Oh."

Greg was perplexed. He wondered if he owed the Duke some money from any card games they had played. But the last time they had, Greg remembered winning.

"May I have a seat?" asked Lord Winthrop.

"Absolutely," Alex said. "I'll leave you to it."

"It's fine," said Greg. "You can stay."

"I think not," said Alex. "If anyone should be here, it should be your wife. Lord Walsh, do you know where the Princess is?"

"I'll send for her," Lord Walsh offered.

"Really Alex, you can stay," said Greg unnerved.

"To be honest, I promised Madeline to meet her for afternoon tea," Alex said.

He left the room. Several minutes later, Sofia appeared in the doorway with Lord Walsh who shut the doors behind her as she entered the drawing room

"What is this all about?" she asked, sitting next to Greg.

Lord Winthrop stood up and bowed, "Your Royal Highness, I've come here on the Duke of Axford's behalf. His will has indicated that your husband is a benefactor."

"The Duke of Axford?" she said confused. "Isn't he-"

She paused. She remembered that he was locked in Curfew Tower the same time she had imprisoned Greg there. She had also thought she had seen him in wanted posters around Windsor.

"It has been assumed that the Duke has passed on," Lord Winthrop went on. "He left a letter at one of his estates. In it, he indicated that he would never return to England and that he would like his affairs put into order according to his will."

"How long has he been missing?" asked Sofia.

"Over a month now. Not a soul has seen him for weeks. Usually, he does tend to contact some of his servants from time to time. But after finding his letter, they believe he is no longer with us."

Sofia cringed. It was obvious what Lord Winthrop was suggesting. The Duke had either disappeared or worse, killed himself. It was an awkward conversation to have.

"So," continued Greg. "The Duke of Axford has left something for me?"

"Yes."

"Ah, that's interesting," Greg said sceptically. "The Duke and I were merely acquaintances. We played cards together at court parties and had plenty of drinks. Nothing more than that. Mind you he was one of the best players. What did he leave me? A deck of cards for good luck at the tables?" Greg smiled.

Lord Winthrop laughed. "Oh, I believe he left you much more than that. He left all his estates and accounts to you."

"Excuse me," Sofia said astounded.

Greg stared at Lord Winthrop, speechless.

"Yes, the Duke was a rather wealthy man and owned many estates," Lord Winthrop went on. "Some in other parts of Europe, too. He didn't have any close family members. Most were distant relatives. He had a goddaughter but it seems that he felt she had no need for his properties. She comes from a wealthy family herself. He left her a few sentimental valuables I think, but that's all."

"Wait," Greg said unable to take in what he was saying. "Do you mean to say, that the Duke of Axford has left me all his property? All his residences?"

"By the looks of things yes, I believe he left you every one of his estates. Oh, and he also left you this."

Out of his waistcoat pocket, Lord Winthrop pulled out a letter and handed it to Greg Both their jaws dropped as Greg took the letter into his hands.

"I'm sorry, Lord Winthrop,' Sofia said, her eyes still wide. "Could we have a moment alone?"

"Certainly."

Lord Winthrop exited to the Green Drawing Room and the two exchanged looks then looked at the letter.

"What do you make of all this?" she began, "Do you think maybe they got things mixed up? Are there any other Umbridges at court?"

"No," Greg laughed, "but I didn't know the man that well."

"Did he not have any children?" Sofia asked tilting her head.

"No."

"Maybe he died lonely and didn't have many friends," she said sadly.

"He was a bit of a recluse. Didn't invite many around to his home. This man acquired a lot throughout his life, though. I'm not exactly sure I'd feel right about taking it."

"If he's left you a letter, maybe he's explaining why," she said gesturing to the letter in his hands.

He tore it open and began to read it aloud to her:

. . .

Dear Sir Gregory Umbridge,

It probably comes as a shock to you that I would give you all my posses-sions and all the estates I owned without dividing it amongst my few personal friends. If this is confusing, I'm sorry. For me, you seemed to be a better choice than them. Not that they were bad people. But many of those closest to me have no need for extras and would not have much appreciation for them.

The reason I've decided to give it all to you is because you remind me of myself. Somewhat. I wasn't a peasant boy, nor as carefree as you tend to be. But I know what it is to be the King's right-hand man and best mate. At times, it can be intolerable. I remember when King Charles was alive, I didn't feel I fit in at court. Quite often, other nobles at court tried to befriend me for their own personal and political gain; this is why I had travelled to other parts of the world, and at times told Charlie I'd never return.

I suppose for that reason, I think you're a better man than myself. You've lived by Alex's side all your life, unable to take a break. You've been judged by others at court for your humble beginnings, and still manage to be polite to those that mistreat you. When you came to the House of Lords and explained all you had done for the King and England and how you deserved a place of your own, I had to agree. No one knows the burden of ruling a country, except the ruler and the rulers' favourite advisor.

I realize that what I have left you may be of little consequence to you. I doubted that you truly wanted to own a place as sorry as Swan Manor. You've never tried to procure a residence for yourself before or since, so if what I have left you is more of a burden than a gift, feel free to sell it.

If you decide to keep it, I'd like to warn you; you may find that inter-esting characters may come out of the woodwork. These people will most likely advise you on what you should do with your new wealth, or try to take advantage of you for their own gain. But if you decide to sell them instead, before selling them, you might consider giving some of the estates to your sisters. I hear you have many.

Whatever you decide, for once, put your own happiness first.

All the best,

Walt

. . .

"BLIMEY," said Sofia.

Greg chuckled, 'Did a Spanish princess just say 'blimey'?"

She shrugged a shoulder, "I don't know what else to say. That is what most English people say when they don't know what to say, isn't it? I just can't believe it. It's so unexpected."

He looked at the next page. It was a list of all the estates. His mouth hung open. It was more than enough to accommodate himself, his parents as well as his sisters and their families. But one residence caught his eye. A manor in Edinburgh.

"It's more than we'll ever need to live our lives," his happiness almost filling him with tears. "These estates are all over the United Kingdom and Europe. There's even one in Edinburgh."

"EDINBURGH!" she shrieked. She jumped into his arms hugging him tightly. "That's perfect. We could stay there on holiday!"

"You don't want to live there?" he asked in shock. "I thought you saw the people of Edinburgh as family? Isn't that the reason we wanted Holyrood House?"

"I did, at first," she confessed. "But these past few weeks here haven't been as bad or humiliating as I thought they might be."

He nodded, "Yes. The court has seemed to accept our marriage."

"It's not just that," she said. "I had always thought it would be mortifying to come back here and assumed rumours would be flying. That people would think I was still in love with Alex. That I was jealous of Madeline."

Greg chuckled, "You don't think the servants and court noticed that you had eyes for me long before going to Edinburgh. You spent most your time with me while Alex was lovesick for Madeline."

"Who could blame me? You're sexy in a roguish type way," she said fighting back a blush. "Besides, Alex was acting fairly odd."

He howled, "Odd? If he were fifty years older, I would have thought he was going senile."

She gave him a playful push on the shoulder, "Enough," she tittered. "In all seriousness though, I liked the Duke's suggestion."

"What suggestion?" he asked raising a brow.

"Giving all your sisters a home. I never had any sisters. I wasn't

423

close with my own family. Wouldn't it be nice to see your sisters more often? You could give them places in London."

"Yes, it would," Greg admitted.

* * *

MADELINE AND ALEX sat in the Octagon Dining Room, having tea together. He rubbed her belly.

"How have you been feeling lately?" he asked.

"Good. The baby has been very active, kicking and moving about."

"In two and a half or three months Madeline, we'll have a whole new person in our world," he smiled.

"It's funny, most couples would have talked about it by now. Maybe because we've had so much going on in our lives," she said grinning.

"I know," he said reading her mind. "I'm surprised we never thought of it either. What to name the baby."

She laughed, "I was thinking Elizabeth if it's a girl."

"After your mother?"

"Well, you have to admit, it's a strong name. Elizabeth the First was a great monarch, too."

He nodded. "But a middle name?"

She pursed her lips, "Haven't thought of one yet."

"Well, as long as we can agree that we won't name her after my mother," he said taking a sip of his tea and putting it down to its saucer.

"What if the baby is a boy?" she asked. "What were you thinking then?"

"I wouldn't want to name the baby after myself," said Alex embarrassed, "if that's what you were thinking."

"Many kings have," she said furrowing her brow. "Why? Don't you like Alexander?"

"I do. But I just rather my son have a name of his own."

"Would you name him after your father?

"Charles? No."

"What about Gregory?" she asked.

"I thought we could name him after Sir Ashton Giles. His middle name was James and I think that's fairly regal."

"I like that. James. What about a middle name?"

"I'm considering Gregory for a middle name," Alex said.

Lord Winthrop entered unexpectedly.

"Your Majesties," he said bowing. "I'm sorry for intruding without announcement."

"It's fine. What is it? Is everything all right?" Alex asked, ready to get up.

"Things are fine. But as you know, I'm legally obligated to be the executor of the Duke's will. He's asked me to present the Queen with something."

Lord Winthrop set a box on the table in front of them and opened it. It was filled with buttons and small swatches of fabric. Then he left the room.

Alex looked at the box, "That's odd. What is this?"

Madeline peered into the box, what she saw looked familiar, "The place I stayed at in Warwickshire. Who's home was it? Was it the Duke's?"

"Yes," Alex confirmed.

She pulled out several pieces of fabric, "If that was his place, then I'm guessing these must be from dresses my mother owned. I found some swatches like these in a chest in Warwickshire along with old copies of The Society Pages. This is from my wedding dress," she said pulling out some lace. She paused, "He must have been the one who gave me her wedding dress."

"Makes sense," Alex agreed. "Mr. Sheffield is the only other person that I would imagine might have it. But if he did, I'm sure he would have made you aware of that years ago." He looked at the fabric, "Hm, if I were to guess, it looks like your mother kept swatches from clothes that had special meaning to her."

She pulled out some of the material and buttons. "Too bad I won't know what they meant."

"Did Walt leave a message for you in the box?"

She began pulling out the swatches and buttons, until she found a small piece of paper, "'All of Beth's happiest memories',"she read and sighed, "Fabric?"

"I think he's trying to remind you of something Madeline," Alex said.

"What?"

"Walt always spoke of how full of life Elizabeth was. I think he resented how no one remembered her for the vibrant person she was. To England, she's a sad story, a murder victim, but she had a life full of happy memories before that. She had so many happy memories, she didn't want to forget them and kept mementos of them. She wasn't some girl that got her comeuppance for not listening to her father and marrying a commoner. She had lived a happy life before her end."

"Did Walt tell you exactly what happened that night?" Madeline asked. "How the fight broke out, how they were killed?"

"No," he said, feeling sorry he couldn't give her an answer. "But he did say that when she went to Swan Manor, she was following her heart and she had your best interests in mind."

Madeline's eyes welled up and she began to cry. He cuddled next to her and wrapped her arm around her.

"It's funny," she said when she finally caught her breath. "All of my life, I thought I didn't matter much to her. But when I read her journals, I felt a spirit in her and thought, someone so full of life that loves everyone in their life would love their baby too, wouldn't they? I know in my heart that she loved me, too."

Madeline rubbed her belly, and felt her little one kick, another tear rolled down her cheek and Alex wiped it away with his thumb.

"The question is, what are you going to do with all these fabrics?" he asked.

She thought a moment, "All these happy memories would make a nice quilt for the baby," she suggested, her hand circling her tummy.

"That's a beautiful idea," he whispered, placing his hand atop hers.

As Alex's hand squeezed hers, she closed her eyes and sighed, feeling at peace. Her mother no longer seemed like a legend or horror story. She felt like a real person that existed; a person who loved and was loved. Madeline smiled, knowing that this was how her mother would want to be remembered. She opened her eyes and pulled out some more of the fabrics, then something nearly blinded her, as the sun shone down on it from the large windows.

Alex's brows raised, "That must have been her engagement ring."

Madeline's eyes bulged. She had never seen a ring quite like it. It was unique. One large diamond among hundreds of colourful smaller ones. She pulled it out of the box and it shone unlike any ring she had ever seen.

"There's an inscription," she said and read it aloud, "'Still not as sparkling as your eyes.' Oh!" she gushed, "that's so sweet."

"In the time I spent with him, I swear Walt's every thought was of your mother."

"Walter," Madeline said, a satisfied look on her face. "James Walter."

"What?"

"Maybe we should name the baby James Walter."

"Sounds good. But royal children have two middle names."

She laughed, "Seriously? Can nothing be simple?"

"Not if you're royal."

NEW MEMORIES

SIX MONTHS LATER
BUCKINGHAM PALACE

Dearest Alex,

Happy to hear the news of the newest little prince. I must admit I was surprised that you named him James. I presume this is to name him after Sir Ashton James Giles? It sounds a little common. Giving the middle name of Duke Walter Axford was a little more respectable, but again it's questionable. Didn't he murder the Swan family? As for his other middle name Gregory. Ugh. Strange to name a future King after a commoner.

Seeing that Princess Sofia has not decided to come home, we here in Spain assume that she has no wish to come back. We've heard that she has taken residence in London with Greg Umbridge. Is it true? Are they married? I still find that difficult to believe!

The reason I'm writing to you is to let you know of our happy news as well as make a few demands. As you may have already heard, I have just given birth to the late Prince Carlos's child. We have named her Isabella Joanna Maria.

We appreciate that you have released the Spanish prisoners from the

Tower of London. But I can't understand why you haven't released my mother. She is a Lady of the court, not your enemy. I demand that you release her immediately and have her sent here.

I have surmised that your release of the Spanish prisoners was a peace offering. I must admit I haven't quite forgiven you for all that you've done. Killing my father, husband, and King Fernando is hardly forgivable. But, once I see my mother, I will do my best to let bygones be bygones and will not retaliate. You may have the greatest navy in the world, but don't forget how cunning I can be.

Her Royal Highness, Princess Susanna of Spain.

ALEX HOWLED in laughter after reading it aloud, "She's something else. Threatening me as though she has any chance."

"You sound a little overconfident, your Majesty," Madeline chuckled, knowingly.

"Haven't I always been?"

He watched her as she cooed over James. He was only a few months old but fairly solid. He stretched his small legs and giggled as she smothered him with kisses on a chaise longue.

"Isn't he adorable?" she said picking him up holding him closely.

"Yes," Alex said marvelling at her; he wished his own mother was nearly as affectionate as Madeline. "But he needs a nap," Alex said. "Being adorable is tiring, wouldn't you say?"

"I don't want to put him down," she said pouting.

"I know, but you know if you don't he'll be grumpy later."

"That's all right," Madeline said. "He's cute when he's grumpy."

"Let's put him down," he said, taking James into his arms. They walked together down the hall to James's room.

"Has he been fed yet?" Alex asked as they entered the room.

"Yes," Madeline said and she set James down in the bassinet. The lids of his big green eyes grew heavy and he yawned widely before drifting to sleep.

Alex came from behind her and kissed her softly on the cheek.

"Why don't we leave him here and spend the afternoon alone together?" he whispered. "I'll get a few guards by the door."

"Mm," she murmured uncertain, "but if he fusses I want to-"

"Madeline, I'm sure one of the nannies can look after him if he does. Besides, I was thinking we could go riding together. We haven't really gone out much since James was born."

She nodded in agreement and he placed his hand on the small of her back guiding her out the door. They went down to the Royal Mews, into Princess' stall.

"I think she's a little angry with me," he said looking at Princess timidly, "I haven't seen her much in the past few months."

He carefully climbed up onto her and hoisted Madeline up with him.

"Where do you want to go?" he asked.

"How about the stream? Remember last time we went?"

He chuckled, "Hard to believe that was two years ago now."

As they rode off, she smiled; it was hard to believe that the last time they rode out to the stream in the forest near Buckingham Palace, she was wearing a maid's outfit and wasn't sure how long he would remain interested in her. Now, she was his wife and the mother of his son, wearing fine clothes. The only thing that hadn't changed was their excitement for one another.

She could hear the stream in the distance, "Remember the first time we came?" she grinned.

"It was a sweet picnic, dolcezza. Why don't we sit by the water?"

They tied Princess to a tree by the stream. He took a blanket off Princess' saddle, and they walked further into the woods. Eventually, they came across a small clearing between the trees and he laid it in the long blades of lush grass by the water. He helped lower Madeline down on it.

AN HOUR later they were swimming in the brook next to the small waterfall. Hues of pink, blues, purples, yellows and oranges painted the sky. Alex sat on a rock submerged in the water. He watched

Madeline as she walked about in the water, unbraiding her long tresses before she drenched her hair beneath the small falls. She had come a long way from being a slave and he no longer had to risk everything to be with her. It was a miracle that they were together, and he was grateful. Despite all their hardships, they still loved and appreciated one another. Nothing had ever stood between them or caused them to hate one another. They seemed to live in their own world, shielded from any harm that might come their way.

She smiled affectionately at him, and he knew she was thinking the same thing. The last time they had come, their relationship was full of excitement, but also fear. Now it was just possibilities and life that lay ahead of them. They were bonded together not just by flesh, but by fate.

"Come to me, dolcezza," he said, waving her over.

She waded through the water and sat down on his lap. He embraced her, warming her cool skin with his large arms.

"Good to know when we get back, there's a beautiful baby waiting for us," she said wrapping her arms around his neck.

"Yes, no secrets to hide, no crazy royals, or questionable family to deal with," he said as his thumb traced her lower lip. "It's finally just us."

Their lips tenderly entwined and they indulged one another in the soft sunlight. They melted into one another like the colours of the sky above them, that knew no beginning or end.

AFTER THEY FINISHED WASHING, stars began to appear and they decided to head back. When they went to retrieve Princess, she was sniffing about a nearby tree.

"What do you think she's got there?" Alex asked as they approached her.

Madeline cocked her head curiously, "No idea."

Once they had reached her, they pulled her away from the tree, "It's the picnic blanket we had when we were here last," Alex said amused. It was tattered and weathered, but as Madeline looked down at it, she realized it was the only piece of clothing left of their time together when they had first met. Unfortunately, she had thrown away all her uniforms and the three dresses he had given her when she was still a servant.

"Alex, give me your dagger," she said, lifting the blanket from the grass.

He unsheathed it from his coat and handed it to her. She cut out a piece of fabric.

"What are you doing?" he asked, though he had a fairly good idea.

"I think we're going to have our happily ever after, Alex. It's time to start saving memories of it.

MAILING LIST...AND MORE!

SIGN UP for my mailing list and get 'Teenage Dream' for FREE! You'll be in the know for hot new releases, other freebies, and ARC opportunities.

https://www.maidformajesty.com/free-novella

ALSO BY AJ PHOENIX

Historical Erotica
STEAM LEVEL 5/5

The Maid for Majesty Series
Maid for Majesty Forbidden Fruit (Book 1)
Maid For Majesty Absence (Book 2)
Maid for Majesty Black Swan (Book 3)

Contemporary Romance
Touchdown
Model Behavior

TEN MAID FOR MAJESTY HISTORICAL FACTS

1. Chinese vases can be pricey. In 2010, a rare vase sold for 53 million pounds!
2. Big Ben the famous clock tower of London was nicknamed Big Ben for the great bell of the clock.
3. The coffee houses of England started the custom of tipping. If you wanted good service at a shop, you'd put money in a tin labelled, 'To insure prompt service.' Or T.I.P.S.
4. Chapstick was made in the Regency era by mixing equal parts of beeswax, sweet almond oil and cocoa butter. Melt in a pot or the microwave, pour into a stick or pot then let it harden overnight.
5. It was proper etiquette to ignore servants at mealtimes.
6. Extramarital affairs were forgivable. In fact, wives were encouraged to ignore if their spouse has a courtesan or mistress. It was improper for a wife to discuss her husbands' infidelities with him or anyone else.
7. Vulgarity was unforgivable. If someone was vulgar, it tainted their reputation. Hence, Greg Umbridges' difficulty in winning the nobles' respect.
8. Stradivarius violins renowned for their incredible sound

are to this day, the world best made violins. Unfortunately, no one knows how Stradivarius made them. They are rare and sell for millions.

9. Today the House of Lords meets in the Palace of Westminster, right next to Big Ben.

10. Ice cream was made from snow saved from the winter.

ABOUT THE AUTHOR

AJ Phoenix is the author of the #1 Best Selling Historical Erotica Series *Maid for Majesty,* and lives on the shores of the Great Lakes in Canada. Her writing is not inspired by real life events. If such events did ever happen to her, her books would never have been written.

Printed in Great Britain
by Amazon

25641611R00260